The Lost Letters
of
PLAYFAIR
STREET

Michelle Montebello

The Lost Letters of Playfair Street

Michelle Montebello

Please note that Michelle Montebello is an Australian author and British English spelling has been used in this novel.

ISBN: 978-0-9876416-5-6

Editing by Lynne Stringer at
Australian eBook Publisher
Book design by Swish Design & Editing
Cover design by Kris Dallas Design
Cover image Copyright 2020

DEDICATION

To Bianca,
For your love and friendship every day...

Hurry up the sun!
Make the days shorter till we meet. I love you, that's all there is to it.

~Orson Welles to Rita Hayworth

The Lost Letters
of
PLAYFAIR STREET

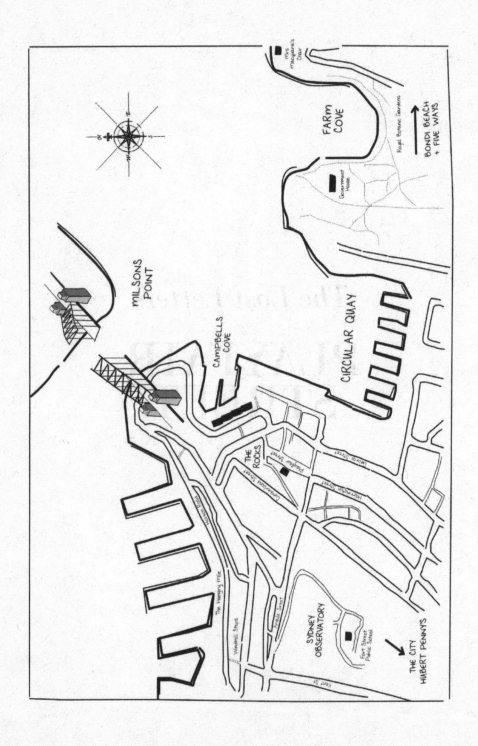

CHAPTER 1

PAIGE

Present Day

'I'm walking up the street now.'

'You mean Playfair? I can hardly hear you.'

'Yes, I'm on Playfair Street. I'm almost at the house.' Paige Westwood pulled her phone away from her ear and glanced at the screen. Despite having full signal on her side, Xavier's voice was coming through distorted. 'Xavier, are you there? Can you hear me?'

'Sorry, bad service where I am. Give me a call once you're inside. Don't be alarmed. It needs a good clean!'

The phone went dead and Paige sighed, dropping it back into her bag. Despite the garbled call, the day held promise. Earlier clouds had cleared to a high golden sun and the air was perfuse with the smell of sea salt and coffee. The Sydney Harbour Bridge arched in the distance, reminding her that seeing it in books would never be as enthralling as seeing it in person.

There hadn't been many reasons to leave Albury in the past, her hometown of thirty-two years, five hours south of Sydney. It was where she was born and raised, where she'd experienced both her first love, and her first heartbreak, by the one person she'd thought could never hurt her. *Christian.* Beautiful, selfish Christian. She had put him above all others, loved him, given him every part of herself, without

1

reciprocation. She'd never been much of a crier, was made of strong country stock, but it was his last words to her before she'd left that always threatened to break the dam of unshed tears.

I asked her to marry me. I wanted you to be the first to know.

Feeling her resolve slip, she pushed thoughts of him away, continuing along the cobblestones, past restaurants and cafes that coloured the street, brushing her long, flaxen hair out of her face and keeping an eye on the numbered shopfronts. She eventually passed the brown brick Cleveland Bond building to arrive at a row of yellow and amber original workmen's terraces.

They were middle to late Victorian with cantilevered balconies, attic windows and chimney pots. Most had been restored and transformed into businesses—solicitors, art galleries and clothing boutiques—but it was the charm and authenticity of the façades that made Paige stop and forget that she had a house to find.

She tore her eyes away to pluck her diary out of her bag, flip it open and check the address she'd scribbled inside. *7 Playfair Street, The Rocks, Sydney.* She glanced up at the row of terraces again. She was definitely in the right place, although the devil was in the detail. It was locating a number amongst the medley of historical houses, restaurants and cafes that would prove the challenge. She kept walking, her long legs covering the distance with ease, sidestepping a small tour group and a family, the smell of lager and hot pizza enticing her grumbling stomach.

Xavier had said the location was fascinating, an old slum that had been transformed in the seventies to a hip and vibrant neighbourhood bordering the city, the perfect location for his new publishing house. She hadn't anticipated it would be the epicentre of where the past and present fused so effortlessly—eighteenth-century cobblestones with contemporary marketplaces, old terraces hosting art galleries, the ghosts of yesteryear with the living. She wanted to poke around in all the houses, follow the laneways as the street urchins must have done, and find the remnants of old homes that had been torn out mid-plague. But she couldn't lose her head yet. She still had to find number seven.

Past the last of the workmen's terraces and before a large Italian restaurant, she saw a 'SOLD' sign out the front of a house and a woman waiting on the street. She was impeccably dressed in a suit and heels, thumbing distractedly through her phone.

'Hi,' Paige said on approach.

The woman glanced up, her eyebrows knitted. 'Oh, hi, are you Paige Westwood?'

'I am.' Paige held her hand out.

'Hi, Jenny from the real estate agency,' she said, shaking it. 'Xavier said you'd be meeting me today.'

'Sorry he couldn't be here. He's back in Albury packing.'

'That's fine.' Jenny dropped her phone into her bag. 'I have the keys so I'll show you around.'

Number seven was larger than the other workmen's terraces, with a honeyed façade, similar chimney pots and an attic window, but this house was freestanding and fully detached. They walked to the front door where Jenny fished in her bag for a set of keys. 'Are you from Sydney?' she asked, unlocking the door.

'No, I'm from Albury too. I've already moved here.' She'd made the move in one swift leap, as quickly as she could, before her heart or Christian could talk her out of it.

'Are you and Xavier married?'

'Oh, no!' Paige laughed and shook her head. 'No, we're good friends. He's starting a business here and I'm his personal assistant.'

Jenny pushed opened the door and they stepped into a small foyer. Stale air rushed upon them and the light was dim. A staircase led upwards to the second floor.

'So this is the main entrance,' Jenny explained. 'These stairs lead up to the second level. And there's an attic up there too, which I believe has a fair bit of junk in it. It's become a bit of a dumping ground over the years, unfortunately.'

She led the way down the hall, pushing doors open as she walked. 'Small office here, dining room and kitchen down there, what I think might have been a parlour once but is now the front living room. You know these old houses and their old room names.'

Paige followed, inspecting each room briefly. Pieces of furniture from the previous tenant remained, as well as grimy windows and walls that hadn't seen a good clean or a lick of paint in years. When they reached the back French doors, Jenny found the correct key and unlocked them.

'Here we have the garden, which is fairly tiny. All backyards in The

Rocks are. Nice view of the Sydney Harbour Bridge, though.'

'This house looks bigger than the others on the street,' Paige said, glancing out. Everything was overgrown. She saw a dwarf apple gum, its delicate white flowers discarded by autumn, carpeting the uneven cobblestones beneath, and an old white table and chairs with peeling paint. At the rear of the yard was a towering sandstone wall and rickety fences along the side to seal off the property from the workmen's terraces next door.

'It is. Much bigger. A family with some money lived here back in the day. Well, not a lot of money, but definitely middle-class.' Jenny held up the set of keys, pointing to each. 'Back door, front door, laundry door and some windows. Sorry, I wasn't given a complete set. Do you want to take a proper look out the back?'

Paige shook her head. 'It's fine. I'll explore later.'

'I'll show you upstairs.'

Paige followed her up the staircase, the boards creaking under their weight.

'So Xavier is going to run a business out of here?' Jenny asked, her phone beeping in her bag.

'Yes,' Paige replied. 'A publishing house for fiction and non-fiction works. It's been a lifelong dream of his.'

'That's exciting.'

At the top, they arrived at a hallway. Jenny's heels clomped along the timber floors as she threw open doors. 'Master bedroom here, second and third bedrooms here and here. Not a lot of the Playfair houses have three bedrooms, so you're lucky to get the extra space. Bathroom here,' she threw open another door quickly then spun around. 'What will he do with these bedrooms if not for sleeping?'

'We'll need office space for editors, designers, marketing, plus room for storage. I'm sure all of these rooms will be put to good use.'

Jenny's phone beeped again in her bag and she plucked it out and glanced at it. 'Oh, before I forget,' she pointed down the hall distractedly, 'the attic is that way.'

Paige walked to the end of the hall reaching a short, dim staircase. 'Up here?' She peered upwards. The air was cold and damp despite the summer heat lingering. Old, lacy cobwebs dangled from the ceiling.

'I doubt anyone's been up there for a while but I believe the door is

4

unlocked if you want to explore.' Then as an afterthought, 'Could be ideal storage space if you feel like clearing out the junk.'

'Who used to live here?' Paige asked as they returned to the ground floor.

'An elderly lady, but she died recently. She was a tenant. The house has been owned by the same family for years, dating back to the turn of the twentieth century,' Jenny said. 'Greene, I believe the family name is. They live in the UK now. They decided to sell it recently.'

Paige nodded thoughtfully. 'And the leftover furniture? The stuff in the attic? Should I give it back to anyone?'

'Give it to charity or throw it out. No one's going to come and claim it.'

'All right.'

Jenny dropped the keys into Paige's open palm. 'Good luck with everything. I have to run. Another appointment. But give me a call if you have any questions.'

She hurried out the door, lost again in her messages.

***

'What do you think of it?' Xavier asked.

With her phone pressed to her ear, Paige walked into the kitchen and found an old wobbly chair to sit on. 'It's not bad. The place has character.'

'Do you think it could work?'

'Isn't it a little late to be asking that? You already own it.'

Xavier chuckled. 'You know what I mean.'

Paige drew a circle through the dusty floor with her Converse. 'It needs a good clean and a few coats of paint. The windows haven't been scrubbed in years. But I think it will do nicely.'

'And the furniture?'

She looked around at the odd pieces that had been left behind. 'It shouldn't be a problem. I'll arrange for them to be collected, although Jenny said something about the attic. Apparently there's a lot of junk up there.'

'I haven't seen the attic yet, but it could be good for storage if we cleaned it out.'

'Yeah,' she said distractedly.

There was a pause on the other end. 'You all right, blossom? You sound sad.'

It was uncanny how he sensed her mood without her having to say anything. 'I don't know. Mixed emotions, I guess.'

'You only arrived yesterday.' His tone was gentle. 'It's okay to feel a bit up and down about leaving.'

Up and down was a good way to put it. One minute she felt exuberant and the next she was terrified. A country girl alone in Sydney without knowing another soul. Without intimate knowledge of streets and with the monumental task of setting Xavier's business up. But she'd made the decision, as painful as it was. New streets meant fewer memories and the chance of ever running into Christian again.

Her voice quivered despite how she tried to keep it steady. 'How's the packing going?'

'Slow. I'm getting resistance.'

'Eric still doesn't want to come?'

'He wants to stay here in Albury. He has no desire to move to Sydney. And I don't mean to rush him, but I have a lot to do and we need to get out of here.'

'Try to be patient,' Paige said. 'He's your husband and he loves you. He knows how important this is. But you need to give him time. This is a big change for him too.'

'So I'm being selfish?'

'I think you have your dreams in sight and you're not seeing anything else.'

Xavier sighed. She could imagine him adjusting his glasses and scratching the top of his head, his dark mop of hair falling over his eyes. 'I suppose you're right. Sound advice as usual.'

Paige smiled at the irony. If only she had sound advice for her own love life.

'Anyway, I should be there next week,' Xavier pressed on. 'In the meantime, can you get started? You'll need to advertise for the new positions. The place could do with a thorough clean and you'll need to order new furniture too. Oh, can you check out laptops, phones, printers and iPads? I've already ordered the electricity back on. Might just need to replace the lightbulbs.'

While Xavier launched tasks at her, Paige glanced around the kitchen. The sun was starting to dip behind the city, casting the Playfair house into shadow. She ought to go before it got too dark, but a strange peace had descended. Despite the state of the house, she liked it there.

'Where are you sleeping tonight?' Xavier asked.

'I'll go back to the hotel.'

'And then?'

'I might set up camp here in one of the rooms, just until I can find an apartment to rent. It would save me a fortune in hotel charges.'

'Are you sure that's a good idea? You know I'll cover your hotel bill. That house might be creepy after dark.'

'It'll be fine once I replace the lightbulbs.'

'Well, if you chicken out, know that you can stay in the hotel as long as you need.'

'Thank you.'

'And Paige?'

'Yes?'

'Go out tonight. Make some new city friends. Kiss a boy. It's time to move on.'

The thought of it caused a reply to clog in her throat. All she could do was nod.

***

After she hung up the call with Xavier, Paige explored the Playfair house. The kitchen was basic and dated. A quick search through cupboards and along the benchtop told her that there was a rodent infestation and that she'd need to add a pest treatment to her list of things to do.

Finding herself at the back doors again, she let herself out into the garden. Although small, it was vastly overgrown and soft moss grew in damp corners. Weeds had sprung up through the cobblestones and flowerbeds to choke what must have once been beautiful. A gardener would be required to strip it all back and plant new flowers. With a table and chairs for clients and a shade cloth or umbrella, it could be an ideal outdoor working space.

There was a sandstone wall at the back which extended the full length of the workmen's terraces next door and when she glanced up the ridge towards Foundation Park, her heart leapt. She saw remnants of old rooms that belonged to former houses, now torn down, likely due to the early 1900s outbreak of bubonic plague and incongruously, amongst them, a lone fireplace still standing in what was left of a wall.

She hadn't meant to squeal, but she did. Xavier had known she would love it here, had known the location of Australia's first settlement would freshen her perspective. Make her forget, just a little, what she'd left behind.

Back inside and in the lengthening shadows, she roamed through the downstairs rooms—the dining room, then the living room, which Jenny had said was a former parlour. She stepped inside, noticing the ornate cornices and ceiling rose. There was an old disused fireplace and a tattered Persian rug on the floor. It was modest-sized, used for formal entertaining back in the day, its name eventually replaced with the more modern term of 'living room'. Paige ran her hand across the fireplace mantel, her fingers tracing through thick dust, imagining the conversations that had been had in that room, of business and politics, glasses glowing copper with neat scotch.

Her inner historian ran wild at the thought. She could see them, hear them, smell them. Some crazy voice inside told her to skip the hotel altogether and stay the night—explore further. But sensible Paige knew she'd have to buy a mattress and supplies and replace the lightbulbs before she could do that.

With daylight slipping fast, she grabbed her bag and headed for the front door, passing the office on her way. She poked her head in, noticing the floor to ceiling bookcase that ran the length of one wall. It was built in and she could tell it had been there for some time, perhaps part of the original structure. This room had once been the library, she realised. Much later, it had been converted into a home office.

When the departing sun finally plunged the house into darkness, it was all she could do to propel herself out the door, lock it and head back onto the street. A sense of purpose cast the trepidation aside and she couldn't wait for sunrise again. She had much to accomplish and she was already looking forward to returning.

And high on her list was to climb those attic stairs.

CHAPTER 2

Brimming with determination, Paige woke early the next morning, dressed, then stepped through the hotel door out onto George Street. The list of tasks she'd mentally compiled had kept her awake most of the night, but she hadn't minded. It made for distraction, excitement even, preventing her mind from wandering to all the places she didn't want it to go, like home and Christian.

I asked her to marry me. I wanted you to be the first to know.

With purpose in her stride, she left the Four Seasons behind and, consulting her map, walked up George Street, cutting through Nurses Walk and Suez Canal to find Harrington Street. At Clocktower Square she purchased food and water for the day along with a broom, torch, lightbulbs and cleaning products.

She stepped back out into the morning sun. The horns of the ferries in Circular Quay drifted on the air, so too the rattle of the trains at the station. She crossed over Argyle and stepped onto Playfair, circumventing eager tourists and eventually arriving at the house, letting herself in the front door.

Stale air hit her, as it had the day before, and the breeze flooded in, sending dust motes spiralling. In the kitchen, she set down her grocery bags, opened the back door and windows to let fresh air in, then consulted her to-do list. It was plentiful; lots of things to tick off before Xavier's arrival the following week.

During the hours before lunch, she replaced the downstairs

lightbulbs, confirmed the electricity was restored, scrubbed the kitchen cupboards and moved all the abandoned furniture to the library for collection by the local thrift store. She stopped briefly to eat a sandwich, dust off her jeans and retie her pale hair back, then she decided it was time to explore the attic.

She climbed the staircase to the second floor, the old steps creaking under her feet. Before reaching the attic, she spent time thoroughly perusing the bedrooms, something she hadn't had the chance to do when Jenny had thrown the doors open in a tailspin.

The rooms were tiny by modern-day standards and littered with the bric-a-brac of former tenants. There were exposed sandstone walls, which Paige was delighted to see had the tell-tale markings of convict hands, lovely old fireplaces, and grimy narrow windows with peeling and cracked sills. It was obvious the house hadn't seen a loving hand in years. It needed repairs, a coat of paint and the floors to be sanded and polished. Paige made a mental note to start ringing contractors as soon as she came down from the attic.

She walked to the end of the hall and stood before the dim attic staircase. It was as cold as she remembered it, a flight of six steps to reach a wooden door at the top. She pushed aside stringy cobwebs, praying their inhabitants wouldn't drop into her hair, and climbed the steps. They creaked in protest and, when she reached the door, she turned the handle. Just as Jenny had indicated, it was unlocked.

She pushed it open and bent low to pass through the doorway, cursing her height as she looked around. The attic was surprisingly spacious and once inside, she could stand upright, the air pungent with time and rodent droppings. The room had a single narrow window that faced the front street and a pull cord for a light that didn't work when she tugged on it. Another lightbulb she'd need to replace.

She went to the window, almost black with grime and, with a great heave of its dirty handles, forced it upwards. A beam of light carved a path through the air to light up a dusty floor littered with sheet-draped furniture, an assortment of boxes and bits and bobs.

Paige pulled back the corners of the sheets to glimpse the objects underneath—an old safe, a grandfather clock, what had once been a beautiful pair of leather armchairs and a brown Chesterfield the colour of burnt toffee. Then, in boxes that belonged to more recent decades—

paperwork and documents, a typewriter, old textbooks and a set of encyclopaedias. The attic was a mishmash of items belonging to different eras that had passed through the house.

Her foot encountered something hard on the ground, just beneath the Chesterfield and, when she bent to inspect it, she found a small, but beautifully carved chest that looked to be early twentieth century, with intricate Edwardian carvings. She dropped to her knees and heaved up the lid, which lifted after a brief spell of resistance. She pushed it back to rest on its hinges and peered into the chest. It seemed to exhale as though it had been closed for too long.

Paige ran her fingers along the curious items inside—bundles and bundles of paper tied with frayed twine. Upon closer inspection, she realised they were letters with neat cursive writing that she'd need to read in better light.

She wondered who the chest belonged to until she noticed a name carved deep into the wood on the front of the chest. *Charlotte Greene*. Her gaze returned to the bundles of letters inside. There could be little doubt as to who the owner was.

Sitting up on her knees, she retrieved her phone out of her back pocket, dialling Xavier's number.

'Hey, how are you?' he said.

'Fine. I'm in the attic.'

'Oh, you are?' He sounded excited. 'Is it any good? Can it be used for storage?'

Paige looked around her. 'It could be, but there's a lot of stuff that will have to go first. I'm not sure what we should do with it all. Some of it is really old and probably antique.'

'Do I need to hire someone to clear it out?'

The idea of 'clearing it out' left her slightly nauseated. There were priceless pieces there, she was sure, and the last thing she wanted was to relegate them to landfill if they had historical value. 'Let me check first. I might be able to separate the junk from the antiques.' If she cast her mind back to her university days and the unit she'd completed on late antiquities, she was fairly certain everything under the sheets belonged to the early twentieth century, including the chest with its Edwardian carvings. Which meant, if what Jenny had said was correct, it would likely belong to the Greene family, who had sold the house to

11

Xavier. 'I have a question for you.'

'Fire away.'

'You purchased the house from the Greene family, correct?'

'I believe so,' Xavier replied. 'That's whose name was on the contract anyway. They're in the steel industry. Why do you ask?'

'I'm certain some of these items belonged to their ancestors. The timeline fits and they could be of sentimental value. I think we should return them.'

'Try calling Jenny. She'll be able to contact them and see if they want any of it back.'

'Okay, I'll do that.'

After she hung up from Xavier, she scanned her contacts list to find Jenny's number and dialled it. After several rings, the agent picked up.

'City Real Estate, Jenny speaking.'

'Hi, Jenny. It's Paige Westwood. We met yesterday at the Playfair house.'

'Oh yes, how are you?' Jenny sounded far away as though she were holding the phone between her ear and shoulder whilst rifling through paperwork.

'Fine, thank you. I'm up in the attic and found some items which I believe belong to the Greene family. I think they could be of sentimental value and should be returned.'

'Uh-huh.'

'Are you able to contact them and see if they'd like them back?'

Noise came down the line, then Jenny's voice again. 'Sorry. Up to my ears in contracts. What is it that you've found?'

'Mostly furniture, but also a small chest containing old letters belonging to a Charlotte Greene. I'm not sure who she was exactly but the Greene family might like them back.'

'Letters? They haven't mentioned anything about letters.' More noise from Jenny's end as if she were adjusting the phone. 'Okay, well, I can drop them an email and ask them. They're in the UK so we probably won't get an answer until tomorrow.'

'Sure. I just thought they'd like to know.'

'Uh-huh.' Jenny had become distracted again as fingers clicked on a keyboard.

'Can you call me tomorrow and let me know how they've

responded?'

'Okay.'

After a hasty goodbye, Paige ended the call and looked around the attic. Twilight had arrived and the light was fading. She could replace the lightbulb and keep exploring, but she still had other things to do, like buy a bed and check out of her room at the Four Seasons. She was determined to stay the night at Playfair, the old house having found its way under her skin, every fascinating room waiting to be explored.

Regrettably, she closed the lid of the chest and secured the sheets over everything again. With any luck, by morning, Jenny would have a response from the Greene family, and it could all be returned to its rightful owners.

***

After she left the attic, Paige caught a cab to Pitt Street Mall and purchased an inflatable mattress, bedding, a pillow and a towel. On her way back to Playfair, she stopped at the Four Seasons, packed her bags and checked out of the hotel.

Xavier would have called her crazy, but there was something about the house and its intoxicating energy that had her intrigued. There was the attic, of course, and those lovely rooms with the exposed sandstone walls and fireplaces. There was the overgrown garden, the former library and the front parlour, as well as the unusual mix of curios left behind by past tenants that had her convinced this should be her temporary home.

It was well after seven when she arrived back there. Confronted with an abundance of dinner options to choose from in The Rocks, she finally settled on Thai takeaway and, after setting up her mattress in the parlour, she sat down on the edge of it to eat.

Maybe she *was* crazy. The house was completely different after dark, despite Paige turning all the lights on to ward off the shadows. It held a different sort of energy, as the walls shifted and the floors creaked, as night bats screeched in the trees and vehicle and pedestrian activity slowed outside. Maybe she should have stayed at the hotel, where the walls didn't exhale the whispers of past occupants.

After a shower, Paige took the torch and climbed back up the staircase to the attic. She picked up Charlotte's chest and lugged it back down to the parlour where her bed was set up. She sat cross-legged on the mattress with the chest in front of her and opened it, peering inside at the letters, four bundles in total.

Hooking her finger around one of the twine-bound stacks, she carefully lifted it and set it in her lap. Likely owing to the darkness of the chest, the paper and ink were surprisingly well-preserved given how old they were. Avoiding direct contact between the paper and her fingers, she let her eyes scan over them. On the topmost letter, under the light, she could just make out the words—*I wonder if your body wants mine the way mine wants yours—the kisses—the hotness—the wetness—all melting together.*

'Good lord!' Paige dropped the bundle of letters back into the chest and closed the lid.

Whoever had written that letter, Charlotte Greene or otherwise, certainly hadn't felt the need for restraint. Paige was embarrassed to feel her cheeks flame. When had she become such a prude? And yet, she was deeply intrigued by the intensity of what had obviously been two lovers. Who were they? What had they meant to each other?

If the words were anything to go by, their romance had been steamy, their love fierce, their encounters passionate. Paige was tempted to take the letters out again and resume reading, but it was almost midnight, and she knew she'd end up reading them all night if she allowed herself. Sense prevailed and she reluctantly pushed the chest against the wall and walked around the house to switch off the lights. She climbed into bed but it took her a long time to fall asleep, her head too full of thoughts of the woman who'd once lived there.

***

In the absence of curtains, for Paige had yet to buy any, early sunlight streamed through the bare windows to light up the parlour. When she rolled over to check the time on her phone, it was five-forty-five. She groaned, rolled back on her side and buried her head under the pillow.

But the list of things she needed to do prevented further sleep and she eventually rose. Pulling on jeans, a shirt and tying her hair into a messy bun, she stepped out into a pearl morning and meandered through The Rocks in search of breakfast.

A hidden laneway off Jack Mundey Place offered an array of cafes and, by eight am, Paige was back at the house drinking coffee, eating a bagel and checking over her list. She began building a website, booked in a pest treatment for the rodents and googled various stores to commence the purchase of furniture, printers, phones and kitchen appliances. By ten she was feeling accomplished and dialled Jenny's number to check on her progress with the Greenes.

Jenny's phone was answered by her chirpy voicemail announcing that she was in a training course for the next three days and would be unavailable. Paige groaned and dropped the phone onto her bed, picking up her laptop instead.

She ran an internet search on the Greene family and was surprised to see multiple results returned. She clicked on the Greenes' official website and read about the success of their family steel business, a multinational corporation and one of the largest steel producers in the UK. According to the history page on their website, they'd supplied steel to several well-known structures, including the Sydney Harbour Bridge.

Paige chewed her lip thoughtfully. She found the 'Contact Us' page and located a generic company email address, deciding it might be the best way to reach out in the absence of Jenny. She wasn't sure if it was allowed, to make contact with prior owners this way, but she would feign ignorance if anyone questioned it.

She typed a brief message in the contact box explaining who she was and what she'd found, added her contact number and hit the send button.

***

The following evening, as she was struggling to work the new coffee machine she'd purchased for the kitchen, her mobile phone rang. She collected it off the benchtop, noticing an international number on her screen. 'Hello?'

'Hi. Is this Paige Westwood?'

'Speaking.' Her attention was piqued by the English accent.

'Good evening. I hope I'm not calling you too late. My name is Ryan Greene. You sent us an email about some personal effects belonging to my great-aunt, Charlotte.'

Paige put down the instruction manual for the coffee machine, surprised to hear from someone so soon. 'Yes, that was me. I wasn't sure where my message would end up but I'm glad to hear from you.'

'On the contrary, we were glad to hear from you. You mentioned in your email that you're Xavier's assistant, the gentleman who purchased the property.'

'That's right. I was up in the attic, preparing to clean it out, and I came across a few items that I think belong to your family.'

'How fascinating.'

'So Charlotte was your great-aunt?'

'Yes,' he replied. 'The younger sister of my great-grandfather, James. What is it that you found exactly?'

Paige leant against the kitchen bench. 'A grandfather clock, a Chesterfield, armchairs; quite beautiful pieces. I came across something else too. An old chest. Inside were four bundles of handwritten letters tied together with twine. They belonged to Charlotte.'

'How do you know they belonged to her?'

'Well, I don't for sure but her name is engraved on the chest.' She recalled the one letter she'd glimpsed days earlier and felt her cheeks redden at the prospect that this well-spoken Englishman might at some point read it too.

'What's Xavier planning to do with the old place?' he asked.

She was brought back to the room. 'Xavier?'

'The guy that purchased the property from us. What plans does he have for it?'

'He'll be running a small publishing house. We were considering the attic as storage space and that's how I came across your family's things.'

'I see.'

'So this house has been in your family for a long time?'

'Since the turn of the twentieth century. Charlotte and James were born there. Our family managed to hang onto it through two world wars and the Great Depression until my father, who it was recently passed down to, decided to sell it. Not a popular decision amongst the rest of us Greenes, but it's done.'

Paige nodded. 'Well, I'm glad to be able to return your great-aunt's things to you. I'd hate for them to be lost to the rubbish.'

'We are truly grateful. Charlotte has remained somewhat of an enigma in our family.'

'How so?'

'Just that she ...' he trailed off. 'Anyway, I don't want to keep you. How should we do this? I mean, the furniture and the chest?'

'I could ship it all to you,' Paige suggested. 'I'm sure if it's packed securely and marked fragile, it will make it to you safely.'

'Yes, you could do that. We'd cover the cost, of course.'

'Could you send me the shipping address and I'll take care of it?'

'I'll have my secretary contact you with the details.'

'There could be other things of Charlotte's too. I haven't had a chance to look through it all yet.'

'Whatever you think belongs to us, just ship it over. We'll pay for everything.'

After saying goodbye Paige returned to the instruction manual for the coffee machine, but the words made little sense. Her head was too full of thoughts of Charlotte and her great-nephew, Ryan, of the Greene family and the Playfair house they'd once owned.

And that little chest of love letters in the corner of the parlour.

***

The next week flew by. Paige was kept busy with a string of contractors who came through the house to paint the walls, replace swollen or rotten floorboards and spray for rodents. She hired a cleaner who whipped through in six hours, removing the heavy cloak of dust and grime that had settled on everything since the last occupant had been there.

She published the company website, bought a fridge and microwave, ordered furniture, and hired a gardener for the backyard. Xavier was ecstatic with the progress she'd made, still bunkered down in Albury with a house full of half-packed boxes and a husband who was resistant to the idea of the city.

'I might not make it there for another week,' he said apologetically.

'It's fine, really. Everything is under control here. Stay there as long as you need to.'

After a particularly busy day making calls and directing

tradespeople, Paige finally lowered herself onto a milk crate left behind in the kitchen by the painters. She made a sandwich for dinner and consulted her notes. Tomorrow would bring a new set of tasks—she would call in the window cleaners, order the printers, iPads and phones, and start searching for a place to live; the floor of the parlour was only temporary.

Balancing a glass of wine and her laptop on her knees, she jolted at a knock on the door. Frowning, she glanced at the time. It was after eight pm and she couldn't imagine who would be calling in at that hour. She'd become accustomed to busy days, with a stream of people traipsing through the house, but after five, everyone went home. And she didn't know a single soul in Sydney to expect house guests.

Paige set her laptop and glass of wine on the floor and walked down the hallway to the front door. She opened it to find a man standing on the porch.

'Are you Paige Westwood?' he asked.

'I am.'

He stepped forward into the circle of hall light and held out his hand. 'I'm Ryan Greene. Charlotte's great-nephew.'

CHAPTER
3

She must have been staring for he cleared his throat. 'Sorry. It's late and I'm disturbing you.'

'No. It's fine. I just...' She shook her head. 'I wasn't expecting you. We spoke on the phone a week ago and you were going to send me an address.'

'Right,' he said. 'I thought about you shipping the items to the UK, then I decided it might be best if one of us came over to inspect them for ourselves.'

She raised an eyebrow. 'You came all the way here to inspect the items? I could have sent you photographs.'

He dipped his head with embarrassment. 'Forgive me. I should have called first. It was rude to turn up like this.' He stepped off the front porch and back onto the street. 'I'll call you tomorrow to arrange a suitable time.'

Paige was the one who felt rude. 'No, wait.'

He turned back.

'You've travelled a long way and you're here now. You might as well come in.'

'Are you sure?'

She opened the door wider. 'Of course.'

He climbed onto the front porch and stepped inside the hallway.

Paige closed the door behind him. Inside, under the hallway light, she could see him properly. Tall, dark hair, an attractive face to match the articulate voice she'd heard on the phone. His eyes were still bright despite the travel, yet his jawline held the first hints of a five o'clock shadow.

Paige turned and led the way into the kitchen.

'I apologise again,' he said, his eyes sweeping over the bare rooms. 'I didn't mean to frighten you. A stranger turning up on your doorstep at night asking to come in would probably scare anyone.'

'You didn't scare me. I was just surprised.'

'And for that I'm sorry. I really should have called first.' He looked so sheepish that she couldn't help but smile.

'We'll put it down to jetlag. Can I fix you coffee or a wine?'

He returned her smile with a look of relief. 'A coffee would be great. I haven't had a decent one since leaving London.'

Paige placed a cup beneath the dispenser of the coffee machine. 'How do you take it?'

'Latte, thanks. One sugar.'

She noticed Ryan eyeing her milk crate. 'Excuse the lack of furnishings,' she said, nodding to it. 'I have furniture on order, but it won't be delivered until next week.'

'It's fine. Completely understandable.'

'So when did you land?' she asked, tipping in a teaspoon of sugar and pressing the latte setting on the machine.

'A couple of hours ago,' he said over the grind of the beans. 'I checked in to a hotel, then I thought I'd walk down here and see the place. Before I knew it, I was knocking on your door.'

'It must have been the house. It has that sort of energy; it pulls you in.'

'Very much so.' He walked around the dining room, running his hands across the fireplace mantel and along the exposed sandstone walls. 'None of us have been here before, but we've always known about it, always thought it a special place.'

Paige carried his coffee to him.

'Thank you. Just what I need. My body still thinks it's ten-thirty in the morning so I'm weirdly exhausted but ready to start the day.'

'That must feel strange. I've never been overseas. Have rarely ventured from my hometown until now.' Paige gestured to the milk crate opposite hers and they both sat. She collected her wine glass from the floor and sipped. 'Tell me about Charlotte.'

'Well, she was the sister of my great-grandfather, James.' Ryan sipped too. 'As far as I know, they both grew up in this house with their father, Walter Greene. James moved to the UK in the late 1920s to expand the steel business there. Charlotte stayed here with Walter.'

'And her mother?'

'I believe she died when Charlotte was a child. She lived her last years in an asylum before she took her own life.'

Paige nodded sagely. 'How sad. You mentioned on the phone that Charlotte remained an enigma to the family. What did you mean by that?'

Ryan cupped his hands around the coffee cup. He looked too tall for the crate but impeccable nonetheless in dark jeans and a khaki jumper with his sleeves pushed up. Smooth, lean arms took his weight as he leaned forward on his knees in a moment of thoughtfulness. 'Charlotte's life became somewhat of a mystery.'

'How so?'

'I don't know a good deal about what transpired. My great-grandfather hardly spoke of his sister but from what I understand, Charlotte disappeared in 1929 and was never heard from again.'

Paige tilted her head. 'What do you mean she disappeared?'

'Just that. Her father, Walter, went missing too. The last contact James had from them was a telegram Charlotte sent on October thirty-first, 1929.'

'What did the telegram say?'

'She asked him to come home to Sydney immediately, that they were sending her away and he was to find her.'

'And that's when it was dated? October thirty-first, 1929?'

'Yes, with a postmaster's stamp from a post office in The Rocks.'

'Interesting.'

'How so?'

'Well, two days before, on October twenty-ninth, Black Tuesday happened. The day the New York Stock Exchange crashed. Actually, it wasn't the first crash, but it was the one the market never recovered from and was a significant cause of the Great Depression.' A coincidence perhaps, but Charlotte and Walter's disappearance at precisely that time intrigued Paige. An accident? Bankruptcy? Many lives had been shattered by the Great Crash and the Depression, and it wasn't unreasonable to think theirs might have been impacted too. 'Did James ever come back and look for them?'

'He did. After he wrote to Charlotte and his father several times with no reply, he made the trip out to Australia. Interestingly, when he got here to the house, it was ransacked, as if someone had been looking for something. In the parlour where Walter's desk was, James knew of a safe his father kept hidden beneath the floorboards. The safe was still there, and inside he found a letter of apology from Walter for leaving so abruptly and a request that James take control of the Australian arm of the business, to do with as he saw fit. The deeds to the company, transferred into James' name, were next to the letter. He then packed up the house, stored as much as he could in the attic, rented it out to tenants, then went back to the UK.'

'Did he try to find Walter and Charlotte?'

'He did, but he didn't have any luck. Eventually, he had to return to England, then the second World War broke out. He was drafted in 1939, sent to France and captured soon after by the Nazis. He was sent to Colditz prisoner-of-war camp in central Germany, where he died. My grandfather and his brother, as young as they were, took over the Greene empire after that.'

'And your family's steel was used on the Sydney Harbour Bridge, correct?'

'Yes, that's right.'

'Before the war, did James see out the bridge contract until it's completion in 1932?'

'I don't believe so,' Ryan said. 'He dissolved the mill and foundry before returning to the UK. Soon after, Greene Steel became an entirely British company.'

Paige let out an incredulous breath. 'That's quite a story. I wonder what happened to Charlotte and Walter.'

'No one really knows. It's been a family mystery, passed down from generation to generation. I'm sure it's become more elaborate over time, as these things do.'

Paige thought of Charlotte's handwritten love letters. 'Do you know if she was ever engaged or married?'

'I believe she was engaged to a banker before she disappeared.'

That must be who she wrote the letters to. 'The chest I told you about, the one I found in the attic, I believe it contains love letters.'

'It could be correspondence between Charlotte and her fiancé.'

Paige nodded. 'Yes, I think it could be. I haven't gone through any, just a quick glance at the top one.' She felt it important to let him know she hadn't snooped, no matter the temptation. 'I'm just glad to be able to return them to you. They shouldn't rot away in an old attic.'

'When it comes to Charlotte, there's never been much to go on,' he said. 'Maybe this chest you found can fill in some of the blanks. Anyway, just coming here and seeing the place for myself is special enough. I can't tell you what it means.'

'Would you like me to show you the rest of the house?'

Ryan's eyes lit up. 'I'd love that.'

They stood, placing their empty glasses on the kitchen bench and Paige led him up the stairs to the second floor. 'You'll have to excuse the fumes up here. I've had the painters in,' she explained. 'The place was pretty rundown when Xavier bought it.'

'We should have looked after it better,' Ryan said, looking sheepish. 'We're a busy family but it's no excuse.'

'So you work for the family business?' she asked as she opened doors and let him roam through the empty rooms.

'I do. Greene Steel and Technologies. I'm the European sales manager, which keeps me busy. I travel a lot. I'm never in one place for long.'

As precious as Charlotte's possessions were to him, Paige still thought it odd that someone so busy would take the unusual step of flying to the other side of the world to chase them down when she could have shipped them to him.

'Where's Xavier now?' he asked as she showed him the bathroom.

'He's back in Albury. It's where I'm from too, a town south of here, near the Victorian border.'

'You grew up there?'

'I did. I'm an only child. My parents retired to Fiji four years ago, so I don't have any family left there. Just Xavier really.'

'And you mentioned you were going to be his assistant.'

'Yes. We worked in a library together. We've been colleagues and friends for years. When his mother passed away, he came into his inheritance so he decided to start a publishing house. Books are his life so it's a dream come true for him. He asked me to join him here to be his assistant.'

'It must have been a big move for you and your partner?' His eyes slid to her bare ring finger.

As he did, she found her eyes sliding to his too. No wedding band.

'I came alone,' she admitted, leaving the bathroom behind and leading him down the hall towards the attic. 'It's been a bit of a culture shock, especially as I'm a country girl. The endless traffic, a city full of strangers, a million different choices for dinner.' She chuckled. 'I really should set up the kitchen downstairs so I can cook each night.'

He did a double-take. 'Wait. You've been staying here?'

'Yes.'

'You sleep here? At night? All by yourself?' He looked incredulous.

She flushed. 'Well, it's convenient. I haven't had a chance to find an apartment yet and the hotel would have been too costly.'

'Of course. I didn't mean ...' He scratched his head. 'It's just a very brave thing to do.'

'You wouldn't stay here on your own?'

He shook his head and laughed. 'Not a chance. I'm not one for sleeping in old ghostly houses.'

'The first night was strange but I'm used to it now. It's a beautiful house. I feel at peace here.' It was true. The walls whispered less, or perhaps she'd learnt to listen to them. The shadows were more fluid, or perhaps she'd learnt to see them.

'You aren't afraid of anything, are you?' he said, fixing her with an admiring gaze.

It wasn't true. She was afraid of lots of things. Maybe not of ghosts and old houses, but she was afraid of falling in love and having her heart broken. Of loving someone for a lifetime and never having the courage to do anything about it. Of escaping to the Big Smoke to find that her feelings couldn't be outrun after all.

'So up there is where I found Charlotte's chest.' She pointed at the attic staircase. 'I haven't replaced the lightbulb yet so it'll be dark if we go in. I didn't bring the torch with me either.'

'Is the chest up there now?' Ryan asked.

'It's downstairs in the parlour where I sleep.'

'Perhaps we could take a look?'

'Sure.'

They retreated down the stairs and she led him to the parlour. 'Pardon the disarray.' She swept up clothes and shoes off the mattress and threw them into her suitcase.

His eyes roamed the room and her makeshift bed.

'Like I said, it's temporary,' she explained. 'I don't plan on staying here long. Finding a rental is on my list of things to do.'

'Brave, brave, brave.' He shook his head.

She nudged him. 'Take a seat. The chest is over here.'

As Ryan perched himself on the edge of her mattress, long legs stretched out in front of him, Paige dragged the chest across and sat down beside him. 'See Charlotte's name here?' She traced the carved letters with her fingertips.

Ryan reached out and did the same. 'Yes, it does say Charlotte. This was definitely hers.' He opened the lid and, on the top of the pile, where Paige had left them a week ago, were the bundles of handwritten notes tied together with twine.

She was about to warn him of the top one, but his finger had already hooked around the twine, pulling it onto his lap. His eyes scanned the words and Paige held her breath as she recalled what was written there... *I wonder if your body wants mine the way mine wants yours—the kisses—the hotness—the wetness—all melting together.*

Ryan's eyes widened and he cleared his throat noisily. 'Ah, right. Well. Um, that's some love letter.'

Paige hid her smile. 'You mentioned that Charlotte was engaged to a banker before she disappeared. It would make sense that she was writing these letters to him and maybe vice versa. Their love was obviously profound. Do you know his name?'

'No, I'm not sure.'

'The rest of the letters might tell you more. Some could even include his name. They have to be handled with care though, as they're probably brittle.'

'Sure. I'll be careful.' Ryan's phone tinged in his pocket and he pulled it out to glance at it. His brow furrowed at whatever he was reading before he shoved the phone back in his pocket a little too forcefully. 'Sorry about that. I've got something going on back home. Anyway,' he glanced at his watch, 'I didn't realise the time. It's after eleven. I've intruded on you long enough. I should get going.'

'Oh. Right. Okay.' Paige stood, surprised at how much she'd enjoyed his company.

Ryan placed the bundle of handwritten notes back into the chest and closed the lid. He stood too, the chest in his arms.

'When's your flight home?' she asked.

'Tomorrow afternoon.'

'And the pieces in the attic? I didn't get around to showing them to you.'

He smiled. 'I'll take you up on the offer of photos.'

She laughed. 'Well, it was lovely to meet you. Good luck with Charlotte's letters. I hope you can find out what happened to her.' She showed him to the front door.

'Thank you again, Paige. It was nice of you to write to us and to let me in to see the old place.'

'It was nothing.'

'Well, I appreciate it all the same. All the best with the publishing house.'

She opened the door for him, and he stepped down onto the footpath. He waved goodbye and, with the chest in his arms and under the haze of the streetlights, he walked down Playfair towards his hotel, taking Charlotte with him.

CHAPTER 4

CHARLOTTE
March 1929

Charlotte Greene had never been to a party before, not in all her eighteen virtuous years. Not a jazz bar or a ball, not even a soirée. It was a solitary existence she kept, something she had done for most of her life, content with books for company rather than people. So she noticed that some were surprised now to see her out, like a rare and exotic creature released from its habitat.

'That must be the Greene girl,' she heard them say from behind mink stoles.

'Wherever has she been?'

'And why now?'

'It's all rather odd.'

'Let them talk,' her father said. 'Let them be curious. We want this engagement on the front page of the paper come morning.'

And so it came to be, that on a warm Saturday evening, the downstairs rooms of their modest Playfair Street house were transformed into the kind of grandeur that could rival a great house. There were glistening chandeliers and extravagant floral arrangements, gold silk curtains and a classical string quartet.

Charlotte sipped champagne lightly from her coupe glass, the same one she'd been holding for the past hour, as the music rippled around her and she became invisible against the wall. It might have been her engagement party but she'd done her best to avoid the guests, especially the women who gathered in circles to size her up from behind their lashes.

Whatever had possessed her to agree to this?

A simple dinner at home would have sufficed, a few of Floyd's closest friends in attendance. She might even have agreed to a small restaurant, but not the two hundred guests he and her father had squeezed into their house, none of whom she knew.

This was all Floyd of course, down to the top hats and furs, the jewels and expensive liquor that people slurped and sloshed around as though turbulent economic times weren't upon them. Floyd was a loans manager at the Bank of New South Wales, a position that afforded him the kind of luxuries the breadline could only dream of. Luxuries like lavish properties and fast automobiles, bright caviar that the wealthy dolloped into their mouths like cheap sweets. It was a life that Charlotte and her middle-class upbringing had little experience of, nor one that she aspired to.

'Charlotte, darling.' Floyd's voice found her from across the room. She turned to see him gliding towards her, a glass of scotch in his hand. 'Wherever have you been hiding?' He reached her, bending exaggeratedly low to kiss her hand.

The morbidly curious turned to watch. She quickly smiled, pushing aside a ribbon of dark hair that had come loose from her clasp. 'Just taking a moment, Mr Clark.'

'Please, you must call me Floyd. Yes, what a party, hey?' He winked at her, his neatly trimmed and combed moustache twitching. 'Are you feeling all right? I've not seen hide nor hair of you all evening.'

'I've been here.'

'Well, come then. Best not to linger in the corner. I want you to meet some important people.'

She hesitated, then fixed her smile again. 'Of course.'

He grasped her hand and led her through the throng of guests, out the back doors and into the small garden. The warm breeze caught her blue satin dress, playing with the hem. Her heels clicked on the pathway as she followed Floyd to the high sandstone wall at the rear where a circle of men stood in a haze of cigarette smoke, beneath the flowering dwarf apple gum.

Floyd's hand was at the small of her back, prodding her forward. 'Gentlemen, I'd like to introduce you to Walter Greene's daughter and my fiancée, Miss Charlotte Greene.'

The men in their top hats dipped their heads in welcome.

'Allow me to make the introductions,' Floyd said self-importantly. 'This is Dr JJC Bradfield, engineer-in-chief of the Sydney Harbour Bridge.'

Charlotte sucked in her breath as Dr Bradfield extended his hand and she shook it. 'It's an absolute pleasure to meet you, sir.'

'And you, Miss Greene. Floyd and your father speak of you often.'

'Good things, I hope.'

He smiled. 'Only good things.'

She breathed, somewhat awestruck. It wasn't every day she got to meet a national pioneer. 'Your bridge is magnificent, if you don't mind me saying.'

In response, the circle turned to look at it across the yard, its majestic half-form rising over the Playfair Street houses to glimmer under a silver moon.

Bradfield's face became fond. 'Yes, it's quite something. And ever-growing. No longer do people have to come all the way into Sydney town to see its progress. They can now witness it from places as far away as Bankstown or Epping.'

'Marvellous. Just marvellous,' said Floyd. 'A true engineering feat.'

'Even in the face of an uncertain global economy, your bridge is a source of hope and employment for hundreds,' said Charlotte with admiration.

Bradfield seemed impressed. 'What do you know of the global economy?'

Floyd's face flushed. 'Charlotte likes to dally with the newspapers from time to time. The fashion pages mostly.'

'I have read extensively on the Wall Street issues,' she said, trying not to let her irritation with Floyd show. 'I'm particularly interested in the stock market reversal we witnessed yesterday. Is it not caused by investors borrowing money from banks to invest in overvalued stocks? Do the banks not have a responsibility with regard to crediting?'

Bradfield nodded thoughtfully. 'Indeed, Miss Greene. You have an eye for detail.'

'I read that the ticker couldn't keep up with the mass sell-off of stocks.'

'The market did recover though.'

'Please, Charlotte dear,' Floyd said, looking uncomfortable. 'You're boring these men with your amateur political talk. Best you stick to ladies' topics, hey?'

As if to ensure not another word left her mouth, he moved her quickly through the rest of the group. She said hello to Lawrence Ennis, director of design and construction for Dorman Long and Co, and Sir Thomas Bavin, the New South Wales premier and treasurer. She'd almost completed a full circle when she came to the last man, Bradfield's chief engineer on the bridge, looking striking in a black tuxedo.

'This is Alexander Young,' Floyd announced.

Mr Young extended his hand to her, their eyes meeting and holding.

She shook it, faltering slightly at the way his intense gaze drank her in and the charming smile he gave her. 'I'm Charlotte Greene. It's nice to meet you.'

'The pleasure is all mine.' His accent was English, his face boyishly handsome, his homburg stylish enough to compete with the arrogance of the top hat. Her cheeks flushed. She glanced around for Floyd in case he'd seen, but he'd moved towards Bradfield again and was apologising on her behalf for the Wall Street talk.

Alexander leant in. 'Mr Clark is a lucky man.'

Her cheeks burned hotter. 'Thank you.'

He smiled again and her mind went blank. She wanted to say more but Floyd reappeared and whisked her once more into the throes of the party.

***

After the cake had been cut and the speeches delivered, Charlotte dissolved once more into the shadows. The crowd thinned slightly as midnight encroached and the band packed away their instruments. The remaining women huddled in groups, gloved hands clutching cigarette holders, while the men gathered around the door to the front parlour.

Charlotte, longing for her bed, glanced down at the Tiffany

engagement ring on her finger. A brilliant diamond solitaire set in twenty-four-carat gold, larger than any piece of jewellery she'd owned before. It still looked at odds with her humble daywear every time she slipped it on.

While she found the whole ordeal daunting, she couldn't deny that Floyd had been a pleasant enough companion during their brief four-week courtship—generous, respectful, a little rigid in his disposition, perhaps, but it was to be expected. He was forty-two to her tender eighteen. 'You have much to learn from him,' her father had said.

Floyd and her father, Walter, shared a financial association. Walter's business, Greene and Son Steel Fabricating, was one of two steelwork enterprises that supplied the Sydney Harbour Bridge with the steel required to build the great arch. Walter ensured Dr Bradfield had enough steel for construction, and Floyd ensured Walter's loans were approved with ease to meet the ongoing demand for product. Her father had said that Charlotte's marriage to Floyd made good business sense. It would ensure the security of her future and the family legacy long after her father retired.

And Floyd would have what he desired. A beautiful, young bride and a clutch of healthy heirs.

Charlotte felt someone approach and glanced up. 'Papa.'

'There you are, love.' Her father leant down to kiss her cheek. 'I've been looking everywhere for you. What are you doing in the corner here?'

'Just catching my breath.' She'd hardly seen him all night as he'd moved from circle to circle and she'd tried her best to meld into the background.

'Quite a party we've thrown. Everyone who's anyone is here.' He sipped his scotch, his eyes eagerly scanning the crowd.

'Yes, it's been wonderful.'

'Did you get a chance to meet Sir Howard Boston? How about Mrs Delia Bligh? She runs a little sewing group for women on Margaret Street.'

'No, I don't believe I did.'

He gave her a knowing look. 'Charlotte, love, I know it's all been a bit overwhelming. Things have moved quickly, but you are Floyd's fiancée now. You must make the effort.'

She felt a pang of guilt. 'I know. I'm sorry.'

'It wouldn't hurt you to make some new friends tonight.'

'It's just that I hardly know these people. We have nothing in common.'

'All the more reason to introduce yourself. They will be *your* people soon. Especially the women. You'll belong to their social circles.'

She'd had every intention of meeting them at the start of the evening, but somewhere between the hors d'oeuvres and their critical dressing-down of her from across the room, she'd lost her nerve. Surely they were wondering if this naive, working-class girl was worthy of their distinguished, upper-class bachelor.

She nodded reassuringly. 'I'll seek out Mrs Bligh and ask if I can join her sewing group.'

Her father grinned broadly then kicked back the rest of his scotch. 'The men are about to retire to the front parlour for brandy and blackjack. I trust you will keep the ladies entertained in our absence.' He patted her arm and left for the parlour to empty his pockets with the other men. Charlotte sipped her champagne and looked around the room, deciding how best to insert herself into the cliques that had already formed. When perfume filled her nostrils and someone brushed against her arm, she turned.

'I can almost hear your brain ticking over,' said a woman beside her. 'And so will they if you're not careful. They'll smell your fear a mile away.'

She was beautiful, her hair cut in a fashionable Eton crop with a red sequined band and feather around her head. Her lips were the brightest red, inhaling back on a cigarette holder, and she wore a striking dress of elegant beadwork. When all other gowns fell to the floor, hers stopped shockingly above the knee as if in defiance. She was exquisite and statuesque, unlike anyone Charlotte had met before, and certainly unlike the other women in the room.

'Am I that obvious?' she asked, blushing.

'A little.' The woman stubbed her cigarette out in a nearby ashtray and extended her hand. 'Estelle Mayfair. How do you do?'

Charlotte shook her hand. 'I'm Charlotte Greene.'

'Oh, I know who you are. Everyone does. You've become quite the sensation.'

She wrinkled her nose at the suggestion of it. 'I don't know about that.'

'Relatively unknown on the social circuit and now you're marrying Floyd Clark. The most desired bachelor in Sydney. Come now.' Her grin was sly.

Despite her awkwardness, Charlotte smiled. Estelle Mayfair had a playful way about her.

'Word of advice,' she said, leaning in so that Charlotte was consumed by her perfume again. 'Don't let them see how terrified you are. They're carnivores. They'll eat you alive.'

A loud giggle bubbled out of Charlotte and she put her hand to her mouth as Estelle giggled too.

Outside, high above the city, fireworks erupted, drawing the women into the garden. Waiters followed quickly with champagne.

'How delightful!' Estelle declared, lighting another cigarette. 'Seems we aren't the only ones having a party. Shall we?'

'You go ahead,' Charlotte said politely. 'I'll be out in a minute.'

Estelle gave her a knowing look before sashaying out to the garden with the other women to watch the colours explode.

Charlotte seized the opportunity and slipped unnoticed into the small library off the hall. Once inside, she eased the door closed, pulled the clasp from her hair, letting her curls unravel down her back, and kicked off her heels, taking her first proper breath of the evening.

The collection of books there was hardly vast, but her mother's library had always been a sanctuary for Charlotte. She'd read everything on the shelves, two, three, four times, much to her father's chagrin. 'Books breed ideas in women's heads that shouldn't be there,' he would often say. 'But read them if you must, until you marry.'

In the four weeks since she'd known Floyd, he'd come to heartily agree. 'You'll be far too busy with marital duties for books.'

She sighed and moved in front of the bookcase that ran the length of the wall, searching the spines for the one she was looking for. Her eyes fell upon its maroon cover and she drew it from its place, taking it with her to the leather armchair. She hiked up her satin dress and sank into the chair, tucking her stockinged legs beneath her.

Love Through the Ages—A Collection of Timeless Love Letters.

She opened the book—a priceless first edition—and breathed in the familiar earthiness of its tea-coloured pages. She'd read these love letters many times before and knew them by heart—Robert Browning to Elizabeth Barret Browning, Oscar Wilde to Lord Alfred Douglas, Beethoven to his Immortal Beloved.

She turned to one of her favourites, knowing exactly where it was— a letter from Napoleon Bonaparte to his wife Josephine, December 1795. She read quietly to herself, the laughter from the men in the front parlour and the excited cries from the women in the garden belonging to some faraway world.

But when she heard the door open slightly, a small creak from its hinges, she turned expecting to see her father or Floyd. It was neither. Standing there was Bradfield's chief engineer, the enigmatic Alexander Young. Charlotte jumped out of the chair, pushed her dress down to cover her knees and cursed her stockinged feet and unpinned hair. A flush grew from her head to her toes.

'Forgive me, Miss Greene. I didn't mean to intrude,' Mr Young said.

She couldn't meet his eyes. 'I thought all the men were in the parlour.'

'I'm not one for gambling or smoking. But I can see I'm disturbing you. I will leave you be.'

'You can come in.' She wasn't sure what had made her say it, but the words had escaped her lips as surely as if someone else had spoken them.

He hesitated. 'Are you sure? Your father thought I might enjoy the library but...'

'It's all right. I was just reading.'

He stepped inside but had the good manners to leave the door open. Removing his hat and leaving it on the small table by the armchair, he walked to the wall of books while she hurried to slip her shoes on.

'You don't have to wear them on my account,' he said, turning towards her. 'You look comfortable as you are.'

She blushed again and left the shoes where they were.

'What were you reading?' he asked.

Charlotte glanced down at the book. 'It's nothing.'

'A lady leaves her own engagement party to escape into the library and read. Must be quite a book.'

She shrugged, feeling embarrassed to tell him. 'It's just letters.'

'Oh?'

'Love letters.'

He didn't laugh but rather held his hand out. 'May I see?'

She handed the book to him, catching his scent as she did. It reminded her of fresh linen and summer days, and she berated herself for liking it, this man who was not her fiancé.

He looked at the cover then flicked through the pages, settling on one. She could see his eyes sweeping over the words. '"No, nothing has the power to part me from you; our love is based upon virtue, and will last as long as our lives. Adieu, there is nothing that I will not brave for your sake. Adieu, my dear heart!"' Mr Young glanced up with an amused smile. 'Voltaire had a way with words.'

Charlotte relaxed and smiled back. 'He wrote often to his many lovers. There are plenty in there from him, far more risqué.'

'What an intriguing book.'

She watched him curiously as he studied the pages. 'Do you like to read?'

'Yes,' Mr Young said. 'My mother's house in London has a library like this. I grew up with her collection—Joseph Conrad, Virginia Woolfe, Ernest Hemingway.'

'We have those authors!' Without giving thought to etiquette, she reached for his arm and led him excitedly to the spot on the bookcase where Conrad, Woolfe and Hemingway stood on the shelves. 'These were my mother's. This was her collection.'

'Your mother?' He glanced at her. 'I don't believe I saw her at the party.'

'She died when I was young,' Charlotte said. Time may have dimmed the sorrow of it, but never had she felt her mother's absence more than on that night.

'I'm sorry to hear that. Was she unwell?'

'She grieved.'

Mr Young bowed his head. 'Forgive me. I shouldn't have asked.'

'No, it's all right. A child born after me didn't survive beyond the first month. He was put to sleep in his cot and never awoke. She had a difficult time recovering from the loss. Still, she always loved it in here. It was a place of peace for her.'

'Among her books. I can understand why.'

'I have a few of her belongings that I treasure. The library is one of them. It reminds me of a bookstore. Shelves full of possibility.' It had become a place of peace for her too, a room to escape within.

'Libraries do hold that promise of transportation.' He was still holding the book of love letters but his eyes were firmly on her, in a way that was intoxicating. No man had ever shown her interest like this before. 'Do you have siblings?'

'Yes, an older brother, James. He lives in England now. My father has another steel mill in Middlesbrough. It's only small but we're trying to expand into Europe.'

'He should do well. There is much need for infrastructure there. Many parts of Europe are still rebuilding, even a decade after the war. So tell me, Miss Greene—'

'Please, you may call me Charlotte. Miss Greene sounds terribly young. Or terribly old, I'm not sure which.'

Mr Young laughed, making her stomach flutter. 'Very well. And please, you can call me Alex. Mr Young sounds like someone's schoolteacher.'

It was her turn to laugh. As she did, she stole a glance at him from the corner of her eye and found he was still looking intently at her. She cleared her throat. 'I'm sorry, you were going to ask me something.'

'Yes, I was going to ask how you knew so much about the economy. You handled yourself well out there. I was impressed, as was my boss.'

She cringed, remembering how uncomfortable it had made Floyd. 'I apologise. I hope I didn't embarrass anyone.'

'On the contrary, it was fascinating to listen to you.'

She smiled, trying to push down her self-consciousness. 'Well, I find the stock market interesting. I read the newspapers and listen to the radio. I'm not an expert by any means, but I do enjoy learning about it. About new things in general.'

'It's important for a woman to be knowledgeable about the world around her.'

'My fiancé would beg to differ.'

Alex leant in. 'Let's not worry about what he thinks.'

Charlotte suppressed a giggle, not entirely sure he was joking.

'So what do you like to learn?' he asked.

'I mostly enjoy English literature. It would be my dream to study at university one day.' She had already discussed the prospect with her father, but then Floyd's proposal had happened and there'd been no further mention of it.

'A degree? How wonderful. Have you enquired about the possibility?'

'I don't think Floyd or my father would allow it.' Not with a wedding to be planned and marital duties to be upheld. Attending university was such a distant hope, she didn't dare to dream.

'That's a shame,' he said, 'Someday perhaps, when the timing is better.'

They shared a look, hers filled with appreciation for his encouraging words. She was aware of how close he was to her, how their shoulders were almost touching and if she reached out her hand just a fraction towards his, their fingertips would connect. This one exchange was unlike anything she'd experienced before. She'd spent several occasions in Floyd's company but had never felt the desire to touch or be touched by him. If he were there now, he'd probably be too horrified by her bare feet and unpinned hair to enjoy the experience.

'So do you associate much with my father?' she asked, turning her thoughts back to Alex.

'Not with your father directly,' he said. 'Though I work with our foreman to ensure we have a constant supply of steel from your mill for the bridge. You may also be aware, your foundry is located on our construction site on the northern side of the harbour, right next door to my office.'

'And you work for Dr Bradfield?'

'I'm one of the chief engineers under his direction. We're from the Department of New South Wales Public Works, although Dorman Long and Co are the contractors who are building the bridge.'

'Do you have much association with Floyd?'

He grinned. 'I can't say I've had the pleasure.'

Charlotte caught the playfulness in his voice and grinned too. 'He and my father are good friends. He helps the business financially. He's quite smart, particularly with money.'

'Then your father has chosen well for you.'

Just as the grandfather clock in the dining room announced one in the morning, her father, Floyd and Dr Bradfield appeared in the doorway. Alex dropped the book into her hands and took a large step away from her.

Floyd's eyes darted between them with suspicion. 'Charlotte, I've been looking all over for you. What are you doing in here? And good lord, where are your shoes? Your hair.'

Charlotte's cheeks burned. 'I was just showing Mr Young our book collection.'

'Ah yes.' Her father stepped into the room. 'I directed Mr Young this way earlier. These are my late wife's books. What do you think, son?'

'You have a fine collection, sir,' Alex said, fetching his hat from the table. 'Miss Greene has been explaining the delights of L Frank Baum to me.'

Floyd looked appalled or confused or something as he swayed from the scotch.

'Did you have any luck on the blackjack?' Alex asked Bradfield.

'Broke even. Mr Greene here was not so lucky.'

'They bled me dry,' Walter said. 'You'll have to join us next time, Mr Young.'

'Indeed,' Alex said. 'For now, though, I should be getting home. I have some paperwork to catch up on in the morning.'

'Working on a Sunday. That's dedication,' Walter acknowledged approvingly.

'Mr Young is one of my brightest engineers,' Bradfield said. 'The bridge can be in no finer hands than his.'

Alex smiled modestly and turned to Charlotte, who was still standing by the bookcase. He put his hat on and tipped it towards her. 'It was a pleasure to meet you, Miss Greene. Thank you for a lovely party and the tour of your library.'

He bid the men good evening and left the room, leaving her to wonder if the last hour had all been a dream.

CHAPTER
5

Charlotte slept late the next morning. It was only when she heard the trill of the telephone downstairs that she opened a sleepy eye and rolled over to stretch. Sunlight streamed through the curtains and the children next door were playing hopscotch beneath her window.

Realising it must be late, she pushed the covers off and rose. After washing her face in the basin, she rolled on stockings then slipped a day dress on, feeling the heat of the morning rise through the floorboards.

She stepped down the stairs just as her father hung up the telephone in the hallway.

'Good morning, love. Did you sleep well?' He gave her a peck on the cheek as she passed.

'I did. What time is it?'

'Just on half eleven. You slept the morning away.'

'I must have been tired.'

As she walked down the hall and into the kitchen, she saw little evidence that her engagement party the night before had ever occurred. The blackjack and card tables had been packed away in the parlour, the furniture in the other rooms returned to their original positions and the polished timber floors were gleaming once more.

'Floyd sent housekeeping staff around to clean up this morning. Can you believe it, housekeeping staff?'

'Goodness.'

'I'm surprised you didn't hear them.'

'Not at all.'

'I think he's trying to impress us. Never mind that, I'm the one who's impressed.' He laughed cheerfully as they entered the kitchen. 'I'm mighty famished love, what with our big night and all.'

'I'm sorry. Let me fix you some breakfast.'

He sat at the small table in the kitchen while she set the kettle of water on the lit stove, and sliced bread for toasting.

'Guess what else happened,' he said. 'We're the top story of the morning.'

The Sydney Morning Herald was folded beside him and he flipped it open, pointing to the front page. There, beside an article about the bridge, was a large column dedicated to her and Floyd's engagement and the people who had attended.

'Isn't that something?' he said with a wide grin. 'It's not often one gets to be on the front page. People all over the city will be talking about our party now.'

Charlotte set down her father's breakfast and lowered herself into a chair. Her eyes were still heavy, despite the late rise. If she was honest, the party had been exhausting. All those people, the forced smiles that had hurt her cheeks…

Then she remembered Mr Young. In her post-engagement weariness she'd almost forgotten about being in the library with him, the conversation they'd shared, the hour she'd spent in his company.

Walter's voice broke through her thoughts. 'What do you think?'

She was brought abruptly back to the room. 'I'm sorry. What were you saying?'

He smiled. 'That's all right, love. You must be on cloud nine after last night. I was saying we should buy a grand piano.'

Charlotte frowned. 'Why?'

'Well, Floyd has a grand piano. I've seen it. A Bösendorfer. It's quite something.'

'But neither of us play the piano.'

'We could get you some lessons. Something to fill in your time with. How about that?'

She shook her head. She didn't want piano lessons. What she really wanted was to enrol in a degree or a course of some kind. 'Perhaps I could enquire at the university for further study.'

He glanced at her sharply. 'Now, love, not that again. We've talked about it.'

'But I could do it just until the wedding in November.'

'It's not becoming of a lady,' he said. 'Certainly not an engaged one. Floyd wouldn't like it.'

A fresh protest sat at the back of her throat but she resisted. It was an old argument that she never seemed to win and it was pointless to try. 'We don't have room for a piano anyway. It'd be a waste of money.'

'We'll move things around. And we're hardly short of a penny. We have the contract with the bridge.'

She closed her eyes. When she opened them, he was watching her closely. 'Charlotte, love, I need you to accept this.'

'Fine, get the piano.'

'Not that. Floyd. Resisting will only make it harder. I know it's difficult to marry a man you hardly know, but you have to try.'

'I am trying,' she said, even though deep down she knew her efforts so far had been lacklustre.

He patted her hand. 'I need a little more from you, okay?'

She chewed her bottom lip and nodded. 'Who was on the telephone earlier?'

'Floyd, checking on his bride-to-be.' Walter picked up the paper again and snapped it open. 'He reminded me that the Governor's Ball is in two weeks. You'll be expected to attend with him. It will be quite the social event.'

'A ball?' Charlotte had never been to one before. She felt a wave of curiosity and panic wash over her equally. A ball with lots of people. People she didn't know. Accompanying Floyd. 'Do I have to go?'

'You do.'

She picked at a mark on the table to avoid resisting again. 'What are your plans for today?'

'I have some business to attend to. As a matter of fact,' he glanced at his watch, 'I should be going. People are waiting for me.'

'On a Sunday?'

'Yes, always busy.' He stood, planted a kiss on top of her head and hurried out of the kitchen.

When she heard the front door close, she exhaled and stood, clearing the table of breakfast dishes and washing them in the sink. As she set them on a towel to dry the telephone rang.

Her first thought was that it was Floyd again and she was almost tempted to let it ring out but didn't want to be unkind. She walked to the hall table and picked up the receiver from the cradle. 'Hello?'

'Miss Greene?'

'Speaking.'

'Charlotte, darling. It's Estelle Mayfair. We met last night at your engagement party.'

'Miss Mayfair?'

'You probably don't remember me.' Her voice tinkled like crystal down the line.

'Of course I remember you.' How could she forget? Estelle had been the striking woman who had made Charlotte laugh by poking fun at the austerity of the upper-class ladies.

'I do hope I'm not disturbing you on a Sunday, but I was wondering if you might be free for afternoon tea today.'

Charlotte wasn't sure if she'd heard right. Never had she been invited to tea before. ' Yes I am free. Did you have somewhere in mind?'

'A tearoom in the city, perhaps?'

Charlotte squirmed at the idea. It would mean she would have to leave The Rocks, board a tram and navigate city streets, all the things she wasn't used to doing. She quickly racked her brain for an alternative. 'May I suggest my house instead?'

'Really?' Estelle didn't seem disappointed. 'How delightful! I will be there at two o'clock.'

After they ended the call, Charlotte stared at the telephone, wondering if somehow she had made a friend.

***

The day had grown warmer by the time Estelle arrived, and although the house was uncomfortably stuffy, the spot in the backyard, beneath the apple gum, was pleasant. Charlotte carried a tray of tea and cake on her mother's finest bone china and set it down on the small table where Estelle sat. She sat too, smoothed her grey pleated skirt and jersey top and tried to quell the flutter of butterflies that had worked their way into her stomach.

'Tea, Miss Mayfair?' she asked.

Estelle smiled. 'Please, if we're going to be friends, you must call me Estelle.' She peeled off her gloves then extended a smooth, bejewelled hand, grabbing the teapot herself, pouring them each a cup.

Charlotte relaxed. 'I do hope you like lemon cake.'

Estelle set down the pot with a wink. 'It's one of my favourites.'

Charlotte placed a slice on each of their plates and they ate as a flock of crimson rosellas landed on the branches above, tweeting in chorus.

'It's quite peaceful out here,' Estelle said. 'Do you get a lot of noise from the bridge?'

'During the week, the creeper cranes can be heard or sometimes the shouts of the men drilling the rivets in. Construction has picked up considerably now that they're bringing the arches together.'

'And your father supplies the steel, I understand.'

'Correct. We have a mill in Silverwater and a foundry on the Dorman Long and Co site on Milsons Point, just under the bridge, although the majority of the steel is imported from England.'

'Is that how your father knows Floyd? Through business dealings?'

Charlotte sipped her tea and set it down. 'Yes. They're associates. Floyd approves the bank loans for the business to ensure we meet the ongoing demand for steel.'

'Must be an extremely profitable venture. All that steel.' She fixed a cigarette to the end of a holder and set a gold lighter to it.

'We only supply a small part of it but yes, it does well.'

Estelle blew a smoke ring and smiled. She looked beautiful in a blue drop-waisted shift and brown heels. A glossy yellow curl from her Eton crop peeked beneath her cloche hat and she exuded the kind of elegance Charlotte could only hope to replicate. The cross of Estelle's legs, the alluring slouch of her shoulders and the petite way she flicked ash from her cigarette all made Charlotte want to stare. Estelle commanded that kind of attention.

'So tell me, dear,' she said, 'how old are you?'

'I turned eighteen this past December.'

'A lovely age. I remember being eighteen once, oh, many moons ago now.'

Charlotte wondered how many moons exactly for Estelle looked ageless.

'I must say, you've become quite the talk of the town. Your engagement to Floyd has ruffled some feathers.' She grinned mischievously as she crushed her cigarette in the ashtray. 'You've managed to snatch away one of Sydney's most eligible bachelors right out from under the noses of the ladies.'

'It wasn't my intention to upset anyone.'

Estelle waved her hand with a laugh. 'Don't be silly. Your father has done well to secure your future with this union.'

'Floyd seems like a nice man,' Charlotte said. 'I'm still getting to know him.'

'He must be delighted with you. A beautiful, young wife half his age to call his own. What a treat. Is he your first?'

'My first what?'

'Lover, of course.'

Charlotte blushed fiercely, realising what Estelle meant. 'I've never... I mean I...'

Estelle's laugh rang out across the yard. 'Oh, dear! I apologise. I've embarrassed you. Let me rephrase. Have you liked another boy before, perhaps someone your age? Or is Floyd the first to court you?'

Charlotte's cheeks were still ablaze. Estelle was unashamedly direct. 'Floyd is the first. I've not been around many boys.'

'But surely you go dancing with them?'

'Not really.'

'Visit jazz bars?'

'No.'

'Drink alcohol? Share cigarettes? Drive in a car with them?'

'Not at all.'

'My goodness.' Estelle, looking confounded, attached another cigarette to the end of her holder. 'What do you do all day?'

Charlotte shifted uncomfortably. She'd always thought her life pleasant and purposeful until it had been cast in a dull light. 'Well, I manage the house.'

Estelle put her hand to her mouth and yawned exaggeratedly. 'You sound like a spinster, darling.'

'And I like to read. I love books and newspapers and education. I want to go to university one day.'

'University?' Now Estelle sat upright. 'A difficult thing for a woman to achieve, but I like that you're considering it. Which one?'

'Perhaps the University of Sydney.'

'How marvellous. Floyd must be thrilled. Beauty and brains.'

Except Charlotte was certain Floyd preferred a little more beauty and a little less brains with his women. 'How do you know Floyd?'

Estelle exhaled a steady stream of smoke. 'Through my husband. They were business associates.'

'I didn't realise you were married.'

'Was married. My dear Augustus died last July.'

'I'm so sorry.' Charlotte felt terrible for bringing it up.

'He was a good man, although he succumbed to his demons and took care of them with a shotgun.'

Most people would have recoiled at the casual way Estelle spoke of her husband's demise, but not Charlotte. She had lived her entire life in the shadow of her mother's similar fate. 'My mother lived in an asylum until I was eight, then she died of her infliction too.'

Estelle nodded sagely. 'I must confess, I was already aware of her death and that is why I asked you to tea today. You are a young woman, and Floyd and the wedding must feel like a formidable ask of you. Without your mother present, you are surely in need of female guidance. I can help you.'

Charlotte had to admit marrying Floyd and navigating this new and daunting world of adulthood felt all the more overwhelming without her mother alive. She would be grateful for Estelle's assistance. 'Thank you. I really haven't a clue what I'm doing.'

Estelle chuckled. 'Nor did I when I married Augustus.'

They giggled across the table.

'Do you live in The Rocks?' Charlotte asked.

'No, I live in Darlinghurst, on the east side of the city. Have you been there?'

'I haven't.' Charlotte reached for the teapot.

Estelle held her hand up. 'Not for me, dear. I must be going.'

'So soon?' Charlotte was surprised at how much she'd enjoyed their time together. 'It's been lovely getting to know you.'

'And you. I daresay the two of us are going to have lots of fun together.' Estelle placed her napkin on the table and stood. 'Would you like to have lunch tomorrow? I know a great jazz bar that makes the most divine grasshoppers. We could go boutique shopping afterwards.'

'Grasshoppers?'

'Cocktails, darling.' Estelle winked. 'It will make the afternoon more fun.'

'You mean you drink alcohol in the afternoon?' Charlotte was astounded. For a man it was acceptable, but for a woman it was considered vulgar.

'Of course. Why not?'

'I just ... I've never done that before.'

'Well now's your chance.'

Charlotte hesitated. She knew how she must seem to Estelle—bland and boring, colourless even. But a jazz bar? Drinking in the afternoon? Her father and Floyd would be appalled. 'I don't know. I'm quite busy here.'

'Doing what?' Estelle laughed huskily when Charlotte flushed. 'Come now. It will be fun. I'll plan a fabulous afternoon. We could get something new and sparkly for your wardrobe.' She cast an appraising eye over Charlotte's simple pleated skirt and top. 'And your hair. Long curls are no longer fashionable, darling. Have you thought about cutting it?'

'Not really.' Charlotte held fast to her curls as she walked Estelle to the front door. The older woman paused to pluck a pen and paper out of her handbag. 'Here's the address for the jazz bar on Pitt Street. Let's meet there at one o'clock tomorrow. We can eat, dance, drink, then shop. The whole afternoon will be ours to do as we please.'

Charlotte accepted the slip of paper as Estelle embraced her.

'Thank you for a lovely afternoon. It's been splendid!' She stepped outside and into her gold Bug Speedster parked out the front. With a toot of her horn, she accelerated down Playfair Street, disappearing around the bend.

CHAPTER
6

Charlotte woke the next morning to the familiar sound of the front door closing as Walter left for work. Instead of the rumble of his Studebaker outside, she heard him greet Mrs Parsons next door, boasting that he was off to catch the ferry to the north side of the bridge.

Because of their contract, he was spending more time at their foundry where they produced the metal castings for the arches, and less time at the Silverwater mill where they smelted the iron ore. Charlotte suspected he liked the foundry better, for the important bridge people he got to rub shoulders with all day long. He was proud of his contract and would tell anyone who listened, particularly their long-suffering neighbours.

Charlotte rose and filled her morning with chores. There was always plenty to do at the house—washing, sweeping, gardening, cooking. After her father left for work, that was how she occupied her days. She didn't mind the cycle, had always taken comfort in it. It was routine and order with no surprises.

As the time edged towards her lunch with Estelle though, her stomach began to flutter. Estelle had been a surprise, one that Charlotte hadn't expected. One that had exploded into her life like fireworks on Bonfire Night. As much as Estelle's dazzling energy had startled her, it had also sparked something inside, a quiet curiosity that at times emerged from her careful and sheltered world.

For their afternoon at the jazz bar, she chose a pale pink and cream shift with a drop-waist and hanky hem, a dress she rarely got a chance to wear, then pinned back her wayward curls and slipped a hat and gloves on. She had told her father about their lunch plans the evening before and he'd been delighted that she'd made a new friend, one who seemed to belong in a similar circle as Floyd. Keeping Floyd happy was of the utmost importance. The part where she was meeting Estelle at a jazz bar and not a tearoom she decided not to share.

She stepped out of the house, locked the door behind her and walked to the end of Playfair Street. From there she cut through to Argyle, then right onto George where The Rocks met the city proper. She halted at a tram stop and when a green and yellow carriage clattered past with the sign 'Pitt St' on its frontage, she boarded. Paying her fare to the conductor, she stepped inside and found a seat, careful to keep an eye on the passing street signs so that she wouldn't miss her stop.

The tram rolled down George Street, carrying her deeper into the business district. She didn't often leave The Rocks, even though it was just next door. The last time she'd ventured into the city was four months earlier with her father for the inauguration of the Commonwealth Bank, when massive crowds had packed Martin Place. Before that, she could hardly remember a time.

The tram curved to the left onto Bridge Street then came to a stop at the intersection of Pitt. Charlotte disembarked and consulted the address of the bar Estelle had given her. Hubert Penny's. She'd not heard of it before and when she reached its front glass windows, she peered inside. It was a decadent establishment of high ceilings and dark timber panelling, red velvet chairs and tasselled brocade lamps.

She smoothed down her dress and pushed open the heavy door. A maître d was upon her instantly. 'Can I help you?'

'I'm meeting Mrs Estelle Mayfair for lunch at one,' she told him.

'Ah, of course.' He lifted his hand. 'Right this way. Mrs Mayfair has a regular table at the back.'

She followed him through the dimly lit club where a cigarette haze clung to the ceiling. Mamie Smith's 'Crazy Blues' played softly in the background. At Estelle's booth in a shadowed corner, Charlotte sat, removed her gloves and waited for her friend to arrive.

When the time nudged quarter past one, the maître d reappeared. 'Miss Greene?'

'Yes?'

'Mrs Mayfair just telephoned,' he said. 'She sends her apologies. Something's come up and she can no longer meet you.'

'Oh.' Charlotte was disappointed. 'I do hope everything is all right.'

'Would you still like to see the menu?'

Charlotte looked around Hubert Penny's. To be there with Estelle was one thing, but to dine there alone may be perceived as something else entirely. 'No, I should probably go. Thank you anyway.'

She slipped on her gloves, collected her handbag and followed the maître d to the front door and back outside onto Pitt Street. A tide of businessmen in suits swirled around her in the lunchtime rush. Charlotte wondered if, now that she was there, she should partake in a little clothes shopping herself or find a more appropriate venue to have lunch in, perhaps one of the tearooms on George Street that she'd noticed on the way. In the end, she decided she'd prefer to go home and turned to walk back towards the tram stop, slamming straight into Alex.

'Miss Greene!' His hands went around her as she stumbled backwards.

'Mr Young.'

'I apologise. I didn't see you there. Are you hurt?'

'No, I'm okay.' She straightened her hat, realising his arms were still around her.

He dropped them quickly. 'It's lovely to see you, even if I did almost knock you over.'

She laughed. In a business suit and hat, he was even more attractive than she remembered him being. Attractive in a way that made her want to stare, even though it was inappropriate to do so.

'You're some way from home,' he said. 'Do you have a chaperone with you?'

'I was supposed to meet someone for lunch but they were unable to make it at the last minute.'

'Your fiancé?'

She blushed at the mention of Floyd. 'No, a friend.'

Alex nodded. 'Are you heading back to The Rocks now? I just finished a meeting and was returning to the bridge. I could accompany you.'

'If it's not an inconvenience,' she shyly.

'Not at all.' His smile was as lovely as his dark eyes. 'Shall we take the tram, or would you care to walk?'

'It's a beautiful day. Perhaps we could walk.'

'All right.'

They fell into step with one another, strolling down Pitt Street towards Circular Quay, carried by the current of pedestrians.

'What a shame you weren't able to meet your friend,' Alex said.

'Yes. I was rather looking forward to it,' Charlotte admitted. 'I don't often come up this way and certainly not for lunch engagements.'

'Are your friends mostly from The Rocks area then?'

'No, I don't really have any.' Then she cringed. Goodness, what a dismal way to paint herself. She cleared her throat, trying to explain. 'What I mean is, I tend to keep to myself mostly. It's just the way I've always been.'

'There's nothing wrong with that,' he said, and something in his voice told her he meant it.

She smiled. 'Well, as a child, I lost my best friend to measles. Her name was Hilda. She was eight. I was so afraid to find another friend in case they died too that I never played with the children in my neighbourhood again.'

'I'm sorry to hear that. How about school friends?'

'I didn't make any. I became a reclusive child.' She probably should have felt awkward at telling him so. Being friendless was not something she freely admitted to people, yet he didn't seem bothered by it.

'You must have been close to your brother then.'

'Yes, I was. My father worked a lot so I only had James for company. But he moved to England a few years ago to oversee the mill there. It's just been my father and me ever since.'

And then, more and more, she'd slipped into solitariness, becoming part of the house, retreating into its corners and settling with its dust. She'd learnt how to become invisible, not because she was aloof or a snob, but because she was painfully shy when it came to social engagements. Now that she was Floyd's fiancée, she was expected to attend events like the Governor's Ball and, of course, her wedding in November, both of which completely terrified her.

'Well, you couldn't be doing too badly, Miss Greene,' Alex said, leaning in slightly. 'Your engagement party was full to the brim with guests.'

'None of whom I knew,' she said with a laugh. 'They were all Floyd's friends.'

'Which makes them your friends?'

'I think they were there out of curiosity mostly. To see the sideshow. Me.'

'Ah, you shouldn't worry about them, Miss Greene. Don't let them make you feel anything less than you are.'

'Mrs Mayfair calls them carnivores.'

'Mrs Mayfair?'

'Estelle. I met her at the party. She's the friend I was meeting for lunch today.'

'Well, she sounds like an excellent judge of character.'

At the intersection of Hunter and Pitt, they waited for a tram to roll by, then crossed the tracks. Soon they would be in The Rocks and Charlotte wished the neighbourhood would pick itself up and relocate someplace else so that her time with Alex wouldn't end.

'Tell me about Hilda,' he said.

She smiled, fond memories of her childhood rushing back. 'She lived next door to us on Playfair Street. Growing up, we used to play a game,' Charlotte explained. 'I still remember it as if it were yesterday. We would write each other clues and leave them all over The Rocks. It would create a trail that we'd have to follow to find each other. These games would last a day, sometimes an entire week, from sunup to sundown. We knew The Rocks like the back of our hands, all its little passageways and staircases, its secret little hiding places.'

'What a marvellous idea.' Alex seemed delighted at the thought. It brought to mind the time she'd mentioned Hilda and the game to Floyd, who'd looked utterly bored, even yawning at one point without the good grace to stifle it.

'The clues would contain a riddle about a certain place or street, and we'd have to solve it to progress to the next clue. All of The Rocks was our playground. I really do miss her.' Charlotte glanced down at the pavement. Thinking of Hilda and that wonderful game, even after all these years, still caused the grief to wash over her as if it were brand new.

'It must have been hard for you as a child to have her there one minute and gone the next. Did you understand what happened?'

'Only that one day we were playing and she was fine, then the next day she couldn't come out because she was unwell. Her mother said she was ill with fever. Five days later she was gone. I saw them carry her body out on a stretcher from my bedroom window. I never got to say goodbye.'

'Did someone explain it to you?'

'My father did, in the best way he knew how, I suppose. He said that people died all the time and we had to find a way to live without them. Then after a while, he told me to stop looking out the window, that she wasn't coming back.'

Alex gave her a sorrowful look, and Charlotte was instantly mortified. 'Goodness, would you listen to how morbid I've become. What a wet mop. I apologise.'

'On the contrary. I've enjoyed every minute talking to you.'

She tried to quell the thrill his words gave her, tried not to beam so obviously at them, but it was difficult. Alex had a strange and exhilarating effect on her.

As they approached Circular Quay, the harbour ferries announced their presence with plumes of hissing steam and horns. The air brought with it the sharp tang of sea salt and the Bushells and Lemon & Co buildings came into view. The roads near the quay were the usual chaotic mix of people, automobiles and tramways, all struggling to coexist on the narrow streets.

'Do you live close to The Rocks too?' Charlotte asked as they skirted around Cadman's Cottage and climbed the steps to George Street.

'No, I live in Paddington, near Five Ways. Have you been there before?'

'I don't believe I have. What brought you to Australia?'

She felt home approaching fast as they reached Argyle Street. She wanted to walk slower, to ask him a thousand questions, to keep him talking. She liked the sound of his voice, the way it felt to stroll beside him, the way he spoke to her, not as Floyd did, but as an equal.

'A friend of mine who works for Dorman Long in London told me about the bridge build,' he explained. 'He was moving here for the project, so I moved too. It was a bit of risk, but he put in a good word for me with Bradfield and I was offered a job with Public Works.'

'And when did you arrive?'

'In 1925, just after the great demolition took place.'

Charlotte remembered it well. Before work could start on the bridge, hundreds of homes, businesses and streets on both the southern and northern sides of the harbour had to be demolished for the approaches. She recalled the public outcry when over two thousand people had been displaced and not a penny of compensation had been received except to those who held freehold land. Luckily, her house on Playfair had not been in the approach line, nor any of the workmen's cottages next door, like Hilda's old house where Mrs Parsons now lived.

They reached Argyle Street and, as they walked past crumbling terraces and shadowy laneways that had become an extension of people's yards, the topic switched to their shared love of books. Children sidestepped them, chasing each other up and down the road with grubby feet and filthy hand-me-down clothes; washing hung from ropes across balconies and inebriated souls tumbled out of public houses.

The slums of The Rocks were a far cry from Alex's beautifully made suit, leather shoes and felt fedora. Charlotte was suddenly self-conscious of where she lived, of her working-class status and inability to offer intelligent conversation. Had she bored him on the way home? Had she talked too little, too much, and of childish and inconsequential things?

Despite her diffidence, it was with immense regret that they arrived at her house on Playfair Street, and she turned her eyes up to him. 'Thank you for walking me home, Alex.'

'The pleasure was mine.'

Then Charlotte had a thought. 'Would you mind waiting here a moment? I'll be right back.'

Alex looked surprised as she quickly unlocked her door, dashed down the hall into the library, found what she was looking for, then hurried back out the door again.

She dropped the book of letters into his hands—*Love Through the Ages*.

He gave her a bemused smile. 'This is your book.'

'Yes,' she replied. 'Would you like to borrow it? You seemed to enjoy it the other night and I thought you might like to take the time to read it properly. Beethoven's letters are quite something, as are Oscar Wilde's.'

She was breathless and rambling, more nervous than she thought she would be at the simple gesture of lending him a book.

His expression was still one of bemusement and it made her wonder if she'd misread the signs. Perhaps he'd been humouring her when he'd said he'd liked it the other night, a show of politeness for the amusing girl who'd fled her engagement party to read love letters in the library.

But then his expression turned to sincerity, then delight as he opened the cover to the first page and ran his eyes down the words. 'Are you sure you want to lend it to me, Charlotte? I'd gratefully accept, but this was your mother's book. It's priceless. I wouldn't want anything to happen to it.'

'Please, I'd be happy if you would. Take as long as you need. Read it from the first page to the last.'

He held the book close to him. 'I shall take very good care of it.'

They parted then as he left for the bridge and she floated inside, her feet feeling as if they were barely touching the floor.

***

The following week Charlotte was clearing the table after dinner when there was a knock on the door.

'Ah,' her father said, dabbing his mouth with a napkin and rising from his seat. 'That'll be Bradfield.'

'I didn't realise we were having company.' Charlotte wiped her hands on her apron. 'Should I prepare a pot of tea?'

'It's just a little business. We'll have brandy and cigars in the parlour.'

Charlotte nodded and carried his plate to the sink. She could hear her father move down the hall to open the front door. Voices travelled towards her, not just her father's and Bradfield's, but a third person's.

Alexander Young.

She slipped off her apron and peered around the corner of the kitchen, watching them congregate in the foyer. Indeed it was Alex, the light from the streetlamps flooding in through the open door and casting him in diffuse light.

'Let's sit in the parlour where we can talk in private,' Walter said.

Alex caught sight of her at the end of the hall and his face broke into a wide grin before he disappeared with her father and Bradfield into the

54

front room.

Sometime later, Charlotte was reading in the library when she heard the parlour door open and voices fill the hall. She climbed out of the leather armchair and went to join them. Walter looked surprisingly sombre, as though the meeting hadn't gone well.

'This will need further discussion, Greene,' Dr Bradfield said seriously. 'Let's meet again soon.'

Walter nodded. 'Of course.' He shook Bradfield's hand, then Bradfield tipped his hat to Charlotte.

'Good evening, Miss Greene.' He stepped out onto the street.

Alex tipped his hat also and made to leave, but then turned back. 'Oh, before I forget.' He reached into his coat pocket and extracted the book of love letters Charlotte had loaned him the week before. 'Miss Greene, thank you for lending me this book. I thoroughly enjoyed it. The letter from Mark Twain to Olivia Langdon was of particular interest.'

She took it from him and their hands brushed. A pleasurable sensation coursed through her and their eyes met. He smiled softly and she smiled back, quickly dropping her gaze, aware that her father was still behind her.

Alex bid them good evening and joined Bradfield out on the street as she closed the door. In the hallway, she turned to face her father. 'Is everything all right?'

'Sure, love.' Walter looked distracted. 'But, ah, best not to mention this visit to Floyd, okay?'

'Why, what happened?'

'No, nothing.' Walter kissed the top of her head. 'Nothing at all. Just business.'

Before she could enquire further, he retreated up the stairs, his footfalls heavy on the boards above her.

Charlotte took the book of letters into the library and curled up once again in the armchair. She opened the cover straight to page thirty, where she knew Mark Twain's letter to his wife, Olivia Langdon, was. And there she saw it, a slip of paper caught in the binding. She extracted it and held it next to the lamp where she found writing that was neat and cursive; the words of a riddle. Her heart skipped. Just like the game she and Hilda used to play, Alex had left her a clue.

CHAPTER
7

PAIGE
Present Day

The morning after Ryan left with Charlotte's letters, Paige was up early to let the painters back in. They had finished the upstairs rooms and were working on the ground level, starting with the former library and the parlour. As the familiar odour of solvent began to waft through the house, Paige returned to her spot on the milk crate in the kitchen and made calls. She set up an appointment with the recruitment agency, spoke to the phone company to arrange more access points, then called Xavier to update him on the progress.

'You're an angel,' he said. 'I couldn't have done any of this without you.'

'It's my job. And a welcome distraction. I needed this.'

'So you haven't heard from Christian?'

Paige's back stiffened. 'No.'

'Juliet?'

'Why would I? I hardly know her.' Nor did she have any desire to acquaint herself with Christian's new fiancée.

'Was just curious,' Xavier said. 'I saw him at the supermarket today. He asked about you.'

'Did he?'

'Yeah. I told him you were great. Amazing even. The ultimate city girl now.'

Her mouth fell open, embarrassed. 'You didn't, did you?'

Xavier laughed. 'No, I didn't. But he was asking me questions about you. Juliet wasn't there.'

Paige sighed. 'Well, thanks for letting me know but it makes little difference now.'

'He misses you.'

'It doesn't matter. I've spent my whole life wanting to be with that man, persevering while he led me on. Then to hear that he's asked someone he's known for five minutes to marry him—' She took a deep breath. It wouldn't do any good to get worked up over it. She'd already spent a lifetime trying to keep up with Christian and the decisions he made. It was exhausting. 'We weren't meant to be. That's all. I've made my peace with it.'

'Have you really?'

'I had until you brought it up.'

Xavier laughed again. 'Okay, point taken. I'll never mention him again.'

They talked more about the tasks he wanted Paige to focus on for the next week, then they ended the call. She stood and stretched the knots out of her back, then went to speak to the painters about the colour choices for the parlour. When she stepped back out into the hallway, she noticed a man in the front foyer carrying a small chest that she recognised instantly as Charlotte's.

It was Ryan Greene.

'Hey,' he said, waving.

Paige couldn't hide her surprise. 'Hey. What are you doing here?'

'Your front door was wide open.'

'No, I mean, what are you doing here in Sydney? I thought you were catching a flight back to London today.'

'I was. I changed it.'

She must have been gaping for Ryan half-turned to leave. 'Sorry, I keep getting you at a bad time. I'll come back another day. Maybe tomorrow?'

'No, it's fine.' She smiled and beckoned him through the doorway. 'Come in, if you can handle the paint fumes.'

'Sure, I love paint fumes!' He shook his head at the lame joke. 'Sorry. I don't know why I said that. I don't love paint fumes.'

She laughed and held up her hands. 'No judgement from me.' She led the way down the hall, sidestepping paint trays, rollers and strips of sheets covering the floorboards. 'Coffee?' she asked once they were in the relative order of the kitchen. 'I also have leftover pizza, a blueberry muffin, which I'm willing to share, and Cornflakes.'

'It all sounds delicious but I'll just have coffee, thanks.'

'Latte, one sugar.'

'You have a good memory.'

Paige placed two cups under the dispensers of the coffee machine and hit the latte setting. 'So the flight?'

'I cancelled it,' Ryan said, placing the chest down on the kitchen bench. 'I spent some time going through the letters last night and if I'm to be completely honest, I felt a bit overwhelmed by it all.'

'Overwhelmed?' She stirred in sugar and pulled the cups from the machine tray.

'I didn't think leaving was the right thing to do. There's more to Charlotte's story and it's here in Sydney and this house.'

Carrying the coffees, Paige indicated they take the conversation into the backyard, out of the way of the painters, and Ryan collected the chest and followed.

'So this is the garden?' he said. 'I haven't been out here yet.'

'It's really overgrown. The gardener will be here tomorrow.' She led him to a table and chairs beneath the apple gum that had lost its flowers for another season. The day was like an autumn postcard. The air was crisp, the sky bright and clear, and the leaves on the trees lining Foundation Park and Gloucester Walk above them had deepened to such a blood-red they looked like they were on fire.

The arch of the Sydney Harbour Bridge could be seen to the north and Ryan paused to gaze at it. 'Greene steel.'

'I'm sorry?' Paige said, setting the coffees down.

'The bridge. It was constructed using Greene steel. Well, we weren't the only suppliers but we were the local ones.'

'Yes, I read that on your website.' Paige sat and Ryan, breaking his gaze from the bridge, joined her, placing the chest on the table between them.

'We were only a small company back then, in the days of my great-great-grandfather, Walter Greene.'

'Where did you manufacture your steel?'

'There was a mill in Silverwater, I believe, but we also had a foundry in Milsons Point that produced the steel castings.'

'Of course,' Paige said. 'Right under the bridge in North Sydney. It's where Luna Park stands now but it would have been used as bridge land back then.'

'That sounds about right. Dorman Long and Co, the English firm who designed and constructed the bridge, used a larger steel supplier from the UK. Eighty percent of the steel came from them. We were just a small piece of the pie, but a part of it nonetheless.'

'Well, contrary to the belief that Australia was the poor cousin of England, we had a lot of money for imports like steel. Before the Great Depression, we'd become wealthy on gold, minerals and agriculture.'

'You know your local history,' Ryan said, sipping his coffee.

'I have a Bachelor of Arts in Modern History, actually.'

'That explains it.'

Paige glanced at the chest between them. 'So, the letters?'

'Yes.' Ryan put down his coffee and ran his hand across the lid. 'I stayed up late last night and went through some of them.'

'What did you find?' she asked eagerly. It had only been twelve hours since Ryan had taken Charlotte's chest, but Paige had spent a fair amount of that time regretting that she hadn't read the letters when she'd had the opportunity. Gifted now with another chance, she could hardly contain her excitement.

'Two styles of handwriting, which supports your theory that Charlotte and another person were writing these letters to each other,' Ryan explained. 'Probably her fiancé. And they weren't just your typical love letters. They were writing clues.'

'Clues?'

'Yeah, like they were playing some sort of game.' Ryan rubbed his jaw thoughtfully.

Paige noticed he was freshly shaven and better rested than the night before when he'd arrived on her doorstep. Then she noticed his eyes again—long-lashed and deep brown, like the colour of cedar. When he caught her staring, she cleared her throat and quickly looked away.

'I think the clues are meant to lead the reader to a location where the other will be waiting,' he said. 'Kind of like a riddle that needs to be solved to find the other person.'

'A lover's treasure hunt,' she said, 'where the other person is the treasure. Now I'm curious.'

'Would you like to take a look?'

'Please.'

He opened the lid and Paige picked up her chair and shuffled it closer to Ryan's. She watched as he lifted the first bundle of letters out by the twine. The bundle was thick and it struck Paige just how many letters Charlotte and her fiancé had written to each other. The game must have gone on for months and frequently too. Judging by the number of them, Charlotte had kept every single one. She hadn't been able to part with them, another sign of her deep affection for the man.

Ryan slipped the twine off. 'From what I can tell, the letters are made up of a clue, plus a romantic declaration of some sort. Like this one.' He placed a letter between them. Unlike the dim light of the attic where Paige could hardly read a word, the bright sunshine out in the garden proved an excellent source.

'"I wish I may find you at home when I carry this letter to drop it in the box, that I may drop a kiss with it into your heart, to be embalmed, till we meet, closer."'

'Quite the expressionist,' Paige said.

'Yes, they had a way with words.'

'And yet, it's the wording that's interesting, not reminiscent of the twenties at all. It sounds older, like decades older.'

'You don't think these letters belonged to Charlotte and her fiancé?'

'I do, but I don't think those words did. They're quoting from something. I'll be back in a minute.' She rose from her chair and hurried into the house. In the kitchen, she found her laptop sitting on the milk crate where she'd last left it and carried it out with her to the garden. Disabling the screensaver, she smiled at Ryan's quizzical look. 'I think they're quoting old love letters. Ones that are well known.'

'How do you know?'

'I studied historical literature.' She sat down in front of the laptop and loaded Google's search page. She typed the first few words of the quote and hit enter. The search returned many results, all on the famed and unconventional writer, Mary Wollstonecraft, mother of Mary Shelley, the author of Frankenstein.

'Bingo. Whoever wrote this letter, Charlotte or her fiancé, quoted from the words Mary Wollstonecraft wrote to her lover, William Godwin, in 1796.'

'That's incredible.'

'Give me another one,' Paige said, her blood starting to pulse a little faster.

Ryan picked up the next letter. '"My heart and I surrender ourselves into your hands, beseeching you to hold us commended to your favour, and that by absence your affection to us may not be lessened."'

'Goodness. They are definitely not the words of the twentieth century. I'm thinking Tudor or Elizabethan.' Sure enough, when she hit enter on the words, they yielded results of Henry VIII. 'A love letter from Henry VIII to his mistress, Anne Boleyn.'

'Charlotte and her fiancé were writing famous love quotes to each other, accompanied by a clue.'

'I wonder where they got the quotes from. They wouldn't have had access to the internet. A book maybe?'

'There wasn't a book with the letters.'

It didn't matter. Just being able to decode the letters, to have an insight into the kind of person Charlotte was, was gift enough—a young woman who'd worn her heart on her sleeve, who'd loved this man fiercely but may not have known how to tell him in her own words.

'What about the clues that go with them?' she asked. 'What are they like?'

Ryan studied a letter and read from it. '"A chair in a garden to gaze out over a bridge. Meet me on Saturday. I'll be waiting at four."'

'A chair in a garden?' Paige racked her brain. 'It could be Mrs Macquarie's Chair. It's located in the Royal Botanic Garden and overlooks the Sydney Harbour Bridge, the whole harbour, in fact. Governor Macquarie had it commissioned for his wife, Elizabeth.'

It was staggering to read these letters now, the private correspondence between two lovers almost a century before. The historian in Paige was running wild, her mind in overdrive. She could see Charlotte and her fiancé writing these letters, incorporating a clue in which to play out a game, one that would have them searching the city to find each other.

'Are the letters dated?' she asked; always an important point to check.

'Some have dates. Some don't. But the ones that do range between March 1929 and October 1929. They were all in meticulous order and nothing later than October.'

Paige tapped her index finger against her lips thoughtfully. 'Last night, you mentioned that Charlotte's brother James received an urgent telegram from her dated October thirty-first, asking him to come home because she was being sent away.'

'Yes, that's right. The letters stopped around that time too.'

'So something must have happened to end the game suddenly and for Charlotte and Walter to disappear.'

Ryan nodded his agreement, then glanced down at the letters. Paige knew he felt it too, that quiet rush when significant and precious history was unearthed, followed by the confusing trail it often left when pieces didn't add up and more needed to be found.

Ryan leant back in his chair and stared up at the sky, through the branches of the apple gum. 'Charlotte has always been a mystery to us—who she was, how she lived and where she died. And I've always had the impression that Walter was full of secrets too—the way he ran the business and his knowledge of what happened to her. Why else would James have been kept in the dark?'

At the back door, one of the painters cleared his throat to get Paige's attention.

'And on that note, I have taken up all of your morning,' Ryan said, returning the letters to the chest and closing the lid. 'I should let you get back to work.'

'No, it's fine,' she said. She did have a lot to do, but once again she found herself enjoying Ryan's company. There was something about Charlotte's story, or perhaps something about Ryan, that compelled her to remain in the garden all morning, her long list of things to do tucked firmly away in the back of her diary. 'Let me just sort out what the painter wants and I'll be right back.'

'Are you sure? You must be busy.'

'Actually, I was thinking I should show you the attic.'

Ryan's face lit up. 'Really?'

'If you're interested.'
'Of course!'
'Great. But let's get lunch first. I'm starving.'

CHAPTER
8

Playfair Street, like anywhere in The Rocks, bustled all day with tourists. It took intimate knowledge of secret nooks to find an equally secret place to eat, of which there were many. In the short time she'd lived in the city, Paige had become good at finding these places, frequented by locals only. She led Ryan to Mill Lane, down a short flight of cobbled steps and into a back alleyway, where there was a row of hidden cafes that sold good beer and excellent food.

'Is all of Sydney like this?' Ryan asked, cutting into his steak.

'Like what?'

'Secret laneways, hidden stairs, old courtyards, a mishmash of streets.'

She laughed. 'Not all of Sydney. The Rocks is unique. It was the site of the first settlement in 1788 and not a lot of thought went into street planning back then. The streets were mostly laid to follow Indigenous tracks. And the landscape is sandstone too; extremely hilly, hence all the steps. But I love that.' She looked around the old courtyard they were seated in, with its several flights of stairs that led in all different directions. 'Everything here is old. It's as if The Rocks is trapped in time.'

'Well, I got lost walking back over here this morning and I'm only five minutes down the road. Even London isn't this confusing.'

She sipped her beer. 'London saw some rebuild after both world wars which might have resulted in a better layout of the streets. We didn't have that here. Even the other capital cities of Australia had the benefit of planning.'

Ryan pointed his fork at her. 'You know, Sydney suits you. You've become a city dweller.'

She chuckled. 'I don't know about that.'

'You must miss your home in Albury, though.'

Paige looked down into her beer, unsure how to respond. She'd been having such a nice time that she hadn't thought once about Christian. 'Yes. And no. It's complicated.'

Ryan nodded contemplatively. 'It often is.'

After lunch, as the painters began to encroach on the kitchen and dining room, Paige and Ryan retreated to the second floor. The stairwell to the attic was dim but free at last of dust and cobwebs after the cleaner had been through. Paige opened the door and they both ducked to make it through the doorway.

Once inside, they straightened, Ryan's head almost touching the ceiling. 'These rooms weren't built for tall people, that's for sure.'

Paige reached up and unscrewed the blown lightbulb from above her. She fitted the new bulb in and tugged on the pull cord. The attic filled with light and Paige looked around. During her previous visit, she'd had to rely solely on filtered daylight from the grimy window, which had barely chased the shadows away. Now the room was brighter and she saw things she hadn't noticed before—a dusty globe, a pile of leather suitcases, an old cast flatiron and a delightful mahogany gramophone from a bygone era. She could almost hear the music of Bing Cosby and Billie Holiday quivering through the brass horn.

'Are you sure you have time for this?' Ryan asked, his forehead crinkling with worry.

'Actually, clearing out the attic is on my to-do list. So you're doing me a favour.'

'Oh well, if it's for the greater good.'

Paige laughed. 'It is.'

'There's so much stuff up here.' Ryan pulled back the sheets on the armchairs and the brown three-seater Chesterfield, coughing the dust away. 'Who does it all belong to?'

'People who have come and gone,' Paige said. 'Unfortunately, everything that wasn't locked away has had a rodent or two feast on it.'

Ryan pressed down on the keys of the typewriter.

'Definitely the sixties or seventies,' she said with a smile.

'What are you planning to do with it all?'

'If we could work out what belonged to your family, you could help decide if it's worth keeping. Then I could call a thrift or antique shop for the rest of it. Some of it will need to be disposed of.'

'What's in here?' Ryan asked, moving to a large chest that replicated the smaller one where Charlotte's letters were stored. 'Looks exactly like the one downstairs.'

'I hadn't noticed that before,' Paige said, pleasantly surprised. 'They look like they're part of a set which means it must belong to Charlotte.' On top of the lid were boxes of old Christmas decorations and large envelopes containing x-rays. 'Let's move all this stuff.'

Together they cleared away the clutter and Ryan ran his palm across the front of the chest. Just like its sister piece, a name was carved deep into the wood. *Charlotte Greene*. 'This was definitely hers.'

They dropped to their knees and prised open the lid. Inside was a protective sheet covering the contents. They pulled the sheet away and found layers of neatly folded clothes, cloche hats, shoes and handbags. An overpowering smell of age escaped as though the chest had given up a weary sigh at being closed for so long.

Paige pulled the top-most garment out—a jade-green dress with a delicate draping of black lace embedded with thousands of tiny crystals. Chantilly, perhaps. The dress was tiny, to fit the slenderest of frames and an obvious piece from the twenties. Exquisite and delicate, it clung to her fingers as though rejoicing at being held again. Placing it aside, Paige pulled out the next garment, a slim satin gown in ivory with a long veil of embroidered flowers. She and Ryan exchanged a look.

'A wedding dress,' he said.

'So does this mean she married her fiancé before she disappeared?'

'I'm guessing so. Which makes it even sadder. He must have been out of his mind with worry.'

Paige gently folded the wedding dress and laid it in her lap, peering inside the chest again. The cloche hats were fascinating, as were the shoes and handbags, throwing her back to a time after the Great War and before the Depression when the world had forgotten how to be humble, living so extravagantly it had upset a delicate and necessary balance of economy. But it was the stray photographs at the bottom of the chest that now caught her attention. 'Look at these,' she said, fishing them out.

'What are they?'

'Photographs. I think they're of Charlotte.' Paige held up the first, a black and white image of a young man and woman sitting on a lounge settee with an older man behind them, the shape of his portly stomach protruding through his vest and suit jacket. Grey hair peeked from beneath the rim of his homburg and his manner was solemn, his hand resting on the shoulder of the younger man.

Ryan leant across her and pointed at him. 'That's my great-great-grandfather, Walter Greene. I've seen photos of him before.'

'The young man and woman must be James and Charlotte.' Paige turned the photograph over in her hand and sure enough, inscribed on the back in writing so cursive she had to strain her eyes to understand it, were the words *'Walter Greene, James Greene, Charlotte Greene—1928'*.

The photo was customary of the decade in which it was taken—straight backs and serious expressions. And yet, Paige thought she detected a glimmer of a smile tugging at the corner of Charlotte's lips. She had a direct gaze and a lovely face that had just reached adulthood.

'She was beautiful,' Paige said, admiring the long, dark plait and the slender ankles that peeked out beneath her dress, which were crossed and tucked to the side gracefully.

'That lounge in the photo.' Ryan pointed to it, then climbed to his feet and went to the Chesterfield he'd removed the sheet from earlier. 'It's the same as this one. It must have been theirs.'

Paige agreed and she became awash with the feeling of wonderstruck when history gifted itself so profoundly to the present. Like a treasure hunter who sifted through the detritus of long-forgotten items to find the precious trove, they had discovered Charlotte's letters, her dresses and hats, a photograph of her sitting on a lounge that was right beside them.

And she wasn't the only one. Ryan's face told her he felt it too. He wore an astonished look as he ran his eyes along the rat-gnawed leather of the Chesterfield. 'What about the other photos?'

Paige held up another. It was of a woman standing in a room wearing sombre hospital garb, her long dark hair tied away, her expression equally serious. Standing next to her was a tall man in a pale overcoat, with a shock of white hair and wire-rimmed spectacles. Paige turned the photograph over to read the inscription on the back. *'Charlotte and Dr Carmichael. December 1929.'*

'Wait.' Ryan leant over. 'That's Charlotte?'

'In December 1929. Two months after the letters stopped.'

Ryan rubbed his jaw, his brow furrowed. 'So is this where she disappeared to? Some sort of hospital?'

'It would appear so. She's dressed like an inpatient,' Paige said. 'Let me Google the doctor's name. Maybe we can find out what kind he was.' She pulled her phone out of her back pocket and typed *Dr Carmichael 1929* into the Google search field. 'Interesting.'

'What does it say?'

'He was a psychiatrist who worked at Gladesville Mental Hospital in the twenties. I guess that's where the photo was taken, which means Charlotte must have been a patient there.' Paige pushed her phone back into her pocket and glanced at the image again. 'But if that's the case, why would someone send Charlotte to a mental institution? And who?'

Ryan shrugged. 'It could have been Walter. His wife suffered mental health issues and died in an asylum when Charlotte and James were little. Maybe Charlotte became unwell too, during those last months of 1929.'

Paige considered this. 'But then Walter disappeared.'

'Yes, apparently.'

'Doesn't that seem odd?'

'Which bit?'

'Well, the bit where Walter puts his daughter in a mental institution, then disappears without a trace. I mean, was she ever let out? And what about her fiancé? Where was he?'

Ryan nodded at the conundrum. Many pieces were falling into their laps and not a single one fit together.

'Okay, this is the last photograph,' Paige said, holding it out so they could both see. It was unmistakably Charlotte again, taken in a bar, on what appeared to be a dark velvet seat. Next to her was a woman with a pale Eton crop and an intricate cloisonné pendant on a silver chain around her neck. They were smiling, almost laughing into the camera. Charlotte's presence in the photo was endearing while the other woman's dazzled with arrogance.

Paige turned the photo over. On the back was the inscription— *Charlotte and Estelle. Hubert's. July 1929.*

'Estelle?' Ryan said. 'A friend perhaps?'

'Looks like it. And the handwriting on the back, it must be Charlotte's. It matches the handwriting on some of the letters in the chest.'

'Yes, you're right. So now we can tell which ones were written by her and which ones were written by her fiancé.'

'It's quite incredible no one ever threw any of this stuff out. It all would have been lost to the rubbish.' Paige returned the photographs to the chest, placing them flat on the bottom again so they wouldn't become squashed by the other items. 'Have you decided which pieces you'd like to ship home?'

Ryan looked around the attic. 'Anything that looks like it belonged to Walter and Charlotte's time, we'll take. Maybe we can restore some of the pieces, reupholster the chairs.'

'I think that's a lovely idea,' Paige said, folding the wedding dress neatly and returning it to the chest as well. 'Perhaps tomorrow we could go to the state library. It's not far from here and we can run some archival searches on the Greene name and see what they turn up.'

'I'd like that,' Ryan said, handing her the jade-green dress so she could fold it and place it on top of the wedding gown. 'It would be good to verify that Charlotte was admitted to Gladesville too.'

'You know we could probably take a trip out there,' Paige suggested. 'I don't think it's too far from here. They might still have patient records on site. How long are you planning to stay?'

'Another few days. Maybe a week.'

'Aren't your family wondering where you are?' The words were out before she could stop them and she cringed at how nosy they sounded.

Ryan shifted on the floor beside her. She saw his Adam's apple bob as though he were working out how to respond.

'Sorry, that's none of my business.' Paige busied herself returning the protective sheet to the chest, laying it over the dresses. 'Just ignore me.'

'No, it's okay. I took a few weeks off work,' he said, not meeting her eyes. 'There's some stuff I've been dealing with back home.'

'You don't have to explain. I shouldn't have asked.'

'My wife and I are divorcing.'

'Oh.' Paige grimaced. It hadn't been her intention to coax it out of him and now that she had, she felt truly awful. 'I'm sorry, Ryan. I didn't mean to pry.'

'No, it's fine.' His smile let her know it was. 'We've been separated for over a year. It's almost finalised. It's just been a bit rough.'

'I understand.'

'Divorce is messy. I don't recommend it.'

She nodded sympathetically. 'So no chance of reconciliation?'

'We tried some counselling a while back but it didn't work. I was mostly to blame. I worked and travelled too much with the job, and she was left alone a lot of the time. I would have walked out on me too.' He shrugged sheepishly. 'They say my great-great-grandfather, Walter, was like that. Married to the business. I guess it runs in the Greene blood.'

She gave him an apologetic look. 'I really am sorry to have put you on the spot like that. I'm mortified actually.'

He nudged her good-naturedly. 'Don't feel bad. You weren't to know. And if I'm to be completely honest, I feel better than I have in months, like I've been able to take a proper breath here, get my head in the right space.'

'Well, I'm glad for that.'

They shared a smile before Paige climbed to her feet, dusting her jeans down. 'I suppose I better check on the painters. They'll be wondering where I am.'

Ryan climbed to his feet too and closed the lid of the chest. 'What about the attic? We didn't get much done in here.'

Paige laughed, looking around. 'No, we didn't. But we can come back up here another day, if you like.'

Ryan smiled at the obvious invitation. 'Sure!'

She blushed and smiled too. He'd barely paused before accepting and she couldn't explain why that made her happy.

He tugged on the pull cord to switch off the light and they closed the attic door, making their way back down the staircase.

CHAPTER
9

Paige rose the next morning with the sun. Its pale fingers shone through the bare window, reminding her that she was yet to buy curtains. That thought, and the mountain of tasks she'd forgone the day before in favour of sitting with Ryan in the attic, made her stretch begrudgingly and climb off her makeshift bed.

When wet painted walls had precluded access to the parlour, she'd been forced to the upper floor. The room she'd stayed in, just at the top of the landing, she suspected had been Charlotte's. An engraving etched into the exposed sandstone wall was the giveaway. *CG.*

She'd been beside herself when she'd seen those letters, down in the corner, where a young child had once crouched with a chisel to signify her room in the house. Paige had felt Charlotte's presence so profoundly then, the walls exhaling her breath, the floors reverberating her steps. She'd had an overwhelming urge to call Ryan, to have him race over immediately to see what she'd found. But while she knew he'd have been thrilled, it had been late at night and late calls to men, in any corner of the world, usually meant one thing and it was not the thing Paige intended.

So she'd laid down on her inflatable mattress, heart skipping a little, staring at the ceiling as Charlotte must have done, wondering what thoughts had passed through her mind, what clues for the game with her fiancé she may have contrived in that very spot.

Now it was morning and, having slept a strange, excitable sleep, she rubbed her gritty eyes and walked down to the kitchen. While she made coffee, she tore pieces off a Danish pastry and ate them against the bench letting the smell and grind of coffee beans wake her.

At eight, she let the painters in for their final day in the house and retreated back up the stairs for a shower. When she returned downstairs to make calls, she noticed a folded slip of paper caught in the brass mail slot in the door. She retrieved it and unfolded it, a slow grin spreading across her lips.

Where there are lots of books. Meet me at two.

Then, in smaller writing underneath, *Sorry, I'm terrible at this!*

She laughed so loudly that the painter poked his head out from the kitchen. 'Did you call for me, miss?'

'Oh, no, sorry, it was something else.'

He shrugged and disappeared again.

For the remaining hours until two, Paige lost herself in her work. She let the gardener in, joined a conference call with Xavier and his accountant, and took her washing to a laundromat. She purchased a toaster while she was out, got lost somewhere near Fort Street Public School, then bought a salad for lunch once she'd found her way back. Then, at one-thirty, she ran a comb through her hair, told the painters she'd return before they finished for the day and stepped outside.

It was the usual chaos around the workmen's terraces, tourists being led by map or tour guides, and locals collecting a late lunch on their way back to work. Paige made her way quickly towards Argyle Street, crossing over to Harrington, then slipping into Suez Canal and Nurses Walk, having discovered the old cobbled back lanes the week before and preferring them now to the rush of George Street.

Cutting through First Fleet Park and Circular Quay, she found the library with ease, at the foot of the Royal Botanic Garden. And she didn't have to search far for Ryan. It was just on two o'clock and he was waiting at the top of the steps, leaning against one of the towering stone columns.

'You got my clue,' he said, hurrying down the steps to meet her. He carried a clear plastic sleeve with him.

'With extreme difficulty, I managed to decipher it,' she joked.

He laughed. 'Obviously, I haven't inherited my great-aunt's knack for riddles.'

'No, your talents clearly lie in steel.'

He laughed again and it was in that happy, relaxed sound and the way his face lit up at her jokes that she found herself relishing unexpectedly in it. He was nicely dressed in dark jeans and a grey shirt, his hair damp as if he'd just had a shower.

Paige's hand flew to her own messy mane and she smoothed it back, wishing she'd thought to put on something nicer than ripped jeans and Converse. Her casual country roots were at obvious odds with his handsome British class.

'Shall we go inside then?' he said, indicating with his hand that she lead the way. 'I'm afraid I'm at your disposal here. I have no idea where we need to go.'

'I studied here once before,' she said as they walked up the steps. 'Just for two days when I was covering a unit on Australian colonisation and Indigenous studies. It's the Mitchell Library Reading Room we want. They have computers that link to the library's archive system. I've always renewed my library card so we can access the resources for free.'

It was two years before that Paige had visited the New South Wales State Library on a study trip and its impressive façade of honeyed sandstone, grand columns and high ceilings had remained with her since. Stepping through the front doors with Ryan and into the large tiled foyer, it still took her breath away. She was a traditionalist and a historian at heart, and it was buildings like these that made her pulse quicken.

They crossed the vestibule, stopping briefly to admire the inlay of the Abel Tasman marble map before Paige led them through the open doors of the Mitchell Library Reading Room. Three tiers of Tasmanian blackwood bookshelves surrounded the floor space, accessed by balconies of brass and timber. Many of the teak desks and bentwood chairs, Paige noticed, were antiquated, seeming to date back several decades, the forties, possibly earlier. The room was well-lit by natural light from the glass ceiling and the southern wall featured two griffins above a clock with the Greek inscription—*In books flows the fountain of wisdom*.

The room was busy that day, but they spotted an empty desk with a computer by a staircase leading to the upper levels of bookshelves.

'I found something exciting last night,' Paige said as she dropped into a chair and flicked the mouse to disengage the screensaver.

'Oh?' Ryan lowered himself into a chair beside her.

'I had to relocate upstairs for the night whilst the parlour dried and I believe I stayed in Charlotte's old room. The first on the right at the top of the stairs.'

'How do you know it was hers?'

'The initials CG were carved into the sandstone wall.'

Ryan looked impressed. 'That's as good an indication as any.'

'I guess there's always the possibility that other people with the initials CG have stayed in that room, but I like to think that it could have been hers.'

'I have something too.' He set the clear sleeve on the table.

Paige could see a piece of paper through the plastic. She leant in for closer inspection and realised it was the telegram Ryan had told her about, the one Charlotte had sent to her brother James in the UK on October thirty-first, two days after Black Tuesday. The paper was crisp and fragile—she would never have dared handle it with her fingers— but the typed messages, the emblem of the Commonwealth of Australia and the Postmaster General's Department stamp were still legible.

'My great-grandfather kept it in an old photo album for years which is why I think it's still in good condition, given how old it is. It was passed down to my grandfather then my father. It's always been in the family.'

Ryan turned the sleeve upside down and allowed the telegram to fall gently onto the desk. It was addressed to Mr James Greene, at a location in Middlesbrough, United Kingdom. The telegram had been a clear plea for help.

> *Dear James. Come urgently. They are sending me away. I*
> *have endured loss. My heart is broken. You must find me.*
> *Yours. Charlotte.*

'Goodness.' The intensity of Charlotte's words caused Paige's heart to pick up pace.

'Yes, it's quite an extraordinary message,' said Ryan.

Paige thought back to the photograph of Charlotte at the Gladesville Mental Hospital, standing beside Dr Carmichael. 'In her telegram she writes "they are sending me away". Do you think someone helped

Walter commit her to Gladesville?'

'Her fiancé might have had a hand in it.'

'It also says she endured loss.' Paige studied the telegram again. 'That her heart was broken. Maybe he ended their engagement.'

'Then sent her away for the grief it caused.'

'Yes, it wasn't uncommon for females back then to be sent to asylums for conditions like hysteria.'

'Sounds like a bit of an overreaction to a simple break up though, grieving so badly she had to be committed to an asylum.'

'Maybe she really loved him.'

Ryan made a dubious sound.

'So after James attempted to correspond and received no reply from his father or sister, he travelled out here from London?' she asked.

'That's right.'

'And he never mentioned anything about Charlotte being in Gladesville?'

'If he knew she was there, he didn't tell a soul. My guess is he wasn't aware. That for whatever reason, it was kept from him.'

But why? What reason could Walter have for keeping his and Charlotte's whereabouts a secret? 'You said when James returned to Sydney, he found a letter of apology from Walter in a safe, along with the deeds to the company.'

'Yes, back at Playfair.'

'Do you have that letter by any chance? I'm wondering if there was more information in it, something that was missed previously but might make sense now.'

Ryan shook his head. 'I've never seen it. It's probably long gone. But it was brief, if the stories are true. There was no explanation as to what happened to Charlotte or Walter. Just an apology and the company was now James' to do with as he pleased.'

'And the house was ransacked when he got there?'

'Yes.'

Paige let out an exasperated breath. 'It's like peeling back a layer to find several more. Nothing adds up.'

'It's always been a bit like that, relying on old stories and hearsay. Unfortunately, James never lived long enough to tell his children and grandchildren what he might have known. The stories came from his wife, my great-grandmother, and her information was sketchy too. I'm not sure how much she knew, to be honest.' He nodded towards the computer. 'Anyway, where do we start?'

'Well, we could see what old newspaper articles we can find on the Greene name from the twenties. Then we wait for the rabbit hole to appear and I guess we dive in.' Paige placed her hand on the mouse and selected the option on the library dashboard for 'newspaper articles', then entered the Greene name and customised the search to the nineteen twenties.

A list of links appeared for various news articles—*The Sydney Morning Herald, The Daily Telegraph, The Australasian Engineer* and *The Australian Banking Forum.* Many of them were related to the Sydney Harbour Bridge construction, which had been widely reported on during the twenties, and the use of Greene steel in its arch work.

Paige and Ryan read as many of the articles as they could, although few of them mentioned Charlotte specifically, instead focusing on Walter Greene and his steel mill and foundry.

Further along, in one of *The Sydney Morning Herald* articles, there was a front-page story, dated March fifteenth, 1929, on the engagement of banker Mr Floyd Clark to Miss Charlotte Greene, daughter of prominent steel monger, Walter Greene. It was Ryan who had found it and there was an audible yelp of discovery from their table, which drew the looks of the others in the reading room.

They lowered their heads together and read of a grand cocktail party held at number seven Playfair Street to celebrate the engagement, and all Sydney's elite had been in attendance. There were no photographs to accompany the article, which Paige found disappointing, for she would have liked to have seen the house she now lived in decorated for a party in the Roaring Twenties. It did little to detract from the moment though. When they finished reading, they both sat back in their seats with satisfied smiles.

'So now we know his name,' she said. 'Floyd Clark.'

Ryan nodded. 'Yes. And we were on the right track too. He was a banker.'

'A loans manager at the Bank of New South Wales. It was a major banking institution for over a century here. It went on later to become Westpac Banking Corporation, one of our four major banks.'

'None of that article tells us what happened to Charlotte though.'

'No, it doesn't. But this article was dated March fifteenth, 1929 and we know that her letters started not long after that. So for the next seven months, she and Floyd must have played the game.'

'Until something dreadful happened.'

The plight of it was sad and although Paige had a million other things she should have been doing, she found herself becoming increasingly drawn to Charlotte's story. Perhaps because she was living in Charlotte's old house and she'd held her wedding gown in her hands. Perhaps because her descendant was sitting beside her, filled with the same gnawing determination to find out what happened to her.

Or perhaps because hidden in Charlotte's letters was more than just a romance.

CHAPTER
10

CHARLOTTE
April 1929

Charlotte set down her father's cup of tea and returned to the sink to wash the remainder of the dishes.

She heard the rustle of his newspaper and the slurp of his tea as she stacked wet plates on the bench to dry. 'What are your plans for today?' she asked.

He turned a page. 'There's a card game over at the Lord Nelson. Was thinking I might drop in.'

'A card game on a Saturday morning?'

'I'll just be watching with some of the lads.'

She wiped her hands on her apron, walked to the table and lowered herself into a chair opposite him. 'It was nice of Dr Bradfield and Mr Young to pay us a visit the other night.' She still remembered the way Alex's fingers had touched hers, ever so slightly, as he'd handed her back the book of love letters, and the soft, prepossessing smile he'd gifted her with, making her whole body react in a way she'd never felt before.

'Yes, they're good folk,' her father said, still glancing at the paper.

'What were they here for?'

'Just business of the bridge.'

'What kind of business?' she persisted. 'Was it to do with our steel?'

Walter closed the paper and set it down on the table. 'We had a small hiccup with production. Nothing to worry about.'

'A hiccup? You mean we're not producing enough?'

He gave a hearty laugh and patted her hand. 'Oh, Charlotte. You're too inquisitive. There was a misunderstanding with the wages and some of our workers weren't paid. They stopped work and it halted production.'

'Will it be sorted soon?' she asked worriedly.

'It already has been.' He waved his hand. 'Bradfield just gets nervous. Like I said, nothing to worry about.'

She ran her palm over stray crumbs on the table, gathering them into a pile. 'Mr Young is lovely.' She hadn't meant it to sound the way it did and she cleared her throat quickly. 'And Dr Bradfield too.'

But it was too late. Walter was eyeing her curiously. 'Maybe we should have Floyd over for dinner soon. It's been a little while since you've seen him. You could prepare a nice meal and serve it up on your mother's bone china. That dinner set is worth a fortune, all the way from Switzerland, you know. Floyd would be mighty impressed to have a meal on that. What do you say, love?'

She nodded obligingly.

'It's important we show him what you have to offer as a wife. He's taking a big chance on us.'

'Of course.'

Walter rose from the table and bent to peck her on the cheek. 'I better head down to the Lord Nelson. The lads will be waiting. What have you planned for today?'

'Just the usual,' she said, sweeping the pile of crumbs into her palm and rising from the table.

'Why don't you have that nice new friend over? What's her name?'

'Estelle.'

'Or better still, head outdoors and see her. You could visit a tearoom for lunch. It's a fine day for it.'

'Yes, I might.'

He left her in the kitchen, humming happily to himself and a moment later, the front door closed behind him.

But it wasn't lunch with Estelle that Charlotte was considering. All morning, the clue from Alex had been burning a hole in her apron pocket and now that her father had left, she fished it out.

Carefully unfolding it, she glanced at the neat, cursive hand of Mr Young.

> *You said I must never tear up a letter after writing it to you and so, I send it.*

She smiled. He'd quoted Mark Twain to his future wife Olivia Langdon, from the page in the book of love letters where he'd slipped in the clue. Very clever. And metaphorical too, for perhaps it spoke of his hesitation to leave the clue at all. Should he tear it up or should he be so bold as to send it? Charlotte wasn't exactly unspoken for. She let the predicament slide and her eyes scanned the rest of his words.

> *A clue for the master of clues.*
> *Find me where a king meets a queen.*
> *Saturday at noon.*

Through the doorway to the dining room, she glimpsed the time on the grandfather clock. It was just on eleven. If she left now, she'd have time to solve the clue and travel to the location, presuming it was in the city, which she hoped it was. Anything outside of it would present a challenge for her.

But did she dare? How clandestine to meet a man who wasn't her father or fiancé. How terribly inappropriate, even if Alex's clue was all in good humour, which she had no doubt it was. He had taken pity on her because of Hilda, because of her lost childhood and the reclusive years that prevailed. Still, she'd never done anything like it before. She rarely left the house and, while this was out of character for her, she couldn't deny the thrill it delivered, the anticipation of cracking the clue and finding Alex.

It took only a minute more to convince herself, then she changed into a dress of yellow lace, slipped on her gloves and hat, wrote a note to her father explaining she'd stepped out for lunch, and closed the door behind her, heading down Argyle Street towards the tram.

The note was securely tucked away in her purse and as she reached George Street, she pulled it out to study it again. *Find me where a king meets a queen.*

Nostalgia washed through her, the memories of her childhood with Hilda, running through crooked alleyways and up and down steep staircases in The Rocks, trying to solve each other's clues. Alex had reinvented a much-loved game of hers. His words were cryptic but she'd been good at this once and doubted that she'd lost her touch. *A clue for the master of clues.* Her only enemy would be the streets of the city. Her infrequent visits over the years could prevent her from navigating them well enough to find him.

She boarded a tram on George Street and handed the conductor ten pence for the fare. Then she fell into a seat behind the driver as the tram clattered on again and they rolled past the large Peat and Harcourt's store and the sought-after ironmongers of Holdsworth MacPherson & Co.

Charlotte glanced down at the clue in her hand. *Find me where a king meets a queen.* Her limited knowledge of the streets told her that George Street could play a part in it. But to meet with a queen? Assuming it *was* streets and not a building or landmark.

She stood and tapped the tram driver on the shoulder. He glanced behind, giving her petite figure an appreciative smile before meeting her eyes. 'What can I do for you, miss?'

'I'm looking for Sydney streets that are named after royalty. Do you know of any?'

He crinkled his forehead in thought. 'Royalty, hey? There are a few in Sydney, probably more ducal titles than anything—York, Sussex, Cumberland, Kent and so on. What are you looking for exactly?'

'Streets named after queens.'

'Streets named after queens?' he repeated. He looked pleased to be asked a question that was in line with his expertise. 'Sydney used to have plenty, but a lot of them were demolished and never replaced. The only principal one left in the city proper, that I can think of, is Elizabeth.'

'And does she intersect with George?'

'No, sorry, love. She runs parallel to George. What's this all about?'

'I'm meeting someone,' Charlotte explained without going into too much detail. 'I believe they'll be at a location where streets named for a king and queen meet.'

'Is that so?' He looked amused. 'Don't you 'ave the address?'

She shook her head. 'It's a long story.'

He pulled gently on the brake lever to avoid accelerating too quickly down the slope of the road. 'All right, then. I think what you'll be looking for is King and Elizabeth. They intersect. That's the best I can come up with.'

Charlotte brightened. 'Are they far from here?'

'Just at the next stop, little lady. You can get off at the King and George Street intersection, turn left then follow King Street east until you reach Elizabeth.'

Where a king meets a queen. The cross street for King and Elizabeth. It had to be. And if it wasn't and Alex was nowhere to be found, then she would have missed the window and the game would be over.

She tapped the driver on the shoulder again. 'What time is it?'

'Going on noon.'

Saturday at noon. She had only minutes to spare.

At the next stop, she disembarked to the amused chuckles of the driver as he wished her luck. This part of the city was bustling with people, out enjoying the cooler weather after the blistering summer heat. Charlotte left George Street behind and, as the driver had instructed, headed east along King towards Elizabeth. Through the crowds she walked, time ticking, her heart beating faster in her chest. And finally, when she reached the intersection, she turned in a full circle, searching for Alex's face amongst the hundreds passing her by. She didn't know where to look, where to focus her eyes, there were so many places he could be waiting.

Then across the road, beneath the street signs that spelled out King Street and Elizabeth Street, she saw him. Her heart soared in her chest and she quickly sidestepped people, narrowly missing an Austin 7 automobile and dodging trams as she crossed the tracks in an attempt to reach him. When she finally did, she wore the widest grin. 'I found you!'

He was smiling just as broadly and for a moment, she thought he might take her in his arms and swing her around. 'Indeed you did, Miss Greene. Well done!'

'It was an easy clue.'

'Really?'

'No, not at all. I had to ask the tram driver for help.'

He threw his head back and laughed. 'But you solved it. And here you are. Can I interest you in a walk through Hyde Park? That is, if you don't have any plans.'

'I'd love to.' She skipped happily beside him as he led her through the crowds past the King Street Courts and St James Church into Hyde Park.

Once inside, the noise of the city fell away as though it were part of another world. The conifers and pines moved with a light breeze, the sun cutting through their leaves to speckle the path with sunlight, and birdsong called from the branches. Everything was slower there; the rush and bustle unwelcome in that place of calm.

'I hope you didn't think me too forward for leaving you the clue,' Alex said as they followed a path lined with ancient Moreton Bay figs.

'No, it was wonderful. The nicest thing anyone has ever done for me.'

'I'm sure your fiancé does lovely things for you all the time.'

Charlotte didn't answer, instead cast her eyes anywhere but the expectant gaze of Alex. She was ashamed to admit she hadn't given consideration to Floyd since her father had mentioned him earlier that morning. Rarely did he entertain her thoughts, not like Alex who seemed to occupy them constantly.

'Well, I enjoyed your book immensely,' he said, smoothing over the silence. '*Love Through the Ages.* An intriguing read. I took the liberty of quoting Mark Twain in my clue.'

'I noticed. The book contains just one of his many letters to Olivia Langdon. Did I ever tell you that the book was a gift from my father to my mother on their wedding night? A first edition, in fact.'

'Is that so? He must have taken her death hard.'

'We all did. Particularly as she died a week before Hilda.'

'Goodness, Charlotte. I had no idea.' Alex's eyes held genuine sorrow. 'First your mother, then your best friend. That's more than any child should have to bear. Is it little wonder you found comfort in solitude?'

'Looking back, I suppose not. Although my father has always worried about me. He'd hoped by now I'd have made a friend or two.' She smiled sheepishly. It struck her again how comfortable she felt in Alex's presence. It was as if no time had passed since she last saw him.

'So your father never remarried?'

'No. I can't ever recall him having a lady friend either. I think he still misses my mother.'

'Do you remember much about her?'

'I have some memories of her being at home, but mostly they are of her in the institution. Gladesville Mental Hospital,' Charlotte explained. 'We were allowed to visit her on the weekends. She was beautiful, even in her sadness. She would often plead with my father to take her home, that she didn't want to be away from her children. I could see it broke his heart too. But the doctors were adamant that she wasn't fit for society and needed further treatment.'

That was how she had spent her weekends as a child, driving out to Gladesville with her father and James, bursting with excitement to see her mother again, but also dreading the oppressive, grey walls that she knew would swallow them up the minute they entered the gates. She relayed stories of the hospital visits and that one brief, precious hour she got to sit on her mother's lap each Saturday, having her hair stroked and a nursery rhyme whispered in her ear. Alex was quiet as she spoke, never interrupting but for the slight nod of his head that told her he was listening.

'Then, one morning, there was a telephone call from the hospital,' she said. 'They informed my father that my mother had committed voluntary death.'

'How devastating.'

'My father put the telephone down and went to his room and didn't come out for two days.'

Charlotte's memories of her mother were slowly dimming with age, but the morning of that call she remembered with disturbing vividness. So, too, the childhood she'd spent worried and confused over her mother's state of mind. In later years, it was panic over her changing body and the blood that had started when no one had warned her to expect it, the culmination of a father and brother who'd had little idea how to nurture the needs of a young female in the house.

It seemed Charlotte's whole life had been spent worrying over one thing or another. None of it had taught her to be brave, rather she felt introverted and cautious, not wanting to give too much of herself to the world, for it would often take and never give back.

They had almost reached the end of Hyde Park North, with Park Street and the entrance to Museum Station across the road. The sounds of people spilling out of St Mary's Cathedral could be heard as Saturday afternoon mass finished and the church bells tolled.

'What's your home like in England?' she asked, wishing the park would stretch forever and with it, the hours.

'I grew up in a house in Finsbury, right near London,' he said. 'But my parents live in the French countryside now. They relocated there after the war. London was a ruin, not that France had fared much better. My mother's grandmother was French and she had left behind a country house that had miraculously remained untouched during the Battle of the Somme.

'After they moved there, I decided to come here. It made sense, especially when I was presented with the opportunity to work on the bridge.'

'And do you like working on it?'

'Of course.' He cast her a smile so beautiful it made her stomach flip. 'I've always enjoyed the mathematics of engineering, have always loved to see the concept of a design become something tangible. And the Sydney Harbour Bridge is nothing short of magnificent. It's a privilege to be Dr Bradfield's right-hand man.'

Charlotte liked the way he spoke of the bridge, as though it were his lover. He was entirely unafraid to express himself, so unlike her father or Floyd, who thought feelings were best kept to oneself.

At the thought of Floyd, she sighed. Alex must have caught her dismay for he eyed her apologetically. 'I'm boring you. I'm sorry.'

'No, not at all,' she said quickly. 'I was thinking of something else.'

'Floyd?'

'Was I that obvious?'

Alex smiled. 'Are you finding the arrangement difficult?'

'A little.'

'It may all seem overwhelming to begin with but I have no doubt your father has forged a suitable match.'

'We're just very different people. I fear we may never find common ground.'

'You're young, Charlotte,' he said kindly. 'And Floyd has an age of wisdom to offer, I'm sure. Give it time.'

Charlotte nodded. It hadn't been her intention to sound so ungrateful. In any case, Alex's assuredness put her at ease. He was right. She would make her marriage to Floyd work for the good of the family, the security of their business and to make her father happy. She would do it because it was in everyone's best interests. 'I'm glad we met, Alex.'

'I'm glad too,' he said.

They reached Park Street and, rather than cross the road to the southern end of Hyde Park, they decided to turn and walk back to King and Elizabeth. They talked more of the bridge and Alex's home in London, and of Charlotte's childhood games with Hilda. She could recall them with ease, and he laughed several times at the stories she told about failed clues and ending up in the wrong place on opposite sides of The Rocks.

Charlotte was disappointed when they reached the outskirts of the park again and were back beneath the streets signs where they'd met.

'Do you know how to catch the tram from here?' Alex asked.

'I do,' she said.

'I would happily escort you home, except your father may not take kindly to me doing so twice in two weeks.'

She wished he would. The afternoon had passed too quickly and she didn't want to leave, didn't want to let go of the last of their minutes together, not knowing if or when she would see him again. Still, she knew he was right. It was not for her to dally in the company of another man, so she extended her hand to shake his. 'Thank you for the lovely afternoon, Alex. And for the clue.'

He took her hand in his. 'The pleasure was all mine.'

She willed her feet to leave him, to cross the road and head back up King Street towards the tram stop on George. And when she looked back to see which direction he'd gone, he was still there, leaning against the lamp post, watching her with a smile.

CHAPTER
11

Charlotte was setting the table the next morning for breakfast when her father appeared in the kitchen. 'Good morning, love,' he said, pecking her on the cheek and sitting.

'I didn't hear you come in last night. Late card game?' She'd been worried about how long she'd stayed out at Hyde Park with Alex and had willed the tram to roll faster towards home. After alighting in The Rocks, she'd run home, bursting through the door, expecting her father to call her into the parlour and ask where she'd been. But he hadn't been home, nor had he returned for dinner.

'Yes, they ran late into the night,' he said as she set a cup of tea down in front of him. 'How was your lunch? I saw your note by the telephone in the hall.'

'My note?' She glanced behind her towards the hall table and sure enough, that lie of a note she'd written the day before was still sitting by the telephone, the one telling her father she'd gone out to lunch. In her haste to get home quickly, she'd forgotten to throw it away. 'It was fine.'

'Who did you go with?'

The next lie came so smoothly she cringed. 'Mrs Mayfair.'

'Superb. I like that you've found a new friend. Puts my mind at ease.'

She gave him a weak smile and cut slices of bread from the loaf she'd baked earlier that morning, arranging them on a plate with jam and butter. She set them down in front of her father. 'Would you like an egg too?'

'No, no. I'll eat this and go.'

'You're heading out?'

'Just to Randwick Racecourse. They have some horses running today for the Autumn Carnival.'

There was a knock on the door and Charlotte, wondering who would be calling in unannounced on a Sunday, walked down the hall to open it. There, on the front step, she found Estelle.

'Mrs Mayfair?'

Estelle leant in to kiss her cheek. 'I apologise for the intrusion on a Sunday. I was in the area and thought I'd stop in on the off chance you were home.'

'I'm glad you did.' Charlotte opened the door wider. 'Come in.'

Estelle stepped into the hall and Charlotte led the way into the kitchen. 'Papa, we have a visitor.'

Walter glanced up. 'Ah, you must be Mrs Mayfair.' He rose to his feet and shook her hand. 'It is lovely to meet you finally. Charlotte hasn't stopped talking about you.'

Estelle smiled demurely. 'You have a delightful daughter, Mr Greene. We've been enjoying each other's company immensely.'

He clucked merrily. 'I heard you had a splendid lunch yesterday.'

Estelle raised an elegantly arched eyebrow. '*Lunch*?' She cut Charlotte a look. 'Oh, yes, lunch was splendid.'

Charlotte burned with a traitorous blush. She turned her face away so no one would see, focusing instead on the kitchen table. 'Excuse the mess. We were just finishing breakfast.'

'Don't stop on my account.' Estelle's eyebrow was still raised.

'Well, it's time for me to head out,' Walter said. 'Good morning, Mrs Mayfair. You are welcome here anytime.' He shook her hand again and left the kitchen.

Charlotte heard the front door close and the familiar rumble of her father's Studebaker ease down Playfair Street. She couldn't meet Estelle's eyes as she gathered up her father's teacup and plate from the kitchen table and took them to the sink. When she returned to wipe the table down, Estelle was still watching her closely.

'Lunch?'

'It was a misunderstanding,' Charlotte said, returning to the sink to shake the crumbs from her cloth.

Estelle set down her handbag and removed glossy fox fur gloves. 'All right, who is he?'

'Excuse me?'

'I wasn't born yesterday, darling. Why else would you lie about being at lunch with me?' She laughed her tinkling laugh at Charlotte's pained face. 'Don't be embarrassed. I think it's fabulous. Not even married yet and you've already taken a lover. How scandalous.'

Charlotte shook her head emphatically. 'It's not what you think.'

'What's his name?'

'You're embarrassing me.'

'Is he marvellous in bed?'

'Estelle!'

Estelle laughed again and waved her hand. 'I'm only playing. You don't have to tell me if you don't want to. But just so you know, I would always keep your secrets safe.' She drew her fingers across her bright red lips and turned an imaginary key.

Charlotte could still feel Estelle's gaze boring into her as she fixed them a tray of tea and led the way into the parlour. When they were seated on the Chesterfield, Charlotte hurried to change the topic. 'I went to Hubert Penny's to meet you the other day but you didn't show. Were you unwell?'

Estelle lit a cigarette. 'Not exactly. I had a small matter to attend to.'

Charlotte poured the tea. 'I hope everything was all right.'

She caught Estelle's moment of hesitation. 'Yes, all was well. I apologise for cancelling at the last minute. I hope you got home all right.'

Charlotte didn't mention that she'd run into Alex and that he'd walked her home, or that she'd met him yesterday and they'd strolled through Hyde Park.

Or that he was starting to occupy her thoughts more than was appropriate. She simply let the crackle of Estelle's cigarette and the clinking of her mother's china settle between them.

'So, what are your plans for next Saturday evening?' Estelle said on a current of smoke. 'I know a great cigar club in Surry Hills. It's underground and opens until late, so we don't need to worry about the six o'clock swill.'

Charlotte sipped her tea. 'Next Saturday is the Governor's Ball. Floyd has asked me to accompany him.'

Estelle froze mid-inhale. Then she smiled. 'The Governor's Ball? Of course. How silly of me.'

'You will be going, won't you?'

She exhaled and crushed out her cigarette. 'I don't believe I received an invitation.'

'Oh.'

Estelle waved her hand flippantly. 'I changed address recently so it must have got lost in the post. Not to worry. I never was one for a stuffy ball.'

'I could see about getting you an invitation,' Charlotte suggested. Although even as she said it, she could see Estelle's nose wrinkle at the prospect of spending an evening in the company of equally stuffy women. Estelle, it seemed, belonged to the correct social circles, but didn't conform to them, existing in the midst, yet on the cusp. She knew the right people and wore the right clothes, but there was more depth and intrigue to her. As Charlotte got to know her better, she realised Estelle was a chameleon, and for that, she liked her.

An hour and another serve of tea later, Estelle stood and collected her bag and gloves. 'I must be going. Lots to do.'

Charlotte walked her to the door and before Estelle stepped out onto the street, on impulse, Charlotte threw her arms around her.

'Goodness.' Estelle seemed taken aback, but her arms went gently around Charlotte too.

'I'm glad we're friends,' Charlotte said.

Estelle pulled away with a curious look. 'You know, I never thought you'd be as nice as you are.'

Charlotte wasn't sure how to take the comment, but it appeared to be complimentary. Especially when Estelle squeezed her hand and smiled at her, before climbing into her gold Bug Speedster and zipping down Playfair Street.

***

Charlotte was reading in the library when her father arrived home later that evening. At the sound of the front door opening and closing, she left *The Call of the Wild* on the arm of her chair and met her father in the hall.

'Hello there,' she said.

He shrugged out of his coat and hat and she took them both, hanging them on the stand.

'Hello, love,' His smile was tired. 'Weren't waiting up for me, were you?'

'No. I was just reading. I can heat up some dinner for you if you like.'

'Not too hungry tonight, thanks. I'll just take a drink in the parlour.'

Despite his refusal, Charlotte went to the kitchen to fix him a cup of tea and a slice of cake. She carried the tray into the parlour where she found him standing in the dark, staring into the unlit fireplace.

'I know you said you weren't hungry, but I fixed you something anyway.' She set the tray down on the table next to the Chesterfield and switched on the lamp. Warm light filled the room.

It was almost a minute before he seemed to realise she was there with him. 'Thanks love, but I might have something stronger than tea.'

She studied him carefully. 'Is everything all right?'

He moved to the decanter on the table and poured himself a whiskey, neat. 'Fine. Just a long day.' He took a full swig, emptying the glass, then poured another.

Charlotte sat on the Chesterfield. It seemed a great weight had settled on his shoulders and she didn't understand why. His mood, compared with earlier that day, had shifted like a pendulum.

Walter took his second glass of whiskey to the fireplace and rested it on the mantel, running his palm over the timber. 'You keep a fine house, love,' he said, holding up his hand to inspect the lack of dust. 'You'll make Floyd a happy man.'

Charlotte shifted on the lounge. 'Can I ask you something?'

Walter turned to her.

'Were you in love with my mother when you married her?'

The hint of a smile. 'I was.'

'So it wasn't an arranged marriage?'

'No. It wasn't.'

She nodded, looking down at her lap, smoothing her nightgown.

'I know you're fretting about marrying Floyd,' he said, 'but you will grow to love him. Many marriages are arranged these days and most of them fare better than the ones that aren't. Floyd is a good match for you. Our family's security depends on it. The business depends on it.'

'But it's a Greene family business. Yours, James' and mine. We don't need an outsider helping us.'

Walter sighed heavily. 'I won't be around forever, Charlotte. I'm growing tired. I want to retire soon. By handing Floyd the Australian arm of the company, we can capitalise on his financial strengths while still keeping everything within the family.'

But at what cost to her? What of her sacrifices? She knew it was too late to say anything about it now, that she should have made her feelings clear the night he'd proposed, but it had all come as such a shock that she'd needed a few days to get her head around it. By then, her father and Floyd had already planned the engagement party. How could she possibly speak up now in a way they would listen?

'What does James think of it all?' she asked.

'He has his hands full in the UK,' he said. 'It's too much for him to run both operations.'

'I could do it,' she said. 'I could run the Australian business for you. You could teach me. I don't need a husband for that.' It surprised her to suggest it, for she had never yearned for the responsibility before, but now that the words were out, she had little doubt she could manage it. She was bright and a fast learner. She soaked up information like a sponge and was always eager to learn. And if it meant keeping the company firmly within the Greene family, it wasn't all that preposterous an idea.

But the dismissal in her father's eyes told her it was. 'The workers would never stand for it. They'd have no respect for you. Besides, your contribution lies within the home. Even if I wanted to put you in charge, the minute you marry, your husband would be entitled to everything. I'd rather that person be someone I can trust, like Floyd.'

'What about the other things I want to do, like go to university and study?'

Walter sighed. 'Not this again, Charlotte.'

'But why not?'

'Because you're a woman,' he said firmly. 'Women do not go to university and they do not run businesses.'

'Some women go to university. Women are starting to become doctors even, not just nurses or midwives, but actual doctors.'

'Oh, love.' Still holding his glass of whiskey, he left the fireplace and sat down beside her on the Chesterfield. It was some time before he spoke again. 'I know this is hard for you, but we all have to do our part. We all have obligations.'

'But you're asking me to give you my entire future. I'm finding that difficult.'

He patted her hand gently but said nothing. Charlotte felt her eyes burn with tears, but she willed them to stay away. She wouldn't spill a single one over this arrangement.

'On your wedding night, Floyd is going to expect certain things from you,' Walter said, eyes fixed firmly on his glass. 'Things that will make you a woman, that will consummate the marriage and hopefully produce a son.'

Charlotte's cheeks flamed.

'In the absence of your mother, it's best you speak to Mrs Mayfair about this. Ask her advice. She can tell you what's involved.'

Charlotte couldn't even look at her father let alone contemplate lying in a bed beside Floyd, his sweaty little body on top of hers.

As a young woman, she'd sometimes wondered what that first time with a man might be like. She'd imagined it would be with someone she loved, someone she couldn't live without, and who loved and respected her in return. Perhaps the books in her mother's library had fanned romantic notions but even so, the fact that she would have to give her virginity to a man like Floyd made her feel truly unwell. And the fact that her father was discussing it with her so openly made it all the more uncomfortable. Never had she longed for her mother more.

Charlotte squirmed on the lounge and her father noticed. He cleared his throat and glanced at his watch. 'Well, I suppose we're done here. I should let you retire.'

'Can I fix you anything before I go to bed?'

'No thank you, love.'

She stood and collected the tray of cold tea and uneaten cake and walked to the door. When she turned back to look at him, he had returned to the empty fireplace, staring into it, lost in thoughts that belonged only to him.

CHAPTER 12

With her father at work all day and no new visits from Estelle, the next week passed idly by. Charlotte was used to the slow movement of time with little more than her own company to fill it, and she simply went about her usual tasks, reading, tending to the house and visiting the local grocer. Despite that, Saturday and the Governor's Ball felt as though it were upon her all too quickly.

As she made her bed that morning, Walter appeared in the doorway of her room carrying a large floral dress box tied with a pink ribbon. 'A package arrived for you, love.'

She looked up from straightening the eiderdown. 'For me?'

'I think it's from Floyd.'

Charlotte took the box from his outstretched hands. 'What is it?'

'Open it and see.'

Her father joined her by the bed as she laid it down and untied the ribbon. Lifting the lid and putting it aside, she pulled from the box a jade-green gown made of the kind of silk that slipped through her fingers like liquid, with a deeply plunging back and neckline. Equally exquisite was the black Chantilly lace that draped over the gown, with thousands of tiny crystals that gave it a prismatic quality. In a separate velvet pouch was a large jewelled hair clip, black silk gloves and a string of black diamantes for her neck.

Charlotte gasped as she held the dress in her fingers, so divine it felt like a cloud. Never had she seen or held anything so beautiful before.

'Floyd had it made for you,' her father said proudly. 'A one-of-a-kind piece. The design was immediately torn up afterwards. No other woman on Earth has one like it.'

Charlotte didn't know what to say. She had been deliberating all week on what to wear to the ball. Nothing in her wardrobe was remotely up to the task, besides her blue engagement dress. 'What a lovely gift.'

'Just be attentive to Floyd tonight when you see him. Show him your gratitude.'

'I wish you were coming,' she said, walking to the wardrobe for a spare hanger. She found one and slipped it through the lace straps of the dress, hanging it from the door. 'I'd feel better if you were to accompany me.'

'That will be Floyd's job now, love.'

Charlotte nodded sagely. She wanted to say that she would always need him, that she didn't want Floyd to take his place, but he patted her hand and left the room as if he knew what she was thinking and was worried she'd voice it.

***

The Governor's Ball, the most glamourous of the autumn events, was held at Government House. Floyd came to collect her at seven in his gleaming silver Duesenberg. As Charlotte carefully pinned her long hair back and secured the jewelled hair clip in place, she heard voices downstairs and knew he had arrived.

She stood from her dressing table and studied herself in the mirror. The woman it reflected was not one she recognised. She looked immensely grown up in the long gown, which moulded to her slender frame exquisitely.

She was nervous about going. She'd never accompanied Floyd out before, nor was it lost on her that she was allowed to go without a chaperone. It felt less about Floyd impressing them and more about them impressing Floyd.

When she came down the stairs in the gown, they were both waiting at the bottom. Floyd's moustache twitched as his beady eyes travelled up and down her body. 'Superb,' he told Walter as if she were a fine cut of meat he was selecting at the butcher. 'The dress fits perfectly.'

'She will look a vision beside you this evening.'

'Indeed.' Floyd straightened his bowtie and smoothed back his oily hair. 'Let's go. I don't want to be late.'

'Shall I wait up until midnight then?' Walter asked, hinting at the time he expected her home.

Floyd brushed at non-existent lint on his lapel. 'I suppose that should suffice.'

Walter handed Charlotte her coat and opened the front door for them. Floyd led the way out to his Duesenberg, the moonlight gleaming off its polished silver surface. He opened the passenger door and Charlotte eased herself into the front seat. She waved to her father as he stood in the doorway looking as tentative as she felt, and she decided if there was ever a time for Estelle and her self-assuredness, it was now.

Floyd climbed into the driver's seat and started the engine. The car, smelling of new leather and wax, purred to life. 'Isn't she something?' he said fondly, stroking the steering wheel.

'She's lovely,' Charlotte said, watching her house and father retreat as the car moved down Playfair Street.

'Do you like the dress?' he asked, navigating them onto Argyle.

'It's beautiful.'

'I had it made especially for you; one of a kind. It was quite expensive. Made with Parisian lace. Chantilly, that is.'

He was fishing for gratitude so Charlotte obliged. 'I can't thank you enough. I've not owned anything like this before.'

'Excellent.' He was pleased with himself. 'Now, there's going to be some prominent people at this event. Please, no talk of Wall Street or politics. It's embarrassing. Stay with the ladies.'

The ride to Government House was short. On Conservatorium Road they entered the Royal Botanic Garden, driving past the Sydney Conservatorium of Music and up to Government House, deep in the gardens, where they joined a queue of waiting automobiles. As they inched closer to an impressive porte cochère, the house rose before them—romantic and beguiling in its Gothic Revival architecture, with castellated towers and stone walls.

A valet arrived to take Floyd's keys and guide the Duesenberg away. Charlotte climbed out of the car and took Floyd's hand as she scooped the bottom of her dress up, careful not to let it catch on the gravel.

At the top of the stairs, Floyd checked in their coats and they joined a line of people waiting to enter the ballroom.

'Floyd Clark, old chap!' There was a slap on the back and a shake of the hand from a man with an exceptionally tall top hat and twinkling eyes.

And so the night began as Charlotte remained on Floyd's arm and he escorted her around the ballroom, making introductions. The conversations in the gentlemen's circles were interesting. It was where she would have preferred to stay, as they discussed the economy and consumer spending and the volatility on Wall Street, which they all seemed to agree was nothing but a series of hiccups, and Charlotte wouldn't have dared offer her opinion. After a quick turn around the room and a meet and greet with the governor himself, Admiral Sir Rawson Stratford de Chair, Floyd deposited her with a group of ladies.

'I'll come find you when I'm done,' he said, hurrying off to smoke cigars in a private drawing room.

She smiled politely at the ladies and listened to their gossip—how Alice's husband had strayed because she'd put on a few extra pounds, and who had mastered the new Singer Model 99 sewing machine with a knee bar. When there was a lull in the conversation, she interjected with talk of literature and her favourite books, which drew a round of uninterested murmurs.

When they eventually turned their backs on her, she made for the open doors to the garden outside. From the steps that led down into the grounds, she could see the half-constructed harbour bridge in the distance and the last of the night ferries as they crisscrossed the water.

She walked down the stairs and strolled along the path, the trees having turned a fierce red in anticipation of winter. The breeze had grown cool and she wrapped her arms around herself, wishing she'd thought to keep her coat on.

With her back to the ballroom doors and with the harbour sprawled before her, she didn't realise anyone was behind her until she felt a tap on her shoulder. She spun around to find Alex standing there.

'Miss Greene, this is a pleasant surprise.'

'Mr Young!' She broke into a delighted grin. 'What are you doing here?'

'It's the perks of being Bradfield's right-hand man. I get an invitation to all the parties.' He smiled at her and despite it being dark out, his eyes still lit with the kind of intensity that could rival the harbour on the stormiest of days. He was handsome in a black tuxedo and top hat, and it almost hurt to look at him, with his finely chiselled face.

'Are you here with your father?' he asked.

She shook her head. 'I've accompanied Mr Clark.'

Brief disappointment crossed his face before he corrected it. 'Of course. Are you cold out here? I'd give you my coat if it wasn't in the cloakroom. We can go back inside if you like.'

'I prefer it out here. It's pretty.'

'Indeed. It has a lovely view. Especially of the bridge.'

'Have you been to the top of it?' she asked.

'Many times,' he said. 'I go up there at least once a week.'

She gasped. 'Is it terrifyingly high? Why, you must be able to see for miles.'

'Yes, for miles in every direction. As the arches cantilever out over the water now, the bridge climbs higher every day. It used to scare me, now I simply climb with it.'

Charlotte turned to look out at the mighty structure. It was so beautiful at night, illuminated by the moon. Her family's steel was proudly on display, for the world to see, from beams that zigzagged through the arches to cables that were embedded in the saddles to support the top chords.

It saddened her to think that once her father retired, Floyd would gain full control of the Australian branch of their business. She'd always imagined her father as lifelong, eternal, never to grow old. But he *was* growing old, and tired, and he wanted someone with youth and energy to take over. But would her family's legacy and their ties to the bridge be lost as a result, for who would remember Greene Steel with a Clark at the helm?

'At the moment each end of the arch is supported by pylons which have been built to deck level only,' Alex continued, and she was drawn back to the garden at Government House. 'Along with the foundation and abutments, they can withstand the pull of the arches and the weight of the creeper cranes. The harbour foreshores are mostly composed of solid sandstone, which is the only reason this could be made possible.

The pylons above deck level, once we finish them, will be purely decorative.'

Where her dress plunged deeply at the back, Alex placed his hand on her bare skin to direct her focus to the pylons, and she could feel the warmth of his fingertips, sending a pleasant sensation through her.

He pointed to the wide gap between the two ends of the arches. 'Once the arches meet in the middle and the span is complete, they'll be joined by a horizontal bearing pin, thus making the arch self-supporting. It's an incredible piece of engineering, if I do say so myself.' He smiled proudly and looked so boyish while doing so.

If it were possible to stop time, Charlotte would have chosen to stop it at that moment, while his hand rested on her back and their bodies were so close she could smell the freshness of his shirt and the cologne he wore.

Alas, people had begun to spill out of the ballroom doors to take advantage of the cool gardens and she heard Floyd calling her name from the top of the steps. Alex dropped his hand quickly and she sensed his shoulders tense in the dark.

'It seems Mr Clark is looking for you,' he said.

Charlotte nodded, her breath held, wishing Floyd and the ball would melt away.

'I better get back to Bradfield and the others. They'll be wondering where I am. As always, it's been a pleasure, Miss Greene.' He bowed his head in parting and dashed up the stairs just as Floyd came down them.

'There you are, Charlotte. I've been looking all over for you.' Floyd was upon her, grabbing her arm, and she noticed the difference between his grasp and the gentle touch of Alex. 'What are you doing out here?'

'Just getting some air,' she said.

'Come then, let's walk for a bit, then we can go back inside for the hors d'oeuvres. I'm starving.'

They did a lap around the gardens where Floyd talked about himself and the important people he'd met. His breath was overpowering with the smell of too many whiskeys and his words had begun to slur by the time they'd completed a full circle. When they arrived back at the steps to the ballroom, he placed both hands around her arms, squeezing too tightly.

'Have I told you how much I spent on this dress?' he asked in her ear.

'It's a beautiful gown,' she said, leaning away from him.

'I didn't ask if you liked it. I asked if you knew how much I'd spent on it.'

'I'd be happy to reimburse you.'

He laughed. 'I don't want your money. You could repay me in other ways though. I can't tell you how happy that would make me.' He moved his face close and forced his lips down onto hers, the stench of the liquor overwhelming.

Charlotte cringed and she had to resist the urge to pull away. He was to be her husband in seven months and, as much as she'd like to, it would do no good to resist his indecorous behaviour, so she clamped her eyes and her lips shut and let him kiss her, praying it would end quickly.

Mercifully, it did, as he swayed from the whiskey and had to catch himself from falling. Still, Charlotte could taste him on her, could feel the tenderness around her mouth where his moustache had scraped her, and all she wanted to do was run to the powder room and wash him away.

'Very nice,' he said, licking his lips. 'Shall we go eat then?' He held out his arm for her to take and she did, turning towards the stairs where she saw Alex staring down at them from the top. His expression was dark, a slight tick of his jaw. He had seen the kiss, maybe even thought she'd enjoyed it.

Every day she was feeling something for Alex, feelings that transcended the bounds of friendship or acquaintance. Every day she thought of him more and more, in ways that she shouldn't. And something told her Alex felt it too. It was in the way his fingers had touched her back earlier and the way he'd looked down at her with that gentle smile, with eyes that seemed only for her. But what would he think of her now having witnessed that kiss, that repugnant, drunken kiss she hadn't fought off?

As Floyd led her up the stairs, Alex turned and disappeared into the ballroom. Despite her best efforts, she lost sight of him amongst the throngs of people as they crowded around waiters with trays of hors d'oeuvres and champagne, hungry, gorging, stuffing themselves.

Floyd led her into the ballroom and towards a waiter, but she tugged on his arm. 'I need to visit the washroom.'

He tut-tutted. 'Fine, but do hurry up.'

She gathered up her gown and hurried away. Navigating around the guests, she moved through the ballroom as quickly as she could and out into the hallway where the cloakroom was.

She had no idea if Alex had left, was praying that he hadn't, and when she asked the attendant if his coat had been collected, he didn't just answer her, he returned with it.

'This is Mr Young's. You'll have to sign here for it,' the man said, sliding Alex's coat and a signature log towards her.

'That's okay, I won't be taking it out. I just need to put something in the pocket. Could I borrow a pen and paper please?'

With a perplexed look, the attendant handed her a piece of paper and a pen. She took them both and leant on the counter to write her clue. Once she was done, with a trembling hand, she folded the paper and slipped it into one of the coat pockets, praying that he would find it.

> *Gone now are the sails of the windmills, where all that remain are the steps.*
> *Meet me tomorrow morning at ten.*

She was talking about Windmill Steps of course, in The Rocks, where the first windmills of Sydney had once stood but were now long gone, and she hoped his knowledge of the area was enough for him to find her there. Because she'd seen the look on his face when Floyd had kissed her and she needed to know if this was more than just a childhood game to him.

And, as if she hadn't already acted boldly enough, before she slipped the note into his coat pocket, she added one last line, a quote from Oscar Wilde's love letter to Lord Alfred Douglas.

> *I feel that it is only with you that I can do anything at all.*

CHAPTER
13

PAIGE
Present Day

With the painters gone and the gardener finished, Paige began to witness the transformation of the Playfair house.

The clutter was removed, the walls were freshly painted, the timber floors were restored and the back yard had a new garden. Some of the furniture had begun to arrive and she no longer had to sit on an uncomfortable milk crate in the kitchen to get her work done. There were white stools along the bench and the dining room had been converted into a meeting room, with a long table, beanbags and a mounted screen for presentations and video conferencing.

For Paige, it also meant it was time to find another place to live. No longer could she squat in the former parlour. Soon Xavier would arrive and the house would be launched into a publishing house.

Paige sat back on the stool at the kitchen bench and rubbed her neck. She had been trawling through rental properties in The Rocks area for the past hour and had noted down two that looked promising and were within her price range, marking their viewing times in her diary.

She glanced at her empty coffee cup and was climbing off the stool to make more when her phone beeped in her pocket. She pulled it out and glanced at the screen. It was a text from Ryan. He was a block down, out for a walk, and asked if he could stop in.

A lopsided grin formed on her face. It had been a few days since she'd last seen him, when they'd both left the library buoyant from their research of Charlotte, despite it revealing more questions than answers. After that, she'd been busy with work and she'd assumed he'd been busy too, for she hadn't heard from him.

She replied to his text and a few minutes later, there was a knock at the door. She opened it to find him on the front step with a tray of takeaway coffees in his hand.

'Hey, thought you could do with one of these.' Smiling, he held out a cup to her. He was fresh-faced and clean-shaven. He smelt good and she tried not to inhale him so obviously.

She took the proffered coffee. 'You're a lifesaver. Come in.'

'Actually, I thought we could take a walk if you have some free time. It's a beautiful day.'

It *was* a beautiful day. The sun was gentle as it lit the harbour, turning the water turquoise. She thought of the rental properties she still had to sift through and decided they could wait a few hours. The fresh air was beckoning and she needed a break from the laptop. 'I'd love to. Have you been over to the bridge yet?'

'No. I've only seen it from afar.'

'Then you're in for a treat. I'm fairly sure I can get us there without getting lost. Would you like to walk under it, across it or climb its southern pylon?'

'Wow, spoilt for choice. Surprise me.'

'Okay.' She locked the door behind her and, with their coffees, they strolled back up Playfair Street, where Paige showed Ryan a narrow laneway that cut through the middle of the workmen's terraces, leading to the rear of them. From there, they took a series of stairs up towards Gloucester Walk, passing through Foundation Park and the remnants of the old pre-plague houses that she could see from Xavier's backyard.

'What have you been up to?' Paige asked as they reached Gloucester and made for Bridge Stairs.

'I went to Windmill Steps the day before last, then walked around Elizabeth and King Streets near Hyde Park yesterday. I've been following Charlotte and Floyd's clues.'

'I can't promise to be a knowledgeable tour guide, but if you ever need company when visiting these places, I'm here.'

'I know,' he said, 'but I'm conscious of eating up your time. I don't want to take you away from your work.'

'It's fine. Most of it is done now. I'm just waiting for Xavier to arrive so we can interview candidates. Though I do need to find a place to live soon or I might be squatting in the attic.'

He laughed. 'Well, if you get stuck, I have a spare bed at the hotel.' As soon as he said it, his ears reddened and he cleared his throat.

Paige smiled shyly. 'Thank you. That's nice of you to offer.' She cleared her throat too. 'So how are you feeling about what we discovered at the library?'

They reached Bridge Stairs and began the climb upwards to Bradfield Highway, the stretch of road that crossed the Sydney Harbour Bridge.

'Or more to the point, what we didn't find,' Ryan said. 'I feel like we should know more by now.'

'It can take time to peel back the layers, especially without decent records.'

'I've been thinking about your suggestion of visiting Gladesville Mental Hospital. I'd like to do that if you could spare a day to come with me.'

'Of course.'

'I looked it up last night and the campus still accommodates some health and community services, although the asylum has been closed for years. You can take a guided tour of the old wards. I'm hoping they will have former patient records there.'

'When are you thinking of going?'

'Tomorrow, if you're free. It looks like a thirty-minute bus ride from The Rocks.'

'As luck would have it, I don't work on Saturdays.'

'So you'll come?' He grinned.

'Sure!'

They reached the top of Bridge Stairs and started on the pedestrian lane alongside Bradfield Highway as traffic whooshed past.

'What made you want to study modern history?' Ryan asked.

'I've just always been fascinated by it,' she said. 'Every day we're making history—social, political, cultural, even fashion and the environment are constantly evolving. I love how it can take an act from every single person who has ever lived to shape the course in some way or another. That's what makes it's complex, what makes us as individuals powerful.'

He nodded. 'I hadn't thought of it like that.'

'Sorry, I become passionate when I talk about it.'

'No, it's all right. I like hearing about it. But why be Xavier's assistant and not a curator in a museum somewhere? As you said, it's obviously a passion.'

It was a good question, but the answer was so pathetically inadequate that she wasn't sure she wanted to say it out loud. 'There were opportunities, a few of them, in fact. One here in a Sydney museum, another in Brisbane and Canberra. But I passed them up and stayed in Albury.' It was all she said and Ryan didn't persist, perhaps knowing they were traversing sensitive ground.

They continued walking along the pedestrian lane, the bridge's arch rising before them.

'Would you look at this view?' Ryan stopped to take in the harbour below them, the Opera House and the Sydney skyline. 'You don't see something like this every day.'

Paige pointed out several sights and he nodded with enthusiasm, a view to enthral even the most well-travelled soul. They spent five minutes gazing out, Paige feeling as small and insignificant as a dust mote, high above a jungle of concrete, water and green parks.

They moved on to reach the bridge's southern pylon. 'We can climb to the top,' Paige said. 'It's a long way up but there's an exhibit inside and an even better view of the harbour from the observation deck.'

Ryan ran his hand along the wall of the pylon. 'Granite?'

'Yes,' Paige said. 'Australian sourced, from Moruya on the south coast of New South Wales. A small town that was virtually unheard of until Bradfield said he wanted his pylons made out of Moruya granite. And then it became the home of every mason in Australia, including two hundred more from Scotland.'

They entered the southern pylon and began the journey up several flights of stairs. Halfway, they paused for breath and stopped to circle the exhibits on display. Ryan took his time looking at the boards of information and the pictures that accompanied them, a small appreciative smile forming on his lips at any mention of Greene Steel.

They strolled around the display cabinets and she was surprised at how knowledgeable he was as he explained the purpose of hinges and bearing pins and lateral chords, as well as the simple tools they used during the construction.

They continued on their journey upwards, walking the remaining flights of stairs until they reached the top. On the observation deck, the view took Paige's breath away. Sydney lay sprawled out below them like a work of art.

'Wow,' she heard Ryan say under his breath.

On the north-facing side of the pylon, the bridge's arch rose beside them, so close Paige thought she could reach out and touch it, and they paused to admire it, as traffic flowed beneath them. 'Isn't she something?' Paige asked.

Ryan was unmistakably awed. 'It's incredible how close you can get to it. And to see my family's legacy right here. I mean, we build things every day. Our steel is everywhere, but this... I can't explain it.'

She watched him closely. 'You must miss home.'

He turned to look at her. 'A little. I'm not missing the breakdown of my marriage or the lawyers or the arguing over settlement, but I do miss home. I never expected to stay here this long. I never even expected to come.'

'What made you decide to?'

'If I'm honest, it was a whim. Although it occurred to me when I was booking my flight that I might have lost my mind. Once I got here, it felt like the right thing.'

'I thought you were a little odd when you appeared on my doorstep that first night,' she said with an apologetic smile.

'I know you did. I'm surprised you let me in, to be honest.'

'Me too.'

He laughed. 'Well, I don't blame you for thinking that. My head wasn't in the right place when I left London. It probably showed.'

'And now?'

'Better. Clearer.'

'I'm glad.' They shared a smile. His candour was refreshing, and Paige had to agree he looked the most relaxed she'd ever seen him. She was glad he was there, standing with her on top of the bridge's pylon, this unexpected friend she'd made.

'And how about you?' he said, eyes held fast on hers. 'Were you mad to come here too?'

Her stomach dropped the way it often did when she was asked about home, when talk of Christian threatened to bruise emotions that still pained. She shrugged nonchalantly, hoping to brush it off. 'Maybe. Time will tell.'

'Do you have people waiting for you back in Albury?'

'Not really.'

'Friends, a boyfriend?'

'No.'

'No?'

She could tell he wasn't going to let her off easily. He'd bared his soul to her and he was expecting the same in return. She sighed. 'There was this one guy I liked. Well, more than liked, I suppose. We'd been best friends for years, since we were children. I don't think I have a single memory that he's not part of.'

He nodded encouragingly. 'And?'

She hesitated. 'And I loved him. Or maybe I loved the idea of him. I don't know. We never did anything about it and, a few months ago, he asked his new girlfriend to marry him. So that's that.' She looked away, out towards the harbour so Ryan wouldn't see how raw she was beneath the surface. How humiliated and rejected she still felt, because all of Albury had thought they would end up together too, and they'd been just as shocked when he'd proposed to someone else.

'What's his name?' he asked.

'Christian.'

Ryan reached out and touched her shoulder. 'I'm sorry that happened to you.'

'It's fine,' she said. 'I've learnt to live with it. It wasn't written in our stars and I'm okay with that. I just couldn't stay around to watch. You know, small town, big wedding. The best thing I could have done was leave and let them be.'

'Does he know how you feel?'

'I think so. And I think he felt the same way. But there were so many missed opportunities and I don't know why. Anyway, it's too late now.'

'He was crazy to let you go, in my opinion.'

She smiled wanly. 'That's nice of you to say.'

'It's the truth. And I think you're exceptionally brave for leaving.' Ryan's smile was so warm, so genuine, that she relaxed.

'I think the jury may still be out on that.'

'You are the only person I know who sleeps in old, ghostly houses and enjoys it. Believe me, you're brave.'

They both laughed and Paige felt a thousand times lighter for the weight that had been lifted off her shoulders. She hadn't realised how much she'd needed to talk to someone.

The wind picked up and sent her hair flying so they left the observation deck and stepped back inside the pylon to an indoor information area. Behind Perspex display cabinets they perused photographs of the different stages of the bridge's construction.

They were completing a stroll around the exhibits when Paige stopped at a photograph of four men standing beneath the bridge at Milsons Point. Construction was still evident in the background and the date stamped on the photo's bottom right corner confirmed it was taken in August 1929, three years before completion.

Paige glimpsed the names of the four men listed in the information plaque beside it. 'Hey,' she said, looking up. 'Isn't this your great-great-grandfather?'

Ryan came to her side. 'Walter Greene. Yes, that's him. Who are the other people?'

'Dr JJC Bradfield and Floyd Clark.'

'So that's Floyd?'

He was a string of a man, with beady, dull eyes and a thick, bristly moustache. If Paige thought back to the striking photo of Charlotte they'd discovered in the attic, she couldn't picture that alluring young woman marrying this man. They hardly seemed a natural fit.

Her eyes fell upon Dr JJC Bradfield, who she recognised instantly from her studies of the bridge, then they shifted across to the fourth person in the photo, a handsome man who looked smart in a single-breasted suit and trilby. An employee of the Department of Public Works and Bradfield's chief engineer, the plaque stated.

His name was Alexander Young.

CHAPTER
14

The next morning at ten, Paige texted Ryan to let him know she'd arrived outside his hotel. While she waited for him by the front doors of The Sebel Quay West with two takeaway coffees, her thoughts wandered to Charlotte and Floyd. What an odd couple they had made— Charlotte, with her youth and that spirited smile lurking in the corners of her lips and Floyd, with his rigid disposition and cold, unfriendly eyes. While she could imagine Charlotte revelling in a game of handwritten clues and cat and mouse around the city, Floyd hardly seemed the type who would enjoy it. Paige was far from being an expert on relationships, and she only had a few photographs to go off, but never had she come across a more unusual pairing.

Her reverie broke when Ryan stepped through the front doors of the hotel and smiled brightly at her. 'Hey.'

'Good morning. Coffee?' She handed him a cup. 'I'm repaying the favour.'

'Ah, perfect.' He took the coffee and sipped. 'All ready for the asylum today?'

Paige chuckled. 'Now that's a line I haven't heard before.'

He grimaced. 'Sorry. I'm a little rusty. Note to self, don't ask girl on date to asylum.'

Paige's stomach flipped at the mention of the word 'date' and she grew shy as they left The Rocks behind and walked to Circular Quay to the bus stop on Alfred Street. They only had to wait two minutes before the 507 to Gladesville arrived and they boarded. They found a seat at the back and sipped their coffees as the bus swung into Saturday morning traffic.

'I read more of the letters in Charlotte's chest last night,' Ryan said.

'Anything interesting to report?'

'Only that I'm halfway through and starting to see their relationship progress. There were lots of guarded words at the beginning, as though they were still getting to know each other, but now I've reached a turning point, around June and July, where they've become more daring, as if throwing caution to the wind.'

'How many more are there to read?'

'Lots. Some are written on scraps of paper, others on proper stationery. It's like, at times, they had to seize the moment to write a clue. It wasn't always planned.'

'I find it a little strange,' Paige said.

Ryan glanced at her. 'Which part?'

'Floyd. He's not her type. He doesn't seem like someone Charlotte would have been attracted to.'

'I hadn't thought about it, to be honest.'

It might have been a minor detail but for Paige, it rankled, and she couldn't explain why. 'Floyd looked too austere.'

'I suppose, but it doesn't mean she didn't love him.'

'I don't think they were well suited.'

'That's a big assumption to make when all we have are a couple of photographs.'

'We have the letters too,' Paige reminded him, 'and the intimate language Charlotte and her man used when writing to each other. Floyd doesn't strike me as being the kind of person who wrote like that. *And* he was far too old for her.'

Ryan's eyebrows went up. 'Well, now you're just being ageist.'

Paige nudged him. 'You know what I mean. Floyd looked like someone a father would choose for his daughter, not someone a young girl would choose for herself. I think their marriage was arranged.'

'Okay, so maybe they weren't a good fit,' he conceded. 'Maybe Walter chose Floyd for her. It doesn't mean they didn't play the game together.'

They would have to agree to disagree on that point. Paige had thought about it most of the night and each time she tried to envision

Charlotte and Floyd leaving clues for one another, of trekking across the city to discover each other's hiding spot, she couldn't. Instead, she would picture Floyd's serious face, the stiffness in his pose, the unyielding eyes that indicated less of a frivolous nature and more of someone who was too spiritless for such pastimes.

'So what's the plan for today?' she asked.

'I want to locate patient records,' Ryan said. 'If we can determine that Charlotte was committed to the asylum and by whom, and what happened to her after that, it might tell us a lot.'

The bus rumbled out of the city and into the inner-western suburbs of Sydney, through Drummoyne and Huntleys Cove. Thirty minutes later, they arrived at a stop on Victoria Road that Ryan said was one of two for the hospital. They took a chance and leapt off, following the hospital perimeter until they found an entrance flanked by heavy metal fencing.

The imposing buildings were nineteenth century and constructed of sandstone, with steel bars on the windows that reminded Paige of a prison. With help from a security officer at the Gatekeeper's Lodge, they found their way to the main reception and stepped inside a small air-conditioned room. A woman called Maggie, as indicated by her name tag, sat at a desk behind a counter, fingers tapping on a keyboard, glasses perched on the end of her nose.

She looked up when they walked in and smiled. 'Hello there.'

'Hi,' Paige said. 'We were wondering if you could help us.'

'If you're looking for the asylum tour, it starts at one-thirty and you'll need to meet the guide at the Punt Road entrance.'

'Oh, we're not here for the tour,' Paige said. 'Actually, we're looking for some information on a possible patient from 1929. Is that something you could help us with?'

'I can try.'

'Her name was Charlotte Greene,' she explained. 'We believe she was admitted to the mental facility here in October or November 1929. We're unsure of the exact date or the reason why she was sent here.'

'Do you know how long she was admitted for and if she died here?' Maggie asked.

'That's what we're hoping to find out,' Ryan said.

'And you're sure it was this asylum? There were a number of them operating at the time—Callan Park, Peat Island on the Hawkesbury, the old Parramatta Female Factory.'

'We're fairly certain,' Ryan said. 'We found a photograph of Charlotte standing with a Dr Carmichael, dated December 1929. It's our understanding he was the treating psychiatrist here.'

Maggie nodded. 'That's correct. Quite renowned for his psychiatry in the day too. Now, we do have old patient records, but not a lot of them. A great deal were lost to the incinerator during an amalgamation with Macquarie Hospital many decades ago, but whatever we managed to salvage, we scanned into the computer. You said her name was Charlotte Greene?'

'That's right,' Ryan said. 'Possibly admitted in October or November 1929.'

'All right, let's see what we can find.' She tapped on her keyboard and leant towards the monitor, peering down her nose at it. 'I have a Marianne Greene. Admitted for grief. Death of an infant. That was in 1915 though.' Maggie's eyes scanned the screen. 'Here we go. Charlotte Greene. I wonder if they were related at all. Anyway, you're in luck. I have Charlotte's patient summary.'

Maggie clicked her mouse and the printer behind her woke with a series of beeps, delivering the summary into the tray. She swivelled in her chair to collect it and set it on the top of the counter so Paige and Ryan could see.

'She was definitely a patient here,' Maggie said, circling a date. 'Admitted on October thirtieth, 1929, at seven forty-five pm, suffering female hysteria.'

'October thirtieth?' Paige glanced at Ryan. 'That can't be. She sent a telegram to her brother on October thirty-first from the post office in The Rocks.'

'Well, she was here on the thirtieth. Her father, Walter, brought her in. She was received by Dr Carmichael. That's his signature there.'

'I'm not sure how she could have been in two places at once,' Paige said.

'Maybe someone sent the telegram on her behalf. Or the postmaster stamped it on the thirty-first, even though Charlotte dropped it in the day before,' Maggie suggested.

'It's possible,' Ryan agreed.

'Oh, now this is quite sad.' Maggie pressed her lips together. 'Her date of death. Seems Charlotte died here too, just a few months later in March 1930.'

Paige watched as Maggie circled the date, seventeenth of March, 1930, when Charlotte's young life had ended.

'What did she die of?' Ryan asked.

Maggie squinted at the piece of paper. 'It just says voluntary death. Nothing more.'

'Voluntary death?'

'Suicide.'

Ryan grew pale. Paige's hand instinctively went to his back, resting it there.

'Does it say anything about how or why she did it?' he asked.

'Not on this sheet.' Maggie glanced back at her screen. 'But it looks like there's a medical report that accompanies the summary. It might detail the treatments she received and her exact cause of death. Shall I print that too?'

'Please,' Paige said.

While the printer delivered Charlotte's medical report into the tray, Maggie handed over the patient summary. 'You keep this. I hope it helps with your research.'

'Thank you,' Ryan said. 'So if she died here, would she have been buried here too?'

Maggie shrugged. 'It's possible, but hard to know for sure. Patients who died here were generally buried in unmarked graves on the grounds unless a family member came to claim them for proper burial. But that didn't happen often.'

'Are there any headstones we could look at?' Paige said.

'There are only five graves with headstones and none of them has the name Charlotte Greene on them. Unfortunately, there are thirteen hundred other bodies in unmarked graves. If she's here, we'd have no way to find her. She could be anywhere.'

Ryan's shoulders slumped. As though the news of her death in the asylum wasn't sad enough, now they wouldn't be able to lay flowers on a grave. *She could be anywhere.*

'You're still welcome to take a walk through the burial grounds but you won't find anything except a path and some trees. Cars aren't allowed through there anymore as a sign of respect but pedestrians are free to walk around.'

Maggie reached for a map of the complex from her desk. She circled various areas with her pen. 'You can find the lost cemeteries here and here. The buildings along the way are interesting too and some should be open. You can have a look inside. But like I said, you won't find much in the way of headstones or marked graves. Gladesville Mental Hospital is one of Sydney's shameful secrets. A lot was done to cover its blemish on history.'

Paige thanked Maggie and gathered up the map.

'Oh wait, you forgot Charlotte's medical report.' Maggie slid a thin stack of papers across the counter and Paige collected them too, placing everything into her backpack.

She and Ryan left the reception area and stepped back out into the sunshine, which seemed cruelly pleasant considering the news they'd just received.

Consulting Maggie's map, they followed a path through the hospital grounds, past craggy sandstone buildings where dangling branches of weeping willows scratched against the windowpanes. It was quiet all around, the soft trickle of a creek and the faraway sound of traffic barely able to penetrate the deep silence. They passed abandoned wards and derelict structures choked with lantana, then a ruined folly crawling with ivy.

They were silent as they walked but Paige knew Ryan was thinking the same thing—how could Walter have left Charlotte in a place like this? What had caused her to tumble into such despair that she'd take her own life? And what had happened to Walter? What had happened to Floyd? Again, so many pieces, a puzzle box full, and a tragic story at the heart of it.

After ten minutes of walking towards the north-eastern corner of the complex, they came to a burial ground. Paige saw the graves Maggie had mentioned, their headstones jutting towards the sky. She and Ryan walked from gravestone to gravestone, inspecting the names. She noticed how quiet he was, his eyes surveying the land around them, the immense roll of sweeping grass that had become the final unmarked resting place of so many lost souls.

'Such a cruel injustice,' Paige said, speaking not only of Charlotte but of the hundreds of others who lay there with no name to identify them.

'Walter left her here to die,' Ryan said dispiritedly. 'By her own hand. What father does that to his daughter?'

Paige felt an overwhelming desire to take him in her arms. To comfort him in a way that surprised her. Everything about that place signified sadness and nothing in the last one hundred years, even closing the asylum down, had changed that.

They walked back to the bus stop on Victoria Road and boarded the 507, returning to the city. When they reached the stop at Circular Quay, they stepped off and headed to Ryan's hotel.

'I'm sorry today didn't go as well as you'd hoped,' Paige said.

He smiled softly. 'You don't have to be sorry. It's just a shame this happened to her, that she died the way she did, and we'll never know where she was laid to rest.'

'Maggie said something about families collecting their deceased relatives for a proper funeral. There's still a chance Walter buried her somewhere else in Sydney. We could search other cemeteries.'

'You think he gave her a proper burial then disappeared?' He shook his head. 'No, Walter committed her to that place and never went back.'

'We don't know that.'

'Honestly, I'm becoming resigned to the fact that we don't know much at all and I have to be okay with that.'

They crossed First Fleet Park by the Museum of Contemporary Art and climbed a flight of steps to George Street.

Out the front of The Sebel Quay West, Paige felt the atmosphere turn strangely electric as Ryan fidgeted, not wanting to say goodbye.

'If you want to talk it through more we could grab a drink at the pub,' she offered.

'It's not that,' he said.

'What is it?'

He looked directly into her eyes and she thought she'd never seen a gaze as intense as his at that moment. 'Do you feel it?'

'Feel what?'

'This. Us. Is it just me or do you feel it too?'

Paige opened her mouth to speak but found the words wouldn't form. She knew exactly what he was saying. It was the very thing she'd been trying to fight since the night she'd first met him, a powerful attraction that would do neither of them good, for he wore the emotional scars of a divorce in Britain and she was running from heartache in country New South Wales. She'd almost conquered the feelings too, pushing them away to a safe place, distracting herself with work and Charlotte's mystery, except now he'd gone and said it out loud and there was no denying it any longer.

'Say something,' he said, dark eyes watching her closely.

She shook her head. 'I'm not sure... I don't...'

'The timing isn't great,' he added quickly.

'No, it isn't.'

'It's complicated.'

'Very.'

'My divorce.'

'And where you live. And where I live. And lots of other things.'

'Tell me you don't feel it. Say the words and I'll leave you alone.'

Her head was spinning, her heart rejoicing, the words stalling on her lips. She couldn't tell him to leave, couldn't ask him to stay, couldn't think straight. 'I do feel it. Of course I do.'

'But?'

Yes, but what, Paige? Why was she hesitating? He was a great guy and she was crazy about him. The decision should be easy. But it wasn't. She thought of Christian and how she couldn't make that work after years of trying, and all the challenges she and Ryan faced suddenly loomed large.

He fidgeted beside her and she looked up at him. A mix of hope and uncertainty had settled in his eyes. She wanted to reassure him, didn't want him to think she was rejecting him. On the contrary, she just needed time to process it. 'Why don't you come by tomorrow? We can talk more once we've had time to get our heads around it.'

'I think my head is around it. It's all I've thought about for the past week.'

She smiled. 'Still, will you come and see me?'

Ryan reached for her hand, squeezing it gently in his. 'You know I will.'

He leant down to kiss her cheek, his lips lingering on her skin before they said goodbye. Paige turned and headed back along Gloucester Street towards Playfair, still unsure of what had transpired and what it all meant, wondering if she'd handled it the right way or if her response had been disastrous. Because she liked Ryan. A lot. The question was, was she brave enough to do anything about it?

CHAPTER 15

It took Paige a long time to fall asleep that night. She tossed and turned, replaying the conversation with Ryan over in her head. She wondered if, four blocks away on Gloucester Street, he was in his bed unable to sleep too. If the same thoughts were running through his mind.

Most of Paige's life had been spent secretly pining for the same person. This newfound possibility of liking someone and having them like her back was a strange and disconcerting notion. Her heart had never indulged in a reciprocated first love before, of giddy romance and stolen kisses. There had been men—a few one-night stands, but nobody serious and nobody who had captured her heart like Christian had. And yet he'd given her nothing. Everything she felt she'd had to lock away, conscious of disrupting the friendship or of being rejected, watching the endless parade of other women date her 'best friend'. She'd placed herself on a shelf, waiting for him to say it, that he felt it too, but it had never come.

And now, suddenly, there was Ryan, someone she liked and who liked her in return. But whenever she thought of him, she also thought of how complicated it would be. They led different lives on different continents. The simple art of dating would have to be played out across the ocean. And he was getting a divorce. He had been the first to admit his life was in disarray. What if he wasn't thinking clearly? Could she put herself back on that shelf to wait again?

The sun had barely risen when Paige gave up on sleep and decided to get up. She showered, dressed, and made a double espresso that she sipped while running through her diary. There were only some things left to do, her list of jobs significantly reduced now that she was waiting on Xavier's arrival. Important decisions had to be made, ones that required his presence, which meant that for the past week she'd been killing time.

Over a slice of toast and another coffee, she spent the next two hours emailing with the graphic designer to prepare the banners, business cards and front signage. She updated the website with new information, cleared her voicemail, tried to call Xavier, who didn't answer, and kept one eye steadfastly on her laptop clock.

At ten am, the knock she was expecting sounded on the door.

'Come in,' she called from her spot at the kitchen bench. She heard Ryan open and close the door, then his sneakers squeak down the hall.

'Hey,' he said, entering the kitchen and placing Charlotte's chest of letters down beside her.

The butterflies she'd worked hard to ignore all morning took sudden flight in her stomach. She tried to keep her voice casual, but it rose several octaves. 'Hey. You brought the letters. Excellent.'

'I thought we could go through them together. It's been a while since you've seen them.'

'It has. We can go up to the attic, if you like.'

'Sure,' he said. 'Finish your work first.'

'I was just clearing emails. There's not much on today.' She met his eyes and waited for him to bring up what they'd spoken about the day before, but he didn't and she let the moment pass. 'Would you like a coffee?' She hopped off the bench stool. 'I bought some takeaway cups so we can pretend they're barista-made.'

He laughed. 'Okay.'

She busied herself at the coffee machine while he walked to the back door and glanced outside.

'The garden looks good,' he said.

'Thanks. I think I can turn it into a nice working space.' She hit the latte setting on the machine and it shot jets of coffee into the cups. 'I have another delivery of furniture coming this week and I'm pretty sure it includes a garden bench and a table and chairs. I think I might have even ordered a birdbath.'

'Nice. And what about your living arrangements?'

She fitted plastic lids over the cups and wiped down the machine. 'I'm going to inspect a few properties tomorrow. Xavier will be here any day now which means we'll have staff starting soon. I don't want to still be sleeping on the floor when that happens.'

She handed him a cup and he collected the chest off the bench, then they walked upstairs to the attic. At the top of the stairwell, she pushed open the attic door and pulled the cord to turn on the light.

The room was as they'd last left it, frozen in time, the only thing still untouched by her renovations. They cleared a spot on the floor and knelt down, setting the coffees and the chest between them.

'Why don't we read some of Charlotte's letters?' Paige suggested.

Ryan's hand went over hers. 'Paige.'

She glanced at him, holding her breath.

'Are we going to talk about yesterday?' Determination sparked in his eyes.

She swallowed and nodded. 'Yes. We should.'

'I didn't mean to spook you,' he said.

'You didn't.' She exhaled. 'Well, maybe a little. But not because I don't feel the same way. I do.'

'And that scares you?'

'It does.'

'It scares me too.'

She stared down at his hand still on hers. 'Other things scare me,' she said. 'Like where we live and how difficult it would be to see each other.'

'I've been thinking about that too.'

'And your divorce.' He went to shake his head but she stopped him. 'I know you don't think that's a problem, but you have a lot going on right now. I don't want to add to it.'

'You wouldn't be adding to it. You'd be making it better.'

'I'm worried you're on the rebound.'

'I'm not on the rebound.'

'You might be.'

'Paige,' he said, turning to face her properly, his expression sincere, 'I've been single for over a year. There's been no one since Sally. Believe me, I'm not confused or rebounding or anything.'

She fell silent, trying to marshal her thoughts into action, but all she could smell was the soap he'd used that morning and the way his body was close to hers. And that if he kissed her, she would let him.

'I never came here expecting anything like this to happen,' he said. 'It was only ever meant to be about Charlotte and getting my head in the right space. But then I met you and well... it's only been a few weeks, but I like you. I haven't been able to stop thinking about you. And if we both lived in the same country, I'd ask you out in a heartbeat. But we don't. And I get that. It doesn't mean I can just walk away either.'

She smiled, feeling her body relax. Yes, it terrified her, placing her faith in someone she hardly knew, after placing it for so long in Christian. But the sincerity in his words and the expression on his face chipped at her defences. She didn't want to lose him. 'I don't know if I can walk away either.'

'I'm going to stay in Sydney another week. See what this is. If you'll have me.' His eyes were hopeful as he watched her reaction.

Of course she would have him, and she said so with the widest grin. He grinned back, a pact made, and he moved in slightly towards her. She leant in too, parted her lips, ready to let him kiss her.

But then the attic door opened and a spill of light from the hallway came flooding in. Paige looked up and squinted.

It was Xavier.

***

'I should be going anyway. You guys have a lot to catch up on.' Ryan reached the front door. Balancing Charlotte's chest under one arm, he stretched out his other hand to Xavier. 'It was lovely to meet you. Paige always speaks highly of you.'

'Thanks. It was nice to meet you too.' Xavier shook Ryan's hand with the same bemused grin he'd worn since he'd caught them in an almost-kiss in the attic. 'Come by again soon.'

'Oh, sure. Thanks. Bye, Paige.'

Paige, grimacing like a teenager who'd been caught making out on the lounge with a boy, waved and closed the door.

'Who was that?' Xavier asked, following her down the hallway to the kitchen.

'Ryan,' she said as nonchalantly as she could.

'I'm aware of that but who is he and what were you doing up in the attic with him?' Xavier was teasing and Paige could feel her ears reddening.

'That's Ryan Greene. The great-nephew of the woman who owns the stuff in the attic. Remember I told you?' She placed two cups under the coffee machine and hit the cappuccino setting. 'And haven't you ever heard of answering your phone? I've been trying to call you all morning. I didn't realise you were coming today.'

'Obviously,' he mumbled, sliding onto a bench stool. A flop of dark hair fell over one eye as he took his glasses off and polished them on his jumper. 'These chairs are nice.'

'I've had one delivery of furniture already, which we'll need to go through. More is on the way.'

'So he's English?' He slid his glasses back on.

Paige raised an eyebrow at him. 'Yes.'

'He came all the way over from England just to look at his great-aunt's things?'

'Yes.'

'Okay.'

It was natural Xavier would want the details, but she was still figuring it out herself and she wasn't sure if she could put any of it into words yet.

'It's just that you never mentioned him in all the times we'd spoken on the phone,' he persisted.

Paige carried their coffee cups to the bench. 'That's because there was nothing to mention.'

'He's cute.'

Paige shook her head with a smile. 'You're relentless. How's Eric? Is he here with you?'

'Yes, we drove up together. He's at the hotel unpacking.'

'Are you staying close?'

'Rydges. It's just around the corner. We'll need to find an apartment soon though.'

Paige brought him up to speed on her search for a rental property, then they went through her notes, diary and emails. 'I couldn't move forward with some things because they need your input. Candidates are already applying so we're going to have to start interviews soon. And I approved all the designs this morning based on what we discussed last week.'

Xavier watched her intently.

'What?' she said. She felt another Spanish inquisition over Ryan coming.

But instead, he pulled her into a hug and held her. 'I've missed you, kid.'

She hugged him back, realising how much she'd missed him too. Setting up the business, transforming Xavier's dreams into a reality had been fun, but it meant nothing if he wasn't doing it with her.

When they let each other go, he looked her up and down properly for the first time. 'You look good. Happy. Glowing.'

She blushed and turned away. 'I'm not glowing.'

'You're definitely glowing.'

She swatted him. 'Come. I'll show you what I've done with the house so far.'

They went for a tour of the property. Paige showed him the rooms she'd had cleared and repainted, the floors and fireplaces that had been restored, the bathroom upstairs that she thought might need renovating, the garden which was now a beautiful and inviting space to sit in, and the boxes of flat-packed furniture she'd squeezed into the library that they'd have to sort through.

He chuckled at her bed on the floor of the parlour.

'I'll be out soon, I promise,' she said, kicking randomly thrown sneakers to the side.

'No hurry. As long as it's before staff and clients start showing up.'

Back at the kitchen bench, Xavier opened his laptop and they spent the rest of the afternoon working side by side. Paige kept a steady stream of coffee flowing and they worked solidly until eight pm when Paige switched coffee for wine and they ordered pizza.

'Does Eric want to join us?' she asked, pouring them each a glass of red.

'He texted me earlier. He's already eaten and happy for an early night.'

'How has he been the last few weeks?' she asked, closing her laptop.

Xavier did the same, pushing it away and taking his glasses off to rub his eyes before sliding them back on. 'He's come around. He'll miss home and our friends, which I understand, but I asked him to give this a chance. Just a couple of months to properly soak up the experience of the big city before he makes his mind up. He's willing to do that.'

'I have no doubt he'll like it here.' Paige smiled fondly for a city that had been a stranger when she'd first arrived, but now felt like an old friend.

Xavier sipped his wine and placed it down on the bench, playing with the stem of the glass. 'I wasn't sure whether to tell you this.'

'Tell me what?'

'I saw Christian before leaving Albury.' He reached down into his laptop bag and pulled out a plain white envelope. 'He asked me to give you this letter.'

Paige hesitated, then took the envelope.

'I'll be honest, on the drive up here, I considered reading it. I also considered not giving it to you at all. I didn't want it to undo everything you've done to move on. But then I realised, as much as I love you, that's not for me to decide.'

Paige nodded and placed the envelope down on the bench, running her palm over it. An old wound that she'd thought had healed began to pain again. It was remarkable how Christian, through a few written words, could wield such power.

'He misses you.'

'I miss him too but...' She shook her head.

'I think he feels a bit lost without you. You've always been together.'

She was saved having to respond when a knock came at the door. The pizza had arrived and she and Xavier sat at the bench and ate and drank, reminiscing about their time at the library and the long hot summers spent swimming in the Murray River. They spoke of everything except the one thing that stared at them like a plain white envelope in the room. Christian.

At midnight, Xavier stood and swayed from the wine. 'I better be going, or my love is going to think I've skipped town on him.' He hiccupped.

'I'll call you a cab. Or let me walk you partway at least.'

Xavier waved a hand. 'I'll be fine. Big boy here.'

'You'll be back tomorrow, right, so we can assemble the furniture?'

He saluted. 'Bright and early.'

'I'll have your aspirin ready.'

They hugged by the front door and she watched him disappear down Playfair Street towards Rydges, humming cheerfully to himself.

Back in the kitchen, she cleared away the pizza box and washed the empty wine glasses. She hadn't realised how much she'd missed her friend until he'd arrived. In the absence of her parents, who had retired to Fiji, Xavier was her only family, the one who always had her back, in many ways, more than Christian ever had.

She collected the envelope from the bench, turned off the kitchen light and walked into the parlour, flicking on the lamp. She sat on the edge of her mattress, collected her thoughts and opened it. There was a single folded sheet of paper inside which she unfolded to find Christian's unmistakable handwriting.

> *Paige,*
> *I hope you are well and enjoying Sydney. I haven't been in contact yet because I know how hard it was for you to leave and I've tried to respect that. I still remember the day you told me you were moving to Sydney, three days after I told you I was marrying Juliet. I know that can't have been a coincidence.*
> *Albury hasn't been the same without you. I've been busy with the wedding but none of it feels right if you're not here. I know proposing to Juliet changed things between us, and I won't lie and say I don't know why. But I still need and want you in my life.*
> *I'd like to come visit you in the city for a few days. We can hang out, just the two of us. Like old times.*
> *I miss you.*
> *Call me once you've read this letter and we can make plans.*
> *Christian*

Paige folded the letter and slipped it back into the envelope. Several weeks ago, she would have jumped at the chance to have a visit from him, her best friend, her secret love.

But Christian was conflicted. She could hear it in his words. He wanted his cake and to eat it too. He wanted to be married to Juliet while having Paige on standby like the familiar security blanket she'd always been. Through every one of Christian's failed relationships, he'd always had Paige to fall back on. To boost him up and make him feel good about himself. He hadn't even realised he'd been doing it, for it was never with intentional exploit or bravado. She was merely a safe haven to slip back to, something she'd equally enjoyed.

But they'd had their chances. Plenty of missed opportunities had passed them by—moments alone and almost-kisses, and they hadn't acted on a single one. She'd finally managed to untangle herself from a very tangled friendship and she was in no hurry to run back and become ensnared. And while she contemplated all this, it was Ryan who occupied her thoughts. Ryan who she couldn't wait to see again.

She took the envelope with Christian's letter inside and slowly and gently tore it in two.

CHAPTER 16

CHARLOTTE
May 1929

A chilly wind blew down Windmill Street, whistling through Windmill Steps as Charlotte sat and waited, retreating further into her coat. The cold southerly had driven the autumn warmth away, as leaves on trees were snatched and hurled into the sky.

She glanced down at her watch, the long hand striding through the minutes, bringing ten am closer. The note she'd left in Alex's coat pocket at the Governor's Ball the evening before was stamped clearly in her mind.

> *Gone now are the sails of the windmills, where all that remain are the steps.*
> *Meet me tomorrow morning at ten.*

Then, more boldly, *I feel that it is only with you that I can do anything at all.*

Her stomach tightened as the step grew colder beneath her. In some ways, she hoped he wouldn't come, that the note would still be in his pocket, missed by accident and lost in the wash. Or that he'd find it and realise she'd misread his intentions, that it had all been an innocent liaison on his part, and he would crumple it up and throw it away.

Despite the disappointment she'd feel, it would be the easier of the outcomes. She could return home, try to forget her feelings for Alex Young and concentrate on Floyd. No distractions, no wondering, just November and a wedding.

Yes, that would be easier, much easier. But it wouldn't make her happy. Seeing Alex appear now, on Windmill Steps, knowing that he felt what she felt and that it hadn't all been a figment of her imagination, would make her happy.

A gaggle of bare-foot children rushed past her, disappearing up Kent Street and into a row of dilapidated terraces. Charlotte glanced at her watch again. Five minutes past ten. Her heart sank as she realised he wasn't coming. She and Hilda had only ever given each other two minutes to arrive. Be on time or lose the game.

Be on time or break a heart.

She felt fingers close around her arm and draw her to her feet, pulling her into the shadow of a dark-brick tea warehouse next door. It was Alex's face she glanced up at and she broke into a relieved grin. 'You came!'

'What were you thinking?' The seriousness of his expression made her smile vanish.

'What do you mean?'

'The Rocks, of all places.' He looked nervously around them. 'Someone might see us. Come on.'

He led her quickly away from Windmill Steps and down Kent where they cut through to Upper Fort Street from Agar Steps. Charlotte held fast to her hat as the wind whistled around her, threatening to seize it.

When she couldn't take his silence any longer, she asked, 'Are you angry at me?'

He led her through an open iron gate into Fort Street Public School, deserted on a Sunday without its children. It was where she'd received her education, the lovely old school high on the hill overlooking the harbour.

When Alex didn't reply, she spoke again. 'If you're angry with me, just say it.'

He led them to a patch of grass behind the main building where he finally stopped and sat. Charlotte smoothed the back of her coat and joined him.

'I'm not angry with you, Charlotte,' he said when she was seated beside him. 'I could never be. But we could have been seen. You live in The Rocks, for goodness' sake.'

'I chose Windmill Steps because it's five minutes from home. I don't know many other places.'

'That's what I mean. Your father or Floyd could have seen us, or your father's friends, associates from the bridge, people who know you in The Rocks.'

Charlotte looked down at her lap. 'I hadn't thought of that.'

'You understand the consequences, don't you? If you were seen meeting a man on a street who was not your fiancé, how that might look?'

'We did walk together in Hyde Park,' she said.

'That was across the other side of the city, not right on your doorstep. The last thing I want is for you to get into trouble.' His look was full of unexpected tenderness, and as their eyes met and held, her breath trapped somewhere in her chest, forcing her to pull her gaze away for fear she'd become lost in him.

From their spot on the school grounds, the bridge construction rose in the distance, all steel and creeper cranes and minute figures working high on half-arches that climbed towards the sky. Below were the terrace roofs and chimney pots of The Rocks, where overcrowding was commonplace, and everyone seemed to live on top of each other.

'Can you hear the men shouting from the bridge?' Alex asked, his tone softer.

'Yes,' Charlotte said. 'It carries on the wind. What are they shouting about?'

'That's the cookers and catchers you can hear.'

Charlotte wrinkled her nose. 'Cookers and catchers?'

'Yes. The men who screw the rivets into place.'

'Why such funny names?'

Alex smiled. 'Well, the cookers carry with them large ovens up to the bridge. They put the rivets in the ovens until they're red hot, essentially cooking them, then, using special tongs, they take the rivets out of the ovens and throw them to the catchers.'

'They throw scalding hot pieces of metal at each other?'

This time Alex laughed. 'Yes. The catchers catch the rivets in a bucket of sand and, while still red hot, they use a set of tongs to drill the rivet into the hole. And that's how it's done.'

'Sounds awfully dangerous.'

He shrugged. 'It takes a good eye and some balance.'

The wind kicked up a swirl of cold air and Charlotte shivered.

'You must be freezing.' Alex made to remove his coat for her, but she shook her head.

'No, I'm fine. I have my coat. Keep yours on or you'll catch your death.'

He took it off anyway and settled it over her shoulders. 'The weather changed so swiftly. It was warm only yesterday.'

They fell silent as Charlotte battled an awkward shyness that crept over her. It was a rare thing for her to be alone with a man, and even though they'd walked through Hyde Park together and talked in the gardens at Government House, she was acutely aware of how alone they were there, in the empty school grounds, sitting so close she could feel his body tremble slightly in the wind.

'Was this your school when you were younger?' Alex asked, looking back towards the main building.

'Yes,' she said, turning too. 'It used to be bigger, but the resumption of land for the bridge took a lot of the playground away.'

'Well, that was rather rude. The bridge has carved quite a piece for itself, hasn't it?'

She smiled. 'Yes.'

'What were your favourite subjects?'

'English literature and art. They were Hilda's too. We needed all that reading and spelling for our clues.' Her thoughts grew wistful, as they often did when she thought of her childhood. 'It was difficult to come back here after she died. I didn't make any new friends. There was no one who I clicked with as I had with her. No one else that I wanted to play the game with. But I still enjoyed school. I became more studious after her death.'

'Did you continue to high school?'

'I did. I was supposed to leave at age eleven to contribute fully to the household because my father worked long hours, but I was able to convince him to let me stay until fourteen, which meant I could attend the girls' high school here.'

'And give you a greater possibility of attending university.'

'Yes, I'd hoped for that, not that I told my father the reason at the time. He balks every time I mention it. It hardly matters anyway. I won't be allowed to attend once I'm married.' The unfairness of it struck her again, that her hopes and dreams could be so easily doused by a man's proposal, that the two couldn't co-exist, for she must be either a dreamless wife or a driven spinster.

Alex watched her intently. 'You are an incredibly bright and beautiful woman. You should have every opportunity this world affords.'

She gulped and dipped her head so he wouldn't see the treacherous colour that had risen up her neck to settle on her cheeks. *Beautiful.*

'Charlotte,' he said solemnly. 'I need to ask you something.'

She kept her gaze on the grass. 'What is it?'

He hesitated. She could feel, if not hear, his mind searching for the words. 'Do you feel it too?'

It was the simplest of questions with all the weight of its meaning. She raised her eyes to his, knowing that her answer, if spoken aloud, had the power to change everything. To change what was otherwise innocent into something fiercely real. 'I feel it.'

He sighed in visible relief and she realised she was not the only one perturbed by this compelling circumstance they found themselves in. His hand crept towards her gloved one, his fingers closing around it. 'I was so happy to get your clue.'

'When did you find it?'

'As soon as I collected my coat. The cloak attendant informed me that a young lady had dropped a note into the pocket. I knew straight away it was you.'

She remembered the reason she'd done it. Floyd's kiss at Government House, Alex's shattered expression, her heartbreak knowing he'd seen it. 'I was worried you might not come.'

'I thought about it; not coming, that is. I don't have to tell you how complicated we've made things.' He gave her a pained look.

'I know. Floyd.' Just saying his name in their peaceful pocket in the school grounds seemed to tarnish the atmosphere. 'I don't love him. I'm not even sure I like him.'

Alex fell silent.

'Sorry. It's inappropriate to talk about him.'

'How can it be inappropriate? He's your fiancé.'

Charlotte wasn't sure why the words stung, but they did. Maybe because Alex felt the need to remind her that she was spoken for, that Floyd existed and she should not forget it. Her back straightened with indignation. 'I'm well aware he's my fiancé. I don't need you to spell it out for me.'

Alex glanced at her. 'Perhaps you do.'

'Well, I don't,' she retorted. 'And what a thing to say. For the record, I wasn't the one who left the first clue. That was you. You started this.'

'And I was a fool,' he said. 'I thought it would be nice to reinvent a childhood game for you.'

'So that's all it was, a game?'

He lowered his gaze to the grass. 'No, of course not. But it should have been.'

'Well, that doesn't help me. Or you. Or any of this.' She crossed her arms and turned away from him, not caring if she seemed petulant. When she heard him laugh softly behind her, she turned back around. 'It's not funny.'

'No, you're right. I apologise.' But he was still chuckling.

'What are you laughing at?'

'You. And how adorable you look when you're angry.'

Despite her frustration, she began to laugh too, softly at first, then in earnest. They both laughed until Charlotte collapsed backwards on the grass and Alex lay beside her, their shoulders touching.

'I'm sorry,' he said sincerely. 'I know I'm not making much sense. I don't mean to confuse you.'

Charlotte felt the same dilemma. 'It's all right. I'm not very good at this either.'

He rolled over and propped himself up on one elbow to look down at her. 'The thing is Charlotte, I enjoy your company. I've never felt so strongly for someone before. But I don't know how to do this. Where do we go from here? Do we even try? I can hardly court you in public. And to do so in secret wouldn't be right.'

Charlotte met his eyes. 'What about friends? We're allowed to be that, at least.'

'Your fiancé wouldn't like it.'

'I don't care what Floyd likes.'

'Your father then.'

'What about what I want? Has anybody considered that?' Was she always to be overlooked? Like the time she'd begged her father to continue school or attend a college to further her studies, and he'd let James go to university instead. To have then watched James waste the privilege by chasing girls around the city with his friends, his failed grades rewarded with building the Greene empire overseas, while she was consigned to the house because that was her place.

'Believe me, I know how difficult this is. It is for me too. Watching you with Floyd...' Alex rolled onto his back and stared up at the sky. She knew he was thinking of that kiss. 'I'm wondering if we should end this now, before we can't.'

Her heart dropped as she comprehended what he was saying. But he was right of course—trying to keep a sane head when she couldn't. She had lost all good sense the night she'd met him at her engagement party, when the force of what she'd felt couldn't be dissuaded. Sometimes at night, she imagined what it would be like to kiss Alex and was surprised at the way her body responded. Floyd had never had that effect on her, quite the opposite. And yet, the unfair ways of the world had seen to it that he would become her husband.

'Please don't be glum.' Alex was on his feet, reaching for her hands and helping her up. 'It hurts me to see you sad.'

'I don't know any other way to feel right now.'

He sighed deeply. 'I feel the same. But let's not waste our precious time together dwelling on what we cannot change. Let's walk, at least to warm up.' He tucked her gloved hand into the crook of his elbow and escorted her back through the school grounds.

More to lighten the mood than anything, she pointed out her old classrooms and the place where she'd once tripped on the hopscotch squares, which had produced a hole in her stockings and a bleeding knee. She told him of her favourite teachers, how she and Hilda had once felt the wrath of the headmaster's strap and the birthplace of the idea for their game, down by the old eucalyptus tree which was still there after all these years.

They walked back through the iron front gate onto Upper Fort Street where they found Agar Steps once more, following them to Kent.

Back at Windmill Steps, Alex looked down at her. 'Will you be able to see yourself home from here?'

'Yes. It's just a few blocks.' She felt the last of their seconds leeching away, felt the startling intensity of his dark eyes on hers and wished they had more time, another day, one more clue. 'Will I ever see you again?'

He didn't answer and she nodded bravely. He was right. End it now before they couldn't.

She thanked him for his coat and handed it back to him, then forced her legs to move, to carry her away from him back to Playfair Street, to the sanctuary of home, where her heart knew how to hide.

CHAPTER 17

Charlotte lifted the flat iron from the stove and carried it to the ironing board where her father's shirt awaited. Careful not to burn herself, she set it against the brown pinstripes and worked through the creases. Even though her father insisted they buy one of the new steam irons on the market, she liked her mother's old cast iron, heavy as it was. Along with the fine china, the books in the library, the collection of chests and the old carriage clock by the telephone in the hall, it was one of the few things she had left of hers.

Two weeks on from her encounter with Alex at Windmill Steps and Charlotte still felt gloom follow her around like an unshakable cloud. Not even a visit from Estelle, with her crystal laugh and flamboyance, had cheered her up. She'd tried to convince herself that there wasn't anything to be sad about, that she was being overdramatic, for she and Alex hardly knew each other. They hadn't courted or kissed or explored what might have been, he hadn't even professed any great love for her. It had been a fling, the whisper of a dalliance. And yet, as brief as it had been, she'd fallen swiftly.

Still, she knew Alex ending it had been the sensible thing to do. He'd drawn on wisdom to do what her inexperienced heart couldn't, for what could possibly transpire while she was engaged to another man? She hadn't been raised to be deceitful, nor did she want to provoke the ire of her father if he found out she was meeting Alex in secret. No, Alex had made the right decision for them both, the only decision that could be made in the end.

It was just before lunch when Walter arrived home. At the sound of the door closing, she returned the iron to the stove to reheat and met him at the coat stand.

'I didn't know you were leaving the mill early.' She took his coat and hat and hung them.

'No, I hadn't planned on it,' he said, 'but I've just had word. We're having guests for dinner.'

'Tonight?' It was already midday and she wasn't at all prepared for an impromptu dinner party. She mentally flipped through the contents of their icebox. 'Who's coming?'

'Floyd.'

Her heart sank.

'And Dr Bradfield.'

'Why is Dr Bradfield coming?' It was rare for them to entertain bridge people. 'Is there a problem with our contract?'

Her father quickly shook his head. 'No, nothing like that. Just some business to discuss.'

He didn't elaborate further and she knew not to ask. 'I've already cut up rabbit for a stew, but I could put that in the icebox for tomorrow. If I hurry to the butcher's, he might have a good cut of beef left.'

'I was thinking fish. I've heard it's Bradfield's favourite.'

'The fishmonger at the docks will have fresh sole I can fillet.'

'Not sole, get salmon. We're going all out tonight.'

Charlotte frowned. 'Salmon's very expensive.'

'Bah.' He waved the pronouncement away. 'And serve it on your mother's fancy china, would you? That'll dazzle them.' He pulled a one-pound banknote out of his pocket and handed it to her. It was more than she would need. 'We're pulling out all the stops tonight, Charlotte,' he declared. 'Spare no expense.'

She reluctantly took the note and retreated to the kitchen. She set the iron aside to cool, left the wood in the stove to burn down and packed away her father's shirts along with the ironing board. Slipping off her apron, she prepared a sandwich for him, grabbed her gloves and hat, and left the house.

***

136

The fishmonger did have salmon and she arrived home from the docks at Towns Place with two wrapped pounds of it. She spent the rest of the afternoon descaling and filleting the fish, peeling potatoes, stringing beans and fashioning a cream sauce. Her father's desire to impress Bradfield was apparent, requiring a menu that was contrary to their usual, somewhat humble dinners. It was tedious work to prepare but at least it took her mind off Alex for the rest of the day.

It was six o'clock and she had just finished setting her hair and slipping her shoes on when she heard a knock at the door. Walter and Floyd's hearty voices travelled up the stairs, followed by the subtle greeting of Dr Bradfield.

She left her room and walked downstairs to find them congregated by the door, shrugging out of hats and coats. But it wasn't Bradfield who stood there. It was Alex, handsome in a grey, single-breasted wool suit and trilby. As he handed his hat to Walter to hang, his eyes caught Charlotte's on the stairwell and there was a sudden smile in them before he checked himself and turned away.

Floyd caught sight of her too and held his hand out to her in a grand and exaggerated gesture. 'Charlotte, my love. You are a vision.'

She walked down the remainder of the stairs and took Floyd's hand. He bent and kissed it, and she was glad she'd worn her gloves as a barrier between her skin and his lips. 'Mr Clark, it's lovely to see you again.'

'Oh please, do call me Floyd. We *are* soon to be married, after all.'

She turned to Alex. 'Mr Young, how lovely of you to join us. I thought Dr Bradfield was coming.'

'He had an urgent appointment to attend and asked me to come on his behalf. I hope it won't cause too much inconvenience.' He spoke but didn't quite meet her eyes and she wished he would. She needed to see if the past two weeks had been hard for him too.

'It's not an inconvenience at all,' Walter said, slapping him lightly on the back. 'Charlotte has been preparing a wonderful meal for us. I do hope everyone likes salmon.'

While the gentlemen took their seats at the dining table, Charlotte retreated to the kitchen to add the final touches to the first course. When she reached the table, her father was pouring champagne into coupe glasses. She set the first course down, a Waldorf salad with warmed bread that she'd collected from the baker on the way home from the docks. The men ate heartily, Floyd crunching on the walnuts, mayonnaise gathering in his thick moustache. Charlotte ate only a little as her stomach somersaulted. Alex was seated directly opposite her and every time their eyes met and held, it both thrilled and unsettled her.

'What a delightful little Waldorf,' Floyd said, dabbing his moustache with his napkin.

'Charlotte makes all our meals here. She runs a fine home,' Walter said, advertising her talents.

'Excellent to hear. She will do well in my large house in Elizabeth Bay,' he said, directing this at Alex. 'I have staff of course—a cook, several housekeepers and a gardener. But once we're married, I'll hand them over to Charlotte to manage as lady of the house. It will give her something to do. Aside from having babies, of course.' He roared with laughter as Alex choked on celery.

'If I'm to have time on my hands, perhaps I could further my education,' Charlotte suggested.

Floyd stopped laughing. He turned to her with a bemused expression. 'Education? What do you mean?'

'I'd like to go to university.'

'*University?*'

Walter coughed loudly.

'I'd like to do something more than manage housekeepers. I enjoy learning.'

Floyd's face turned puce. 'Whatever are you talking about, girl? Have you had too much champagne?'

'I haven't had any.'

'Goodness Walter, your daughter has quite the imagination then.'

Walter wiped his mouth with his napkin and cleared his throat. 'Charlotte does have a fondness for knowledge,' he explained diplomatically. 'Perhaps you could indulge her with a library in your house. All new books, shelves of them. Something of a wedding gift. She'd rather enjoy that to occupy her time.'

'What a marvellous idea, Walter,' Floyd said, smacking his lips together. 'A room full of books to idle her time away. Excellent. I'd much prefer that to this university nonsense. I dare say, do they even accept women into university?' He laughed rambunctiously, banging his palms on the table.

Walter, looking visibly relieved, laughed politely with him.

'I think university is a fine idea,' Alex said, setting his fork down and dabbing his mouth with his napkin.

Floyd was brought to silence again. 'Excuse me?'

'University. For Miss Greene. It's a fine idea. And to answer your question, Mr Clark, yes, women *are* being accepted into university. The numbers are small, but they're there.'

Charlotte almost beamed with pride as Floyd's eyes widened. He leant towards Alex, resting both elbows on the table. 'And you would entertain this notion for your wife? Allowing her to traipse off to university, indifferent to her responsibilities at home?'

'If I were married, yes.' Alex's eyes drifted across to Charlotte and she stared back, her breath held.

'See, that's why you're not married,' Floyd said, nodding triumphantly as if he'd solved Alex's problem. 'Women like to know their place, even if they challenge you with wild ideas about education and whatnot.' He threw back his glass of champagne and pushed it towards Walter for a refill. 'You have to show them you're in charge. Always.'

The table grew quiet. Floyd was twitching beside her, fuelled by alcohol and possibly the dislike of being challenged by the handsome young bridge engineer that was seated across from him. Walter refilled his glass and Floyd took a huge swig, leaning forward again on his elbows. 'So, what do the public works pay bridge boys?' he asked, leeringly.

Alex raised an eyebrow. To talk of one's salary was inappropriate, even Charlotte knew that, but somewhere between the first champagne and the salad, Floyd had become roaring drunk and had misplaced his manners.

'They look after me,' Alex replied.

'Mr Young is one of the bridge's finest engineers,' Walter said.

'The bank looks after me too,' Floyd boasted. 'I've made a tidy fortune as a loans manager. I'm on a salary, plus I earn commission for every loan I approve. And I approve plenty.' He winked at Walter, who shifted in his chair. 'I have two cars—a Duesenberg and a Mercedes-Benz S-

Series, both personally imported by me from the United States of America.'

'You're well-established,' Alex said. 'You must have worked hard after returning from the war.'

'I didn't fight in the war.' Floyd chugged down his champagne and pushed the glass towards Walter again.

'You didn't?' Alex frowned. 'And why is that?'

Floyd's moustache quivered. 'I'm a money man. They needed strong minds here on home soil.'

'You sought an exemption from the draft?'

'So what if I did? The war wasn't fought solely on the battlefields, my boy.'

'I think you'll find it was,' Alex said. 'That's where a lot of good men gave their lives for king and country.'

Floyd's nostrils flared. 'Oh and I suppose you fought heroically on the front line.'

'I was only a child when the war broke out, Mr Clark. I'm far younger than you.'

Charlotte stifled a smile. Feeling a different kind of war about to break out in her dining room, she rose from her chair. 'Shall I bring in the main course?'

***

After dinner and a dessert of pineapple upside-down cake, the men withdrew to the parlour while Charlotte cleared the table. Talk of business kept them behind closed doors for some hours and she sat outside on the back step in the cool night while she waited for them to emerge.

When they eventually did, a serious mood accompanied them into the hall and she wondered what had been discussed.

'Thank you, Mr Young,' Walter said, shaking Alex's hand. 'We appreciate you coming this evening.'

'The pleasure was mine. I'll update Dr Bradfield in the morning.'

'Very good. Charlotte will see you out.'

Floyd and her father retreated into the parlour and closed the door. Charlotte walked Alex down the hall, retrieving his coat and trilby from the stand and handing them to him. 'How was the meeting. Is everything all right?' she asked worriedly.

He leant close to her, his voice soft and low in her ear. 'Your fiancé is intolerable.'

She suppressed a giggle.

'Take this.' He handed her a small note and she shivered as their fingers touched. 'You make me question everything, Charlotte.' His eyes were on hers, fathomless pools of dark brown that always seemed to reach deep into her soul to the parts she never shared with anyone. 'Tonight shouldn't have been, but it was. And now I can't stop myself.'

He slipped on his coat and hat and kissed her cheek softly, his lips lingering, setting her skin alight. She opened the door for him and he gave her one last look before stepping out into the night.

She closed the door behind him and turned to place her back against it, his note in her hand which she unfolded and read.

I wake filled with thoughts of you. Your portrait and the intoxicating evening which we spent have left my senses in turmoil. Sweet, incomparable Josephine, what a strange effect you have on my heart.

Charlotte closed her eyes and smiled. It was a letter from Napoleon Bonaparte to his wife Josephine. And in Napoleon's words, Charlotte saw a little of what Alex was trying to say. He couldn't let go of this any more than she could, this strange, intoxicating effect they had on each other.

Her eyes dropped to the next clue in the game—*Icebergs in the sun. Meet me this Saturday, noon, by the sand. I can't wait to see you.*

There were hundreds of beaches along Sydney's coastline and she wasn't sure which one he meant. She reread the clue, knowing the answer was somewhere in the words. In any case, she had three long days until Saturday to figure it out. She would study it mercilessly, every precious vowel and consonant, every delicate curve of his hand.

The weekend felt like an eternity away.

CHAPTER
18

Saturday rolled about so slowly that Charlotte wondered if it would ever arrive. Her anticipation was such that every tick of the grandfather clock felt agonisingly prolonged. There were the usual chores to occupy her time and another visit from Floyd on Friday evening but other than that, her week was quiet and unfulfilled.

On Saturday morning she woke at first light. When her father arrived for breakfast, she dropped a plate of pancakes down in front of him.

'You're up early,' he said.

'With the birds,' she replied, watching him take a painfully slow bite, hoping he would hurry along so she could wash the dishes and run upstairs to change.

'I see you've been busy already.' He looked past her to the rows of washing strung across the backyard.

'Wanted to get a head start.'

He nodded and returned to his pancakes, sliding the paper towards him so he could read it. Charlotte grimaced. The grandfather clock chimed nine on the hour and she knew if she had any hope of meeting Alex on time, she would have to leave soon.

'What are your plans today?' her father asked.

'Chores.'

'Anything else?'

'Maybe a walk.'

'Lovely. Perhaps I'll accompany you.'

She gulped.

'On second thought,' he said, 'maybe I'll head out to the racecourse. There are some good horses racing today. Do you mind?'

'Not at all.'

He set his knife and fork down on his empty plate. 'How about a cup of tea, love? And another plate of those pancakes. They were delicious.'

'What? More pancakes?'

Walter seemed to think twice of it, patting his stomach. 'No, you're absolutely right. I should watch my waist. Not getting any thinner.' He laughed good-naturedly. 'I think I'll head off instead.'

Charlotte let out a relieved breath.

He disappeared upstairs, returning ten minutes later to call out a goodbye then closing the front door. She cleared away his breakfast dishes, too nervous to attempt breakfast herself, then flung off her apron and dashed up the stairs to change. She rifled through her closet and selected one of the prettiest day dresses she could find, of sky-blue chiffon with a drop waist and a matching cloche. She paired this with comfortable white heels that she could slip off easily on the sand and a white parasol.

She'd finally cracked Alex's clue, the one he'd slipped into her hand after dinner. At least, she hoped she had. She'd read in the paper recently that a new association had been established at Bondi Beach called the Bondi Icebergs Winter Swimming Club. It was the only place she could think of that fit the clue—*Icebergs in the sun. Meet me this Saturday, noon, by the sand.* It would take a tram to get there and it was further than she'd ever ventured on her own before, but she was certain it was where Alex would be.

She reached for her handbag and stepped out the front door, colliding with Estelle who was standing on the front porch. She started, almost dropping her parasol.

'Charlotte, darling.' Estelle pulled her into an embrace.

'Estelle? What are you doing here?' She hadn't meant to sound so inconvenienced but the timing of it couldn't have been worse.

'I was in the area and thought I'd stop by. How about a sneaky drink at Hubert's?'

Charlotte looked up and down Playfair. 'Did you walk here? Where's your car?'

Estelle faltered briefly, then righted her expression. 'A little trouble with the clutch. I'm having it fixed. But we could catch the tram there.'

Charlotte smiled apologetically. 'I'm sorry, I was just on my way out. Perhaps tomorrow?'

'Oh, where are you going?'

'To an appointment,' she said vaguely.

'On a Saturday?' Estelle's eyebrows raised with suspicion. 'How peculiar. Perhaps I could tag along for company.'

Charlotte squirmed. She was fast losing time and taking Estelle along with her was not an option. 'I'm sorry, not today.'

Estelle blinked away a flash of hurt. 'I see. Well, it was rude of me to call in on you without telephoning first.'

'Perhaps I could walk with you some of the way back,' Charlotte suggested. It would eat up precious minutes, but she felt awful. It had been a long time since she'd had a friend and it seemed her tact had got lost along the way.

Estelle waved her hand. 'No, it'll only slow you down. Off you go.'

Charlotte glanced at her watch. It was already quarter to eleven. 'All right. But please come by tomorrow. We'll have tea.'

Estelle smiled before kissing Charlotte on the cheek and walking back down Playfair Street. Charlotte watched her go, unsure if it was her imagination or if Estelle cut a lonely figure as she moved away from the house.

But there was no time to ponder. She had to get moving. She knew that a tram left Bridge Street at ten past eleven and took forty-five minutes to reach South Bondi, where she believed Alex would be waiting near the winter swim club, Icebergs. She had spent the previous afternoon studying tram times from a timetable she'd collected at the post office, finding the one that would get her to Bondi by noon.

She gathered pace, hurrying directly through the quay, past vendors hawking everything from vegetables to animal skins to candied apples. She reached Loftus Street, following it to the intersection of Bridge Street and the tram stop. She took a moment to collect her breath and wipe a bead of sweat that had formed on her brow from the frantic walk over.

It was ten past eleven. She was worried the tram had already come and gone but then she saw it, clattering down Bridge Street towards her, its destination of Bondi Beach clearly labelled on the sign beneath the driver's window. She hopped on, slipped through one of its doors and squeezed between people to find a seat at the back.

The forty-five-minute journey felt like an age as she clenched her hands tightly around her handbag and parasol, wondering what on earth she was doing. She didn't want to imagine her father's reaction if he found out who she was meeting, nor did she want to become lost in Bondi, unable to find Alex or her way home again. By the time the conductor strode through to collect her fare, she was a bundle of nerves.

Down Oxford Street, where rows of fashionable boutiques had sprung up along the tramline, the tram clattered into Bondi Junction before reaching Bondi Road and the steep gradient that led to the ocean. It came to a complete stop on Campbell Parade and Charlotte alighted, along with most of the passengers. She hurried straight to the edge of the walkway, grabbed hold of the railing and looked out across the beach.

The water was edgeless and blue, twinkling like a thousand tiny sapphires under the sun. She couldn't remember the last time she had been to the seaside, which was a depressing thought really, since Sydney was hemmed by glorious coastline. She'd just never had anyone to go with, and perhaps no desire.

It was exactly noon and her gaze searched the sand and the thousands of bodies that lay in the sun. There were a million places Alex could be waiting and her heart began to pound as she wondered how she would find him amongst all those people. She pushed off from the railing, deciding she'd start at Icebergs and work her way down. She turned and found him standing right beside her.

'Alex!' She almost threw her arms around him, catching herself before she did.

He grinned broadly, the sun and sea reflected in his eyes. 'Did you get here okay? I was worried the clue was too much.'

'I don't think I've ever been this far from home before,' she said, elated. 'But, yes, I made it and it was easy!'

He pointed to the tram stop. 'I've been here for the past two hours watching every tram arrive. I didn't want to risk missing you in case you got here early and wandered off into the crowd.'

'You would never have found me.'

'No, I wouldn't have.'

They laughed again, deliriously happy that somehow Alex's adventurous clue had worked out.

He put his hand on her back and guided her away from the beach. 'Shall we settle in a tearoom for lunch, then we can go for a walk along the beach?'

'Okay.'

They crossed Campbell Parade, avoiding bicycles and cars and the rattling trams that wended their way up the cliff towards the last stop at North Bondi. The salty air smelt fresher here than it did at the wharves at Circular Quay or the docks on Hickson Road. There was something cleansing about the wide, open ocean, more so than the water in the harbour.

They settled in a tearoom next door to the Hotel Astra, finding a table at the back where a scratchy Jimmie Rodgers song trebled from the horn of a gramophone.

A waitress arrived to take their order.

'They make the best rhubarb frappes here,' Alex told Charlotte. He ordered them a plate of tea sandwiches, slices of chocolate cake and the fruity rhubarb drinks that she noticed many of the diners were drinking.

The waitress wrote down their order, collected the menus and left the table.

Charlotte removed her gloves and placed them in her handbag. When she looked up, Alex was smiling at her. 'What?'

'I'm proud of you.'

'Of me?'

'Yes. For being brave and coming here.'

'Well, it was only Bondi. If your clue had suggested Africa, I might have had some trouble.' He laughed at her joke and it pleased her that he thought she was funny. The tangle of nerves she'd felt on the way over started to loosen in her stomach. 'To tell you the truth, I was a little anxious about not finding you; that I'd catch the wrong tram or that I'd miss it altogether. I got delayed, you see, when I left the house.' She meant Estelle and she still felt a pang of self-reproach at the way she'd slighted her.

'Did your father ask where you were going today?'

'Yes, but I was vague. He's spending the day at the racecourse. A blessing, really, for if he were to have stayed home, I would have had a problem leaving. He knows I don't go out much.'

Alex nodded thoughtfully. 'I worry about that.'

'About what?'

'You having to lie, to be secretive.'

'I haven't told too many.'

'It's just that I enjoy your company, more than I ought to, given your circumstance.' He glanced down at her engagement ring, then looked away as though the sight of it dismayed him.

She placed her hand on his arm so that he would turn back to her. 'I enjoy your company too. Why does that have to be wrong?'

The waitress arrived and Charlotte smartly removed her hand, placing it back in her lap. Their rhubarb frappes were set down on the table with a plate of mixed sandwiches cut into petite triangles and two slices of chocolate cake.

The waitress left and they sipped their drinks, the tense mood lifting when Charlotte laughed at the rhubarb moustache Alex had purposefully allowed to form on his upper lip. Having skipped breakfast she was famished, and they ate and talked, slurping on their frappes which she decided was the loveliest thing she'd ever tasted. Afterwards, Alex paid the bill and they left the tearoom, heading back across Campbell Parade to the beach. They walked down the steps to the sand and Charlotte slipped her heels off, tucking them into her bag and letting her feet sink in.

'Let's go closer to the water where it's easier to walk,' Alex suggested.

They navigated around wet bodies baking gently in the sun. Down at the water's edge, the sand was firmer to walk on. Charlotte opened her parasol as the water rushed over her toes, the lovely cool feel of it mingling with the sight of the golden-fleshed lifesavers carrying out drills and the squeals of children chasing waves. She took a deep, salty breath and must have made a pleasurable sound for Alex glanced at her.

'You had a lovely look on your face just then,' he said. 'What were you thinking?'

'Just that I feel extremely carefree.'

'Ah, yes, the ocean will do that,' he said. 'Living in London, I didn't visit the beach often as a child. That's not to say we didn't go on holiday to the seaside, but coming to Sydney and realising I could visit the beach any day of the week was quite something.'

They strolled along the sand towards North Bondi.

'Do you have siblings, Alex?' she asked.

'I had an older brother, but he died.'

'Oh, I'm awfully sorry. In the war?'

'No, some years later. He was killed in a construction accident back home in London. He left a young family behind. It was tragic.'

'That's awful. What was his name?'

'Johnny. A lovely man and my best friend. His death was swift, which was at least a blessing.'

She knew how the loss of a loved one never really healed, how it haunted dreams and weighed heavily on the soul. 'You must miss him terribly.'

'Every day,' he said sadly. 'The timing of it made me question whether I should come to Sydney. His death was a great shock to us all. In the end, my parents convinced me to make the journey. What good would it have done to stay in London and mourn? Johnny wouldn't have wanted that.'

She thought of her mother and Hilda and what they would have wanted for her. She was certain they wouldn't have wanted her to grieve as long as she did. Standing there on that glorious beach with the sun turning the sea into a bed of jewels, it now seemed a strange waste of her years, locking herself away in her Playfair house, afraid of getting close to people, a self-imposed recluse.

'What are your plans once the bridge is built?' she asked. 'Will you stay in Sydney or return to London?'

He shrugged. 'I'm not sure yet. I like it here. The sun agrees with me and if I have something to keep me here, then I'll stay.' He gave her a meaningful look that made her heart swell. 'I still don't know where we go from here, Charlotte. I've racked my brain over it and all I know is that we must be half-mad to do this.'

'Then let us be mad,' she said resolutely.

'We're not making it easy for ourselves.' He stared out at the ocean. 'I try to tell myself we're not doing anything wrong. We simply enjoy each other's company, as friends do. But I'd be lying if I said I thought of you only as my friend.'

She watched his dismayed expression, realising how conflicted he was. While she was ready to throw herself at this with reckless abandon, he was trying his best to employ sensible logic—the hopeless romantic and the wise engineer.

He reached for her hand and tucked it into his elbow as they walked. There was no one on the beach to recognise them, no one who knew who they were. To the average onlooker, they were simply a young couple enjoying an afternoon stroll along the shoreline. If Charlotte could bottle up that moment of simple freedom and capture it forever, she would.

'Your friendship is special to me, Alex,' she said.

'And yours is special to me, Charlotte. More than you could possibly know.'

She wanted to tell him that he made her wildly happy, that she couldn't imagine her life if he wasn't part of it, that he'd opened her eyes to new experiences and had encouraged her out of her own shadow. She wanted to say all of it and more but fought for restraint.

'What happens when November comes?' he asked.

'I don't know,' she replied honestly.

'Perhaps the question is, can I give you up then?' He looked down at her for such a long time she felt trapped in his gaze. 'I'm not sure I'll be able to.'

CHAPTER 19

PAIGE
Present Day

The arrival of Xavier catapulted Paige's days back into action. They installed all the required software onto new laptops for the design, marketing and editing teams, then they spent two days constructing furniture from flat packs. Ryan arrived on the second day to help and by one o'clock every room except the parlour resembled some version of an office.

'Now to fill it with people,' Xavier said as they stopped for a break in the kitchen. 'I've got an appointment with the recruitment agency at two to start longlisting the candidates. I'd better head over there soon.'

'I'll come with you,' Paige said, gulping down the last of her water and setting the glass in the sink.

'And I'd better get out of your hair.' Ryan placed his empty glass beside Paige's.

'No need to. Eric's coming with me,' Xavier said. From behind Ryan's back, Paige caught his wink.

She raised an eyebrow. 'I should be the one to go with you.'

'It's just longlisting, darling. Eric and I can handle it. You need a break.' Xavier waved his hands to indicate that she run along. 'Go on.'

'Are you sure?'

'Positive.'

Paige collected her coat and handbag as Xavier ushered them out of the house. It was a cool June morning, a winter sun summoning what meagre strength it could to warm the cobblestones.

At a nearby café on Playfair Street, they stopped to buy coffee.

'That was nice of Xavier,' Ryan said, paying for their lattes.

'It was cheeky. I know what he was trying to do.'

Ryan grinned. 'So do I, but I like it.'

Paige laughed, collecting their coffees from the barista. 'Okay, so where would you like to go?' She had an unexpected afternoon off, a man that she liked by her side and a whole city to explore.

'Anywhere. We can just walk and see where it takes us.'

She liked the idea and they soon found themselves climbing Bridge Stairs and cutting through to Upper Fort Street. At Sydney Observatory, they roamed the grounds, stopping to watch boats on the harbour, then strolled past Fort Street Public School. They found Agar Steps and climbed them down to Kent and High Streets, arriving onto Hickson Road.

'Did you know, this entire stretch of street is known as The Hungry Mile?' Paige said as they walked. 'They termed it that in the lead up to the Great Depression, when hundreds of unemployed men would queue here for a day's work on the docks.'

'Rather a depressing thought, excuse the pun,' Ryan said ruefully.

'No, you're quite right. It was a terrible time. They would shuffle along this road, waiting their turn to go from dock to dock, seeking work. Anything to feed their starving families. It would have been a heartbreaking sight.'

They finished their coffees and tossed the empty cups into a bin.

'The clerks on the docks selected workers based on a system where only the fittest and strongest men were chosen,' Paige explained. 'It was brutal and completely unfair, leaving many capable men without a chance. You can imagine the protests and fights that broke out down here.'

'It's a shame you have yet to do more with your history degree,' Ryan said. 'I could picture you as a tour guide or working in a museum.'

She smiled. 'That would be nice.'

'But?'

She shrugged. 'I committed to helping Xavier so that's what I'm going to do. Maybe I'll look into a curating role later down the track.'

'You should,' he said. 'And you should travel. There's a whole world of history out there. Like in England.'

Paige caught the last of his words and wondered if he had meant it as an invitation or a flyaway comment. She was reminded again of how far England was, a world away from her own, and that this was just one of the many challenges they would face when he went home.

They continued walking along Hickson Road, arriving in Millers Point and The Steps to Nowhere.

'Well, this is unusual,' Ryan said, glancing up, his hand over his eyes to shield them from the sun.

'Oh yes, I've read about these. The Steps to Nowhere. It used to be a functional flight of stairs but each end was boarded up at some point, probably when the plague hit and they demolished a lot of old streets.' She pointed to the sequence of steps embedded in the sandstone that indeed led to nowhere—no way in and no way out.

They fell silent, heads tilted, taking in the odd sight, and Paige wondered if she and Ryan were a little like those steps. No way forward and no way back, stuck somewhere in the middle between two continents.

'Have you found anything else of interest in Charlotte's chest?' she asked, as they moved past them and continued along The Hungry Mile.

'Just more clues and declarations of love.' He chuckled. 'I'm up to July now. Their meetings have become more frequent and the words they wrote to each other bolder.'

'I think it's special that you get to witness their bond growing, even from a century on.'

'It's remarkable really. They were a sweet couple. I feel sad that they met with such a demise.'

Paige agreed, but then she remembered the photograph of Floyd and felt that niggling doubt again that he'd been the one to play the game with Charlotte. His austere image had stuck firmly in her mind, the rigid disposition that didn't quite reconcile with a man who had traipsed adoringly across a city to find her. Still, there was no evidence to suggest otherwise so she had to accept that in this instance, she'd judged a book by its cover, and that a picture was not always worth a thousand words.

They headed down Windmill Street, Ryan placing his hand on Paige's back as they crossed the street.

'I want to talk to you about something,' he said.

'Uh oh. Sounds serious.'

'I was thinking I might stay in Sydney a while.' He cast her a sideways glance. 'Just a couple more months. How would you feel about that?'

Despite being surprised by the news, for she'd always known Ryan would eventually return home, the idea of two more months together almost lifted her off the ground. She grinned. 'I'd love that.'

'You would?' Ryan grinned too. 'Great. I'd keep out of your hair, of course. I know you've got a lot on.'

'No, it's fine,' she said quickly. 'You don't have to.'

'Really?' His face lit up. 'Okay!'

They arrived at Lower Fort Street and crossed over to Trinity Avenue.

'How do your parents feel about you staying here?' Paige asked. 'They must be wondering when you'll return to work.'

'I've been able to handle some of it from here. Not everything, obviously. I'll have to go home at some point. But for now, they're okay with it.'

'Aren't they curious as to why you're staying?'

'They are. And I've told them.'

'Of course. Charlotte's story.'

'It's not about Charlotte.' He fixed his eyes on her. 'I'm staying here for you, Paige.'

Her heart skipped in her chest. *I'm staying here for you*. They were simple words but for Paige, no less powerful. All she'd ever known were the games Christian had played, the constant emotional dance of hoping and wondering. But with Ryan, everything was out in the open. There were no secrets, no feelings withheld. He was so transparent it made her head spin and for that, she liked him even more.

When they reached Garrison Church, he stopped walking and pulled her close to him. She lost all train of thought. Under the midday sun, with the historic terraces of The Rocks around them, he leant down and kissed her. As their lips moved together, the earth began to tilt, and it was only Ryan's hand circling her waist that caused her to stay upright. Her pulse quickened and she made a soft sound in his mouth which made him pull her even closer, until they were one. It was only the need to come up for air that finally caused them to part.

He smiled down at her, leant his forehead against hers and she smiled back. Everything about his kiss felt right. Everything told her to trust in it. Everything said they were nothing like those steps to nowhere.

***

Ryan left her at the Playfair house with another kiss.

'Do you want to come in?' she asked, their fingers entwined.

'I'd better let you get back to work. I've stolen your whole afternoon as it is.'

'You haven't stolen anything.' *Except my heart*, she wanted to add, which left her both thrilled and terrified in equal measure. 'Although I'd better catch up on emails.'

'I'm going to crack on with some more of the clues in Charlotte's chest. Want to grab breakfast tomorrow?'

'I'd love to.'

He leant down and kissed her again, their fingers untangling regrettably. He waved at her and started down the street and, when he turned back to look at her, she felt the most ridiculous smile break out across her face.

In the kitchen, she found Xavier poring over paperwork. He looked up. 'Hey, how was your afternoon?'

'Great,' she said, opening the fridge door and reaching for a bottle of water. 'We walked down to The Hungry Mile and around Windmill Street. How did your appointment go with the recruitment agency?'

'Good. I'm impressed with our list of candidates. We're going to start the first round of interviews next week.'

'Where's Eric?'

'He's gone back to the hotel for a swim. I've got a mountain of foreign contracts to go over before I send them to the lawyer.'

'Can I help?'

He glanced up distractedly. 'You could go through the list of interview questions the recruitment agency has prepared and tailor them.'

'Sure.'

For the next hour, they worked side by side, until the sun started to dip behind the sandstone wall out the back and Xavier finally stretched. 'Coffee?'

'I'd love one.'

He made them each a cup and brought them back to the bench. 'So how was the walk with Ryan? Don't think I didn't see your smile when you came in.'

Paige's offending grin reappeared. 'He's going to stay in Sydney a couple more months.'

'He is? How come?'

'So we can spend more time together.' The statement caused her cheeks to flame and she looked away.

Xavier broke into a grin. 'That's great, darling. I'm happy for you. But what about his job? He works for his family's big steel company, right?'

'He does. He's covering some of it from here. He'll have to go home eventually for work and to finalise his divorce.'

Xavier's eyebrows went up. 'He's married?'

'Yes. But not for much longer.'

He nodded thoughtfully. 'What do you think about that?'

If she were honest, it played on her mind more than she would have liked. Not because there was another woman in Ryan's life, for Paige understood that that part of his life was over, but that he might not be emotionally ready to move on with someone else. He could return to England and realise the need to be on his own or to explore other relationships. That what they'd had was nothing more than a holiday romance. 'I'm worried he's on the rebound.'

'Have you asked him about it?'

'Yes. He says he isn't.'

'Then maybe you should trust him.'

'I don't want to get hurt again.'

He smiled. 'Look, honey, everyone has baggage. The older you get, the more of it there is. It's a fact of life. If he says he's ready to move on, and he likes you, you have to go for it. Take the risk. Lord knows you deserve to be happy.'

'It still comes with an expiration date. He'll have to go home at some point.'

'Yes, but long-distance relationships can work. Don't write it off just yet. And it doesn't have to be long-distance forever. One day at a time.'

She wasn't sure why she was talking herself out of it, only that when she was with Ryan, everything felt perfect, but as soon as she was alone, old doubts crept in. She reached for Xavier's hand and squeezed it, grateful he was there to restore perspective, her best friend in the world, the only one who understood her. Christian had been that person until a silent love had muddied the waters.

She had no regrets about refusing to see him in Sydney. She'd finally closed that chapter of her life, one that had grown to be neither nurturing nor fulfilling. Reading his words, then tearing the letter in two, had been remarkably healing, as though her eyes were finally open and she was no longer held back by empty promises.

'Tell me about this mystery woman, Charlotte Greene,' Xavier said, sipping his coffee.

'She's Ryan's great-aunt. She used to live in this house with her father, Walter. Their steel can be seen in the Sydney Harbour Bridge. I found a chest belonging to her when I went up to the attic to clean it out.'

'And what was in the chest?'

'Clues.'

'Clues?'

'Yes. Charlotte and her fiancé wrote clues that would lead each other to various places around Sydney. It was a game they played. Accompanying the clues were quotes from famous love letters— Napoleon to his wife Josephine or Oscar Wilde to Lord Alfred Douglas.'

'Incredible,' Xavier said. 'Where's the chest now?'

'Ryan has it. He's been going through them, trying to find more information. He came here originally to collect the chest but also to understand what became of Charlotte. She and her father Walter disappeared in late 1929 and what happened to them has been a family mystery ever since.

'We found out that Charlotte was institutionalised at the Gladesville Mental Hospital in late October 1929, just before the Great Depression, and we also learnt that she died a few months later at the hospital due to voluntary death. But the whereabouts of her father and her fiancé remain a mystery.'

Xavier let out a small whistle. 'Wow. What was she institutionalised for?'

'Her patient summary says female hysteria, though we're not sure what she grieved for.'

'Who was her fiancé?'

'A man called Floyd Clark, a loans manager at the Bank of New South Wales.'

Xavier's coffee had lost its steam as he sat forward, engrossed in the story. 'So you know what happened to Charlotte, but you can't be sure what happened to Floyd or her father. And all you have is this box of clues to go on.'

'Pretty much. And when her brother James came back from the UK to find them, he discovered this house ransacked.'

'By whom?'

'No idea.'

Xavier shivered and looked around. 'I have goosebumps.'

Paige felt the same exhilarating thrill. 'It's fascinating, right?'

'So what will you do next?'

'Well, the trail has grown cold. We know that Charlotte died at Gladesville, but we don't know much else.'

'Will you keep searching for Walter and Floyd? For who ransacked this house?'

'We'll try. But some ghosts aren't giving up their secrets so easily.'

CHAPTER
20

After weeks of procrastinating about finding a place to live, Paige could put it off no longer. Xavier was finalising the second round of interviews with candidates and any day now, her parlour-turned-bedroom would become the office of the editor. Armed with a list of rental properties, she set aside time one cool and sunny Tuesday morning to view them with Ryan.

Their first stop was a terrace on Argyle Street near Garrison Church. There was a fair turnout to inspect what was otherwise a cold and narrow house with a smell of mould and naphthalene. The rent was out of Paige's price range but, given her circumstance, she was not in a position to be selective.

The second property fared no better—an apartment on Kent Street near Wynyard Station that was the size of the Playfair house kitchen, barely enough room for a bed let alone a dining table. She ended the day with a share house in Darlinghurst, a little further than she'd wanted to move to and, while not in the market to house share at all, found herself filling out an application form out of sheer desperation.

They grabbed burgers on the way back to Playfair and ate them at the kitchen bench.

'How busy are you this afternoon?' Ryan asked. 'Can you get away early?'

Paige chewed and swallowed. 'Not sure. I need to unpack Xavier's office. He can't keep working at the bench. Why, what were you thinking?'

'Just that I might read more clues. Thought you could join me.' He leant over and nuzzled into her neck.

She giggled, tempted to postpone Xavier's office, but knew she shouldn't.

'I might go to the library too and see what else I can dig up.'

'You're going to look for Walter and Floyd?'

'I'm going to try,' he said.

'Lunch tomorrow?' she asked hopefully.

He moved from her neck to her lips and kissed her, the kind that made her stomach rise and fall like the ferries in the harbour. 'Definitely lunch.'

She was still grinning stupidly all the way to the front door to see him off. He kissed her again and she wriggled in close to him, his hands firmly on her hips as though he didn't want to let her go.

After Ryan left she set to work on Xavier's office. In the former library, the room he'd chosen for himself, she unpacked stationery and the printer she'd ordered weeks ago, then she set her sights on the bookcase that ran the length of the wall, lining it with his books and photo frames and some small potted succulents she'd found at the markets. By five, the sun was disappearing to the west and she stood back to survey her work. Pleased with her progress, she ran upstairs to take a shower. She was undressing when Ryan called.

'I found something,' he said.

She ran the hot water, old pipes groaning behind the walls. 'Can you be a little more specific?'

'Something you need to see. Can you come now?'

She paused. 'Right now? Okay. But what is it?'

'Meet me at my hotel. I'll show you when you get here.'

***

Paige finished her shower, dressed and hurried out the door as the sun finally dropped and the city lights came on. She reached Ryan's hotel and texted him from the lobby.

I'll come down and get you, he replied.

A minute later he was striding towards her as she stood waiting by the concierge. He bent to kiss her, then they walked together to the elevator.

'So what did you find?' she asked.

The doors pinged open and he swiped his room card to activate the ride to his floor. 'I'll show you upstairs. I made printouts.'

On level twenty-three, the doors opened and he led her down the corridor to his room. It was an impressive three-bedroom penthouse apartment with sweeping views of Sydney Harbour and as far east as the Heads and the Tasman Sea. Below them, Circular Quay bustled with commuters heading home under dark clouds. It was the first time Paige had been inside Ryan's hotel room and the first indication as to the extent of his wealth, for a prolonged stay in a Sebel Quay West penthouse, with a view of the harbour, didn't come cheap.

He walked to a large oak desk by the window and picked up a thin stack of printouts which sat beside Charlotte's chest. He held them out to her. 'I went to the library this afternoon after I left you. I wanted to find out more about Floyd.'

Paige took the papers and flicked through them. They were photocopies of handwritten documents.

'I ended up on the New South Wales State Archives site, then eventually in a section that stored old documents from the Bank of New South Wales.'

'That's where Floyd worked.'

'Right,' Ryan said. 'These were written by him. See there?' He pointed to the photocopies in her hand, and Paige glanced down. Surely enough, she was looking at bank documents written in a swirling copperplate script. Floyd's signature was on the bottom of each.

'Okay, so these were written by him,' she said. 'What am I missing?'

'His handwriting. Look at it. It's not the handwriting that's on the letters in Charlotte's chest. Floyd wasn't the person she played the game with.'

Paige looked down at the handwriting again. It had been some weeks since she'd seen the clues and she moved to the chest where it sat on the desk. 'Can I see a comparison?'

Ryan lifted the lid and retrieved a bundle of tied clues. He slipped off the twine and separated the ones written by Charlotte from the ones they thought had been written by Floyd. Paige picked up a clue and compared it with Floyd's sloping handwriting on the bank documents. It wasn't a match.

'So Floyd didn't write any of these clues?' she asked, looking up.

'No, he didn't.'

She tried to collect her thoughts. 'Charlotte was engaged to Floyd, but she played the game with another man.'

'Yes. And I found something else.' He handed her another thin stack of papers which Paige recognised as the medical report Maggie from the Gladesville Hospital had printed for them. 'I finally got around to reading it this afternoon. It has her reason for death.'

'Voluntary?'

'Yes but look.' He pointed to more cursive writing almost too eligible to read.

'"Voluntary death due to female hysteria caused by death of lover",' Paige read aloud.

'She played the game with another man, then he died,' Ryan said. 'It sent Charlotte into a mental decline and she took her own life.'

Paige sank into the armchair by the table. The news was validating and flooring all at the same time. She'd always had an inkling that Charlotte hadn't played the game with Floyd, that she'd been in love with another man, but to learn that that man had died, perhaps tragically, which had caused Charlotte to take her own life, was devastating.

She glanced down at the medical report again, then to Floyd's handwriting, then to the clues. 'I wonder who the mystery man was? And where they met?'

'It could have been anyone.'

'What about Walter? Were you able to find anything on him?'

Ryan shook his head. 'No, I ran out of time, but I'm planning to go back to the library tomorrow. I wouldn't mind finding out more about Floyd too. And to see if we can track down Charlotte's lover.'

'So much for the trail growing cold.' She smiled ruefully. On the contrary, it had flared again in a big way. She had an urge to reach into the past and shake the answers out of Charlotte. To know what had happened to them all. She sighed and ran a hand through her hair. 'I don't know if I'm relieved now or more confused.'

'Tomorrow we might know more.'

'I'll come with you to the library.'

There was a bright sizzle of light that briefly lit the sky then seconds later, a loud thunderous crack.

'It's going to storm,' Paige said. 'I didn't bring an umbrella. I'd better head back.'

'I'll walk you down.'

They returned to the elevator, the mood more sombre than when she'd arrived. They were both quiet and absorbed in thought, listening to the loud thunderclaps as they waited by the lift. They arrived in the lobby and Ryan walked her to the front doors but as they stepped through them, the heavens opened and rain began to pelt down. Paige's clothes were immediately soaked as she made to dash up the street, but Ryan's fingers closed around her hand, pulling her back.

'You can't run home in this!' he yelled above the deluge.

Her hair was already stuck to her head and her Converse were full of water as the wind whistled up Gloucester, driving the rain every which way.

'Come back up and dry off. We'll wait for it to stop,' he said.

She hesitated, but the longer they stood in the rain, the more drenched they became so she relented and headed back inside the lobby. Their shoes squelched on the tiles as they returned to the elevator and once inside, they dripped little puddles of water on the lift floor as they rode back up to Ryan's room.

Inside again, he handed her a thick towel. 'You can dry off in the bedroom.'

She gratefully accepted it and followed him into his room. There was another impressive view of the harbour and a king-sized bed with hotel-typical pillows and a white quilt. He rifled through a set of drawers and produced a large Manchester City FC t-shirt. 'This should fit you.'

'Thank you.' She clutched it to her chest. It was two sizes too big for her and smelt of him.

'Well, I'll let you get changed,' he said, stepping towards the door.

Before she knew what was happening, her hand closed around his and their eyes locked. 'Don't go,' she said.

He hesitated for a fraction before he pulled her to him, pressing his lips down onto hers. She kissed him back, a kiss that spoke of everything she hadn't had the courage to tell him. That she liked him more than she dared to admit, that she wanted him and was trying not to be afraid by this almighty leap of faith.

He slowly peeled away her wet clothes, dropping them in a heap on the floor. When she shivered, he quickly removed his shirt and jeans, tossing them away too and drawing her into him. 'You are so beautiful, Paige.'

She looked carefully into his eyes for signs that he might just be flattering her. She didn't think she was beautiful, with her slightly downturned mouth and too-large eyes, her pale hair and lanky limbs. Christian had called her beautiful too but had never felt compelled to do anything about it. And yet here she was, with a man who seemed to want her, who was wrapping his arms around her bare skin, who had stayed in Sydney for her, and she berated herself for doubting him when he'd always been honest with her.

Ryan caressed her shoulder with his fingertips, his hand gliding down her stomach, his broad chest against hers, making her skin tingle. She pulled him back onto the bed, lost in the feel of him as he collapsed on top of her.

'I've wanted you for so long,' he said into her ear, his lips carving a path down her neck to her collarbone, then even further, circling lazily near her hips until she could take it no more.

She arched her back and wrapped her legs around him as he moved inside her, and the world ceased to exist. She didn't know if the thunder had stopped clapping or the rain had stopped falling. Everything beyond the window receded. All she could see and feel was Ryan as he became lost in her too.

When a glossy moon appeared through scattered clouds to cast a glow across the city, they finally separated, tumbling onto opposite sides of the bed. Ryan found her fingers from across the sheets, threading them with his own, a quiet declaration of his feelings. Neither of them moved, their breathing laboured but blissfully content, everything they felt and thought and wanted sweet in the air.

CHAPTER
21

When Paige woke, it was morning. Ryan still slept soundly, arm around her waist, his face nuzzled into the back of her neck where she suspected he had remained most of the night. Careful not to wake him, she eased herself out from beneath his arm and slid from the sheets, her feet touching the carpet.

She had never spent the night with a man before. Her dating life had been reduced to a few meaningless one-night stands, no one ever able to compete with the guy she'd stacked all others against. And now, here in Ryan's bed, where she'd spent all night locked in his arms, she was surprised at how comfortable she felt.

She found her phone in the next room and brought it back to bed with her, checking her emails. It was almost eight am and her stomach growled, having skipped dinner the night before.

Ryan stirred beside her, hair ruffled, eyes sleepy. 'Good morning.'

She smiled lazily at him. 'Good morning.'

'Sleep well?'

'Too well. I'd forgotten what a real bed feels like.'

He laughed then pulled her close, kissing her on the lips, a long, slow, sensual kiss that had them ducking back beneath the covers, the time and her appetite forgotten.

When they emerged again, Paige curled up against him and stretched, her body aching pleasurably and her lips bruised.

'Would you still like to go to the library later?' he asked.

'Yes. I just have a few things to get done first.'

'I've got some work to do too. I can meet you there.'

Paige nodded then rolled over to face him, running her fingertips along his arm. 'Can I talk to you about something?'

'Of course.'

'I'm not sure how to bring it up exactly.'

'Just tell me.'

She hesitated. 'This penthouse.'

'What about it?'

'It must be costing a fortune.'

Ryan watched her closely. 'It's something I can afford.'

Paige pursed her lips.

'That seems to bother you.'

'It doesn't bother me. I just didn't realise you were...'

'Wealthy?'

She blushed. 'Well, I figured you might be. Your family runs a large corporation. I just didn't think you were...'

'*That* wealthy?'

If the bed could have swallowed her up, she would have allowed it to. 'I guess.'

He chewed his lip with a pensive expression. 'Contrary to what you might think, I wasn't handed everything on a silver spoon. My parents have always had money, but we weren't spoilt as children. We were taught to respect and earn our wealth. Everything I have, I've worked hard for. Too hard. The breakdown of my marriage is testament to that.'

His face changed as he said this, an edge to his voice, and Paige felt a pang of regret for bringing it up. 'I'm sorry. I didn't mean anything by it. I was just a little surprised when I got here yesterday.'

'I understand that, but I'll be straight with you. I don't talk about money. I don't like it getting in the way. Whatever I have, I will always share, but my whole divorce has been about money and I'm sick to death of it being the focus of everything. So what I need to know is can *you* get past it?'

Paige shrugged, wanting to be honest with him. 'I guess I'd be worried that I wouldn't be able to afford the lifestyle you're used to. I couldn't even afford the hotel when I arrived, hence the reason I'm sleeping on the parlour floor. I make peanuts, just so you know. Can *you* live with that? With me being financially inadequate.'

'I don't want your money or your peanuts.'

Despite their seriousness, she couldn't help chuckle.

'I just want you and I want you to want me. Only.' He ran a hand over his jaw. 'I must say, this is the strangest conversation I've ever had. Most women love the money.'

'I like a simple life.'

He kissed the tip of her nose, then her lips. 'Well, that's good because I like simple too.'

She kissed him back and felt the anxiety slowly slip away. The more she opened up to Ryan, the more she liked the person he was and the more secure he made her feel. She was starting to glean a future for the two of them. And it didn't seem all that daunting.

***

When Paige reached the Playfair house it was already ten am. She unlocked the front door, wearing Ryan's oversized Manchester City FC shirt and carrying her wet clothes in a plastic bag. She prayed Xavier wouldn't be there, but when she walked past the former library, he was at his desk, typing on his laptop.

He looked up as she snuck past and she was forced to take a step back and pause in the doorway to say hello, pulling the shirt down around her thighs and blushing so profusely, her ears grew hot.

'Good morning,' he said pointedly.

She grimaced. 'Sorry I'm late. I won't make a habit of it.'

A smile tugged at the corner of his lips. 'I didn't think your bed had been slept in.'

'I stayed at Ryan's. The storm last night.'

'Right. The storm.' He smirked.

Paige's ears grew hotter, but she swallowed her embarrassment and lifted her chin. 'I'm going to have a shower now, put proper clothes on, then we can plan our day. Do you think you can stop laughing long enough for me to do that?'

This time he snorted. 'Oh, it'll be tough.'

She poked her tongue out at him and left the doorway.

They spent the rest of the day tucked away in Xavier's office, laptops set up opposite each other, alternating between phone calls, emailing, brainstorming across the desk and drinking coffee.

At three, Xavier sat back in his chair and stretched. 'I'm done for the day. I need to drop into the supermarket, then I'm going to finish this marketing plan at the hotel.'

'I'll stay and load these website updates.'

Xavier closed down his laptop, slid it into his bag, then stood and kissed the top of Paige's head. 'You can do that tomorrow. Take the rest of the afternoon off.'

'Really?'

'Sure,' he said. 'We'll meet back here in the morning at eight-thirty.'

Xavier left and Paige shut down her laptop and reached for her phone. She texted Ryan to find out where he was and his reply was immediate. The state library.

She threw on a jumper, combed her hair and stepped out, locking the door behind her. A June sun struggled to warm the city, its sporadic slide through the clouds throwing dappled light across the ground. It took her ten minutes to reach Macquarie Street and the library where she found Ryan in the Mitchell Reading Room at their usual desk.

'Hey,' she said, taking the seat beside him.

'Hey. I wasn't expecting you until later.' He leant across and kissed her in a way that reminded her of the night before.

'Xavier called an early mark. Have you found anything interesting?'

Ryan angled the computer screen towards her. 'I've been searching some of the local cemeteries to see if they have a record of Charlotte.'

'So you don't think she was buried at Gladesville? You think Walter gave her a proper burial?'

'I don't know. I figured it was worth a try. But it didn't matter anyway. No one had any record of her so we're back to square one on that. But I did run a search on Floyd Clark and came up with something.' Ryan tapped the writing pad beside him, scribbled with notes.

'Do tell.'

'I found him alive and well after the Great Depression, although no longer working for the bank. I believe he experienced a somewhat spectacular fall from grace, having approved an obscene amount of credit to customers prior to the stock exchange crashes in October 1929. And, as the over-issuance of credit contributed to those market falls, a lot of heads rolled for it, including Floyd's.'

'Where did you find him?'

'Living in Alice Springs with his new wife and her four children. Seems he married shortly after Charlotte died,' Ryan referred to his notes, 'to a Mrs Dorothea Baker at Town Hall, then they were run out of Sydney. They lived out their days in a dusty outback town where they eventually died in the fifties. I found obituaries for each.' He pointed to printed obituaries of Floyd Clark and Dorothea Baker.

Floyd had passed first from a heart attack, then three years later, Dorothea had suffered a fatal bout of pneumonia. Paige thought Dorothea looked strangely familiar, but she couldn't think why.

'Poor Charlotte. She almost married that wretch of a man. I knew he was bad news. I'm also certain he was behind whatever happened to her lover.'

'You think he did something to the guy she played the game with?'

'Yes, I think he discovered Charlotte was in love with someone else, became enraged, then intervened. He may have taken it out on Walter too.'

Ryan rubbed his jaw. 'I haven't seen anything to suggest that.'

'If we find Charlotte's mystery man, we might find out what happened to them both.'

'Well, we're at a dead-end there. I still can't work out who he was, and I don't know what happened to Walter. Aside from some news articles indicating contract tensions between him and the bridge, he seems to have disappeared into thin air.'

They spent a further hour at the library, then Ryan walked Paige back to Playfair Street for an overnight bag before they headed to Sebel Quay West. They ordered room service and watched a movie, then went to bed early where sleep was the last thing on their minds.

Paige had never known anyone like Ryan. He wasn't afraid to tell her she was beautiful, to follow it with a kiss or a touch, the peeling off of her clothes. He was genuine and attentive, the kindest person she knew. He wanted her relentlessly, with an insatiable appetite that she was starting to match.

That night, as the city slept and they lay spent in each other's arms, he told her he'd fallen for her.

***

The next morning, Paige woke to find Ryan standing by the window. He was already dressed, his hands in his jeans pockets, staring out at the quay as though lost in thought.

She climbed onto one elbow. 'Hey you. What are you doing up so early?' She patted the space on the sheets beside her. 'Come back to bed.'

It felt like an eternity before he turned around. 'I had a call from my lawyer.'

'Oh?'

'He wants me back in the UK. Looks like Sally's ready to finalise the divorce.'

'When does he want you back there?'

'As soon as possible. I'm booked on a flight later today.'

'Today?' Paige felt the wind knocked out of her. 'But we had two more months together. You were going to stay.'

'I know. That was the plan, but I need to get this divorce settled. We've reached an agreement that we're both happy with. I can't afford to have Sally back out now. I don't have it in me to do another year of this.'

Paige tried to process his words, but it was all coming at her too quickly. She drew her knees up to her chin and pulled the sheets over her.

Ryan left the window and sat on the edge of the bed, reaching for her hand. 'Come with me.'

She gave him a sad smile. 'You know I can't.'

'Why not?'

'Because of Xavier, the business. We still have so much to do.'

'Just come for a few weeks, a month even. Or two. Whatever you can manage.'

'But I still have to find a place to live here. I've put applications in. I can't pack up and leave now.'

'You can manage all that from the UK. That's the funny thing about England, we have internet too.' He grinned playfully but she couldn't find the humour in it.

'Can't you come straight back after you finalise your divorce?'

'My parents wouldn't like that. I've put a lot on hold to be here. Once

I'm home, I'll have to get back into the office, see my team, attend meetings in person. I wouldn't be able to turn around and fly back out again.'

Paige nodded, feeling an all too familiar low seep into her bones.

'Please, will you at least think about it? You don't have to come with me today. Maybe you could come tomorrow or by the weekend once you've told Xavier.'

'I don't have a passport.'

'Apply for one. We'll get it fast-tracked, then you can come. I'm not ready for us to be long-distance yet. I want to wake up to you every day.'

While Ryan packed, Paige dressed, feeling mechanical and in shock, as though a rug had been ripped hard and fast from under her. She found herself at an inevitable crossroad, one she hadn't thought she'd be at this soon. Did she go to the UK and let Xavier down or did she disappoint Ryan and stay? No matter her decision, she was going to hurt someone.

At the door to the penthouse he held her, burying his face into her hair and she felt him breathe her in. She clung to him, trying to will the tears away.

'My flight is at three. Do you think you can make it to the airport? Not to say goodbye, but to say see you soon?'

She nodded into his chest. 'I'll try.'

Ryan seemed buoyed by the thought. 'Great. Message me later?'

'Okay.'

'And say bye to Xavier for me. I'm sorry I won't be able to see him in person.'

'I'll tell him.'

He kissed her and she left the hotel, walking back to Playfair in a daze.

At the house, she could hardly concentrate on a word Xavier said. As the minutes edged towards Ryan's flight, she chastised them both for jumping in without thought. Their relationship had always come with an expiration date, but she'd figured they'd had time, two glorious months to be entirely frivolous before decisions had to be made.

Now, out of nowhere, Ryan's divorce called and he was going home. He was asking her to go with him. Even if only for a few weeks, how could she leave Xavier, the business, the task of finding a place to live? She'd just found the courage to set down roots and now she was being asked to rip them up.

Just before three Ryan called, and she slipped out of Xavier's office and into the parlour to answer it.

'You're not coming, are you?' he asked.

'I'm so sorry Ryan,' she said.

'I didn't mean to freak you out.'

'Either I'm freaked out or I'm thinking really clearly.'

'Okay. I don't know which one I prefer.' He sighed and she could hear his frustration. 'You still could have come to the airport.'

'Was there any point?'

'Wow, all right.'

She cringed at her lack of sensitivity, at the words that tumbled out without a filter. 'I didn't mean it like that. I'm just really thrown by it all.'

'I'm not asking you to the moon, Paige. It's just London. And it's for a few weeks.'

'I know that. But I can't leave right now.'

'You can't or you won't.'

'It's not just now. What about in the future when you're busy and I'm busy and it becomes a year before we see each other again? How is that going to work?'

'Okay, Paige.' He made an exasperated noise. 'My plane's boarding. I have to go.'

'Don't be angry. I'm trying to explain.'

But he'd already hung up.

CHAPTER
22

CHARLOTTE
July 1929

Following their declaration of friendship on Bondi Beach, Charlotte and Alex played the game in earnest. She challenged him to seek her out on Market Street in the middle of bustling Market Row, far from The Rocks, where no one could recognise them, a place she'd visited as a child with her father and James and had always remembered.

Alex had found her by a treacle toffee cart. They'd chewed on toffees and sipped hot chocolate as they'd talked the entire day away, until the sun dropped so low she'd had to scramble to catch the last tram home.

Then he'd challenged her to find him on a ferry, amidst the many that crisscrossed the harbour. She had and they'd sailed down Parramatta River where he'd pointed out sights like Goat and Cockatoo Islands. She'd followed this with a trip around the City Circle on the train, where she hadn't set just one clue but many, and he'd been led on a journey through the carriages and stations to find her.

Their meetings had become frequent—mostly on the weekends, but sometimes during the week when Alex's work hours permitted it. They were increasingly creative with their clues, more daring with their destinations and bolder still with the quotes they took from the book of love letters. Their assertion of friendship had been one thing, a safe guise in which to play the game, but the quotes began to say what they weren't fearless enough to voice.

Then, on an otherwise uneventful Tuesday morning, when Charlotte walked past her front door, she spied a piece of paper on the floor beneath the mail slot and knew Alex had been. She immediately threw open the door and ran out to the street to see if he was still there but Playfair, with its usual comings and goings, was unchanged. She closed the door and leant back against it to read the note.

I wish I may find you at home when I carry this letter to drop it in the box, that I may drop a kiss with it into your heart, to be embalmed, till we meet, closer...

She beamed. He'd quoted Mary Wollstonecraft, the eighteenth-century English writer and philosopher, mother of Mary Shelley. It was a letter to her then-lover, William Godwin, in 1796. The clue read—*A chair in a garden to gaze out over a bridge. Meet me on Saturday. I'll be waiting at four.*

Charlotte's knowledge of Sydney was improving every week. Although she had lived on the fringe of the city her entire life, her self-imposed isolation had kept her close to The Rocks, and only with Alex had she properly begun to explore. But *a chair in a garden*? That could be anywhere.

She dashed upstairs to her room. From beneath her bed, she dragged out a small wooden chest that had once belonged to her mother. Edwardian in style, it came as a three-piece set. Her father kept the middle-sized chest in the parlour to store ledgers in and the larger chest, which sat against her bedroom wall, now housed the one-of-a-kind jade-green dress Floyd had had crafted for her. One that she'd wrapped carefully in tissue paper and placed away, unsure if she'd ever wear it again.

But in the smaller chest, which she'd carved her name into, she now secretly stored all the clues she and Alex had ever written to each other—the carefully penned ones when time permitted and the hastily scribbled ones when time was of the essence. She'd asked Alex to give her the clues she'd written to him, so they could all be kept together, and he'd handed them over with a partly amused, partly adoring smile.

Now, when the days seemed to stretch until the next time she saw him, she would open the chest and reread the words they'd written to each other, carefully tied together with twine so they wouldn't be damaged.

She placed his latest clue inside—*a chair in a garden to gaze out over a bridge*. Saturday seemed an age to have to wait, but it did afford her some time to crack the riddle, to extract whatever information she could from newspapers and books, perhaps a well-angled conversation with her father in the hope that he might know. She had never failed to find Alex before, had always solved his clues, and she wasn't about to fail this one. Because if she didn't find him, it would be a whole afternoon wasted that they could have spent together, and with the November wedding drawing near, every minute spent with him was a gift.

The telephone ringing downstairs broke her reverie and she quickly closed the lid of the chest and pushed it back under her bed as far as it would go. She hurried down the stairs and snatched up the receiver.

'Hello?' she said.

'Darling, it's Estelle!'

Charlotte smiled. She'd been neglecting her new friend lately and was happy to hear from her. 'How are you?'

'Oh, fine. Just missing you terribly,' Estelle teased. 'Where have you been hiding? You've been impossible to reach.'

Charlotte fidgeted, twirling her finger around the coiled cord. 'I'm sorry. I've been busy lately.'

'Indeed. Do you have plans for the rest of the day?'

'I'm free, actually.'

'Excellent. A cocktail at Hubert Penny's then?'

Charlotte glanced at the carriage clock beside the telephone. It was only midday. 'All right, I suppose we could.'

'Wonderful. I'll meet you there in an hour.'

***

Charlotte took the same route she'd followed the first time she was to meet Estelle at Hubert's, only this time, she hoped her friend would show. She caught the tram on George Street, alighting at the intersection of Bridge and Pitt, and at Hubert Penny's she pushed through the heavy front doors, stepping into the shadowy jazz bar.

The maître d arrived to greet her and she told him she was meeting Mrs Mayfair. 'Of course. She's waiting for you at her usual table.'

Charlotte followed him past the dark timber panelling, red velvet chairs and tasselled brocade lamps she remembered from her previous visit. There was a lunch crowd inside and a jazz band was playing on the small stage, the brassy beats of the trumpet and the sultry reeds of the saxophone electrifying the air. Faceless silhouettes slinked in dark corners, cigar smoke curled towards the ceiling and waitresses in short dresses carried trays of cigarettes and drinks to patrons.

The maître d delivered Charlotte to Estelle's table once again, deep in the back, and this time she was there. Estelle rose from the booth. She wore no hat, her Eton crop sleek and fastened in place with a large diamond clasp. Her dress was navy blue, sitting well above the knees and bejewelled, and around her neck was an intricate cloisonné pendant on a silver chain. On her right ring finger sat the largest ruby Charlotte had ever seen.

'Darling!' Estelle held her cigarette holder out the way with one hand and grabbed Charlotte with the other, pulling her in close. 'It's lovely to see you.' Her voice rose above the deep bursts of the trombone.

'That ring is stunning.' Charlotte reached out to touch the exquisite red rock.

Estelle winked. 'Isn't it just?'

Charlotte removed her coat and sank into the booth, happy to hide her plain tea dress which stuck out amongst the glittering sequins and fishnet stockings. 'It's quite lively today. They have a jazz band playing.'

Estelle sat too and placed her cigarette holder between her bright red lips, dragging back. 'Yes, the band always brings in a crowd. Aren't they fabulous?' She signalled for service and a waitress appeared. 'A grasshopper, please. What will you have, Charlotte?'

'A pot of tea for me,' Charlotte said.

Estelle burst out laughing. 'I don't think they serve tea here, darling.'

The waitress hid her smile. Charlotte's cheeks grew hot with embarrassment.

'Make it two grasshoppers,' Estelle told the waitress.

Once the woman was out of earshot, Charlotte leant forward. 'I'm not sure I should have alcohol. It's only one in the afternoon and I haven't had lunch yet.'

'Don't fret. We can ask them to add a cherry on the side for you.' Estelle threw her head back, chortling at her own joke. 'I'm just kidding. But isn't this place marvellous? A woman can be anyone she wants to be in here. No rules, no men telling her what to do and how she should act. And no prohibition. God bless New South Wales!'

Charlotte cast her gaze around the room. The music had enticed couples onto the dance floor and they began to kick out their legs to the Charleston. Estelle and others clapped in time to the music as the dancers flapped wildly and the band grew livelier, encouraging them on.

Walter and Floyd would have had a pink fit at the sight, but Charlotte thought there was something intoxicating, if not liberating, about it. Meanwhile, out on Pitt Street, just two doors up were the likes of demure tearooms and upper-class fashion boutiques. It was incredible and just a trifle audacious, that a place with such freedom and provocation, with dim, smoke-filled corners and rebellious women perched on the laps of men, could blatantly exist among them.

'So tell me,' Estelle crushed out her cigarette, 'what have you been doing lately? It feels like an age since I saw you last.'

Charlotte removed her gloves and hat and sat them beside her on the velvet seat. 'I apologise. I've been busy.'

'Oh, I can imagine,' Estelle said. 'Pulling a wedding together by November. That's no small feat.'

Charlotte looked away guiltily.

'I must say, you haven't once called on my help.' She raised her eyebrow. 'I assume it's all going swimmingly then.'

The waitress arrived with their grasshoppers and set them down on the table. Charlotte eyed the mint-green drink in the martini glass warily. Estelle picked hers up and drank. 'Ah, divine. Go on. It's refreshing.'

Charlotte raised the glass to her lips and sipped. She tasted cold mint and the burn of crème de menthe. It hit the back of her throat, causing her to cough, but the cream was quick to soothe and she soon found the experience pleasant.

'I told you you'd like it,' Estelle said. 'You won't even need lunch after a few of these.' She attached another cigarette to the end of her holder and touched her lighter against it, puffing until the end glowed red.

A man holding an aluminium Kodak Brownie appeared, cupping Estelle under the chin as she beamed up at him.

'Bertie!'

'Dollface,' he said affectionately. 'Can I interest you ladies in a photo? It's on the house today.'

'Oh Bertie, you know how to make a girl's day.' Estelle scooted across the seat to sit close to Charlotte, leaning in, her perfume tickling Charlotte's nose.

Bertie held the camera up, aimed and clicked down on a button. The camera flashed, taking their photograph. 'If you're going to be here a while, I'll drop home, develop it and bring it back.'

'You're a sweetheart, Bertie. We'll be here!'

'Anything for you, dollface.'

Estelle waved as he left with his camera to take photographs elsewhere. 'Bertie's an old school friend. I've known him for years,' she explained. 'You can keep our photograph once it's developed. Something to remember our little friendship by.' She took a long, thoughtful drag of her cigarette. 'So how is Floyd?'

'He's okay.'

Estelle looked pointedly at her. 'Just okay?'

Charlotte shifted her eyes from Estelle's questioning gaze, fixing them on her drink instead.

'You know,' Estelle said, leaning forward, 'when I married Augustus, he was twenty-five years my senior.'

Charlotte looked up. 'He was?'

'Yes. My father fixed the union. They were best friends, you see. The world was still at war and I was in love with a much younger man, a soldier, in fact. We were engaged to be married. But my father didn't want me to be left widowed and heartbroken, so he arranged my wedding to Augustus instead.'

Charlotte played with the straw in her drink, thinking about Estelle's words. She hadn't realised how alike their tales were; they almost mirrored one another. An arranged marriage, an older fiancé, a heart that yearned for someone else. 'So you married him.'

'I had to. My father forbade anything less. Augustus was a rich man; the heir of a large textile's empire. He treated me like a princess. He was generous with his wealth and paraded me around like a prize. He wasn't everything I'd hoped for in the bedroom, but one can hardly expect it all.'

'What about the man you loved? The soldier?'

'He did die in the war and my father was proven right, that had I married him, I would have been left a heartbroken widow.' Estelle crushed out her cigarette, her features soft and sad in a rare, unguarded moment. 'So you see, I understand how you feel about Floyd because I've been in your shoes. He's much older than you and not everything your heart desires. It's natural to resist him.'

'I don't think I could ever grow to love him. He doesn't understand me at all. He hasn't even tried to.' She didn't bother to hide the defiance in her voice.

'That's because he has no interest. You're a prize, darling, just like I was to Augustus.'

'My father chose Floyd so that he can run the business once he retires.'

Estelle looked scandalised at the thought. 'If it's just for the sake of retirement, why can't he pick someone else? Someone you like. There are plenty of Floyds in this town.'

'He trusts him. Floyd is good with money.'

'Yes, but at what cost to you?'

Charlotte sipped her drink. If it wasn't for the cool mint and the alcohol warming her insides, making her muscles relax, she might have cried into her grasshopper. 'My father says I'll have to consummate the marriage on the wedding night.'

'Does that trouble you?'

'Yes,' Charlotte said grimly.

'The best thing you can do is lie there and pretend you're enjoying it, even when you're not. You must convince him of this, otherwise he'll take a mistress.'

'Maybe that would be for the best.'

Estelle eyed her curiously. 'Goodness, you really don't want to marry him, do you?'

'No.'

Her expression became serious. 'Then tell your father. You're not a child anymore. Women are liberated these days. If you don't want to marry Floyd, you need to say so.'

'He won't hear of it.'

'Just tell him what your heart wants.'

Charlotte couldn't tell anyone what her heart wanted. A bridge engineer, the freedom to be with him, to wish it had been his proposal she'd yes to, and not Floyd's.

'Let me give you a little tip,' Estelle said, sipping her cocktail and lighting another cigarette. 'I married Augustus because my father said it would secure my happiness. When Augustus took his own life, he left me a widow anyway. I might as well have married my soldier, who I actually loved. Men don't know everything, not even our fathers. You must look after yourself, Charlotte.' She threw her head back and let the smoke escape her lips. 'Otherwise, you'll just become another desperate woman in this godforsaken town.'

CHAPTER
23

Estelle was right. Three grasshoppers later and Charlotte's appetite for lunch had all but abated. She stayed long into the afternoon at Hubert's, the alcohol loosening her limbs and making her a trifle daring. She got up to dance when the band played an upbeat version of Fats Waller's 'Ain't Misbehavin', then tried a little of Estelle's cigarette, which made her cough uncontrollably for two minutes, much to her friend's hysterical laughter, who was equally drunk.

As the six o'clock swill drew to a close and the public houses and bars closed for the evening, she reluctantly left Hubert's and caught the tram home, clutching Bertie's photograph of herself and Estelle, grinning at it. It had been the most perfect day, filled with laughter and dancing, but when she arrived back at Playfair Street, the walls of her house had an instantly sobering effect.

In her room, she scribbled an inscription on the back of the photograph, stowed it away in the larger chest with her jade-green dress, away from her father's prying eyes, changed out of her smoky clothes, then swished water around in her mouth as he called up the staircase to enquire where she'd been.

'Just out with Estelle,' she called back, hurrying down to the kitchen to start dinner.

The mere mention of Estelle's name caused Walter to nod approvingly before disappearing into the parlour. It wasn't a lie, for Charlotte had been with Estelle, but she didn't tell him that she'd danced to jazz music, drunk alcohol and smoked a cigarette, and it didn't stop the twinge of self-reproach for all the other things she'd been keeping from him.

***

The rest of the week passed ordinarily until at last Saturday arrived. Before leaving to follow Alex's clue, Charlotte tried on several dresses, deciding on a green belted tweed frock, tailored but softened with a silk vestee and crushed bow, a lovely outfit she had rarely worn but was pleased still fit. She rolled on stockings and fixed a velvet cloche over her pinned hair, then decided on rayon gloves at the last minute, green to match her dress. And to cover her engagement ring.

Walter, thankfully, was at the Lord Nelson Hotel for a card game and Charlotte left the house without the need for an excuse, walking quickly towards the closest tram stop on George Street. She boarded a tram bound for the far side of Circular Quay, to Bennelong Point near the tram depot. From there, she alighted and set off on foot through The Royal Botanic Garden for a famous chair she knew was carved into the shoreline's sandstone. Mrs Macquarie's Chair—*A chair in a garden to gaze out over a bridge.*

This time she'd worked out the clue quickly, reading from a book in her mother's collection about Colonial Sydney. In a few paragraphs dedicated to Governor Lachlan Macquarie and his wife, Elizabeth, she'd read about a chair by the harbour carved in stone and was certain it was the one Alex referred to. The magic of her childhood had started to weave its way back into her subconscious, a passion for discovery and adventure, of imagination and good old-fashioned sleuthing, making her feel alive again.

Charlotte followed the path along the shoreline until she finally reached the peninsula, taking the steps down to the chair where she found Alex sitting. He must have heard her approach for he rose with a smile. 'Charlotte, you found me!'

'Alex.' She rushed to him, stopping short of their bodies colliding.

He reached for her hands, taking them in his, his thumbs caressing them with unspoken words. His eyes held hers for a moment long enough to block out the world, then he led her to Mrs Macquarie's Chair.

'Have a seat. You can see the entire harbour from here.'

Charlotte sat beside him and revelled in the view. The half-formed bridge was to the west, just behind Bennelong Point where she'd disembarked the tram. Across to North Sydney, she spotted Admiralty House, then the twin-gabled, gothic-style dwelling of Kirribilli House, a residence of the prime minister.

The afternoon sun was mild as it slid westward towards the horizon and a gentle breeze lifted off blue and rippled water. Charlotte breathed deeply, a mix of sea salt from the water and sweetness from Port Jackson fig trees in the botanic gardens filling her lungs. How wonderful it was to sit outside, to enjoy as natural a sight as the sun setting, to be in the company of someone she felt deeply for, someone she could have enjoyed many sunsets with.

'The Governor of New South Wales, Major-General Lachlan Macquarie had this chair commissioned for his wife, Elizabeth,' Alex said, running his hand over the sandstone. 'Convicts carved it in 1810. Mrs Macquarie was fond of the view and was known to sit out here for hours.'

'It's extraordinary that someone would craft such a chair for another person.'

'He must have loved her dearly,' Alex said, meeting Charlotte's eyes, then pulling away. 'Did you have any trouble getting out today?'

'My father went to the Lord Nelson Hotel for a card game. He won't be home for hours.'

Alex nodded. 'Are you cold?'

'I'm fine.'

'In about an hour, the sun will set just over there,' he said, pointing. 'Sydney sunsets, whether I'm at the top of the bridge or just here by the water, are the loveliest I've ever seen. I wanted you to experience it too.'

Charlotte glanced up at the sky. White scribbled clouds were slowly turning a fierce peach as the sun dragged the remaining light with it. It was a beautiful spectacle, and pointless to fill it with perfunctory words, so she simply sat, as did Alex, quiet and comfortable in each other's company.

'I went to Hubert Penny's on Tuesday,' she said after some time.

'*You* went to Hubert Penny's?' Alex chuckled. 'And here I've been taking it easy on you.'

182

She laughed.

'Who did you go with?'

'My friend Estelle.' At his questioning expression, she clarified. 'Mrs Mayfair. Remember, I told you about her.'

'Ah yes, I recall. And did you listen to jazz music?'

'I did.'

'How scandalous of you.'

'I smoked a cigarette too.'

He feigned shock. 'Rebellious even!'

'I like Estelle. She's been a good friend to me. And she's a confident woman. I only wish I could be more like her.'

'You're perfect the way you are.'

She grinned, giddiness rushing over her in waves, making her lightheaded. *You're perfect the way you are.*

They both grew silent again. Ferries drifted past, rising and falling on the swell and the sky grew more fierce with the fading sun.

'Do you know what I wish for?' Alex asked, staring out at the water.

Charlotte turned to him. 'What?'

'To have met you one year earlier when you were unspoken for. Then I would be able to say all the things I want to say.'

'Can't you say them now?' she asked boldly.

He gave an infinitesimal shake of his head, barely enough to stir the air, but enough for Charlotte's heart to sink. She cast her eyes back out to the water. 'Estelle said I shouldn't marry Floyd.'

Alex looked at her. 'You know I can't have an opinion on that.'

'Tell me, Alex. Tell me to end the engagement and I will.'

His expression was dismayed. 'Charlotte, I can't.'

'Why not?'

'Because if you do that, you will jeopardise your relationship with your father. I can't ask that of you.'

'You can't or you won't?'

'I'm trying to be a good man, to do the right thing.'

'You think sneaking around is good?'

Alex lowered his head and sighed deeply. It was some time before he spoke again. 'If you had any idea how I feel about you, you'd know why I leave you clues. Why I turn up to meet you each time even when I know we're playing with fire. It's because I can't help myself, because every minute of every day I think about you.

'And I know that's not right, that you're not mine to think about, but I have to stop short of telling you to end your engagement. It's a decision you have to think through properly, for ending it will come with repercussions.'

That's what made it so difficult. She didn't care a whit for Floyd or his feelings and would happily see him gone, but she loved her father and was loath to hurt him, to feel his disappointment or bear the brunt of his anger. She would never be able to make him see reason when it came to Floyd, not if she explained it a million different ways or in a thousand different languages. His mind was made up.

It was all the more torturous to hear Alex say he thought about her every minute of every day and know that little could be done about it. She wanted to stay at Mrs Macquarie's Chair with him forever, to stave off the dying sun, for once it fell, their time would be up until the next clue.

Alas, it was going down all too fast and Alex reached for her hand and pointed. 'Look Charlotte, it's about to set.'

She watched it, a shimmering, blazing ball being swallowed by the end of the Earth. 'I've never seen anything so beautiful.'

'Look what it does to the sky.'

They sat, hands held, bodies close against the breeze, watching the sun sink slowly, casting the sky in an inferno of orange. Twinkle by twinkle, the lights of the city came on, the golden ball disappeared and darkness descended.

'I should get you home,' Alex said.

Her hands were still in his, their knees and shoulders touching. She shivered, but it had nothing to do with the cool night air. His face was inches from hers, his lips within kissing reach and she wanted to feel them on hers. She wanted him to kiss her.

But he seemed to come to his senses and pulled away, the moment lost. He cleared his throat, stood and helped her to her feet. 'Come, my Charlotte. I'll walk you to the tram.'

They left Mrs Macquarie's Chair as the last of the warmth was stolen from the sandstone, and they walked back through the botanic gardens to the tram depot at Bennelong Point.

Before Charlotte boarded the tram, Alex looked down at her with such an intense longing that she almost didn't climb aboard. How had they got to this point? Why had they allowed themselves to be so indulgent? Alex was right. They were playing with fire, but neither seemed able to douse the flames.

She waved goodbye to him as the tram rolled away from the stop, back towards the city, and they locked eyes until he became a tiny figure in the distance. As the tram curled around Circular Quay, she wondered if she'd ever be able to stop wanting him, if when November came, she'd be able to switch off her feelings like a light switch. She suspected not, for what she felt was unlike anything she'd experienced before, both terrifying and electric.

Gone was that tame and invisible girl who'd once shut herself off because she'd been too fragile for the world. It was that girl who waited for her in marriage to Floyd, a meek little thing who would run his household and have his babies and be treated to a book every now and then to appease her spirit. She thought of what life would be like with Alex. Adventurous, loving, full of laughter; a tonic for her soul.

But her worlds were set to converge, and she didn't know how to stop what seemed an inevitable collision.

CHAPTER
24

Charlotte was furrowing inside the oak sideboard in the dining room when her father appeared in the doorway. 'Love, are you in here?'

She poked her head out from behind the sideboard doors. 'Yes, I'm here. I'm looking for Mama's bone china set. Have you seen it?'

He cast his eyes upwards in thought. 'No, can't say that I have.'

'I've searched everywhere. It seems to have grown legs and walked off.'

'You might have put it someplace else.'

'Yes, I probably did. Anyway,' she stood, dusting her hands and skirt down, 'what are you doing home so early? It's only midday.'

'I left the mill early. Bradfield has invited us to the bridge for the afternoon.'

Charlotte's heart leapt. 'The bridge?'

'That's right. To show us some of the day to day operations. The invitation was extended to you and Floyd, since Floyd will be taking over the business soon. But he has a bank meeting to attend so I've invited Mrs Mayfair instead.'

Charlotte, still grappling with the idea that she might see Alex there, caught the last of his words. 'Mrs Mayfair?'

'Yes. I ran into her on the street earlier. She gave me her telephone number.' He beamed at this. 'I thought it would be nice to have a companion in Floyd's absence, so I invited her along. I know how fond you've grown of Floyd lately, and how you'll miss his company today.'

Charlotte grimaced on the inside. It was deceitful to allow her father to think that she'd warmed to Floyd. Just the other week he'd visited for dinner and Charlotte, fresh from an afternoon spent with Alex, had been overly cheerful in his presence, her father clearly accepting this as a good sign.

'So did Estelle say yes? Is she coming?' She followed Walter into the kitchen.

'Indeed. She sounded thrilled. She'll be here in one hour.'

'I'd better fix us a quick lunch then.'

She cut bread from a fresh loaf baked that morning and made sandwiches. They ate quietly at the table, her father humming to himself as he sipped ginger ale.

'James wrote,' he said, flipping open the paper.

'Oh, he did? How is he?'

'Doing well. Says the business is prospering over in Middlesbrough.'

'Did he say when he'll be coming home?'

'He might travel in November for the wedding. He's met a young lady. She sounds nice, from a good English family. You never know, we may be arranging two weddings this year.' He laughed heartily and took a bite from his sandwich. 'Speaking of which,' he said, wiping the corners of his mouth with a napkin, 'have you given thought to the arrangements?'

'Arrangements?' Charlotte took a bite from her sandwich.

'Yes. For your wedding. There's much to do and November will be here before we know it.'

She forced herself to swallow a lump of bread. 'No, I haven't done anything yet.'

He looked puzzled. 'Now that's interesting. I thought that's what you've been doing on all your recent outings. Looking for a dress and flowers and such. Where have you been going then?'

She stammered. 'Just... out.'

He gave her another puzzled look. 'Well, Floyd has been asking me about it and I have to tell him something. He won't like to hear we haven't started yet.'

'I don't know where to begin,' she confessed.

He smiled gently at her. 'Nor do I, love. I'm a little out of my depth too. Your mother would have been good at this sort of thing. Maybe Mrs

Mayfair could help you.'

Charlotte looked down at her engagement ring, the large Tiffany diamond set in a twenty-four-carat gold band. The ring Floyd had given her when he'd proposed in the parlour only months earlier. It had come as such a shock that before she could register what had happened, her father had accepted on her behalf and the ring had been shoved onto her finger, Walter and Floyd toasting each other's achievement with a brandy.

She collected her plate with her barely eaten sandwich and rose from the table. If her father had noticed the tremble of her hands, he didn't say anything. His eyes were still on the paper.

'Phar Lap is racing at Randwick on the weekend. Odds look good. I might put a bet on.'

***

Charlotte had already worn all of her prettiest dresses on outings with Alex and it took an age to find something new to wear. There was no guarantee she would see him at the bridge when they arrived, but she was filled with hope all the same.

She eventually settled on a pink wool dress with a drop waist, silk stockings and matching pink heels. She took care to pin her hair, setting a curl so that it peeked out from beneath her cloche like she'd seen Estelle wear. She pulled on white mesh gloves, sprayed perfume from an atomiser and placed a hand on her stomach to quell the butterflies that had started to flutter.

There was a knock at the front door, then voices downstairs. Estelle had arrived. She reached for her handbag and headed down the stairs.

'I was delighted to receive your invitation.' Estelle was in the hallway talking to Walter.

'Not as delighted as I was that you accepted.' His cheeks grew uncharacteristically pink.

Charlotte had to wonder if her father had another reason for inviting Estelle. A slight fancy for the woman perhaps, and not just as a companion for his daughter.

Estelle caught sight of Charlotte. 'Darling!' Beneath a luxurious white fur stole, she held out her arms to her. 'How lovely you look.'

Charlotte stepped down to her and they embraced. 'I'm glad you could make it.'

'Wouldn't have missed it for the world.'

Walter, beaming, reached for his coat and hat. 'Shall we be off then?'

***

They caught a ferry from Circular Quay to take them across the harbour to Milsons Point. Charlotte and Estelle sat outside, clutching their hats to save them from being snatched by the wind. When the ferry sailed beneath the shadow of the half-formed bridge, they both shrieked with delight.

Charlotte threw her head back and gazed up at the gentle curve of the arches as they reached across the sky for each other, the glint of sunlight off each beam of steel. An exhilarating thrill surged through her as she thought about the incredible work of Alex and her own family's contribution.

The ferry charged across the harbour, rising and dipping with the swell. It took only minutes to reach the north side of Sydney where most of the fabrication work for the bridge was conducted, and where the Greene steel foundry was located. It was also, Charlotte knew, where Alex was stationed, in the public works office on the Dorman Long and Co site.

Her father's foundry had been in operation there for two years, coinciding with the age of their contract. She'd only visited the foundry once, when it was first built, but hadn't returned since, her father insisting it wasn't a place for women. Nor had she ever been invited to the bridge before and wondered briefly if Alex had had a hand in it.

The ferry halted alongside a wharf big enough to receive large international vessels and Estelle squeezed her hand. 'How exciting!' she said, still clutching her hat. 'This is not something one does every day.'

Charlotte nodded.

'Are you quite all right? You look peaky. The boat ride perhaps?'

It wasn't the boat ride. It was the thought of Alex being only feet away, with no game, no clue, no pretence to hide behind, just a perfectly acceptable scenario that would land them in each other's company. Life dealt disappointments sometimes, but it could also follow through with the sweetest apologies.

Charlotte adjusted her expression and smiled. 'I'm fine. Just excited.'

They disembarked, the wharf hand helping Charlotte and Estelle down from the ferry. They followed Walter along a path that led directly into the Dorman Long site, a huge expanse of excavated area lined with fabrication workshops, including the Greene steel foundry. The site was a flurry of workers and construction, air heavy with the smell of industrialisation.

A myriad of small and large cranes swung through the air, and trucks and horse-drawn carriages moved rubble and steel around the site, while the great shadow of the bridge loomed large above them. Charlotte wanted to cast her eye everywhere, for never had she seen such activity and it was not something that could be seen in any great detail from the city side of the harbour.

'This way,' Walter said, guiding them around the site. 'This here is all Dorman Long and Co. The wharf is theirs too. It receives regular shipments of steel from England. The cranes then come down to the wharf and unload it all. Of course, England doesn't supply all of the steel for the bridge. Greene Steel supplies twenty percent,' he boasted proudly to Estelle.

She raised an elegant eyebrow. 'That's quite impressive, Mr Greene.'

'Ah, please. Call me Walter.' He hitched up his pants as they walked, puffing his chest out slightly. 'Usually, the public isn't allowed to walk around this area but it's all right if you're with me. The Greenes are as good as bridge family.'

They followed a dusty path past rows of fabrication workshops until they reached a small building that appeared more administrative than industrial.

'And this is the public works office where Bradfield and his men work from,' Walter explained, leading them up a small flight of stairs. The door was open and he knocked on it to announce his arrival.

It was one large room with multiple desks where draftsmen sat hunched over plans and paperwork. Dr Bradfield looked up from his desk, which was neither closed off nor set apart from any of the others. The draftsmen stopped what they were doing to look up also, their eyes pausing on Estelle in her slinky fur stole and long legs.

Dr Bradfield rose and walked over to greet them. 'Walter, good to see you.' He turned his attention to Charlotte. 'And I see you've brought your daughter, Miss Greene.' He shook her hand, a kind smile in his eyes.

'And this is Mrs Estelle Mayfair,' Walter said. 'A friend of Charlotte's.'

Estelle extended an elegantly gloved hand to Bradfield, her expression coquettish.

'And Floyd?' Bradfield asked. 'Will he be coming?'

'He has a meeting at the bank,' Walter explained. 'Seems there was some volatility on Wall Street overnight.'

'I did read something about that this morning,' Charlotte said cautiously, recalling Floyd's accusation that she'd bored the men at their engagement party with amateur political talk.

But Bradfield turned to her with interest. 'Indeed, Miss Greene. I read of it also. Seems that a stock tumble occurred. There has been an alarming number of them lately.'

'Perhaps too many of them to be an isolated occurrence,' Charlotte said.

'I agree.'

'They say we are a society of reckless and extravagant spenders, that the economy has grown too rapidly,' she added.

'And yet wages are decreasing, unemployment has risen and we have a proliferation of debt,' Bradfield said.

Walter looked from Charlotte to Bradfield with a ruffled expression. 'Ah, pay no heed to the nonsense of economists! They're doom-mongers. We have strong banks and good investment. Why, would you take a look at that bridge out there. Finest example if I've ever seen one.'

'While my bridge is impressive, I tend to disagree with you about the banks, Walter,' Bradfield said. 'They are adding to the issue with over-lending. Don't you think, given the rising unemployment, that they should curb credit to those who cannot possibly repay?'

'Floyd can tell you better than anyone that talk of over-crediting is balderdash,' Walter argued. 'Wall Street is fine. Our banks are fine. The global economy is fine. So what if we have a little unemployment?'

Bradfield looked briefly annoyed, then corrected his expression. 'Never mind. Shall we get on? I'm keen to show Miss Greene the ropes.' He walked them along the desks and they were introduced to the draftsmen, then through another door to meet the newest engineers and foremen that had joined the team. All the while Charlotte kept her eyes peeled for Alex, but he was not in the office with the engineers, nor did it appear he was anywhere in the public works building.

Bradfield positioned her in front of a large steel hinge and explained to her the importance of weight-bearing in an enormous steel structure like the Sydney Harbour Bridge. 'It's all down to these hinges, which the bridge has four of, two at either end.' He indicated with his hands. 'They support the full weight of the steel and even allow it to expand and contract during changes in temperature.'

'Fascinating,' Charlotte said, staring at the cast steel rod encasing the hinge. 'How much weight can these hinges take?'

'Each bearing, which weighs three hundred tonnes, can handle a load of twenty thousand tonnes.'

'And did your engineers design it this way?'

'Indeed, they did,' Bradfield said. 'My engineers had to be particularly innovative when creating this design, for the Sydney Harbour Bridge contains the heaviest steelwork ever used in construction.'

'And Greene Steel contributes to that?'

'It does. While you are not our primary steel provider, your family's production is crucial to ensuring we are never without supply while we wait for overseas shipments to arrive. That's why it's important for the bridge and your family to continue a strong working relationship and to comply always with the strict code of the contract.' He gave her a pointed look that she couldn't quite interpret.

Before she could ask him to elaborate, Walter cleared his throat. 'Floyd is the one who will handle the matter of contracts after November,' he said. 'Not Charlotte.'

'It is my opinion that Miss Greene is also quite capable,' Bradfield said, smiling at her.

Walter flushed. 'Well, ah, yes. I suppose she could assist in some small way once they're married and business decisions are transferred to him.'

Bradfield frowned as though the answer was less than satisfactory.

After a few minutes, Walter led Estelle away to look outside the window. Once he was out of earshot, Charlotte turned to Dr Bradfield and asked quietly, 'Is your chief engineer here today?'

'You mean Mr Young?' If he was surprised by her query, he didn't show it. 'He's up on the arch at the moment. He should be down soon.'

She nodded politely and allowed him to roll out the plans for the pylons and explain to her their decorative purpose and the exhibit and observation deck he had planned for the southern one. It was twenty minutes later, after a cup of tea and a short tour around the fabrication workshops with Bradfield, that they ran into Alex outside.

'Mr Young,' Walter said, shaking his hand eagerly. 'It's wonderful to see you again.'

'And you, Mr Greene.' He nodded to Charlotte. 'Miss Greene.'

Charlotte tried to contain her beaming smile. 'Hello, Mr Young. This is my friend, Mrs Estelle Mayfair.'

Estelle's thickly lashed eyes travelled the length of Alex, smiling appreciatively. 'How lovely to meet you.'

'We were just finishing a tour of the site,' Bradfield explained.

'Perhaps I could take Miss Greene down to the northern pylon to show her the bridge up close,' Alex suggested.

'Marvellous idea.'

'I'll come too,' said Estelle.

'I thought you might prefer to see the Greene foundry,' Walter suggested. 'It's just over there. We can meet up with Charlotte and Mr Young in a little while.'

Estelle, who looked as though she'd have much preferred a visit to the northern pylon with Alex too, fixed a bright smile. 'Of course, Walter.'

Dr Bradfield bid them good day and returned to the public works building. Walter guided Estelle towards the foundry and Charlotte followed Alex down the path towards the bridge. He was quiet along the way, his expression serious. Few words were spoken until they'd reached another small cluster of buildings by the waterfront, directly adjacent to the northern pylon. He pulled her onto a narrow walkway between two buildings and there, in the shadows, they halted.

Charlotte glanced shyly up at him. 'Hello.'

He smiled down at her. 'Hello.'

'I didn't think we'd see each other so soon after Mrs Macquarie's Chair.'

'Yes, this was quite unexpected. I couldn't stop smiling when Bradfield told me he'd invited you here.' His hand dropped to her waist and the other reached out to graze her cheek gently. 'I've missed you.'

'We only saw each other a few days ago.'

He laughed. 'Far too long in my opinion.'

She giggled. 'I've missed you too. I thought this might have been your idea.' She relaxed into his touch. Never had they been so brazen as to caress each other before, the gift of a chance encounter imparting some bold, brave reaction in them.

'I wish I was free to make decisions like that. I'd have you here every day.'

'Were you really up on the arch?'

'Yes. I had to inspect some rivets going in.'

She traced her fingers along his forearms, feeling the strength in them. 'Why did Bradfield invite us here?'

Alex chewed his bottom lip as though wondering how best to respond. 'He's keeping a close eye on your father and Floyd. He's worried about the contract.'

Charlotte pulled back slightly. 'The contract? What's wrong with it?'

'They probably don't want you to know but I think you should.'

Dread dropped into her stomach. 'Know what?'

They both jumped at the sound of Estelle's voice calling out for Charlotte. Their stolen moment together, all too fleeting, had come to an end.

'That's your friend. You'd better go. Here, take this?' Alex held out a folded piece of paper.

Charlotte's heart leapt as her hands folded around the next clue. She slipped it deep into her coat pocket.

Alex leant in, his body so close she thought she could hear his heart beating. He kissed her cheek, his lips lingering by her ear as he whispered, 'You have all of me, Charlotte. Always and completely.'

Her pulse raced. She could barely think straight as he took her hand and led her out from the shadow of the building and back onto the path just as Estelle appeared.

'Oh, there you are,' she said. 'I've been looking all over for you.' Her eyes darted from Charlotte to Alex, then to the side of the building where they'd just emerged. A slow, wicked smile spread across her lips. 'I see.'

Charlotte swallowed. 'Mr Young was just showing me the workshops.'

Alex nodded quickly. 'That's right. We have a granite offloading system down here.'

'I bet you do,' Estelle said, grinning.

An awkward silence fell and Charlotte fidgeted.

'Your father would like you to come back now, Charlotte. We're catching the ferry home.'

'Of course,' she said.

'I will leave you here then, Miss Greene. Will you be all right to find your way back?' Alex asked.

'We'll be fine.'

'Then I'll say goodbye.' He tipped his hat. 'Mrs Mayfair, it was lovely to meet you.'

'The pleasure was all mine,' Estelle said, and the way she smiled at them made Charlotte uncomfortable. They couldn't have looked guiltier jumping out from between those buildings and while she was dying to tell Estelle about Alex, she couldn't risk anyone knowing for fear it would get back to her father and Floyd. And how dreadful a position it would put Alex in.

She forced composure, although it seemed too little too late. As soon as they were back on the path towards the wharf, Estelle linked her arm through Charlotte's and leant in. 'The bridge engineer? Really? How fabulous!'

Charlotte shook her head. 'It's not what you think.'

'Oh don't be coy with me, Charlotte Greene. I know what it feels like to fall in love.' She sighed wistfully. 'And you, my darling, have it written all over your face for that boy.'

CHAPTER
25

PAIGE
Present Day

It was two weeks since Ryan left and Paige still searched for distraction. She threw herself into work with an almost ruthless efficiency, finalising interviews with candidates and joining late-night calls with foreign publishers. She inspected rental properties, aware that her stay in the parlour was on borrowed time, and applied for all of them, even the ones that were damp with mould and would cost her an entire week's salary. She did this because she needed to validate the way she'd treated Ryan, to prove to herself that her decision had been the only one she could make. After all, she lived in Sydney and he lived in London, and if they couldn't make a simple trip happen now, what hope did they have of making one happen in the future?

For the most part, the distraction and denial worked. During the day, she flew through her tasks but at night, when Xavier went home to Eric and she was alone in her bed, she was reminded of what she'd said no to—an amazing guy who'd wanted to be with her, despite the geographical distance. He'd looked towards solutions while she'd focused firmly on the challenges. At times, she wasn't sure what had prevented her from going to London. Maybe it was the risk of getting hurt again, or of letting Xavier down at a time when her presence was crucial, or of not believing happiness was attainable. She suspected it was all of it.

Xavier wasn't blind to it either, for Ryan's sudden absence and Paige's newfound work obsession could hardly go unnoticed.

'You know it's Saturday,' he said, watching her fingers hit the laptop keys.

'Really? I hadn't noticed.'

He frowned.

'What do you think of this for the launch party?' She turned her laptop towards him, pointing to an image of a cake. 'The lady said we can add your logo and decorate it to suit your branding. The balloons, guest list and invitations are all done too. I'm going to start on gift bags and catering next week.'

'Will you stop that and talk to me?'

Paige looked up. 'About?'

'Eric and I asked you to dinner three times this week. You didn't accept once.'

'I was tired.'

'You're miserable.'

Paige returned her gaze to the screen, determined not to acknowledge the truth in Xavier's words. 'Have you finished downloading the software your accountant gave you?'

'Stop deflecting.'

'We still have a lot to do.'

'It can wait a minute.'

'The launch is in six weeks.'

Xavier gave her a stark look, enough for Paige to finally sit back in her chair and pinch the space between her eyes.

It was Saturday afternoon and they were sitting in Xavier's office. He'd spent the morning on the phone trying to entice her out, first to The Rocks Markets, then a walk along the quay, then lunch at William Blue, but she'd declined it all until he'd finally given up and tut-tutted his way into the house to find her working.

'Have you spoken to Ryan?'

Paige shook her head. 'Not since he left.'

'Why not?'

'Because I don't think he'd feel like speaking to me right now, not after the way I treated him.'

'You should still call.'

Paige opened her mouth but found she couldn't conjure any words. Truth was, she was too afraid to call him, to hear the disappointment in his voice, for him to tell her that she'd wasted his time. He could have returned to England months earlier, back to his job and his family, back to finalising his divorce. He could have taken Charlotte's things with him and completed the search on his own, had a whole team of people helping him. Instead, he'd chosen to stay in Sydney with Paige and she'd let him down.

She swallowed past her guilt and took a breath. 'Anyway, no point dwelling. It is what it is. Maybe we just found each other at a bad time. He was in the middle of a divorce and I was leaving Christian behind.'

'What a load of rubbish.'

Paige started. 'Excuse me?'

'Call him.'

'Why don't you just download that software? Your accountant wants it done by this weekend.'

He played with a pen, rolling it back and forth along the desk. 'You're not doing it for me, are you?'

'Doing what?'

'Breaking it off with Ryan. Staying behind in Sydney. Are you doing it out of loyalty to the business?'

Paige looked down at her laptop keys until they blurred. 'This is where I'm meant to be.'

'That's not an answer.' Xavier sighed and stood, walked around to the part of the desk where she sat and kissed the top of her head. 'I'm going back to the hotel. Come by at seven for dinner? Eric misses you.'

She nodded. 'Okay.'

But she wouldn't, and she knew he knew it too.

***

'So what do you think?' the real estate agent asked.

Paige smiled, trying not to fixate on the swollen floorboards or the dank smell or the cockroach she'd seen scuttling along the skirting boards. It was yet another property, one in a long list of dim rooms and poky kitchens. She hadn't stumbled across anything remotely like the

Greene's Playfair house, where the rooms had character and she felt completely at home. Still, new employees were starting in three weeks and time had run out. She had to vacate the parlour.

'It's nice,' she said, looking around. 'I think it could work.'

'Great.' The woman handed her an application form. 'Now, I've had a lot of interest in this one, so the quicker you can get this back to me, the better.' Her phone rang and she glanced at it. 'Sorry, I have to get back to the office. Call me if you have any questions.'

Paige watched as the woman hurried back to her car, climbed in and drove away. She took one last uncertain look at the ramshackle terrace before folding the application form and slipping it into her bag.

It was four pm and a cool July sun splayed the last of its rays on the city as it made its way to the horizon. When she arrived back at the house, she let herself in and dropped her bag to the floor. Her phone rang and she retrieved it from her pocket, stunned to see it was Ryan. Taking a deep breath, she answered. 'Hello?'

'Hey, how are you?'

She walked into the kitchen and leant against the bench, her heart in her throat. 'I'm good. How are you?'

'Doing well.'

She wasn't sure what to say, where to start, or if words could even mend what had happened. 'What time is it there?'

'Seven in the morning. Are you okay to talk? I can call you back.'

'No it's fine. I've finished for the day.'

'It's five pm there, right?'

'Just after four.' The small talk was excruciating. 'Ryan...'

'I'm not sure what happened in Sydney,' he interjected. 'I've been turning it over in my head but I still can't work it out. I knew there was a chance you wouldn't come to London, but I thought at least you'd see me off at the airport. Did I do something to upset you?'

Paige dipped her head, ashamed again at how she'd acted. 'You didn't do anything wrong. It was me. Everything happened so quickly and I couldn't process it. My instinct was to shut down.'

'It was a lot of decisions to make at once,' he said. 'I get that, and I apologise if I put pressure on you.'

'You didn't. I just handled it badly. I couldn't drop everything and leave and I didn't know how to tell you that.'

'I suspect you did, but I refused to listen.'

Perhaps so, but her biggest regret would always be the way she'd treated him and the obsessive worry about protecting her heart to the detriment of the relationship. She hadn't been able to see past her own fears to consider a future with Ryan. At the first hurdle, she'd stumbled.

'Anyway, I'm calling to offer a truce,' he said. 'We can be friends, at least.'

She exhaled with relief. It was more than she'd expected. 'I'd like that.'

'All right then.' His words carried a smile she knew well. 'That's the hard stuff out of the way. Now, what's been happening?'

She smiled too. 'Well, we're launching the business in six weeks, so we've been madly preparing for that. We have new staff coming and I'll have to vacate the house soon.'

'Have you found a place?'

'Not yet but I looked at somewhere promising today. How about you?'

'Busy with work too. Had lots waiting for me when I got back. And I'm now divorced.'

'You mean it's done?'

'Yes. It's all over.'

The news was bittersweet. 'Ryan, that's great. I'm happy for you.'

'It's been the longest twelve months of my life. I'm glad it's behind me. I've been getting out a bit, trying to move on, see new people.'

See new people. Paige's smile vanished. 'Right, of course.'

'Anyway, I called because I discovered something.'

'Oh?'

'In Charlotte's chest of letters. I finally got to the last clue.'

'You did?' Paige stopped slouching and stood upright. 'Did it tell you anything new?'

'Yes. I know the name of her lover.'

She was momentarily speechless. 'Oh my God. Who was it?'

'A man called Alex. The first initial of his last name was Y. That's how he signed it. *Alex Y.*'

'Her lover signed his name?' Paige was surprised. 'Was there a quote included?'

'There was. I googled it. It was from John Keats to Fanny Brawne in

1818. "My love has made me selfish. I cannot exist without you. I am forgetful of everything but seeing you again. I could die for that—I could die for you."'

'Alex wrote that to Charlotte?'

'It was the last letter in the chest. This final clue was played out before everything collapsed.'

'What was the clue?'

'"My bed awaits. You know where."'

Paige arched an eyebrow. 'So they'd become proper lovers. They'd had an affair. I doubt they could have got away with that here at the house. They must have been meeting at his house, hence the clue—*my bed awaits*.'

'I thought that too. Ironic also that the quote he chose speaks of dying for her and their love.'

'You think he was aware of his fate?'

'Hard to know. But now we have his name. Alex Y. And I keep thinking we've come across it in our research before, but I don't know where.'

Paige chewed the inside of her cheek. Ryan was right. The name sounded familiar. She stretched her mind to its farthest corners, trying to remember. 'Gladesville Hospital?'

'No, I was thinking the library,' Ryan said, 'We must have retrieved him in a search.'

And then it struck her. 'Neither. It was the southern pylon.'

'The pylon?'

'Yes. At the Sydney Harbour Bridge, up on the observation deck. There were photographs in display cabinets there.'

'Which ones? We looked at a lot of display cabinets.'

Paige's pulse raced. 'I'm going over there now.'

'*Right now?*'

'Yes. I'll call you back. I won't be long.'

'Okay. I'll keep my phone close.'

They said goodbye and Paige snatched up the house keys and rushed out the door. Taking the narrow alley through the workmen's terraces, Paige darted up to Foundation Park, cutting through Gloucester Street to Argyle and finding Bridge Stairs. She took them two at a time, her lungs burning by the time she reached the top, then ran down Bradfield

Highway, barely taking stock of the harbour view, until she arrived at the southern pylon.

She was gasping for air, still with two hundred steps to climb to the observation deck. She willed her legs on, her body screaming for her to stop as she went up, her face flushed and a trickle of sweat making its way down her back. She paused at the exhibits level and the cinema, gulped down air, then kept climbing. At long last, she reached the observation deck and went straight to the display cabinet where she knew the photograph was.

She found it instantly, the black and white image she'd seen when she'd visited with Ryan weeks earlier, of four men standing beneath the bridge at Milsons Point. It was mid-construction and the photograph was dated August 1929, at the height of Charlotte's love affair with her mystery man. But it was a mystery no more, for Paige knew who he was.

She traced her fingers along the plaque—Walter Greene, Floyd Clark, Dr JJC Bradfield. Then she reached him. The last man on the right, the one who had captured her eye the first time she'd seen the photograph because of the kind and handsome face that had peered back at her. The employee of the public works department.

She snatched her phone out of her pocket, took a snap of the photo and texted it to Ryan. Then she called him. 'I know who he was.'

'Who?' Ryan asked.

'Alexander Young. He was Bradfield's chief engineer.'

'He worked on the bridge?'

'He didn't just work on it. He was key to its design and construction. He's the one Charlotte played the game with. The one she loved.' She glanced down again at the photograph. 'Now we just need to know what happened to him.'

202

CHAPTER
26

By the time Paige left the southern pylon to return to Playfair Street, the sun had stolen the last of the daylight to cast on another part of the world. She'd wanted to head straight to the New South Wales State Library to do an archival search on Alexander Young but had given up when the lights of the city flickered on and buildings began to close for the evening.

The next morning she woke early, dressed and headed straight for the Mitchell Reading Room. She found the oak desk she and Ryan had always sat at, turned the library computer on and called him. It was eleven pm in London, but he sounded wide awake.

'Sorry, is it too late to do this?' she asked.

'Not at all. Are you at the library?'

'Yes, I just got here.'

'All right. I'm ready. Let's recap.'

'Okay, so on Tuesday, October twenty-ninth, 1929, the last crash of the New York Stock Exchange occurred. They called it Black Tuesday,' Paige said, sketching the timeline on a pad beside her.

'Right,' said Ryan.

'Then, the following day, on Wednesday, October thirtieth, Charlotte was admitted by her father to the Gladesville Mental Hospital. She was received by Dr Carmichael.'

'Correct.'

'The following day, a telegram from Charlotte is sent to her brother

James in the UK, pleading for help, dated October thirty-first.'

There was the rustling of paper on the other end, then Ryan said, 'Yes, the telegram was sent after she was admitted to the hospital.'

Paige chewed the end of her pen. 'Which is odd, but somewhat explainable.'

'Maggie said the telegram could have been sent by someone else on Charlotte's behalf. Or that it was dated a day later by the postmaster when he sent it. In any case, we know she was admitted to the hospital, without a doubt. That part holds.'

'Yes,' Paige concurred. 'And we know she died there. Her medical report confirms she took her own life in March 1930 due to grief caused by the death of her lover.' She glanced over her notepad, tapping one name that stood out with her pen. 'Alexander Young. We need to know what happened to him. He's the key to all this. To Charlotte's grief, Walter's disappearance and the house being ransacked.'

'Do you still think Floyd found out about the affair and had Alex taken care of?'

'I do, but we need the records to back it up. And it doesn't explain Walter's disappearance.'

'No, it doesn't.'

Paige felt that frustrating dead-end loom again. It was time to cast their net wider and search for Alexander Young in state library archives.

Ryan sipped something, then there was the sound of a glass settling gently on a table. There was faint conversation in the background, like the television was on.

'Is it getting too late for you?' Paige asked. 'You can go to bed if you like. I'll keep going with this.'

'No, it's fine. I had a friend over earlier but she just left.'

'Oh.' Paige's heart sank. 'Right. Well,' she quickly rambled on to fill the awkward silence, 'I did some internet searches on Alex last night but was only able to find basic information. He was an engineer for the Department of Public Works, which we knew. He was Bradfield's right-hand man on the bridge construction. He was also English, you may be interested to know.'

'Is that so?' Ryan said. 'Must have been an all right lad then.'

Paige laughed. 'I'm hoping that the state archives will give us what the public domain couldn't.'

'Alexander Young's cause of death.'

'Exactly.' She spent the next several minutes searching through archives and catalogues. There was a wealth of information about the bridge construction and Bradfield, about Alexander and the public works department. Even his address—a small terrace off Five Ways, Paddington, on Broughton Street.

Then she found a document that caught her interest. 'I might have found something.'

'What is it?'

'A list of all the men who died working on the bridge. It's in a closing report dated June twentieth, 1932, a couple of months after the bridge was completed.'

'You mean men who fell to their deaths from the top?'

'Some fell from the top, but some died as a result of other injuries,' Paige explained. 'One man was crushed by a crane, another two were killed while cooking and catching, and one even died from tetanus after accidentally driving a rusty nail into his foot.'

'Sounds like a highly pleasant job.'

'Yes, and not something the government was interested in promoting at the time, for they only wanted positive stories associated with their new bridge. Until recently, a lot of these men were forgotten. I'm not surprised to see this hidden away in a closing report.'

'Anything in there about Alex?'

'This is where it gets interesting. A lot of the original writing is faded due to age. Some of the men's names are incomplete. It seems the state archives scanned it into the computer simply the way they found it, without restoration.'

'Is Alex's name there?' She could hear Ryan getting impatient.

'I think so.' She touched her finger to the screen. 'A man fell to his death from the northern arch on October twenty-four, 1929. His name is mostly faded but I can definitely see an A, E in his first name and a Y in his surname.'

'It's got to be him,' Ryan said. 'The date is too coincidental. He died on the bridge a week before Charlotte was admitted to the mental institution.'

Paige felt certain too. A shiver crept up her spine at the discovery. 'The timing fits, the letters are there. It's Alex.'

Ryan sighed. 'I'm kind of devastated really.'

'I am too. I'll still need to verify it properly, but it says he was struck by a creeper crane. It knocked him from the top. They found his body the next day in the water.'

'Goodness.'

'No wonder Charlotte was beside herself,' Paige said. 'What a tragic way to lose someone you love.'

'Do you still think Floyd was involved? Seems to me like it was an accident.'

'Maybe it was made to look like one.' But the theory sounded far-fetched even to Paige.

'I need to digest this,' Ryan said, sounding tired suddenly. 'I've spent months reading Charlotte and Alex's letters. I've come to know them. I just... I don't know how I feel right now.'

'I understand,' Paige said. She wished he was next to her so she could put her arms around him. So she could lay her head on his shoulder and tell him she understood in more ways than just words. But she couldn't, nor did she think he would welcome it with a new woman in his life. A dull ache settled over her in the reading room as she realised they'd figured out Charlotte's mystery and that there would be few reasons to pick up the phone and talk again.

He yawned. 'Well, it's getting late here. I suppose I should go to bed.'

'Ryan?'

'Yes, Paige?'

She took a deep breath. 'I just wanted to tell you how much the last few months have meant to me. I know I didn't end things well, but the time we spent together was still special.'

There was silence. Then, 'It was special for me too.'

She wasn't sure if he meant it and felt it probably didn't matter. The damage was irreparable. She was here and he was there and that's how it would remain.

'Look after Charlotte and Alex for me,' she said, turning the library computer off.

'I will.'

'And good luck with everything. With work and life.' *And moving on.*

'Thanks. You too.'

They said goodbye and ended the call. It took Paige a full minute to drop her phone back into her bag and leave the library. On the way home to Playfair Street, the winter sun disappeared behind clouds, leaving her cold and hollow. She'd just said goodbye to Ryan for a second time. And not just to him, but to Charlotte and Alex, Walter and Floyd, all of whom had kept her company in this big, lonely city, filling her days and nights with their stories. They'd brought Ryan to her and for that, she'd always be grateful.

As she crossed the quay, she stared up at the Sydney Harbour Bridge, solitary and stark against the sky. It represented everything about that family in 1929. It was the underpinning of their tragic story, of a love that had eclipsed boundaries and a death that had extinguished the light of a young man and woman.

Paige had always admired the bridge for its exceptional engineering, its representation of local labour and its strength in times of great economic depression. But now when she looked at it, she felt sorrow for everything that had been lost, for Ryan, who was far away in another country, and for the life she'd chosen in Sydney, which now seemed empty and lacking.

CHAPTER
27

A few days later, Paige was returning from her lunch break when Xavier called out to her. 'We need more storage space,' he declared when she arrived in his office doorway.

'Okay.'

'I'm finalising the floor plan and we don't have enough room. I've tried to rework it three times. If I put design and marketing together upstairs I could free up a room for storage, but it will be squashy.' He looked down at a large plan on his desk, sighing with exasperation.

'What do you want to do?'

'The attic,' he said.

Their eyes shot upwards to the ceiling.

'What about it?' She dreaded the answer, knowing she hadn't done anything with it yet. She'd been absorbed in Ryan and the business and Charlotte and Alex's clues, and the attic had made a steadfast decline to the bottom of her list.

'Have you cleaned it out yet?'

She half-nodded, half-shook her head. 'Sort of. Not really. There's heaps of stuff up there.'

'Can you get it sorted?'

'I'll take care of it first thing tomorrow.'

'Thanks, love.'

She lingered in the doorway. 'Have you and Eric heard back from any of the rentals you applied for?'

'We have, actually,' he said. 'We're approved for a place in Surry Hills. We'll be moving there in two weeks.'

'That's great!'

'It's just another thing to get done before the launch but yes, it's a relief. You?'

'Nothing yet.'

'Didn't you fill out an application recently?'

'Yes. I'm waiting a response.'

He nodded with distraction. 'If it falls through, you can sleep on our lounge until something comes up.' He bent his head over the floor plan again.

The next morning, while Xavier was out meeting his accountant, Paige rose, dressed and padded up to the attic. At the foot of the staircase, she breathed in the musty air that seemed to only permeate this section of the house. The rest of the house had been restored and repainted, the smell of new furniture muting the age. It was here, and here only, in that dim, dusty room overlooking Playfair Street, that Charlotte and her story still seemed to exist.

Paige climbed the steps and pushed open the door. Weak light from the hallway cast a beam across the floor, meeting the slivers that spilled in from the small window opposite. The attic sighed. Dust motes hung motionless.

She walked in, saw the Chesterfield lounge and the old grandfather clock, the gramophone and large Edwardian chest that matched the smaller one Ryan had taken home with him. She could see the disturbed circle of dust where she and Ryan had last sat; the first time he'd almost kissed her before Xavier had walked in on them. Her heart tugged and she swallowed down the lump of regret she always felt when she thought of him.

'Right, need to get on with it,' she said to the quiet, cluttered attic. 'No time for moping.'

The idea was to make four piles. One for immediate rubbish removal, like the rodent-gnawed encyclopaedias and boxes of paperwork that couldn't be salvaged; another pile for pieces she wanted to keep for display downstairs, like the typewriter and dusty globe; a third pile for items that could be given to the thrift store; and a fourth pile. The Greenes' pile. Items she would need to send back to Ryan.

She spent the next three hours sifting, sorting and jumping when she uncovered the occasional dead mouse. She coded everything with a sticker—green for the Greenes, yellow for rubbish, blue for the thrift and pink to stay. Wiping sweat from her brow, she finally stretched and observed her handy work. Now that she could see the walls and floors better, the attic held the promise of good storage and she knew Xavier would be pleased. But she also felt a sense of loss as though the house's century-old grip on this final room of treasures had at long last been loosened.

Downstairs, she washed her hands and face, gulped down a glass of water and was finalising details over the phone with a rubbish removal service when Xavier returned. He slid a coffee and pastry along the bench towards her and she put the phone down, smiling appreciatively. 'Thank you. I forgot to eat breakfast.'

'How is it going in the attic?'

'Good,' she said, sipping the coffee. 'I booked the rubbish removal and thrift pickup for Wednesday. That will take care of most of the stuff. I also saved a couple of items, like a globe and a typewriter that's been protected in its case, circa 1964. Thought we could keep them down here for display.'

'An ode to the house. I like it,' Xavier said.

'Then there's the Greenes' items.' Paige took another deliberate sip of her coffee.

'You could call Ryan and ask what can be done with them.'

'I'll just email him.'

Xavier shot her a look over the rim of his cup. 'Whatever you think is best.'

He disappeared into his office and Paige pushed her sleeves up, retied her long hair away and trudged back up the stairs. Inside the attic, she set her sights on the pile of Charlotte's belongings marked with little green stickers.

Her eyes swept over the Chesterfield lounge and armchairs, the grandfather clock whose time had halted long ago, the brass gramophone and a beautiful antique rotary telephone she'd unearthed, not having noticed it before. And of course, the Edwardian chest that stored Charlotte's wedding gown as well as another—a jade-green dress swathed in delicate black Chantilly lace. Also in the chest were the photographs of Charlotte, her father and her brother, the one taken at Hubert's with Estelle, and one of Charlotte at the Gladesville Mental Hospital, standing beside Dr Carmichael.

Paige felt melancholy settle over her like an opaque cloud, not unlike the moment she'd discovered that Charlotte and Alex had died. It was so terribly sad what had become of them. Love deserved to flourish. If it was bold and brave and true, it deserved life, and theirs had been extinguished far too soon.

Alas, there was no time to dwell on what couldn't be changed all these years later. The day was getting on and she still had the rest of the attic to organise. She wanted to complete an inventory of the pieces she needed to ship back to Ryan so that she could email him, then she needed to work out how she was going to get all of it down the staircases. A conundrum for another day.

She ran her fingertips along the arm of the Chesterfield, through the dust that had settled on the gramophone horn, along the newly discovered telephone, until she found herself behind the grandfather clock. There, wedged against the attic wall, to Paige's surprise, was a third Edwardian chest she'd missed earlier. It was clearly part of the existing set—the small one that stored Charlotte's letters and the large one that housed her wedding gown and jade dress. This chest was the middle piece and a gurgle of elation bubbled out of Paige's mouth. She thought she'd been through everything of the Greenes.

She tried her best to get behind the clock, pushing away cobwebs that stuck to her hands and hair, hoping spidery inhabitants had fled elsewhere. She crouched down, wrapped her hands around the chest and heaved it out. When it was finally free of its spot she knelt down, gripped the lid with her fingers and worked it open. It was good fortune really that none of the chests had been locked. Securely fastened and stiff in the hinges, but not bolted shut.

She peered into its contents. There was a thin stack of plastic records for the gramophone as well as several fountain pens with dry inkwells, an empty decanter and tumblers, some old books, three leather-bound ledgers and a strange rotating contraption in a bronze case that she realised was a Rolodex. She picked it up and turned it over to inspect it. It was heavy and the bronze wore a thick coat of patina. There was a rectangular window cut into the bronze to view each contact card and when she turned the dial on the side, stiff at first, but which eventually yielded, she watched as people's names, phone numbers and addresses turned through the viewing window.

Dr JJC Bradfield, Mr Floyd Clark, Mrs Estelle Mayfair, The Bank of New South Wales, the Silverwater mill, the Milsons Point foundry, and many others. It was like peering through the looking-glass, a snapshot into what she was sure had been Walter's world.

She placed the Rolodex back into the chest and gently rifled through the rest of the contents. It was paperwork mostly, nothing of consequence, until her fingers closed around an envelope which she pulled out, addressed to the Playfair Street house.

The letter inside was long gone, which made it an empty envelope, but the front indicated it had been intended for Charlotte and the date of the postage stamp, albeit faded, read February 1930. Someone had sent Charlotte mail around the same time as her death, obviously unaware of what had happened to her.

It made her think instantly of James. He was the likeliest candidate, for he hadn't known that Charlotte was at Gladesville or that she'd died there, and was at that time trying to elicit a response from both her and Walter. But Walter had disappeared too, so who opened the envelope and where was the letter inside?

When she turned it over to look at the sender's address on the back, her curiosity piqued further. It had been sent from France.

Xavier's voice echoed down the hall. 'How's it going up there?'

Paige placed the envelope back in the chest and stood, meeting him at the attic door. 'Good. I'm just about to take an inventory of everything so I can email Ryan.'

'I thought you'd disappeared down a rabbit hole.'

She smiled. 'Almost.'

'I'm heading out to run errands. Want me to grab you dinner on my way back?'

Paige started, realising the time. It was almost four pm. She'd spent the entire day up there. 'Yes, please, if you could. I'll keep going in here.'

Xavier waved goodbye, his footsteps retreating down the hall. She returned to the collection of Greene items and considered them. Taking her phone out, she typed an inventory of the pieces into it and turned the light off. As an afterthought, she went back for the envelope before heading downstairs.

At the kitchen bench, she opened her laptop and powered it on. She hadn't made a dent in her to-do list all day but once she emailed Ryan, she could finish her work in the attic and finally award Xavier his storage space. As she created a new message and typed his email address in, her eyes drifted to the envelope on the bench beside her. How to explain that in an email?

The time was seven-thirty am in London. He'd probably still be in bed. If she called him, she could explain the envelope in better detail. But if he was lying beside company...

Paige chewed her fingernail, her foot kicking the under panel of the bench, wondering what to do. Eventually, she gave in, reached for her phone and dialled his number, her heart in her throat.

Ryan picked up on the third ring. 'Hello?'

'Ryan, hey. It's Paige.'

'Hi.' He chuckled. 'I knew it was you. Your number came up on my phone.'

'Oh. Right. Yeah. How are you?'

'Good, thanks.'

Her mouth was so dry it felt like cotton wool. 'Have I got you at a bad time? I can call back later.'

'No, it's all right. I was just getting ready for work. What's up?'

'I finally cleaned out the attic.'

'Oh, yes.'

'And I wanted to know where you'd like me to ship your family's items to. I can email you the inventory. There are some big pieces, like the Chesterfield and the grandfather clock, then some smaller items, like the gramophone.'

'Okay, can you send me an email describing each piece? I'll get my secretary to arrange the shipping.'

'Sure. And Ryan?'

'Yes.'

'I found something else.' She picked up the envelope, turning it over in her hands. 'There was another chest behind the grandfather clock. It belongs to the same set as the one you took home and the larger one that's still here. It's the middle piece.'

There was silence, as though Ryan had stopped what he was doing.

'Another chest?'

'Yes. I went through it. There were some records for the gramophone, a Rolodex and some other office particulars like fountain pens and ledgers. And I found an envelope.'

'What kind of an envelope?'

'Well, an empty one. The letter that was inside is gone. There's a postage stamp which reads February 1930, but I can't tell the exact date. It was addressed to this house, attention to Charlotte Greene. On the back, I found the sender's address. It's had some water damage but I can just make it out. A place in France.'

'France?' He was repeating her words, clearly as surprised as she was. 'Who was the sender?'

'It doesn't say,' she said. 'But who would be sending Charlotte a letter from France, especially one that would have arrived in Sydney after she died?'

'It could have been James. He wouldn't have known what happened to her.'

'That's what I thought too. Did your family have property in France?'

'We have property in a lot of places and James did too. It shouldn't be too hard to confirm. I'll ask my grandfather. Can you send me the address?'

'Sure.'

They ended the call and Paige immediately compiled an email to Ryan with the inventory of pieces that needed shipping, as well as the address on the back of the envelope.

Afterwards, she sat back on the stool and considered this strange new sequence of events. A sender had tried to correspond with Charlotte, someone who may not have been aware of her incarceration at Gladesville. Someone else had intercepted that letter when it arrived at Playfair Street. They'd opened it, no doubt read it, taken it with them, then stored the empty envelope in the chest in the attic. Had it been Walter or someone else? What message had the letter contained?

And where was it now?

CHAPTER 28

CHARLOTTE
August 1929

August was drawing to a close. Winter sunshine, pale and gentle, cut through the leaves of the apple gum, lighting up the kitchen. Charlotte slid two eggs and a piece of toast onto Walter's plate as he took his seat at the table and reached for the paper.

'Good morning.' His voice was gruff, not like his usual self.

Charlotte glanced furtively at him. 'Did you sleep well? I didn't hear you come in.'

'Late night on The Hungry Mile.'

'The Hungry Mile? What were you doing down there?'

'Went to watch a couple of boxing matches.'

'Men are boxing down there now?'

He didn't reply, just snapped open the paper with too much force, causing a tear in the crease.

'Do you know where the antique carriage clock has gone?' she asked, ignoring the mood he seemed to have woken with. 'The one that was by the telephone in the hall?'

'How would I know where it's gone?'

She frowned at his tetchy tone. 'I just thought you might know. It was there and now it's not. Things seem to be walking off around here.' Or maybe it was her constant state of distraction that had caused her to misplace them.

'I'm sure it will turn up.'

She set down his tea and pointed to an article in the paper. 'The news out of New York is worrying. Wall Street had another bad trading day. Economists are predicting a crash the world won't recover from.'

'Utter nonsense,' Walter said, making a point of flipping past it. 'Floyd is well aware of what's happening on Wall Street. He says there's nothing to worry about. The banks hold the world up, not the stock exchanges.'

'Worldwide production is declining and unemployment is rising. It's left stock prices higher than their actual value. I think it's worth reading the article. We'll need to be prepared.'

His disregard of her comment was blatant. 'The hounds are racing today. Odds look good. I might take a trip out to Richmond.'

Charlotte shook her head with frustration. If James or Floyd had made the suggestion, he would have paid attention. He would have hurried them into the parlour for brandy and cigars to discuss it at length, but because it had come from her, a woman, someone who couldn't possibly hope to understand such a topic, it was considered insignificant.

'You should spend less time worrying about the stock exchange and more time on this wedding,' he said, as if to read her thoughts. 'What's happening with it? It's already August.'

Charlotte bristled at his tone. 'I don't know what's happening with it.' She hadn't a clue how to start its preparation, nor could she summon the inclination to. Nothing in her being could motivate her to want to organise that wedding.

'I'll have Floyd arrange the dress.'

'I can have my own dress made,' she retorted.

'Obviously you can't or you'd have consulted with a dressmaker already. And where's your friend, Mrs Mayfair? Why haven't you asked her for help yet? Do you think this wedding is going to magically create itself?'

'Maybe we should put it on hold for a while. It hardly seems the time.'

Walter slammed down the paper, spilling his tea. 'We're not putting it on hold! This wedding will happen. It must. And I don't want to hear another word of resistance from you.' He stood, threw his napkin down and stormed out of the kitchen.

Charlotte heard his hat and coat being ripped off the coat rack and the front door slam behind him. She stared at the kitchen table, at his plate of uneaten breakfast and the tea that had spilled all over the newspaper, soaking through the pages.

She was tired of his incessant mood swings, exuberant one minute, bad-tempered the next. She couldn't imagine what had got into him lately. Perhaps if he were more compromising, if he'd offered to accompany her to a dressmaker or a fashion boutique to select a gown, she'd be more inclined to take part. But his unprovoked aggression served only to make her an unwilling participant.

Charlotte untied her apron, draped it over the back of a chair and left the kitchen. He could clean his own spilt tea. She wanted out of the house as quickly as possible, a place she was struggling to derive any comfort from lately. She took the stairs two at a time up to her room and from under her bed, she dragged out the small chest and opened it. Alex's latest clue, the one he'd slipped into her hand before Estelle had almost caught them at the bridge, was sitting on top of all the others. She unfolded it gently.

My heart is full of you,
None other than you is in my thoughts,
Yet when I seek to say to you something not for the
world,
Words fail me,
If you were here, we need not talk at all,
Our eyes would whisper for us,
Your hand fast in mine.

It was the raw and beautiful words of prolific poet Emily Dickinson to her sister-in-law, Susan Gilbert, quoted from the book of love letters. They had been close and affectionate friends for most of the late nineteenth century, the true extent and interpretation of their relationship only realised decades later, when hundreds of Emily's letters to Susan were unearthed. 'Be my own again and kiss me, feel so eager for you, feel that I cannot wait, feel that I must have you now.'

Charlotte brought the clue to her chest and held it there. When she thought of what Emily and Susan had felt for each other, the love they'd had to conceal for fear of being looked upon unfavourably, she was fuelled with determination that she wouldn't be like that. She wouldn't love in secret. For what was love if it had to be hidden away?

Her eyes travelled down to the clue.

My dear, sweet Charlotte, I grow more curious of you every day.
Escape with me to where the rooms are hushed and the shelves are full of possibility.
Sunday noon.

His words sang of a library and she was reminded of her own, when she'd first met Alex, on the night of her engagement party. They'd stood facing the books and she'd said those exact words to him, that the shelves were full of possibility. He'd remembered and her heart leapt a dance all of its own. There was only one library in the city and she was certain this was where she would find him. The Public Library of New South Wales.

It was not quite noon so she washed and dressed, pinning her wilful curls back and pulling a hat on. To wait out the time, she didn't clean the kitchen or sweep the floor as she would normally have done for her father. She sat in the library and read *Love Through the Ages—A Collection of Timeless Love Letters.* Her mother's book, now her book, and it was guiding her on a journey of self-discovery, leading her each time to Alex. From some distant and untouchable place, it felt like the greatest gift her mother could give her.

When the grandfather clock edged towards midday, Charlotte placed the book back on the library shelf and left the house. She crossed busy Circular Quay as ferry horns rang out across the harbour and the trams rattled on their tracks. On Shakespeare Place, she found the entrance to the library, with its vast stone columns and rising steps. But she couldn't see Alex. He wouldn't have made it that easy, she was certain, to simply wait on the steps for her. His clue spoke of hushed rooms and shelves of possibility. He was hiding somewhere, and she'd have to find him.

She quickly covered the cool stone floor of the Mitchell Wing foyer, the sound of her shoes echoing. She didn't visit the library often, having always been content with her mother's collection at home, but now that she was there, she looked up in wonder at the high ceilings and multiple doors and corridors that led into different parts of the building.

She started in the small reading rooms in the Mitchell Wing, going from room to room, scanning rows of long, dark oak desks with soft lamplight and heads bent studiously low. Bookcases lined the walls and everyone was silent, little more than the clearing of a throat, the flitter of a page, the crack of a book spine.

Having not found Alex in the Mitchell Wing, Charlotte quickly left, conscious of time, and traversed the rabbit warren of dim corridors, heading into the Dixon Wing. She passed more rooms, some doors open, some locked, as she was carried deeper into the belly of the library, trying to seek him out. After she'd explored what felt like every room and corridor, she made her way back towards the foyer, perplexed.

She'd felt certain his clue had hinted at the state library, so why was he not there? Surely he hadn't left the city, expecting her to travel to some faraway suburb to find him. Because if that were the case, she couldn't possibly. She didn't know how. It was on this panicked thought that she passed a door, felt a gentle hand close around her arm and pull her inside.

The door closed behind her and she turned to find Alex, smiling down at her, his finger to his lips, bidding her quiet as she leapt into his arms.

'I was about to give up!' she whispered.

He chuckled. 'I saw you go past and when you came back, I thought I'd better stop you.'

She let him go and looked around. 'What is this place? Why are we in here?'

'It's called the David Scott Mitchell Room and it's especially for archives,' he said. 'But we must be quiet. A friend of mine works here and let me in for a few hours.'

'He did?'

'Yes. It's not usually open to the public. You need appropriate access. But I told him someone very special to me would love to see it.'

Charlotte's heart swelled. 'What do they store in here?'

'Works that are historically significant and need to be preserved for future generations.'

The area was small—two leather armchairs, a small table in the middle with a stack of books on top, a tall brocade lamp and a wrought-iron chandelier casting diffuse light against the walls. The room was windowless and carpeted with mahogany bookcases resting against oak-panelled walls. There was a smell of age and a time well passed that was pressed into the shelves.

Alex took her hand and led her to the bookcases. 'This room holds valuable treasures, whether donated or purchased at auction by the state. Like the papers of James Cook and journals from Lachlan Macquarie and his wife, Elizabeth. Over there are items belonging to Abel Tasman and Matthew Flinders.'

'Incredible.' Charlotte wasn't sure where to cast her eye. Her lessons at school had been one of the redeeming features of her childhood after her mother and Hilda had passed, and she remembered listening with avid curiosity to her tutors as they taught Australian history and literature. It was just like Alex to present her with a day that would reach deep into the heart of who she was.

'Look here,' he said, as they faced a row of navy blue leather-bound journals. He was behind her and his hand folded around hers, raising it to touch the spines. Her whole body shivered as she felt his chest against her back. 'These are Elizabeth Macquarie's botanical journals. Remember the time you met me at Mrs Macquarie's Chair? She had a fascination for flora, as is evident throughout the Royal Botanic Garden.'

She was in his arms and she took a breath and spun around to face him.

'Charlotte,' he said, reaching up to touch her cheek.

'I think about you all the time,' she blurted.

He smiled. 'I think about you too.'

'I've never felt like this before and I'm confused. I don't know what to do about it. Tell me, what should I do?'

Alex was staring at her so intently her heart almost stopped. 'I want to kiss you.'

'Then kiss me.'

He drew her to him and pressed his lips against hers. The feel of him on her flayed her open and grounded her all at the same time. She returned the kiss timidly at first, but then with more fervour, trying to drink him in.

His hands were on her back, beneath her coat, and she could feel his fingers clenching the fabric of her dress, bringing her closer still, and she wanted to be close, as close as she could be, because for months she'd been at arm's length, conflicted with feelings that had battled inside her.

'I want you in ways I shouldn't,' he said against her lips.

'I don't belong to him,' she whispered back.

'Some would say you do.'

She could hear the tiniest tremor in his voice, as though the thought caused pain and she knew he felt it too, the confusion about what they were doing and what November would bring, that these last few months could well be the end of it.

The thought made her wrap her arms around his neck and hold onto him tighter, to want him more deeply, to graze her lips against his and savour every moment before it was once again time to go home.

'I don't want you to get into trouble, Charlotte. If your father found out about us...' He rested his forehead on hers. 'I don't care for me. I care what will happen to you.'

'He won't find out.'

'What about your friend, Mrs Mayfair? She almost caught us at the bridge.'

'She knows,' Charlotte said. 'She questioned me all the way down to the ferry and finally got it out of me.'

Alex pulled away, looking agonised. 'You told her?'

'I couldn't help it. She was persistent, as Estelle can be. And it's not like she didn't have an inkling anyway. She's been suspicious for weeks now.' At Alex's continued anguish, Charlotte tried to placate him. 'Don't worry. She won't say anything.'

'Because if she did...'

'She won't. She's my friend.'

He still looked uncertain.

'I don't want these last months to be shadowed with doubt. I want to make the most of them.' She traced her finger down his cheek, trying to get him to smile. 'Please. Will you make these the happiest days?'

His expression relaxed; his eyes determined. 'I will make them the happiest of your life, my darling.'

'Then I have my next clue.' She brought her lips to his ear and whispered.

His eyes widened. 'Are you sure, Charlotte?'

'Yes.'

He nestled into her, holding her so tight her breath almost left her. 'Then I'll tell you where I'll be. Tomorrow at two.'

CHAPTER
29

Walter's mood had not lifted the next morning.

'What are your plans today?' he barked at Charlotte over breakfast.

'I was thinking of taking a trip to Pitt Street to look at the shops.' It was a blatant lie but she couldn't tell him she was meeting Alex and, strangely, she didn't feel all that guilty about it. Not after his treatment of her the day before. She was rebelling, perhaps, but she was also an adult, the only one in the house apparently, if his petulant behaviour was anything to go by.

'Make sure you're home by five.' His eyes didn't leave the paper.

'Why, what's at five?'

'Just don't be late.'

He left shortly after that, to where, Charlotte had no idea. She pottered around the house, tending to the washing and dusting, the chores that had once given her purpose but now seemed like a waste of her day when there was a world to explore outside.

After lunch, she dressed and slipped on her coat, checking her reflection in the mirror above her dressing table. A familiar swirl of butterflies erupted in her belly and she pressed her hand against her navel to calm them.

At one-thirty, she left the house and walked to the tram stop at Circular Quay. She boarded a tram bound for Five Ways in Paddington, tapping the driver on the shoulder once they began to move.

'Excuse me, sir.' She showed him the address Alex had given her. 'Is there a tram stop near this address?'

He squinted at the paper. 'Indeed there is, miss. That address is right by Five Ways, near the Royal Hotel.'

'Thank you.' She sat on a seat, placed her hands in her lap and fixed her eyes on the streets and buildings gliding by outside. They rounded Saint Mary's Cathedral and the tram clattered towards Oxford Street and the Eastern Suburbs. At Paddington, the tram curved around Glenmore Road, eventually slowing at a large intersection where five streets cascaded in different directions.

'Five Ways, Paddington,' the tram conductor called over his shoulder. 'This is your stop, miss. And the Royal Hotel is right over there.' He pointed to a cream building wrapped around a steep corner.

She thanked him and alighted from the tram, watching it roll away towards Edgecliff. Drawing a deep breath, she crossed the intersection, heading towards the Royal Hotel and was surprised to see Alex already waiting for her. She ran straight into his arms, far enough from home to feel a sense of anonymity.

He held her close, pressing his face into her hair as though they hadn't just seen each other the day before. 'I'm so happy you're here. Did you have trouble finding it?'

'Not at all.'

'You're quite the confident traveller now,' he said with a touch of pride. He tucked her hand into the crook of his elbow and they walked down Broughton Street, fringed with neat, narrow terraces painted in blues and greys. Chimney pots and attic windows dotted the rooflines.

'So this is where you live,' she said as they walked.

'Yes, for the past four years. There are mostly young families here, which is nice. It's just far enough from the razor gangs in Darlinghurst to be peaceful.'

He stopped outside a pale blue terrace and opened the gate for her. At the front door, he fished a key out of his pocket, turned it in the lock and swung it open. She stepped through the threshold of his home. Jarrah timber floors ran the length of the hallway, down to the back of the terrace. The layout was similar to that of her own house on Playfair Street, although smaller. There was a library filled with books but no parlour or dining room, just a kitchen that led out to a little courtyard and a narrow staircase that climbed upwards to the second floor.

The hallway walls were decorated with photographs of the Sydney Harbour Bridge in various stages of construction, and some of Alex with Dr Bradfield and other members of the public works department. Everything was neat and minimally furnished, exactly how she'd imagined Alex's house would look.

'Do you live here alone?' she asked, shrugging out of her coat and removing her gloves, placing them on the kitchen table with her hat and handbag.

'Yes. Just me.'

'It's a lovely home.'

They shared a smile, then Alex seemed unsure of what to do. He ran a hand nervously through his hair. 'Shall I fix us some tea?'

'That would be nice.'

He prepared a tray and set it out in the courtyard on a small table. When they were seated, he poured.

Charlotte brought the cup to her lips. 'My father's upset with me,' she said, setting it back on the saucer.

Alex's face fixed in concern. 'How so?'

'He's cross that I haven't done anything about the wedding. November's getting closer but I can't seem to get started. I just don't have it in me.' She shook her head, felt on the verge of tears.

Alex's hand went over hers. 'I know it's difficult. Perhaps Mrs Mayfair can help you.'

'I can't do it. I don't want to marry him.'

'Your father isn't going to let you off the hook. There's so much more at stake than just hurting Floyd's feelings.'

'My father wants long-term security for the company. I understand that. But when did that become my burden to carry? The company is doing fine. One day, James might even come home to run it. The company will survive without me having to marry Floyd.'

Alex pulled his lips into a thin line.

'What is it?'

'The company won't survive, Charlotte.'

Surprise choked her words so they sounded hoarse. 'What do you mean?'

He leant forward and took her hands in his. 'It's what I was trying to tell you at the bridge the other day. Before Estelle arrived.'

She watched him carefully.

'Your father has a gambling problem, a terrible one. He's gambled all the company profits away. He's gambled every cent and has nothing left to run the steel mill or the foundry with. Workers have been striking, they haven't been paid in weeks. Production has stopped. It's a mess.'

The blood drained from Charlotte's face.

'Floyd has been propping him up with bank loans, lots of them, but your father has gambled those away too. Bradfield is livid. He's about to void your contract. Your family will be left with nothing if your marriage to Floyd doesn't go ahead.'

Charlotte gripped the edge of the table, anchoring herself as Alex's small courtyard tilted around her. 'I'm marrying Floyd to save the company from going under?'

'Yes.'

'I thought I was marrying him so that a male could take on the Australian operations and my father could retire.'

'It's bigger than that. There won't be a business in a few months' time if you don't marry him. The contract with the bridge will be over and you'll be plunged into bankruptcy. I suspect Floyd's been feeding your father these loans knowing full well he can't control himself with the money, purposely sinking you into debt. Then, with your hand in marriage, Floyd can assume full control. Once that happens, nothing will stop him convincing your father to transfer the deeds.'

'But the company is James' to inherit.' Her hands were still in Alex's and they began to tremble.

'Floyd wants it and he will bankrupt you if he doesn't get it. The bank will take your house, your car, your family's assets, including the Middlesbrough mill. He's got your father right where he wants him.'

Charlotte gulped. How could she have been so stupid? How could she not have seen the signs? Her father's recurrent trips to the races and card games, the innocent bets here and there, the missing items around the house which she was now certain he'd pawned. The antique carriage clock and her mother's precious bone china set, the few things she had left of her, almost certainly gone.

She wasn't wise to the world at all. She hadn't seen what had been in front of her the whole time, her father gambling their entire fortune away, Floyd signing over loan after loan. He hadn't just handed her father the noose, he'd placed it around his neck.

'I'm so sorry, my darling,' Alex said. 'Are you okay? Can I fetch you some water?'

'I just need a minute,' she said. 'Do you have a washroom?'

'It's upstairs.' Alex helped her to her feet and held her hand, leading her back into the kitchen and up the staircase to the second floor. He showed her the washroom and she stepped inside, closing the door behind her.

She glanced in the mirror over the vanity and let out a shaky breath. Anger and betrayal swirled like a cyclone. Any hope of delaying the wedding or changing her father's mind had been dashed. Their motive was clear—marrying Floyd was not simply about strengthening the company's foundation for future generations, it was to save it from ruin by her father's own hand. And if Alex was right, it was already on the brink of collapse.

She splashed cold water on her face, patted it dry with a towel hanging by the sink and opened the door.

Alex was waiting in the hall. He looked heartbroken for her. 'Are you all right?'

'I'm not sure,' she said. 'I think I'm still in shock.'

'Would you like me to walk you back to the tram stop?'

She shook her head. 'I don't want to go home. Can I stay here with you?'

He reached for her hand. 'Of course you can.' He pulled her close to him and held her and she wrapped her arms around his neck. She felt safe when he was near, like she could blot out the world with his kindness and sincerity.

She felt his hands stroke her back and she pulled away to meet his eyes. It was an attraction that had been there since the first day she'd met him, one that had worked its way under her skin and into her heart. She loved him, she realised with perfect clarity. She loved him more than she'd loved anyone.

He sensed her need, dipping his head to meet her lips and he kissed her so passionately, her breath caught in her lungs. She returned it with everything she had, an urgent and aching need for him overwhelming her senses.

He stepped backwards through the doorway of his bedroom.

Charlotte fumbled with the buttons on his shirt so that Alex could slip it off, her hands finding his bare skin underneath. He shuddered at her touch and drew her closer. She offered her lips to him and he pressed himself down on them again with crushing need, too long denying what had always felt natural.

They stumbled back towards his bed, Alex helping her slide her dress up over her waist and shoulders, dropping it to the floor, leaving her in her petticoat and stockings. She hesitated, never having been seen in her adult flesh like this by anyone.

'We don't have to,' Alex said gently. 'We can stop if you like.'

She swallowed and shook her head, sliding the petticoat off and rolling her stockings down over her legs and feet. Alex stroked her collarbone, circling her breasts and forging a path to her hips where she sucked in her breath. Her head tipped back and he kissed her neck until their breathing came in short, sharp bursts and she couldn't stop, didn't want to stop.

'One day, my love, I will find a way to make you mine,' he said, unpinning her hair and letting it unravel. 'Whether it's in this lifetime or the next.'

'Promise me,' she said.

'I promise you.'

Then, in a moment that seemed to stretch forever, that belonged only to them, he laid her down on the bed and made love to her, as gently and exquisitely as the letters they wrote.

***

When Charlotte woke, it took her a moment to realise where she was. The sun had already set and the room was dark. Open French doors led to a small balcony and a cool breeze ruffled the curtains.

She lay on a pillow, her hair fanned out around her, a light brown sheet pulled up to her waist. Footsteps sounded on the staircase, then Alex was in the doorway. He wore trousers only, his bare chest reminding her of what they had shared in his bed only hours before.

He carried a cup of tea to the small side table next to her, then leant down and kissed her. 'You slept so soundly, my love, I didn't want to wake you.'

She stretched, then sat up, pulling the covers to her chest. 'I must have needed it.'

He sat on the edge of the bed beside her and played with the curls that fell over her shoulders. 'Your hair is beautiful. I've never seen it out before.'

'It's not the ways of a lady to wear her hair unpinned.'

'If you were my wife, you could wear it any way you wanted to.'

She smiled, then it fell away, reminded again that she would never be his wife. Alex had promised to make her his, but could any amount of promises erase what Floyd and her father had done? Her whole future had been signed away as a means to repay a debt, like another household item pawned.

'You're thinking something sad,' Alex said, stroking her cheek. 'I can see it on your face.'

'I've decided if I have to marry Floyd, if there is no way out of it, then I'll do it for my father, but I won't consummate the marriage and I'll take you as my lover. I'll spend every night in your bed.'

Alex's smile was full of love and heartache. 'I could never let you tarnish your reputation like that.'

'I don't care about my reputation.'

He sighed deeply but said no more.

A clock downstairs chimed the hour and Charlotte started. 'What time is it?'

'Seven o'clock.'

'I have to go.' She kicked the sheet away and climbed off the bed. 'My father gave me a curfew this morning. I was to be home by five. He'll be furious.'

'I'll walk you to the tram stop. They should still be running.'

She pulled on her stockings and petticoat and Alex found her dress. She hurriedly slipped into it and pinned her hair, and they dashed down the stairs together. On the kitchen table she found her coat, gloves, hat and handbag, and Alex led her out the door and onto the street.

It was an agonising fifteen minutes until the next tram rattled along the tracks to halt outside the Royal Hotel. Alex kissed her and they held each other before she climbed into the carriage and took a seat at the back. As the tram pulled away, the anxiety caved briefly to the mysterious and pleasurable discovery of becoming a woman. Of becoming Alex's. A moment so achingly perfect she could have burst. Except it was another secret to pile on top of the others.

CHAPTER 30

Her feeling of exhilaration, as swiftly as it arrived, was soon defeated. By the time the tram reached Oxford Street, Charlotte's hands were clenched tightly in her lap. Her father had instructed her to be home by five o'clock, and the idea of him pacing the parlour waiting for her caused her knuckles to turn white. Perhaps he'd been delayed at a card game and was not yet home either. She berated herself for wishing such a distraction.

She finally reached Playfair Street and let herself into the house, hanging her coat and hat and setting her bag and gloves on the hall table beside the telephone, in the spot her mother's carriage clock once stood. Her heart broke at its absence. Voices drifted from the parlour and she glanced up, following them to the doorway.

Her father was standing by the lit fireplace, a glass of brandy in his hand, burnished copper in the firelight, talking to Estelle, who was sitting on one end of the Chesterfield, wearing a glossy mink stole, long legs crossed, a polite smile on her bright lips. Draped over the opposite end of the lounge was an ivory satin gown that made Charlotte's heart squeeze in her chest.

Walter saw her in the doorway and Estelle, who had noticed his attention shift, stood and faced her too, her hands wringing nervously.

'Well, it's almost eight o'clock.' He snapped open his pocket watch. 'You're three hours late. What do you have to say for yourself?'

Charlotte looked from her father to Estelle. 'I went for a walk. Time got away from me.'

'Time got away from you?' The look on his face told her that he didn't believe it for a second, but it also seemed he had no idea about Alex. 'We'll talk about it later. Come in and sit down.'

Charlotte stepped into the room. She didn't sit, instead eyed the ivory satin dress with its slender bias cut and tea-length hem, a long veil of embroidered flowers resting beside it.

'Mrs Mayfair graciously leant me her time today to help select a gown for your wedding.'

Charlotte glanced at Estelle, who wouldn't quite meet her eyes.

'We also spoke to the minister at Garrison Church and arranged a lunch at the Coffee Palace.'

'I told you I'd have a dress made,' Charlotte said, staring at the boutique-bought gown.

'And when were you planning to do that?' her father challenged. 'You've had months to get started and haven't done a damn thing.'

Estelle cleared her throat. 'Walter, may I offer a suggestion? Perhaps Charlotte needs more time to adjust. This is still a lot for her to take in, especially as she's lacked female guidance most of her life.' She smiled demurely at him. 'Couldn't you and Mr Clark afford her an extra six months? I'm sure that's all she needs.'

'There will be no delaying this wedding,' he said sharply.

Estelle flinched.

'My father has a deadline, you see,' Charlotte said, the wedding dress and her father's behaviour stirring something brave inside her. 'The company finances have got away from him.'

Walter turned puce, the jowls under his chin quivering.

Estelle's uncertain eyes darted between them both. 'You know, I've just realised the time. Perhaps I should be going.' She collected her handbag and gloves from the Chesterfield and nodded at Walter. 'Good evening, Mr Greene.'

'Mrs Mayfair.'

Charlotte left the parlour to walk Estelle to the front door.

Once there, Estelle gave her an apologetic look. 'I'm sorry, darling. I had no idea he was going to ask me to help him with those things. Otherwise, I would have made an excuse when he telephoned.'

'It wasn't your fault.'

'He invited me out to lunch. I met him here, but he took me straight to the Garrison, then the Coffee Palace, then to buy your gown. Your father and Floyd have already agreed on the wedding date. Saturday, November thirtieth. Oh darling, you must be firm with him now if you don't intend to go through with it.'

'He won't listen.'

'Make him.'

She shook her head helplessly. Before today, she'd had hope of changing his mind, but not now. *He's gambled every cent and has nothing left...*

'Where were you tonight?' Estelle searched her face with questioning eyes. When Charlotte looked away guiltily, she nodded. 'I see. The engineer.' She pursed her lips. 'Talk to your father. Make him understand this wedding can't go ahead.'

She held Charlotte close, then she opened the door and stepped out onto the street, her heels clicking along the pavement until she disappeared into the haze of mist and street lights.

Charlotte closed the door behind her and returned to the parlour. Her father was facing the fireplace, his back to her, sipping his brandy.

'Did you really gamble all our money away?' she asked.

He half-turned but wouldn't meet her gaze. 'We've had some financial difficulties, yes.'

'How much do we have left?'

She heard his sigh, deep and tired. 'It's the recession.'

'It's not the recession.' Her voice rose and quivered. 'You don't even believe one is coming, so don't lie to me. How much do we have left?'

His shoulders fell like someone broken. 'Nothing. There's nothing left.'

Charlotte sank into the Chesterfield. 'When did you last pay our workers?'

'Months ago.'

'What about the loan money Floyd has been giving you?'

He turned to look at her completely this time. 'How do you know about all this? Who's been talking to you?'

She stared him down, resolved to show him it didn't matter how she'd found out, that he'd betrayed her with his weakness, his inability to exercise a shred of self-control.

He nodded resolutely. 'The workers, I imagine. It was only a matter of time before they spoke out. They're upset, on strike, production has stopped. They have families to feed. And Bradfield is calling me constantly for the next order.'

'Where has all the money gone?'

He shrugged. 'The cards, races, boxing matches down at The Hungry Mile. I place bets, I win big, I bet higher, I lose it all. I try again.' He swallowed, his eyes bloodshot with the weight of his troubles. 'I can't seem to stop myself.'

'And my mother's chinaware? The carriage clock?'

He hung his head. 'Gone.'

Charlotte's hand went to her mouth. She had known, yes, but his admission was like a blade to the heart. He'd stolen from her, sold away things that could never be replaced. 'Was it worth it?' she asked through thinly veiled disappointment. 'Stealing from me.'

'I got a pittance for them.'

'And now you want to pawn me off in the same way.'

His eyes turned pleading. 'Floyd will save us from going under. You don't have to love him. You don't even have to like him. All I'm asking is that you do this for our family so that we don't lose everything.'

'Why don't we just give him the company?' she said. 'If he wants it that badly, he can have it. Then I won't have to marry him.'

'I'm not giving it away. I've worked too hard for it, built it from the ground up. It's Greene Steel and it will remain Greene Steel. The deeds stay within the family. I only want Floyd to take the financial matters out of my hands. I can't be trusted with them.'

'Then a year down the track, he'll go for the deeds. He'll take everything from us. He's the one who can't be trusted. Don't you see that?'

Walter shook his head sadly.

'What does James think of all this?'

'I haven't told him yet.'

'You mean he doesn't know?' She should hardly be surprised. Her father was too proud to confess to her brother the predicament he'd resigned them to. Better to let his heir believe all was fine and trade off his daughter instead.

'He doesn't and I don't want him to. I need him to focus on the business in England. And Floyd will be based here. It's a good solution. We just need you to do your part now.'

Charlotte stood. 'I'm writing to James. He needs to know what's happening.'

Walter set his glass of brandy down on the mantel and in one solid stride he was beside her. He reached for her arm, not in a show of aggression, but in an authoritative manner. 'Charlotte, you're emotional and you're a woman. I don't expect you to understand this. Let Floyd and me handle it. Show some interest in the wedding. That's how you can help.'

She wrenched her hand away and left the parlour, taking the wretched wedding gown and veil with her. Up in her room, she opened the large Edwardian chest and pulled out the jade-green dress that Floyd had given her, the one-of-a-kind piece he'd made her wear to the Governor's Ball in April. She still remembered the repulsive kiss he'd planted on her in the governor's garden. The thin, wet lips and wiry moustache that had defiled her. How different from the soft touch of Alex.

She thought of poor Estelle, who'd been caught in the middle, grateful she hadn't exposed Charlotte's secret, angry at her father for the position he'd put them all in and loathing Floyd, who was destroying her family. Once they married, he wouldn't stop at the simple management of daily operations. He would move to take over the Greene empire, to rip the floor right out from under James and her father. Give him an inch and he'd take a mile and leave them with nothing.

Charlotte folded the wedding gown and veil and placed them in the chest, lying the jade-green dress over the top of it and closing the lid. She'd never hated anyone before, but her heart was full of hate for Floyd.

***

It didn't seem to matter that Charlotte had confronted her father about his gambling ways. The next week saw little change. Walter was avoiding Bradfield and the foundry, so he spent his days at the mill instead. He always left early, before she woke, and stumbled home with empty pockets well after midnight. She had no doubt where he ended up after the mill closed at five—a shady card game at a sly grog shop or an underground cockfight on the wrong side of town, anywhere he might seek to further his money.

This saddened Charlotte, but she was resolved not to sit at home and wait for him, to obligingly prepare a meal he wouldn't eat or to dwell on what she couldn't change. No amount of pleading or chastising would change his actions. She left each afternoon for Alex's house, where she met him after his day on the bridge. In his bed, she could escape the troubles of home.

On a blustery day that threatened rain, she stepped off the tram and hurried along Broughton Street off Five Ways to his house. She knocked and he was at the door immediately, picking her up and swinging her around, carrying her backwards into the hallway. His kisses were immediate, on her lips, her face, her neck, the twenty-four hours since they'd last seen each other too great a time to endure now that they knew what it felt like to properly be with one another.

In his room, he laid her down on his bed, taking the time to gently remove her clothes, unrolling her stockings with the gentlest touch, slipping her petticoat off like a whisper. 'I've missed you,' he said.

She met his eyes, felt swallowed by them. 'I always miss you, even when I'm with you.'

His bedroom had become a sanctuary, a place she could love and be loved, a world away from her fractured life and the deceit that had invaded her existence. Everything about Alex was pure and true, his love for her clearly pronounced in the way he made love to her, the way he drew her to him afterwards and held her close until she had to reluctantly pull herself away to return home.

And now, as he brought them both to the kind of pleasure she'd had no idea their bodies could reach, she sighed and he rolled onto his back, gathering her up in his arms. 'Are you happy, my love?' he asked, his voice low in her ear.

She pressed herself closer to him, resting her head on his chest. 'Yes. So happy that it scares me.'

He didn't reply and she could almost hear his thoughts whirring in the quiet room. They were her thoughts too. The week of afternoons they'd spent together brought only temporary peace, a sliver of a moment in which they could disappear until reality presented itself again.

After some time Alex spoke. 'We lost a man today.'

She looked up at the pained expression on his face. 'Where? How?'

'On the bridge. He was at the top of the southern arch, working alongside the crane. He lost his footing. Just like that.'

Charlotte was speechless.

'They recovered his body from the water. I had to call his family. He had a wife and small child.'

'Will they be all right?'

'They'll receive an additional week's salary, but who knows after that.' Alex's chest rose and fell with his sorrow. 'I knew him. He was only a young lad. A hard worker, his whole life ahead of him. He came to work this morning and never went home.'

Charlotte closed her eyes and laid her head back down, her heart heavy. 'I worry about you being up there. What if you fall too?'

'I'm not up there every day.'

'But you do go up. You've told me so. What if you lose your footing, if the crane strikes you or the wind is too strong? I couldn't...' She buried deeper into him.

He kissed the top of her head. 'I'll be careful, my love. You don't have to worry.'

But despite Alex's words of reassurance, Charlotte couldn't find comfort. She was sure that young man who had lost his life had been careful too. He would have known the top of the bridge like his own hand, where to step and where not to. All it had taken was one wrong move and he'd fallen.

She held Alex a little closer after that, feeling his sense of loss as keenly as if it were her own. And when they made love again before she left, she was more attentive, more giving, taking him and all that hurt inside her.

Later that night, on the tram ride home, it occurred to her how invested she had become in Alex. It was fierce and unrivalled, like nothing she'd felt before or would ever feel again, she was certain. It meant the real chance of loss, of a greater height to fall from, of her world collapsing if anything should happen to him. She loved him that much; a first love, a true love. Marrying Floyd might have been terrifying, but it was what she felt for Alex that kept her up at night.

CHAPTER 31

PAIGE
Present Day

The piles destined for the thrift store and rubbish had been taken away and the attic was looking cleaner than it had in decades. The Greenes' items were neatly stacked by the attic door, waiting transportation to the London address Ryan's secretary had sent, and all that remained were the cobwebs, dust and the few pieces she was saving for display downstairs in their new reception area.

Paige was pushing a broom through the muck on the floor when her phone rang in her back pocket. It was Ryan. 'Hi,' she said, surprised.

'Hey, what are you doing?'

'Sweeping.'

'I found that place in France. Where the letter was sent from.' He sounded excited. 'It's a country residence, a cottage in a small town called Ovillers-la-Boiselle. It's north of Paris, right in the heart of Somme.'

'Wow. Okay.' Paige set the broom against the wall. 'And you think James might have sent it from there?'

'I don't know. I checked with my grandfather. He said James had a few properties in France but he's not sure about some of the locations. Somme could be one of them.'

'Is there any way we can confirm it?'

'I'm working on it. But I do know who lives there now.'

'Who?'

'A Miss Delphine Beaumont.'

'Not Greene?' Paige asked hopefully.

'No, not Greene.'

'How did you find this out?'

'I've been researching all night.'

Paige glanced at her watch. It was eleven in the morning in Sydney. 'What time is it there?'

'Two am.'

'God, you must be exhausted. Go to bed and we can speak later when you get up.'

'Meet me in Paris.'

Paige almost fell over. 'What?'

'Meet me in Paris. We'll take a drive out to this Ovillers place, we'll find out who Delphine Beaumont is and if she can shed any light on who sent this envelope.'

'Ryan...' It was a crossroad they'd been at before, one that hadn't ended so well.

'I know it sounds crazy.'

'It's the timing. I have the launch in three weeks. And I don't have a passport.'

'Apply for one today, mark it urgent. Then meet me in Paris next week, just for a few days, and I'll have you back in Sydney before the launch.'

'I don't know,' she said.

'Paige, I want you to do this with me. We started it together. We should finish it together.'

She leant against the wall, considering his words. Maybe he was right. They had started it together. Ovillers might hold the key to the mystery sender or it might hold nothing at all, but the thought of discovering it in person, after all they'd accomplished so far, was greatly tempting. And it was a chance to see Ryan again, even though she knew she shouldn't think that.

'I'll have to speak to Xavier.'

Ryan gave a whoop.

'No promises. If he hates the idea, you'll have to go without me.'

'I won't go without you.'

She smiled at the unexpectedness of his words.

***

'France?'

'Yes. I found the envelope in the attic from a sender in Ovillers-la-Boiselle, a town in Somme. It was addressed to Charlotte and arrived here shortly after she died in 1930. Whoever sent it must not have known she was deceased.'

Xavier turned the envelope over in his hands. 'So who sent it?'

'We think it was her brother, James. It's the only possible explanation. He wouldn't have known she'd died and the Greenes had property in France, quite likely that house.'

Xavier was quiet, eyes skimming over the sender's address. 'So where's the letter that was inside? What does it say?'

'We don't have it. It wasn't inside the envelope and I went back up to the attic to see if it was there, but it's not.'

Xavier smiled ruefully. 'So you don't have the letter, you don't know who the sender was and you don't know if it helps your cause at all. I'm not sure if you've uncovered some great mystery here or if you're embarking on a wild goose chase.'

'Agree, it's a long shot.'

'And you want to go all the way to France for it?'

'Well, if I got my passport in time, I could leave next week,' Paige explained. 'I could spend a few days there at most and be back before the launch. I'd take my laptop with me, keep up with my work so I don't fall behind.'

Xavier was silent.

'I know it's not convenient. A terrible idea, in fact, this close to the launch date.' She hated asking, could only imagine what Xavier was thinking. 'If you don't want me to go, just say it and I'll stay.'

He gave her a long and steady look. 'It's not ideal,' he said. 'And I'll be in an absolute flap without you.'

Paige held her breath.

'But we do have some new people starting soon. I'm sure if you hand everything over to us, we could manage for a few days.'

'I could do that.'

'And you'd have to be on call, whatever the time, in case we need you.'

She nodded emphatically. 'Any time, day or night. Just call me.'

He sighed and looked at the envelope again. 'Then I guess it's a yes from me. Of course you can go.'

She flung her arms around his neck and hugged him so tightly he began to choke. 'Sorry. Sorry.' She let him go. 'I promise I'll do a thorough handover. I won't leave any loose ends. I'll make sure everything is ready before I go.'

'I know you will, darling.' He smiled. 'You're excited, aren't you?'

'I've never been overseas before.'

'No, I mean about seeing Ryan again.'

She sucked in a tiny breath, the excitement of the morning almost too much for her, and even though she wasn't prone to emotional outbursts, she thought she might dissolve into tears. 'I'm trying not to be. I think he has a girlfriend now.'

***

Her urgent application for a new passport was fulfilled three days later. She booked her return ticket to Paris for the following Friday, which gave her just enough time to vacate the parlour for the editing team to move in, store her belongings in the freshly-cleaned attic, send the Greenes' precious antiques to the UK and hand over her work to Xavier.

On the morning of her flight, she sat across from him in his office, running through her handover one last time.

'I'm trying not to panic,' he said.

'Just remember the editors are starting this week, the design team next week. All their welcome packs are in that box over there.' She pointed to a cardboard box in the corner of his office. 'If they don't have much to do in the first few days, have them follow up on RSVPs for the launch. If you want manuscripts to work on, we'll need as many authors and agents to attend as possible.'

Xavier made notes on a pad beside him. 'Anything else?'

'Only that I'll be online at every possible opportunity, so email or call if you need me. Other than that, everything's done.'

'Thanks to you.' He shook his head. 'I couldn't have done any of this without you. You've made my dream possible.'

'And you gave me a new beginning.' She thought back to the day she had first arrived with little more than a suitcase and a broken heart, the city so bewildering, so far from home, she'd worried she'd never adapt. Gone now was that girl who'd doubted every decision she'd ever made, who'd been beaten down by rejection. She was confident and happier, and she knew that no matter where the world took her, she was in the driver's seat.

When emotion uncharacteristically clogged her throat, Xavier stood and walked around to her side of the desk. 'Don't start with the waterworks or you'll get me going.'

'Sorry,' she said, sniffing. 'I don't know what's come over me lately.' She stood too and they hugged.

'I'm going to miss you,' he said.

'I'll only be gone a few days.'

'It will be the longest few days of my life.'

She smiled. 'It might be the quietest, actually. I won't be here to nag you.'

'I like your nagging.'

'You say that now.'

He laughed. 'Go finish packing before I change my mind.'

She took no chances, closing down her laptop and hurrying into the parlour to finish packing her suitcase. There was a train to the international airport departing Circular Quay at two pm, so she lugged her suitcase onto the front step, gave Xavier one last hug, then set off on foot towards the station. She texted Ryan as she walked.

I'm on my way.

***

Sleep on the flight was thin, partly from the thrill of seeing Ryan but also from the turbulence that hit over the Bay of Bengal and didn't ease until the Mediterranean Sea.

Arriving in Paris was like a dream Paige hadn't realised she'd wished for. The day was gloriously blue and crisp, torn clouds sailing across the tip of the Eiffel Tower and the spires of Notre Dame. The taxi carried her to the hotel address Ryan had sent her earlier that week, La Maison Champs Elysée, just off the tree-lined avenue of the same name.

La Maison was quintessentially Parisian, with wrought-iron balconies and grand double front doors. Paige had been adamant about paying for her room but that hadn't stopped her buckling slightly when she'd seen the rate per night. Five star, a stone's throw from the Champs Elysée and Arc de Triomphe, in the heart of Paris. But she'd pushed the concern aside, refusing Ryan's offer to cover the charge, and had handed over her credit card details. Now, standing before it, she was glad. It was worth every cent of her hard-earned money.

The taxi dropped her at the front doors and the concierge was upon her, welcoming her to Paris with a pleasant accent and taking her suitcase from the boot. He led her into the foyer and pointed to a large marble reception desk where she could check in.

'I'll just text my friend,' she said. 'He's already here.'

'Do you mean Monsieur Greene?'

Paige was surprised. 'Yes, that's right.'

The concierge beamed. 'He is our special guest here. We see him often. He mentioned earlier that he was expecting you. Come this way.' He indicated towards a bank of elevators. 'He has already checked you in and is waiting upstairs.'

She followed him through the lobby as he rolled her suitcase behind him. At the lifts, he pressed the button for her and smiled politely. 'Monsieur Greene is in room four-eleven and you are adjoining him in room four-twelve.'

The doors opened and they stepped inside. He pressed the button for level four, the doors closed and they glided upwards. The elevator was smooth, soft opera playing from the ceiling. Paige felt a twinge of exhausted excitement. She was unsure of the time in both Paris and Sydney, her body clock humming to a strange imbalance.

On the fourth floor, the elevator doors chimed open and the concierge led her to room eleven, knocking on the door. A moment later, Ryan opened it and broke into a wide grin. 'Paige. You made it!'

'I'm here,' she said, not sure whether to hug him or shake his hand.

He seemed unsure too, glancing at the concierge with a smile. '*Merci*, Emile.'

'*Vous êtes les bienvenus*, Monsieur Greene.'

Emile retreated down the corridor and Ryan held the door wider for Paige, allowing her in and taking hold of her suitcase. 'How are you? How was the flight?'

'A little bumpy, but otherwise good.'

'You must be tired.'

'I'm not sure what I am at the moment.' She looked around the room with its white marble bathroom, queen-sized bed and small lounge area. The balcony doors were open and she stepped out onto it, a view of the Eiffel Tower greeting her. She squealed at the sight.

Ryan laughed behind her. 'Great, isn't she?'

'Just beautiful.'

'Made of iron rather than steel.'

'Really? I didn't know that.'

He leant against the balcony railing to gaze out too. 'Even though steel was available, Mr Eiffel chose iron because he was experienced in iron design. It was also, in his words, the best and most robust of materials. They used to puddle the iron, basically stripping it of its carbon content to leave it in its purest form. It could have been a completely different-looking tower had they built it with steel.'

Paige looked out across the green parks and spires of Paris, at the monuments and boulevards and grand avenues. All the pieces were laid out beneath them, like coloured patchworks on a quilt. The balcony was small and Ryan was close beside her, pointing out the River Seine, the Louvre and Versailles. She was aware of every brush of his arm against hers, every moment his hand landed on her back to direct her gaze to something new. Her feelings hadn't changed at all since she'd last seen him. She still felt a quiet rush at his closeness.

'By the way, this door leads to your room,' he said, returning inside and pointing to a closed door beside the television. 'I hope you don't mind that we're adjoined.'

'Not at all. Thank you for organising it.' She followed him in. 'When did you arrive?'

'Late last night. I came after work. Here, take a seat.' He cleared away a jumper and bath towel from the bed and tossed them onto a chair. 'It's good to see you.'

'And you.'

'Did Emile look after you?'

'He did. He was lovely. How do they know you so well?' She sat on the edge of the bed, taking him in. He looked relaxed and tanned, having spent weeks now in a European summer. He wore jeans and a black shirt; hair wet from the shower. Her heart squeezed, remembering what it had felt like to be his. Those fun and easy months, the days they'd spent traipsing around the city, that last week in his bed before she'd decided a life with him would be too difficult.

'I'm a regular,' he said. 'I travel to Paris a lot for work and I always stay here. I used to live here once. Had a place upstairs that I rented for ten months.'

'Oh. Wow.'

'I was setting up a new office around the corner. Anyway, do you want some coffee? The good Parisian stuff.'

'Actually, I might take a raincheck.' She stood. 'I could kill for a shower.'

'Oh, sure. Let me get your bag.' Ryan collected it from beside the settee and unlocked the adjoining door. 'We can grab dinner later if you like. I know lots of good places around here.'

'That'd be great.' She stepped through to her room, a carbon copy of Ryan's.

'Well, have a good rest.'

'Thank you.'

'Shout out if you need anything. I'll be right here.'

She watched him pull the door closed, knowing that if she was going to survive the next few days with him, she'd have to get her feelings in check.

***

Later that night, she knocked on the adjoining door and Ryan opened it.

'How are you feeling?'

'Like I'm in a daze.'

He laughed. 'You'll sleep well tonight. Are you hungry?'

'Starving.'

'I know the perfect place. It's not far.'

She grabbed her bag and they headed down to the lobby and out onto the street. The sun had already sunk below the city, having splashed the sky with lavender on its way down. Ryan led them away from the Champs Elysée towards the Seine, to a small restaurant in a cobbled lane tucked out of sight of the main thoroughfare.

The evening was pleasant so they sat outside and watched the canal boats drift by on the river, the water lit by city lights. They ordered and as they waited for their meals, they sipped wine and ate from the bread basket.

'So how far is Ovillers from Paris?' Paige asked, almost inhaling the bread. She'd spent the afternoon fighting sleep and catching up on emails, snacking only on peanuts and a chocolate bar from her room.

'It's about two hours north of here, depending on traffic.'

'And will we drive?'

'Yes. We'll pick up the rental in the morning.'

'I assume you know how to get there.'

Ryan laughed, that deep wonderful sound she'd missed. 'I do. I even know how to drive on the other side of the road. I used to live here, remember?'

Paige smiled and sat back, letting the bread and wine hit her stomach and relax her. Sleep would come hard and fast later but for now, she was pleasantly sedate. 'So what's our plan? Do we just look around? Do we knock on the door? We might be a surprise for this Delphine Beaumont.'

'I say we knock on the door,' Ryan said. 'Why not? She might have something to share or she might not. It would be a shame to go all that way not to at least knock.'

Paige agreed.

'So how are things back home?' he asked. He played with the stem of his wine glass as though trying to appear nonchalant.

She did the same, picking at a chunk of bread. 'Busy. The launch is in a few weeks.'

'It was good of Xavier to let you come.'

'He was great about it actually.'

'And you?' He finally met her eyes and she saw more than a question there. Regret. 'How have you been?'

She shrugged. 'I have my days.'

Ryan nodded. 'Look, Paige, there's something I've been meaning to tell you.'

The waiter interrupted, arriving with their food, setting plates down in front of them. Napkins were laid, more wine poured, the bread basket refilled. *Bon appétit!*

The waiter retreated and Paige picked up her knife and fork. She didn't want Ryan to explain about his new girlfriend, to tell her that he'd enjoyed their time together, but he'd moved on with someone else. That it was serious and he was happy and to please not get the wrong idea about Paris, for they were solely there for Charlotte. She hadn't had enough wine yet for that conversation.

'Dinner looks delicious,' she announced, tucking straight in, thwarting his opportunity.

He smiled softly and she wasn't sure if it was disappointment or relief that crossed his face.

CHAPTER
32

Paige slept like the dead that night and felt better by the morning when Ryan knocked on the adjoining door.

'Great, you're awake.' He smelt fresh of aftershave and soap. 'It's eight so we should probably hit the road.'

'Ready when you are.'

Twenty minutes later, they were in Ryan's rented Audi, hot coffee and croissants balancing on their laps. The interior smelt of new leather, Ryan at the wheel as he comfortably navigated them through the streets of Paris and out onto the open motorway, heading north towards Somme.

The dense jumble of housing remained with them for the first thirty minutes until it fell away and the road began to wind through open fields green with summer rain. The morning was grey, thick pockets of clouds toying with the sun. An hour into the trip, at Beauvais, a drizzle fell and mist clung to the hills, turning them blue.

Charlotte's chest of love letters rested on the seat in the back. During a stop to stretch their legs and take in fields that reminded Paige of Albury, she brought the chest to the front to sit on her lap. 'Is it all right if I take some of the letters out to read?'

'Of course. They're as much yours as they are mine.'

It was a nice sentiment, even if it wasn't entirely true. She opened the lid and pulled the topmost bundle out, resting the chest on the floor at her feet and setting the letters on her knees. She read quietly to herself, reminded again of the love Charlotte and Alex had shared, their sense of playfulness and adventure, the way they'd relied on written words to express what they'd felt when to utter them was forbidden.

Then she pulled the envelope from the attic out of her bag, protected in a plastic sleeve and she handed it to Ryan.

He glanced at it briefly before handing it back to her, returning his eyes to the road. 'The ink is in poor shape. Must have got caught in the rain at some point. It's too bad we can't compare it to anything.'

'If we had a sample of James' handwriting, we could probably try.'

'What if the letter wasn't from James?' Ryan said. 'What if it was from someone else?'

'Like who?'

'I don't know. Walter?'

She shrugged. 'It's possible. Maybe this is where he disappeared to. France.'

'Or it could have been her friend, Estelle.'

'Also quite likely,' Paige agreed. 'The fact is it could have come from anyone. We don't know the extent of Charlotte's relationships. She might have had a French pen pal for all we know.'

'What intrigues me is that someone had to have intercepted the letter in Sydney,' Ryan said. 'It was sent to the Playfair house, attention to Charlotte, yet someone else opened it, took out the letter and placed the envelope in the chest in the attic. Who would have done that? Where is the letter now?'

'And what did it say?' Paige added. It was all the questions that had circled her head since she'd found the empty envelope.

The car continued to roll north and when they reached the main town of Amiens, divided in two by the Somme River, Ryan drove them through the Quartier Saint-Leu's narrow streets. The sun had found a spot to nestle in between heavy-bottomed clouds, lighting up the cathedral's gothic spires.

'It's a straight run from here to Ovillers. About forty minutes to go,' Ryan said as they returned to the motorway.

The rest of the trip passed by, as did the villages that grew more scattered and infrequent as they went. They finally reached Ovillers-la-Boiselle just before lunch, a small town of four hundred and forty-eight, according to the welcome sign as they entered.

'Such a quiet place,' Paige said.

'Would have been even fewer people than that back in the twenties and thirties,' Ryan said. 'Hardly anyone around at all.'

'And yet, someone from this tiny pocket of the world knew Charlotte.'

As they drove through curving and narrow tree-lined roads, they spotted a huge crater to the east, like a giant had scooped out a massive chunk of earth with a spoon, scars of a Great War which had remained long after the fighting had ceased.

'Can you show me that envelope again?' Ryan asked, pulling to the side of the road and tapping the GPS screen on the Audi's dashboard.

Paige handed him the plastic sleeve.

He turned it over to read the address on the back, then tapped the screen again. 'Judging from the GPS, it's not far from here. Two minutes, tops. But it seems to be down a private road or track.' He pointed to lines on the map. 'Must be deep in the fields.'

He navigated them back onto the road and they bumped along a winding stretch of old gravelly bitumen, with low crumbling walls at the verge. The turnoff for the house came quickly, by a copse of common oaks, and Ryan swung the Audi onto a dirt track. There was an open gate with a letterbox beside it and brambles that ran unchecked along the fence line. The road led down through fields, bordered by large stones and pockmarked where recent rain had filled the holes with muddy pools the colour of dishwater.

They drove for another two minutes, as if to disappear into the horizon, until the track rose and fell over a hill and abruptly ended. Through an opening in a low wall, there was a two-storey house made of grey stone. Patches of yellowing lichen coloured the walls and voracious ivy had stolen over the lintel. The windowsills were white and peeling, the roof steeply pitched and gabled, and chimney pots stood resolute at either end, thin grey smoke twirling out of them.

Ryan parked the car at the side of the house, tires rolling and crunching on the tiny driveway rocks. 'Looks like someone's home if the fireplaces are lit.'

Paige collected Charlotte's chest of letters and the sleeve with the mystery envelope and they climbed out of the car, doors closing with a metallic echo that rolled over the fields, disturbing a flock of birds in some distant part. They walked to the front door and Ryan knocked.

There was soft noise inside, shuffling, then quiet. Ryan raised an eyebrow at Paige, then knocked again. The door opened a fraction.

The sliver of a woman's face appeared; young, with brown eyes and dark hair that fell over one shoulder. '*Oui?*' she said.

Ryan cleared his throat. 'Hello, we're looking for a Miss Delphine Beaumont. Is she home?'

The woman's eye darted back and forth between them. '*Qui êtes vous?*'

'I'm Ryan Greene and this is Paige Westwood. We drove up this morning from Paris, from La Maison Champs Elysée. We're looking for Delphine.'

She remained silent.

'Sorry, do you speak English?' Ryan asked. '*Parlez-vous Anglais?*'

The young woman shrugged, harder to penetrate than the stone wall of a castle.

'Right, we'd like to speak to someone about this house, and a former tenant who used to live here back in the thirties. Can you help us with that?'

They were met again with her deadpan stare.

'Please,' Paige said. 'We're looking for some information about a letter that was sent from this address in 1930. We're keen to know who the sender was.' She balanced the chest of letters in one hand while she held up the envelope with the other.

The woman stared at both the envelope and the chest. '1930? That was a long time ago,' she replied finally, in perfect but heavily-accented English.

'Yes. And we realise it's a long shot,' Ryan said. 'But we thought you might have some information.'

'I'm sorry. I don't know,' she said. 'I can't help you.'

'Wait, how about Delphine? Can she help us?'

'Sorry, no. She cannot.' The door closed in their faces.

Shoulders sagging, they walked back to the car and climbed in as the clouds prevailed and a soft rain began to fall.

'That went well,' Ryan said.

'Maybe she doesn't know anything,' Paige said. 'It *was* almost a century ago.'

'She was kind of rude.'

'She was surprised that two people turned up on her doorstep out of nowhere.'

'Kind of like what I did to you that time?' He gave her a mischievous grin.

She laughed. 'Yes, kind of like that.'

'Except you let me in.' He met her eyes and for a moment, Paige thought he was going to reach across and take her hand. He didn't. Instead, he reached for the ignition button, then the handbrake as he manoeuvred them back down the private track and onto the main road.

***

'It was all a big waste of time, if I'm honest,' Ryan said, letting them into his room at La Maison. 'Not sure it was even worth coming.'

They'd returned to Paris that afternoon, taken the Audi back to the rental depot and strolled along the Champs Elysée, led by the smell of baked baguettes and cheese. Famished, they'd found a place, eaten and had several glasses of red wine, trying to wash the disappointment of the day away, before heading back to the hotel.

'It wasn't a total waste of time,' Paige said, tossing her backpack onto the settee. 'Now we know where the envelope leads to.'

'Yes, some cottage in the middle of Somme where a random woman lives.'

'Did your grandfather have any luck with James' properties in France?'

'There's no record of a Somme residence that he could find. It doesn't mean there wasn't one, we just don't know about it.' Ryan sighed and sat on the edge of his bed. 'I think I'm drunk.'

Paige laughed and dropped down beside him. 'I think I am too.'

'It is nice though. Being drunk in Paris.'

'Yeah, it is.'

They sat that way for a time, as the day slid towards the other side of the world, leaving a burnished sunset behind.

'I'm glad you're here.' His voice was soft. 'That's not the alcohol talking, by the way. Although it does give me the nerve to say it.'

Paige's stomach flipped. 'I'm glad I'm here too. Even though we didn't find out much, it was important to do it for Charlotte.'

'Yes, for Charlotte.'

Their shoulders touched lightly, their knees brushed. Paige wasn't sure whether to call it a day and return to her room or remain there, pretend like their bodies weren't that close, like they were just friends casually talking.

Ryan spoke first. 'Do you wonder what could have been if I'd stayed in Sydney?'

Her heart stumbled on a beat. 'Yes.'

'Or if you'd come to London?'

'All the time.'

His gaze fell to his hands in his lap. 'I thought I'd get home and everything would feel normal again. But it hasn't yet. Far from it.'

She nodded. 'I know.'

He glanced up at her. 'Are you seeing anyone?'

'No. You?'

'No.

Paige was confused. 'But I thought...' The girl who'd been at his house, the comments about moving on.

'What?'

She shook her head. 'Nothing.'

'No, go on. You thought what?'

She felt a blush creep up her neck. 'I thought you'd met someone.'

'Why did you think that?'

'We were on the phone that time and you said a female friend had just left. It was late. I'd assumed she was your new girlfriend.'

Ryan frowned, then chuckled. 'Oh, that was my best friend's wife. She came to pick up his football gear. He'd left it at my place. She was there for fifteen minutes catching up and then left. So no, definitely not someone I was seeing.'

'Oh.' Her blush burned fiercely now. She wanted to run and dive under the settee. 'I'm sorry.'

He was smiling. 'Don't be. I'm glad you asked.'

'So there hasn't been anyone?'

'Not since a girl I met in Sydney.'

All this time she'd imagined Ryan with another woman, had felt hurt at the ease in which she'd thought he'd moved on. To hear that he hadn't, that there had been no one since her, made her feel silly and relieved all at once.

'In fact, nothing has felt right since then.' He took a deep breath and ran a hand through his hair. 'The thing is, I don't think there's room for me in your life. You've just settled into a new city and a new job. Just getting you here to Paris took some planning.'

'Is there room for me in yours? You're busy too.' She spoke gently. It wasn't an accusation.

He nodded. 'To be fair, you're right.' He turned to her. 'I guess what I'm trying to say though, is that we've been here for one day and already I feel like myself again. You have this happy, relaxed way about you. You don't take yourself too seriously and that makes you comfortable to be around. I've never met anyone like that before. And so, when I'm not with you, I feel, well... not all that happy.'

The alcohol had certainly loosened his tongue. Paige tried not to beam at his words.

'So what I'm trying to say is that I still feel something. And it's not going away. And I don't know what to do about it because we're so insistent on making it more complicated than it needs to be.'

Her fight for composure was lost. Elation burst out of her and she broke into a wide grin.

'Is that a happy smile?' he asked.

She nodded emphatically.

'That's good.' He looked pleased. 'Happy smiles are good.'

'Since we don't have anywhere to be tomorrow, maybe we could spend the day together in Paris,' she suggested,' before I have to go home.'

'I'd love that,' he said. 'We could rent the car again. I could show you a few places. Maybe even hold your hand?'

Her belly fluttered. '*Only* if you hold my hand.'

He glanced at her and when their eyes met, they dissolved into teenage giggles.

'All right, I think it's time for bed,' she said. 'I'm still jetlagged.'

'Right you are. I will stop talking drunken nonsense.'

She chuckled and stood, reaching for her backpack on the settee. 'Breakfast tomorrow?'

'I'll be ready.' He stood too and leant in to kiss her softly on the cheek.

Back in her room, Paige felt warmth spread through her like a sure and giddy thing as she undressed and stepped into the shower. The day may have yielded disappointing results when it came to Delphine Beaumont and the sender of the letter, but they'd managed to make progress on that other mystery. The one of Paige and Ryan. The way forward was still unclear, fraught with a complicated geography, but there was hope, and that was as good a start as any.

She climbed out of the shower, dried her hair and wrapped the towel around her. When she opened the door, she jumped when she saw Ryan sitting on the edge of her bed. 'Goodness, you scared me.'

He grinned sheepishly. 'I'm sorry. I just need one more minute. I thought of something else to tell you.'

She went to him and wrapped her arms around his neck.

He sucked in his breath. 'Paige.'

She put her finger to his lips and let her towel drop to the floor. His hands were on her instantly, running up her bare thighs, pulling her close to him and kissing her so intensely she ran out of breath. They were lips she knew well, hands that understood her body, a man she'd grown to love more than anything.

She removed his shirt as he kissed her wet skin, devouring every inch of her. His hands found her breasts, her waist, the space between her legs. She pushed him backwards on the bed and he took her with him, refusing to let her go. And never did she want him to again.

The time for words was over.

CHAPTER
33

The next morning, Paige awoke to the pleasurable feeling of Ryan in her bed. She rolled over, pushing her hair aside and watched him as he slept—the grey shadow of day-old stubble on his face and long lashes that swept the top of his cheeks. He was beautiful in repose, a strong jawline and full lips that she'd enjoyed kissing most of the night. Her heart felt full, her body pleasantly tired, her arms wanting to close the space between them because in two days, when she returned home, there would be oceans of space again.

He opened a sleepy eye and smiled. 'You're staring at me.'

She blushed. 'I'm sorry. You're nice to stare at.'

'As are you.' He pulled her to him. 'Did you sleep well?'

'I'm not sure either of us did a great deal of sleeping, but yes.'

He kissed her softly and she rolled onto him, her hair falling around his face. He pushed it to the side, his hands and eyes travelling up and down her body. 'You make me so happy.'

'Four days together hardly seems fair.'

'No, it's quite like torture,' he said with a wry smile.

'What are we going to do about Delphine and the house in Ovillers?'

He ran his hand through her hair, letting it slip between his fingers. 'I'm not sure there's much we can do. We know what happened to Charlotte and Alex. That might be as far as the story takes us.' He brought her down to his lips, grazing them along her neck. 'I hope you're not hungry.'

'I *was* thinking about coffee,' she murmured.

'I had something else in mind actually.'

'Like what?'

He kissed her long and slow, rolled her onto her back and showed her what he meant.

***

An hour later they rose and, while Ryan showered, Paige checked her emails. Overnight Xavier had reported that preparation for the launch was going well, that the editing team had commenced their first day at Playfair Street and that they'd received numerous RSVPs for the party. He also wrote that he and Eric had moved into their new flat over the weekend, which reminded her that when she returned to Sydney, she'd be homeless. The front parlour was no longer hers to sleep in nor any of the other rooms in the house.

She replied to his email, filling him in briefly on their encounter with the woman in Ovillers, then closed the laptop and joined Ryan in the shower before breakfast.

Ravenous, they ate at the hotel restaurant downstairs, their plates piled high with food.

'What would you like to do today?' Ryan asked, biting into his toast.

'I don't know. I wasn't expecting to have all this free time.'

'Your flight isn't for another two days. Let's make the most of it...' he trailed off, but Paige knew what he meant. Make the most of it before they went their separate ways again. It was another reminder that they'd yet to work out the logistics of their relationship. The night before, under the lustre of wine, it had all seemed uncomplicated—easy words, simple objectives. But in the cold light of day, reality prevailed and the old challenges of long distance presented themselves again.

She pushed the thought aside, not wanting to cloud over the time they had left. 'I'm happy for you to play tour guide. Wherever you want to take me, I'll go.'

They finished breakfast, agreeing to start at the Tuileries Gardens before moving on to the Latin Quarter, then Versailles. Ryan reached for Paige's hand and they left the restaurant together, exiting back through the lobby when Emile hurried over.

'*Bonjour*, Monsieur Greene,' he said. 'Sorry to disturb you.'

'That's okay, Emile. What's up?'

'You have a visitor. She arrived ten minutes ago. I tried your room but there was no answer. I told her you might have gone out, but she said she would wait.'

'A visitor?'

'Just over there on the lounge.'

Paige and Ryan turned towards the lounges. The woman from the cottage sat perched on the edge of one, spine straight, looking as uncomfortable as if she was a predator's prey. Her eyes darted around, her hands clasped tightly in her lap.

'It's all right, Emile. We know her. Thank you.'

Emile bowed his head and retreated to the concierge desk. The woman caught their eyes and stood. Unable to have seen all of her the day before through the partly closed door, Paige saw her now for the first time. Young, in her early twenties. Lovely dark eyes, high cheekbones, arresting features on a serious face as she watched them approach.

'Hello,' Ryan said, as they reached the bank of lounges. 'It's nice to see you again.'

She nodded.

'How did you find us?' he asked.

'Yesterday you said you drove from Paris. From La Maison. I found you here.' She dropped her gaze to the floor as though she'd done something wrong.

'No, that's great,' Ryan said. 'We're glad you did.'

The woman raised her eyes to them.

'Does that mean you're Delphine Beaumont?' Paige asked.

'*Oui*. I am Delphine.'

Paige exchanged an excited glance with Ryan. 'You came a long way to find us again. Why?'

Delphine took a moment to reply. 'Because yesterday you asked me if I knew who used to live in the house.'

'That's right.'

'And who might have sent that letter.'

'Yes.'

Delphine looked around the lobby. 'Is there some place we can talk?'

CHAPTER 34

CHARLOTTE
September 1929

Gusty winds buffeted the city, snatching away crisp leaves that clung valiantly to branches. Charlotte buttoned her coat and drew it up to her neck as the gale grew brisker and storm clouds gathered.

She was standing in a line that snaked around the grocer at Susannah Place in The Rocks. This was strange in itself, for never had she needed to wait in line before, nor had she witnessed such worried faces emerge from the store with only a few provisions. By the time her turn arrived and she entered, she noticed a substantial price rise in everything and the shelves of bread, eggs, milk and flour were empty. She purchased what she could and left.

The docks on Hickson Road fared no better. The Hungry Mile was teeming with men seeking a day's work. They clogged the streets and fights broke out, the fishmonger forced to move elsewhere for fear of being pillaged. Charlotte didn't have the energy to follow him. She made do with her meagre purchases from Susannah Place and headed home.

The inflated grocery prices were of no surprise. All week, the New York and London stock exchanges had been gasping. The Dow was volatile, up and down like a nervous investor. Wall Street bankers had feverishly bought shares to stabilise it. It had worked temporarily, but the falls that followed had been significant. There was panic.

Economists were warning of a catastrophic collapse.

But it was the scene at the front of her house that made her truly concerned. Men, two dozen of them, chanted angrily in protest at her door, demanding her father pay their wages. They were from the Silverwater steel mill and the foundry on Milsons Point, men who had a look of hunger and desperation in their eyes and whom she didn't trust to let her through to the house without incident.

The neighbours had come out to watch the commotion and Charlotte caught the eye of Mrs Parsons, the woman who lived next door in Hilda's old house, and who beckoned her over. 'Come, child. You can cut through to your house from my yard.'

Charlotte gratefully accepted her offer and followed her into her narrow hallway. It had been ten years since she'd been inside that house and she felt a wave of nostalgia sweep over her. She'd spent her childhood tearing down that same hallway with Hilda, bursting out into her backyard to climb fences into other neighbour's yards, Hilda's mother chastising them in her half-hearted way as she'd hung the washing out. Mrs Parsons' wallpaper was different, so too the furniture, but Charlotte knew that house like she knew her own. It left her breathless by the time they reached the yard.

'Quite a spectacle you've got out there,' Mrs Parsons said, wiping her hands on her apron, strands of grey hair falling from her bun into her face. 'What's the problem?'

'They're from my father's steel plants. He hasn't paid their wages.'

Mrs Parsons looked surprised. 'Hasn't paid their wages? Why not? Can't be short of a penny, surely. Not with that fancy bridge contract we keep hearing about.'

'It's complicated.'

She shook her head sadly. 'Terrible time to be hurtin' people. They say a big recession is coming.'

'He means to pay them,' she offered feebly.

'Means to pay and paying them are two different things.' Her tone was disapproving as she pushed a wooden vegetable crate towards the fence she shared with the Greenes and helped Charlotte up. 'Don't snag your stockings there. That's a girl.' She gave her a boost and Charlotte threw one leg over the fence, followed by the other, before lowering herself down onto a crate in her yard.

261

'Tell that father of yours to do the right thing,' Mrs Parsons said, a sliver of her reproach visible through the fence palings. 'Those workers and their families can't survive on air.'

Before Charlotte could thank her or say any more, Mrs Parsons shuffled back inside her house and closed the door. Charlotte sighed and walked to her back door, opening it and stepping into the kitchen. She could still hear the men outside, chanting their disfavour, calling for Walter Greene to face them.

Mrs Parsons was right. Her father needed to do the right thing. But what *was* the right thing? He was buried in debt; he couldn't pay his men if he wanted to. Floyd was the only answer, and that meant Charlotte had a part to play too. Hunger was an impelling thing and those men were desperate, bare cupboards and empty stew pots greeting tiny mouths at the dinner table. It was an unbearable thought at an inconceivable time and Charlotte, with one small sacrifice, had the power to change it.

She dropped the groceries and her handbag onto the kitchen table and, without removing her hat, coat or gloves, she went in search of her father. At the partially closed parlour door, she heard voices inside.

'She's been resistant. More so than usual.' Walter's voice sounded low and tired.

'Then make her see reason,' came Floyd's brusque reply.

'She won't accept it without a fight.'

'I don't want to hear your pitiful excuses, Greene. You owe me. Make it happen.'

Charlotte pushed open the door and both men looked up—Walter, who was standing by the unlit fireplace and Floyd, seated in an armchair with his legs crossed. He wore a pale blue pinstriped suit, bowtie and white wingtip Oxfords. A cane and boater hat were beside him on the table, next to a glass of brandy. He looked as though he were holidaying by the seaside, rather than sitting in the front parlour of a house in the slums of The Rocks.

His beady eyes rested on her before he rose and went to her side. 'Charlotte, darling. You are more radiant than ever.' He kissed her cheek, his wet lips and moustache lingering on her skin, making it crawl. 'Come, sit down. We were just discussing you.'

'The men outside,' she said, unmoving. 'They're protesting for their wages.'

Floyd straightened. 'We're well aware of what they're doing. And they're becoming a nuisance. We've already called the police. They'll be here soon to move them along.'

'But we need to pay them. Somehow. They need money to survive.'

Floyd looked at her father. 'Indeed, they do. Walter, explain to Charlotte how we intend to pay them.'

Walter fixed a weary gaze on her. 'We're bringing the wedding forward.'

Charlotte's breath caught in her throat. 'What?'

'It'll be in three weeks' time at Town Hall. We've cancelled Garrison Church and the Coffee Palace for end of November. They won't be needed.'

Charlotte moved to the Chesterfield and sat down.

'We talked about this, love,' her father said, eyes pleading with her not to serve up a fresh round of protests. 'The business needs you. It needs Floyd. Together, the two of you can turn things around.'

'You want those men to get paid, don't you?' Floyd said. He may not have known her well, but he knew how to exploit her weaknesses. Empathy towards others. Kindness of the heart. The difference between right and wrong. She despaired for the souls outside who, through no fault of their own, had been left penniless by the greed and failings of others, and Floyd knew it.

'Well, Charlotte?' he said, pointedly.

'Sorry, Mr Clark, but this can't be the only way.'

'It is. Your father has bled the company dry. He's in a mountain of debt. I've propped him up as much as I can, but even I can't help anymore. If the bank knew how much I'd loaned him, I'd be in a lot of trouble.' He placed his hand on his chest in feigned consternation.

'Then perhaps you could write a loan in my name. I'll handle the money, ensuring the workers are paid and the bank repayments are met on time.'

Floyd laughed. 'But that's preposterous.'

'Why?' Charlotte argued. 'It's not illegal. Women have the right to borrow money.'

'Perhaps, but it's rare for a female to borrow on her own accord. She usually requires her husband to be in attendance for joint endorsement. I'm afraid the bank won't like your proposal at all. Meanwhile, time is ticking. You have Bradfield breathing down your neck.'

Charlotte turned to her father, unable to tolerate Floyd's smug face any longer, the insinuation that he was the saviour and not the swindler. 'Papa, we can sell our car, our other assets too. Even the house. We can scrape together enough money to get some of the men back into the mill. It would be enough to resume production and keep the bridge happy. Bit by bit, we could build it up again. Small steps. You just have to stay away from the gambling.'

Floyd scoffed. 'Utter rubbish.'

Walter looked like a broken man staring into the fireplace. 'I can't sell the house, Charlotte. Your mother's memory is here.'

'You didn't mind selling her chinaware or her carriage clock,' she said curtly, a fresh wave of betrayal rising up her throat.

He shook his head miserably. 'I was a fool.'

'You still are.'

'I'm trying to make amends.'

By selling me off too, she wanted to say. To this horrid, weasel of a man. She thought of Alex and how dear he was to her. How November now seemed like a gift when faced with a Town Hall wedding in a matter of weeks. How could she tell him their time was over, to acknowledge it herself? No more clues, no more beautiful afternoons in his bed, no more dreams to which they'd wrapped themselves in for comfort.

'Charlotte? Did you hear what I said?'

She was brought back to the room. 'I'm sorry?'

Floyd was staring at her. 'Have you arranged a wedding gown?'

'One was purchased,' Walter said. 'It's upstairs. Charlotte's friend helped pick it out.'

'At least someone has their wits about them,' Floyd said.

'Yes. I'm terribly sorry.' Walter shook his head. 'I omitted to inform you. Charlotte's friend, Mrs Estelle Mayfair, helped select it. It's a delightful gown. Modest and pretty, like our Charlotte.'

Floyd grew still. 'Who did you say helped you?'

Walter looked confused. 'I beg your pardon?'

'That woman. The one who assisted with the dress. What's her name?'

'Estelle Mayfair.'

Floyd's face paled and he visibly gulped. 'And you say this woman has befriended Charlotte?'

Charlotte sat straighter in her chair. 'Yes, she's my friend. Why?'

Floyd sat back, his fingers gripping the arms of the chair, turning his knuckles white. 'I know this woman and she is of questionable morality.'

'Why do you say that?' Walter asked with scepticism.

'She has a reputation around town and it's not for her sewing skills, I can assure you.'

'Whatever do you mean?'

'She's a harlot. A prostitute. She beds men for payment.'

Charlotte felt her pulse quicken. 'That's terrible of you to say. Estelle is no such thing.'

'She's gutter trash. I forbid you to see her. To have anything to do with her again.'

'You can't tell me what to do. You're not my father.' She was furious. The nerve of the man.

'I'm your fiancé and you will listen to what I say!' Spittle flew out of his mouth, landing in his moustache and on the Chesterfield. He took a composing breath, smoothed back his oily hair and straightened his bow tie. 'You really don't have a clue about her, do you?'

'I know enough.'

'Foolish girl. Why do you keep calling her Estelle, then?' He grinned cunningly.

Charlotte faltered, her conviction slipping. 'Because that's her name.'

Floyd nodded, his beady eyes lit. 'Is it now? Interesting.'

'For goodness sake Mr Clark, what is it you're trying to say?'

He smacked his lips together. 'Her real name is Dorothea Baker. Widow of Augustus Baker, a pathetic businessman who took his own life, then left her with four grubby children and a debt longer than The Hungry Mile.'

Charlotte sat extremely still. 'You're mistaken.'

'I don't believe I am.'

The telephone shrilled loudly and Walter, looking the colour of putty, pushed off from the fireplace and disappeared into the hall. The call was answered. Walter made small sounds of acknowledgement, bid the person good evening and returned.

'Positive news,' he said. 'That was the constable. The police have moved on the protestors. Some peace and quiet at last.'

But no one in the parlour was rejoicing.

CHAPTER
35

As soon as Walter left for work the next morning, Charlotte climbed out of bed and hurried downstairs into the parlour. Floyd's words still echoed in her ears.

'Really, how could you have not known who she was?' he'd said upon leaving. 'It's a travesty that she lied to you. You should pick your friends more carefully.'

Walter had remained ashen faced for the rest of the evening, hardly touching his dinner and retreating early to the parlour, closing the door behind him. She'd heard brandy being poured, the fire lit and a heavy sigh amidst the crackling flames. She'd wondered as to his thoughts, the melancholy he might feel over the realisation that Estelle, or Dorothea, was not the woman he'd thought she was. Another fracture in his tower of burdens.

Charlotte returned her focus to the parlour now, determined to get to the bottom of Floyd's claim. She knew that her father kept office particulars in that room on a small desk—ledgers and paperwork. There was one item in particular that she'd hoped was there and, after scouring the top of his desk, she found it easily, beside his fountain pen holder and two ink stamps. A Rolodex.

She knew that Estelle had given Walter her phone number the day he'd invited her to the bridge. With any luck, she might have shared her address too, and he'd recorded it in his Rolodex. It didn't escape Charlotte that she'd never been invited to Estelle's house before. They'd always met at Playfair Street or Hubert Penny's. Why was that so?

Charlotte had never thought to question it. She didn't have many adult friends to compare such oddities. But now, after hearing Floyd's words, she wondered if she knew Estelle at all. Or Dorothea. Whatever her name was. Floyd had painted the picture of a woman so far removed from the Estelle Charlotte knew it was almost laughable. Harlot and prostitute. Four children. A mountain of debt.

In any case, Charlotte considered herself a fair person. She wasn't one to judge until she knew the facts, so she pulled the Rolodex towards her and grasped the bronze side dial in her fingers. Flipping through the contact cards, which she viewed through a rectangular window cut into the bronze, she noticed they were categorised in alphabetical order according to surname. She turned the dial which turned the cards, all the way until she came to M.

Mayfair, Mrs Estelle.

Walter had captured her phone number but not her address. Charlotte wrote the number down on a slip of paper and took it with her out into the hall where the telephone sat. She would call Estelle, ask to visit for tea and get to the bottom of what Floyd had accused her of.

She dialled the number. It rang, eventually answered by a young girl. 'Hello?'

'Good morning. Is Estelle there please?' Charlotte asked politely.

'I don't know anyone called Estelle,' the girl said.

Charlotte frowned. Even the child didn't know her as Estelle. It gave weight to Floyd's claim, much to her chagrin. 'I'm sorry. Is Dorothea home?' she tried again.

'She's gone out. She'll be back soon,' the little voice replied.

'I'm a friend of hers and I'd like to pay her a visit. Can you give me your address please?'

The trusting child did not hesitate, happily rattling off a street in Darlinghurst in the city's east. Razor gang territory. It was a thuggish neighbourhood, one that Estelle had clearly wanted to keep them from seeing. It took Charlotte less than a minute to thank the child, hang up the phone, grab her gloves and hat, and dash out the front door.

She reached the tram stop at Circular Quay and waited ten minutes until a tram arrived with a Darlinghurst sign affixed. She climbed aboard, paid her fare when the conductor passed through and sat with her hands clutched tightly around her handbag as the tram wended its way through the city towards the east.

At Oxford Street, the tram veered left onto Victoria, passing by St Vincent's Hospital, then coming to rest at the intersection of Burton Street. Charlotte alighted and cast her eye warily around. An unsavoury duo in brown tweed and suspenders passed her by, their leering gaze travelling the length of her figure.

'Lost, little lady?' one of them said with a toothless grin.

'Want some help finding your way?'

When she didn't respond, they blocked her passage until she was forced to push past them, their cackling laughter making the hairs on the back of her neck rise. Without haste, she put distance between them and found West Street, turning into it, eyeing the row of dilapidated Victorian terraces with their tumbledown fences and rotting windowsills. Gardens were unkempt and tenacious ivy was free to roam. Kids who should have been in school tore up the street playing a game of gangs and pretending to slice each other with razors, a reminder that she'd crossed into the territory of crime matrons Kate Leigh and Tilly Divine, and that it was best not to dally.

She found Estelle's terrace and unlatched the gate. It yawed back at her in protest. Side-stepping a beaten-up tricycle, she reached the front door and knocked tentatively. She hoped Estelle was home.

After an agonising minute, she knocked again, then footsteps sounded down the hallway. The door creaked open a fraction.

It was Estelle, at least a version of her—grey, splotchy skin, drab hair and dark circles under pale eyes, a far cry from the woman Charlotte knew, of bright rosy cheeks, a silky Eton crop and lips as glossy as toffee.

'Charlotte?' Her surprise was obvious as she held the door firm.

'Estelle.' Charlotte swallowed. 'I apologise for calling in on you like this.'

'What are you doing here? How did you get my address?' Her eyes, visible through the sliver of doorway, darted left and right.

'I came alone. I needed to see you.'

Estelle's hand flew to her hair as though trying to tame it into submission. 'Darling, you could have dropped me a note. We could have met at Hubert's.'

A young cry erupted from the back of the house, then another, as though children were squabbling over a toy.

Estelle looked behind her, then back at Charlotte. 'I'm sorry. I'm not fit for visitors today. It's a bad time. Let's meet tomorrow. I know a great place on George Street—'

Charlotte stuck her foot in the doorway. 'Please, I need to talk to you.'

Estelle pulled her lips into a thin line. As she contemplated, the squabbling escalated and she turned to look back again before her shoulders drooped and she sighed, opening the door. 'Fine.'

Charlotte stepped into a narrow hallway, walls peeling with paint and timber floors dull and scuffed, having long lost their lustre. Estelle, wearing a faded purple dressing robe and brown threadbare slippers, led her through to the back of the house, which opened into a kitchen with a small round table. There were age and neglect in every corner, but Estelle kept a tidy house. Three children ceased their arguing and watched as Charlotte walked in. Another child sat at the kitchen table, her hair wet and a comb and bowl beside her.

'Lice,' Estelle explained, watching Charlotte's eyes roam the table. 'They've all got it. The school won't let them come back until it's out. Wretched things. I've tried everything to get rid of it. Clove, eucalyptus, cinnamon. It just keeps coming back.' She pulled her robe tighter around her. 'Can I fix you something? A drink?'

Charlotte held up her hand. 'No, thank you.'

'Would you mind waiting here a moment then? I'll run upstairs and make myself presentable.'

Estelle left the room, her footsteps hurrying up the stairs and along the floorboards above the kitchen. While Charlotte waited, the children stared at her—two boys and two girls. The youngest, presumably the one who'd answered Charlotte's call earlier, grinned from her spot on the chair, her thin legs dangling over the edge, kicking the table leg.

'What's your name?' the eldest boy asked.

'I'm Charlotte Greene, your mother's friend.'

He appraised her quizzically. 'My mum doesn't have any friends. Not lady ones anyway.'

'Are you here to buy Mama's jewellery?' the eldest girl asked with large round eyes.

'No,' Charlotte said. 'I'm not here to buy jewellery.'

Before they could interrogate her further, Estelle returned. She wore a maroon and white dress complete with heels and a long bejewelled necklace looped several times around her neck. Her lips and cheeks were coloured, and her hair had been combed and set, a white headband fitted with a large gemstone brooch sparkling from the side.

Just like that, Estelle was shiny again, her old skin shed and a fresh one rolled on like a mink coat. She drew her shoulders back with renewed confidence and went to the child on the chair. 'Scoot now. We'll finish this later.' She turned to the others. 'Go on. All of you. Outside.'

They hesitated, then took off at a roaring pace, down the hallway and out the front door with peals of delight.

Estelle turned to Charlotte with wringing hands. 'I'm sure you have questions.'

Charlotte did, many of them. So many that she didn't know where to start. 'Your children are lovely.'

'They can be a handful,' Estelle said, a fond smile touching her eyes. 'It's been difficult raising them on my own, but I manage.' She cleared her throat and turned to the table, scooping away the bowl and comb. She dusted off the chair and beckoned to Charlotte. 'Please, take a seat.'

As she did, Estelle fussed behind her, making a pot of tea.

'What are their names?' Charlotte asked.

Estelle pulled two chipped cups from a cupboard and set them on a tray. 'Frederick. He's ten, the eldest. Then there's Marie, eight, Archie, six and Helen is five.'

'Who watches them while you're out?'

'Frederick. He's more than capable, the man of the house, really. Otherwise they're at school.'

'I didn't know you had children,' Charlotte said gently. She didn't want it to sound like an accusation. 'You could have told me. I wouldn't have minded.'

Estelle considered her a moment. 'How did you know about them?'

'Floyd told me.'

Estelle faltered briefly, then righted herself and carried the tray to the table. 'I see.'

'He said you had children and were placed into debt by your late husband. He said other things too.'

Estelle set the tray down and sat opposite her. 'I'm sorry. I don't have any cake or biscuits.'

Charlotte shook her head, trying not to let pity show. Estelle would cringe if she saw it. 'Tea is fine.'

Estelle stirred sugar into her cup and brought it to her lips, taking a slow and deliberate sip. She set the cup down. 'It's true, about the debt. When Augustus died, he left me a dreadful mountain of it. So much that I had to sell our lovely home in Point Piper. I sold our cars, my furs and jewels. I even sold our furniture and artwork. Everything we owned I had to part with, hundreds of thousands of pounds worth. I paid as much back as I could, then I moved my children here, to this place.'

She looked around with disdain. 'But still it wasn't enough. He owed so much money. Not to good people either. They threatened to kill us, to burn our house down while we slept, to tie rocks to my children's feet and throw them in the harbour.' Estelle's bottom lip quivered, her palm gathering stray crumbs on the table in a stoic attempt to compose herself.

'So I had to make a decision. We die, or I try to pay back the rest of what was owed. They were all gambling debts, you see. Augustus had a terrible problem. The bank kept propping him up with loans but he even spent that money. He was a coward, taking his own life, leaving me to clean up his mess.' Her expression darkened.

'Bank loans, you say?' Charlotte said. 'The Bank of New South Wales?'

Estelle averted her gaze as if she'd said too much. 'I guess.'

'How did you pay back the rest of the money?'

She pressed her bright red lips together. 'I did what any desperate woman would do. I had to or we would have died. It's all repaid now.'

'Floyd called you unsavoury things.'

'I'm sure he did.'

'Are they true?'

Estelle looked away. When she looked back, her eyes were defiant. 'I have gentlemen friends, yes. They shower me with gifts. They buy me cars and expensive jewels. But I'm not a prostitute. I'm simply a mistress to many. There's a difference.' Her voice held conviction, as though trying to convince herself.

'Is that how you survive now?'

'I do whatever it takes to feed my children.'

'How do you feed them with cars and jewels?'

Estelle shrugged. 'First I wear them, drive them, enjoy them, then I sell them off for food and rent.'

Charlotte was reminded of the expensive gold Bug Speedster Estelle had arrived in for her first visit to tea at Playfair Street. Shortly after, the car had disappeared, Estelle claiming it had a clutch problem. She thought of the fur coats, the ruby ring, the jewels, so many of them. She had assumed her husband, being a wealthy man, had left Estelle a sizable fortune. On the contrary. The only thing he'd left her was a sizable mess.

'If Augustus hadn't taken his own life, I would have killed him myself for what he did to us,' she said. 'We had a wonderful life. We were social royalty, had invitations to all the best parties. My children went to private schools. We had nannies and house staff and a swimming pool. Augustus ruined us!' Her face screwed up tightly, her breathing laboured as though the very frustration of her social collapse might cause her to pick up the tea tray and throw it.

'So you changed your name and became someone else?'

'I couldn't very well be Dorothea Baker anymore. People in this town will forget a face but they won't forget a name. I recreated myself.'

Charlotte sat still, her tea untouched, growing cold in the cup. She could hear the children shrieking outside as they raced up and down the street.

'Your wedding to Floyd,' Estelle said, 'is it still going ahead?'

'They want to bring it forward. Three weeks' time at Town Hall.'

'Bring it forward?' Estelle looked stunned. 'But I thought it was set for the end of November? I thought you were trying to delay it.'

'The men from my father's steel mill haven't been paid. It's an awful mess. Floyd means to take over the business and restore it. But I can't marry him. The idea repulses me.' She was still holding onto a glimmer of hope that her father would see reason and find another way.

Estelle narrowed her eyes. 'You really should stop your whining about it.'

Charlotte blinked. 'Excuse me?'

'You're a lucky girl. You may not love Floyd, but your life is going to be one of ease and wealth. You won't have to scrape for a meal or wear your stockings until their last thread. You'll have everything your heart desires. I'd give my final breath to be in your position.'

Charlotte was taken aback. If there was one thing she'd always been able to count on, it was Estelle's support, someone who saw things from her point of view. Now it would appear Estelle had changed her mind. 'I can see you're no longer on my side.'

'It's not about sides,' Estelle replied brusquely. 'It's about reality. And frankly, your ungratefulness is starting to irk me.'

Charlotte swallowed back her hurt. 'I don't know what to say.'

'It's the truth. I'm not trying to be unkind.'

The room started to feel hot and airless. A cold glass of water would have been nice, but Charlotte wanted to get away from Estelle as quickly as possible. Nothing was as it seemed anymore. Everything felt blurred and wrong and confusing. She touched her fingers to her forehead as a dull ache brewed behind her eyes. 'I've intruded on you long enough. I'll be going. May I use your washroom first?'

Estelle sat back in her chair and crossed her arms. 'We have a small one inside. Upstairs and to the right.'

'Thank you.' Charlotte left the kitchen and headed for the stairs at the front of the house, climbing them, feeling the rough and swollen timber beneath her shoes.

At the top, she found the washroom, closed the door behind her and leaned against the small porcelain vanity. Much had transpired in the past twenty-four hours, yet it was Estelle's comments downstairs that were most upsetting. Not her chameleon appearance or the children she'd kept hidden or that her name wasn't even Estelle Mayfair, but her stinging words of envy. The jealousy she must have felt every time they'd sat down together and spoken of Floyd and the wealthy marriage Charlotte would enter into, every conversation now cast in a different light.

She straightened her dress, fixed her hat in the cracked and speckled mirror and took a deep breath, then opened the washroom door and stepped back into the hallway. She should have gone downstairs, but an inquisitive urge crept over her and, careful not to disturb the floorboards, she trod lightly down the hall, away from the stairs, to explore. She passed a room with three mattresses side by side on the floor, fitted neatly with sheets, blankets and pillows. The room of the three eldest children, Charlotte decided.

Further along the hall, she found a second bedroom with a double bed, also neatly made with a small ragged teddy missing an eye propped against one of the pillows. There was a bedside table, Estelle's purple robe and tattered slippers in a pile on the floor where she'd hurriedly discarded them, and a dark oak double wardrobe. It was the main bedroom, one Estelle must share with young Helen.

Charlotte stepped in and looked around. There was little evidence of Estelle's duplicitous life in there. To a stranger's eyes, she was a poor, single mother living on the wrong side of town, struggling to make ends meet. But Charlotte knew better. She walked as quietly as she could to the oak wardrobe and pulled open the doors.

Inside was the Estelle she knew.

A white fur coat, a grey mink stole, an array of tea and cocktail dresses, embellished with gemstones and sequins, and a row of heels. The wardrobe contained a set of drawers and she opened them one by one, finding satin petticoats, silk stockings, lace and ribbon brassieres, cloche hats and leather gloves.

There were rouge and lipstick, atomisers filled with fragrances, a beautiful enamel hair comb, strands of pearls and necklaces, headbands, opal paste rings and sapphire brooches. All the sparkling things that allowed Dorothea Baker to become Estelle Mayfair. To reinvent herself for a few hours each day to bring home the bacon.

Charlotte was about to close the wardrobe doors when a fragment of black lace poking through the other garments caught her attention. She leant closer to inspect. It wasn't just black lace, rather Chantilly, delicate and exquisite, for she knew how it slipped through the fingers like liquid. Floyd had had a dress fashioned for her with similar lace. An original one-of-a-kind piece. No other woman owned its replica.

Curious and unconcerned that she'd been gone for some time, she pushed aside the other dresses and reached deep in the back for the gown. She pulled it out by the hanger, her heart stopping.

It was a jade-green dress, draped in black Chantilly lace, exactly like hers. And not so one-of-a-kind.

CHAPTER
36

'If you wanted to borrow something, you could have just asked.' Estelle was in the doorway.

Charlotte jumped, dropping the dress from its hanger to the floor.

Estelle walked to the wardrobe and bent to scoop it up from the floorboards. 'Lovely, isn't it?' she said, letting the fabric slip between her fingers. 'It's delicious to wear.'

'Where did you get it?'

'One of my gentleman friends had it made for me. A one-of-a-kind piece made with Parisian lace. I'm the only woman to own one.'

'Which man?'

'Nobody you know.' But the way Estelle avoided Charlotte's eyes told her she did know.

'How long have you and Floyd been together?'

There was a flicker of hesitation before Estelle slipped the gown back onto the hanger. 'Excuse me?'

'The first time you came to my place for tea, you said Floyd and Augustus were close business associates.'

Estelle opened her mouth to speak but then closed it, placing the gown back into the wardrobe and closing the doors. Finally, she turned around. 'I don't recall ever saying that.'

'You did. I remember.'

'Well, you must be mistaken. I hardly know your fiancé.'

'I think you do. And I know it because I have that same dress. Floyd had one made for me and I wore it to the Governor's Ball in April with him. He told me it was an original piece, a one-of-a-kind. No other woman had one. It seems he had two made.'

Estelle's face paled.

'Is he one of the men you slept with to repay your husband's debts?' Her blood began to pulse. 'Are you still sleeping with him for gifts? Did he do to Augustus what he's now doing to my father?'

Estelle's laugh was unnaturally high. 'Goodness! What a load of wild accusations. You have gone quite mad, Charlotte.'

'Why are you lying about it? Like everything in your life. It's one big lie. Dorothea.'

Estelle straightened, jutting her chin out, her eyes glacial. 'Why are you even here?'

'Because I can't take any more lies.'

'What do you want me to say?' Estelle fired back. 'That yes, I've been sleeping with Floyd. That I have been since before Augustus died because his debts were mounting long before he took his own life. That I did and will continue to do, whatever it takes to keep a roof over our heads. So don't sit there, in all your righteous ways, Charlotte Greene, and lecture me.'

The room grew tensely still. Estelle took a deep breath, sat on the edge of her bed and hung her head. Her bejewelled necklace sat like a puddle of sparkles in her lap. She was a broken piece of crystal, once beautiful, now cracked, but not beyond repair, for if Charlotte knew Estelle at all, it was that she was a fighter. And would continue to be long after that day.

'Why do you care?' Estelle asked, lifting her head. 'You don't even like Floyd. What does it matter who he goes to bed with?'

'I care because he's ruining our lives. He's doing to us what he did to you.'

'You can be so melodramatic, Charlotte. You don't know what a ruined life is.' Estelle reached across to her drawer and pulled out a pack of Camels and a cigarette holder. She fitted a cigarette to the end of the holder, struck a match to it and inhaled deeply. 'Did Floyd really speak poorly of me?'

Charlotte nodded.

'What did he say exactly? Tell me. I want to hear it.'

'He called you a harlot and a prostitute. Gutter trash. He forbade me to see you again.'

'Did he really?' Estelle threw her head back and laughed, but it sounded hollow.

'Yes, he did.'

The laughing stopped and a brief shadow of hurt crossed her eyes before she blinked it away.

'Do you love him?' It was a horrible thought, but Estelle was full of surprises lately.

She lifted her shoulders dismissively. 'I suppose I do.'

'Does he love you?'

'Love is a strange thing for Floyd Clark,' she said. 'I'm sure he does, in his own way.'

'Then why would he call you those names?'

'To deter you. If you'd found out about us, it would give you more reason not to marry him.'

Did Charlotte need any more reasons not to marry him? The man was truly awful. Many lives had been broken by his hand. He'd done to Augustus what he was now doing to her father. Enabling a gambler, then sitting back to watch them fall, ready to reap the rewards.

Her stomach churned. 'Don't you hate him for what he's done to you? What he's still doing to you?'

Estelle dropped the packet of Camels back into her drawer and closed it. 'I hate Augustus more.'

'You're deluded.'

'I'm a realist. There's no point hating Floyd now. He keeps food on my table.'

'He's a man with puppet strings tied to you and you're allowing him to use them.'

Estelle shrugged.

'That first time we were to meet at Hubert Penny's and you didn't show up, were you with him?' Charlotte asked.

Estelle crossed her long legs gracefully. 'Yes. He called. He'd gone home for his lunch break and wanted to see me. So I got in my car and drove to him. When I got there, he had a Tiffany watch waiting for me and we spent the afternoon together. I did apologise to you for standing you up. You do remember that, don't you?' Her voice was defensive, as if by that apology she should be absolved of it all.

Charlotte closed her eyes and opened them again. She felt betrayed and stupid. The whole ordeal was humiliating. She'd become a pawn in Floyd and Estelle's games and the deception of it sent her mind reeling.

She had one last question for Estelle, then she would leave and never return. 'Was our friendship real?'

Estelle exhaled a steady stream of smoke towards the ceiling. 'Not always. I just wanted my enemy close.' She gave her a long look. 'But I did grow to like you, I really did, even if you don't believe me.'

That was the thing about liars. It was hard to believe anything they said.

***

The afternoon sun was setting as she left Estelle's house. Charlotte hadn't realised the whole day had passed, but now, the dying rays stretched their fingers across the sky to grasp the last of the light and drag it to the horizon. The children were at the far end of the street, a billy cart race in progress, oblivious to her exit. She loathed to linger anyway, not another second in that street, but she didn't want to go home either.

She wanted to see Alex, to talk to someone she could trust about Estelle, so she found the nearest tram stop, outside St Vincent's Hospital, and boarded it. It was destined for Kings Cross, in the opposite direction, but Charlotte had learnt to navigate the city with ease, to move from tram to tram and to recognise streets and landmarks without fear of becoming lost. The game she played with Alex had taught her to be a confident and steady commuter.

In Kings Cross, outside The Paris Café on Darlinghurst Road, she disembarked from one tram, dashed across the tracks, and boarded another bound for Five Ways, Paddington. She paid her fare and remained standing, holding onto the bar above her. It wouldn't be a long trip. The five minutes to Alex's house would give her a moment to catch her breath and reflect on what had transpired with Estelle.

Lies, betrayal, a friendship that should never have been. How Estelle must despise her. To have to bear witness to the wealth and social status Charlotte would be gifted by the very man who had taken it from her must have filled her with hatred. So instead, Estelle had kept her close, watching her, filling her head with notions of female liberation, trying to dissuade her from marrying Floyd. And perhaps that had been a good thing, except it had come from a dark place, and that's what hurt Charlotte the most.

At Five Ways, across from the Royal Hotel, she hopped off the tram, certain Alex wouldn't be home from work yet, although happy to sit and wait for him on his porch. She started along Broughton Street but halted a few houses down when she caught sight of him standing by his front gate. She almost waved until she realised he wasn't alone. He held a small boy in one arm and with his other, pulled a woman close to him. Charlotte turned cold, her heart tripping on an unpleasant beat, compelled to watch but wanting to tear her eyes away.

The scene was too inexplicable, too unexpected for her to understand and, in the end, she didn't want to be caught lurking so she hurried away, back along Broughton Street, jumping on the first tram that came rattling along.

Numb and in shock, she sat, turning the scene over in her head. Alex with a family? A wife and child? Surely not. She would have known. She'd been in his house lots of times, had spent whole afternoons in his bed, had roamed the rooms. She would have noticed if a woman and child lived there too. What if they didn't live with him, for some reason they boarded elsewhere? She shook her head. Did it matter? The way he held that child, the way his arm had pulled the woman into him spoke of a closeness, an intimacy, of family.

Charlotte couldn't and wouldn't let the tears fall while on the tram, packed with afternoon commuters, but as soon as she alighted, somewhere south of Pitt Street, and began walking home, they fell. Her gloved hands wiped them away and still more came until she was back in her bedroom, letting them run unchecked across her cheeks to soak her pillow.

***

The next morning, Charlotte still lay in the same position on her bed, fully clothed, eyes bled dry. She had slept fitfully, dreams of Alex and Estelle morphing together so that their deception became one and the same. Alex holding Estelle. Their arms linked and bodies pressed together. Her children skipping happily around them.

It was after midday when she finally pushed herself to a sitting position. She washed, dressed and went down to the kitchen. Housework held no appeal, nor did food or the day outside, which was so bright it seemed to mock her mood.

It wasn't as though she'd never experienced pain before. She'd lost her mother at a tender age, then Hilda a week later. Her father and Estelle had disappointed her in inexcusable ways. But Alex? He had hurt her the most. His betrayal had been an unexpected dagger to the heart. The words he'd whispered, the letters he'd written, the way he'd kissed her and held her and laid her down in his bed, all seemed now like a blatant lie.

She shuffled into the library, eyes gritty like sand. This room had always been a sanctuary for her, a place of safe walls and make-believe worlds, where the unkind world could be kept out. Why had she ever chosen to leave?

She trailed her fingers along the books pressed neatly together on the shelves, resolved never to let the outside in again. When her fingers encountered an empty slot where a book should have been, she straightened with apprehension. Peering closer, she realised that a book was missing, which was unusual, for there should be no empty slots in her mother's bookcase. Her brain began to fire, heart beating quicker. *No, no, no, no.* It couldn't be. *Please, not that book.*

She scanned the shelves for the title she prayed was not missing. She hadn't moved it, had replaced it the last time she'd read from it. She remembered doing so. Then why wasn't it on the shelves anymore?

Charlotte looked frantically around the library, flinging shawls away, moving cushions, searching under chairs, but it was nowhere to be found. She raced to the parlour, then to the kitchen, then up to her room and into her father's room, just to be sure. It wasn't anywhere. The book of love letters, her and her mother's most treasured book, and their last link, was gone.

***

When her father returned home, Charlotte was upon him in an instant.

'Where is it?'

He removed his hat and coat, giving her a wary glance. 'Where's what?'

'My mother's book.'

He sighed. 'You'll have to be more precise than that.'

'*Love Through the Ages*. What have you done with it?'

'I don't know what you're talking about.' He shuffled up the hall towards the kitchen and fell heavily into a chair.

'You do know what I'm talking about. And I want it back.' Dread coursed through her.

'Please, Charlotte,' he said, pinching the space between his eyes, 'it's been a long day. Can we do this tomorrow?'

'No, we cannot.' She stood in front of him, arms crossed.

He glanced tiredly up at her. 'You have hundreds of books in that library. Read one of those.'

'That book is a first edition. It's worth a fortune, not to mention it's irreplaceable. I want to know where it is.'

He closed his eyes, but when he opened them again, he didn't meet hers.

'You sold it, didn't you?' Charlotte sank into a chair across from him. It was the most precious of all things left by her mother; it signified everything that was Alex. That book had meant the world to her. Now, like all the other things her father had stolen, it was gone. 'Why?' she asked, heartbroken. 'Why would you sell it?'

He shook his head sorrowfully. 'I thought if I could double my money on the hounds, I could put it back into the business, pay the workers. Floyd won't grant me another loan.'

'Is it any wonder? He's got you right where he wants you. Desperate and broke.'

'I'm trying to fix things.'

Her father looked haggard, beaten down by his own actions. She loved him, but she was empty of patience or forgiveness. Only anger seemed to remain for what he'd taken from her, what he was still trying to take from her.

'I'll buy you another book, something better,' he pleaded.

'You're despicable.'

Walter made a wounded sound.

She wrapped her arms around herself, feeling empty, like a shell. She searched for light at that moment, something to grasp onto, something to give hope to the future, but there was nothing. Bleak.

'I'm sorry, love,' her father said dejectedly. 'I'll make it up to you. Once you marry Floyd, this will all be better. I'll stop the gambling, the business will be set right, we'll be rich. You'll see.'

She closed her eyes. 'I'm alone.'

'What did you say, sweetheart?'

'I have no one.'

He put his hand over hers. 'Don't be like that. You have me.'

She opened her eyes and regarded him squarely. 'No, I don't'.

CHAPTER 37

It had been two weeks since Charlotte had seen Alex outside his house with the woman and child, and none of the shock had abated. He'd left her two clues since then, both hand-delivered through the mail slot of her door, but she couldn't muster the strength to read them, let alone follow them, so she placed them in the chest of letters underneath her bed and pushed it to the far wall. He would have waited for her at those meeting places, unable to understand why she hadn't shown. She had never not shown before.

The image of him holding the child, pulling the woman in close, would forever be etched in her mind. Together with the truth about Estelle and the book of love letters her father had pawned off in his latest attempt to line his pockets left Charlotte feeling like she was teetering precariously on a cliff's edge.

The past couple of weeks had taught her what she'd realised so simply as a child. People didn't stay. It's why she'd closed her heart all those years ago. The loss of her mother, then Hilda, then her brother James had left. Even her father, in his own way, had retreated into himself, finding solace in gambling rather than the joy of raising his daughter. She'd known these lessons, had learnt them most harshly as a young girl. Why, then, had she turned her back on all she knew to be dealt the same cruel blow?

It was four days until her wedding. Just she, her father and Floyd would be in attendance. It would be a brief ceremony at the registry office at Town Hall. They would sign on the dotted line, place Floyd at the helm of the Greene empire, deliver her father a reprieve from his sins, and pay the workers. Afterwards, she would move to Floyd's house, turn a blind eye to his continued affair with Estelle—whatever kept him away from Charlotte—and grieve in private for a man she'd loved but who hadn't loved her enough in return.

With the wedding close, attention had turned to the ivory satin dress that no one would see on the day, but which Walter had insisted she still wear in some feeble attempt to make the occasion meaningful. They were in the front parlour, Charlotte being pinned at the waist by a dour seamstress he'd called in.

'It's too loose here,' she said through a pin clenched between her teeth, gathering the dress at Charlotte's sides. 'It has to be taken in.'

'Looks like you've lost some weight, love,' her father said. 'All right. Let's take it in. How long before it'll be ready?'

'This is delicate fabric. I can't rush it.' The seamstress pulled the pin from her mouth and pierced it through the dress. 'Maybe two weeks.'

'We need it by this weekend. How much will it cost to get it done in three days?'

'Papa, I can wear it as it is,' Charlotte said. 'We don't need to spend money on it.'

'Nonsense. How much?' he insisted.

'It'll be triple the price. I'm very busy,' the dour woman said.

'Done.'

The seamstress finished pinning the waist, then Walter left the parlour and Charlotte undressed, handing the gown to the woman and sliding back into her day dress. After the seamstress left, Charlotte collected her gloves and hat and made for the door. Walter must have heard her, for he stepped out from the kitchen into the hall, wearing an apron. He looked comical with his huge belly protruding through it.

'Going somewhere, love?' He'd been on his best behaviour the last few days, arriving home at appropriate hours, cooking dinner, speaking to her in soft, dulcet tones as if she were a delicate piece of porcelain that might shatter.

'Just out for some air. I won't be long,' she said.

He walked to the door and glanced down at her, eyes full of concern. 'You're doing the right thing, love. Marrying Floyd. It's the only way now.'

She slipped her gloves and hat on.

'He might even surprise you. He could turn out to be someone you care for over time.'

Care for, not love. For once her father didn't mince words.

He patted her arm. 'I'm off to the mill shortly. I've fixed you some lunch.'

'Thank you.' Before he could trap her in any further conversation, she closed the door and stepped out onto Playfair Street. The truth was, she didn't know where she was going, as long as she was out of the house and away from her father. She wanted to move, to feel open space around her and the scurry of people going about everyday business. She walked through Argyle Cut, past Trinity Avenue and Garrison Church, up towards Hickson Road.

The end of October was upon them, whispers of warmer weather on the heels of spring. The trees that lined this part of The Rocks were sprouting with rejuvenated life, the scent of new buds tickling Charlotte's nose. The city was alive, glorious, in stark contrast to how she felt inside, as cold as a frost-bitten winter's morning.

On The Hungry Mile, she side-stepped those waiting in that despairing line of hope for a day's work. The line of hunched shoulders and fedora hats stretched further than she'd ever seen it, cigarette smoke and stale sweat heavy in the air. Feet shuffled slowly towards the inevitable disappointment at the end, for there was only so much work to go around on the wharves, and the thousands who queued with some fragile thread of expectation would likely be turned away to go hungry another day.

Charlotte thought of the men in her father's employ, the ones who hadn't been paid in months, whose desperate protests at the front of their house were met with the threat of jail time from the police. Their pleas for owed wages had Walter stressed and Floyd agitated, so that any suggestion by Charlotte to delay the wedding was instantly shut down.

'Can't you hear that racket?' Floyd had snapped at her when she'd dared to ask again to change the date. 'Not everything is about you, Charlotte.'

'Yes, love. We must proceed as soon as possible,' her father had said in a gentler tone. 'It's the only way to put the company back in sure hands. You want the workers to be paid, don't you?'

So yes, she would marry Floyd. She would do it for the hundreds of families who relied on Greene employment. Whose husbands and fathers were in that line, who needed her to see them through darkening times. And was there any point resisting? Alex had betrayed her. Estelle had lied to her. Charlotte could have done away with the last six months, for all it had done was land her back at the start.

She kept walking, head bowed low, keen to get past The Hungry Mile and through to High Steps, where she could link up with Agar Steps and reach calmer ground. As she passed the men, they catcalled, asking her for a spare shilling. She reached High Steps, climbing them quickly, able to take a proper breath once she'd reached the top, only to collide straight into Alex.

His hands reached out to steady her as she gasped, but he didn't seem surprised she was there. 'Are you okay?'

'Alex? What are you doing here?'

'I followed you. Thought you might come up this way, so I took High Street instead to catch up.'

He was the person she least wanted to see and yet the only one. If she bottled up all the hurts into a jar, it was Alex's that had slipped between the gaps to fill the hollows, making her heart the heaviest.

'You shouldn't be near The Hungry Mile on your own,' he said. 'It's not safe.'

She pulled away from his grasp and kept walking. 'I can look after myself. I've done so for a long time.'

He jogged to reach her again. 'Why didn't you meet me the last couple of weeks? I left you clues.'

She said nothing, kept her head bent low and on towards Agar Steps.

'Were they too difficult?'

She almost laughed. The nerve.

'Charlotte, wait a minute. What's going on?'

They climbed the steps and at the top, emerged onto the ridge where The Rocks unfolded below them. Charlotte headed for Upper Fort

Street, the narrow road that circled Fort Street Public School.

Alex was beside her, still looking bewildered. 'Charlotte, please, would you just stop for a minute? I don't understand.'

She didn't stop, didn't slow.

'Did something happen with your father and Floyd?'

'Are you going to pretend you've done nothing wrong?' she said.

'Pretend? What?'

'That you haven't lied too? You're no better than the rest of them, Alex.'

He reached for her arm and pulled her to a stop. She gave in, tears starting to slide down her cheeks, but he seemed to know better than to bring her to him. Instead, he reached for her hand and they stepped into the open gate of the school, around the classrooms to the spot on the hill overlooking the bridge construction, where they had sat during Charlotte's Windmill Steps clue.

Charlotte stared out across the cluttered roofs and chimney pots of The Rocks, anything to avoid Alex's expectant gaze. It was Tuesday afternoon, the school's students had left for another day and the city was beginning to slow for supper.

They sat on the grass and Alex spoke. 'Charlotte, tell me what's happening, please. I left you two clues, one for Taronga Zoo and the other for my house, but you didn't meet me at either.'

'I saw you,' she said.

'Saw me where?'

Charlotte finally met his eyes. 'Outside your house. I came to visit you and you were standing by the gate with a woman and child.'

Alex's gaze slid sidewards as if trying to remember.

'Please don't lie to me,' she said. 'I've heard enough of them to last me a lifetime. Just admit it and leave me be.'

'Charlotte...' Alex said.

She dropped her head, tears falling again.

He reached for her hands and gently turned her face towards his. 'Look at me, my darling. Please.'

She turned but couldn't lift her eyes to his. She would see in them everything that had been lost.

'That woman you saw, that child, they aren't who you think they are.'

Charlotte blinked and took a shuddering breath.

'That was my sister-in-law and my nephew. They moved here from England with her parents. Remember I told you about my brother, Johnny? He was killed in a construction accident back in London.'

For the first time, Charlotte met his eyes.

'I haven't seen them in years, and she met me in Paddington for a short visit. She set up a homestead with her parents here in Canterbury, just something small. If I'm honest, it's lovely to have them close, to know I can see my nephew grow. It's been so long since I've seen family.'

'Your brother's wife?' A sliver of realisation cast light through the fog.

'Yes.'

'Not *your* wife? Your lover?'

'Goodness, no.'

Charlotte dropped her head into her hands and sobbed in an outpouring of relief. Her shoulders shook from exhaustion, so consumed with the ups and downs of the past weeks that when Alex pulled her to him, she let him, burying her face into his chest and allowing his strong arms to fold around her.

'Charlotte, my love.' He soothed her, stroking her hair. 'Come now, what's happened? It can't be this one thing alone.'

Her sobs turned to great gulps for air. She couldn't speak, couldn't look at him. She waited for her body to calm before she raised her head and found her voice. 'Everything has fallen apart.'

'What do you mean?'

'Estelle. She wasn't who she said she was.' Charlotte told him of her duplicity, how she was once the socialite Dorothea Baker, married to Augustus Baker, who had taken his own life due to insurmountable debt. He'd left her and their four children to brave the world without a penny to their name, resulting in Dorothea's spectacular fall from social grace and the impoverished hand she'd been dealt. She told him of Floyd and his involvement in Augustus' affairs, just as he was involved in Walter's, of his liaison with Estelle, of the intricate and cunning web of deceit that Charlotte had found herself in.

'Oh, Charlotte, I didn't realise how awful things had become. Estelle and Floyd? I'm shocked.' Alex held her close again.

'Everything's a mess. And my book of love letters is gone. My father sold it for money, then he gambled it all away.' She dipped her head again into her hands and cried. It felt good to let it out, but it would do little to reverse the damage.

Alex held her hands to his face and pressed his lips against them. 'No matter what, my love, you have me. You'll always have me.'

'But I won't,' Charlotte said, lifting her head. 'The wedding has been brought forward. I'm to marry Floyd this weekend at Town Hall.'

Alex's eyes widened. 'What? That's in four days. What happened to November?'

'They're getting desperate. Time's running out.'

'We haven't received a steel supply from your father in weeks. Bradfield's about to tear up the contract. But...' He squeezed his eyes shut then opened them again. 'I thought we had more time.'

That was the problem. They'd been so arrogant that they'd cast Floyd and the wedding to the back of their minds like some distant quandary they could forget about amid their games. Charlotte had thought if she protested enough, her father would cave, if out of sight out of mind, Floyd would simply go away. But he wasn't going anywhere. They'd underestimated his cunningness and resolve to take what wasn't his.

Alex stood. 'I'm going to speak to your father.'

Charlotte climbed to her feet too. 'What, *now*?'

'Yes. It's something I should have done ages ago. I was a fool not to.'

'What are you going to say to him?'

Alex's face set in determination. 'Exactly what I've always wanted to say. That we want to be together.'

Charlotte's heart beat faster. 'You won't catch him at the foundry. He doesn't go there anymore.'

'I'll try the mill instead, otherwise, I'm coming to the house. We'll tell him together. Be ready.'

Charlotte let Alex take her by the hand and lead her out of the school. He had renewed purpose in his step and a steely look in his eyes as they walked back along Argyle Street towards The Rocks. She was worried about how her father would take the news. She knew it would be met with belligerence, for she'd witnessed his moods before when he was backed into a corner.

The sun slunk low in dusk. Old terraces sparked on in the darkness, some with electricity, others glowing faintly with kerosene lamps. They hurried through Argyle Cut and at the top of Playfair Street, in the shadows between two streetlights, Alex kissed her goodbye. 'I'll see you soon and we'll put this right. I promise.'

She clung to him, the merest whisper telling her they might be making a mistake.

CHAPTER
38

Charlotte waited all evening for her father to come home or to hear word from Alex, but neither prevailed. Later, with her mind full of worry, sleep became elusive, slinking around her before scurrying away. In the early morning, when she heard voices in the parlour, she leapt out of bed, dressed and hurried down the stairs, certain that it must be Alex talking with her father. But when she reached the parlour doorway, she found Walter by the fireplace, not with Alex, but with Floyd, who was sitting on one end of the Chesterfield, smoking a cigarette.

He caught sight of her and stood, crushing it out in the ashtray. 'Ah, Charlotte. We were just talking about you.'

Charlotte hesitated in the doorway.

'Don't linger. Come in. Your father has been telling me a fascinating story.'

She took a tentative step into the room.

'He was just informing me,' Floyd said, 'that Mr Young, the engineer that works for Bradfield, visited him last night. He found your father at a card game over on Cleveland Street.'

Charlotte's eyes strayed to her father, but he wouldn't look at her.

'Yes, that's right. Mr Young must have embarked on some impressive sleuthing to have found your father across the other side of the city. Must have had something really important to discuss with him.' Floyd's moustache twitched. 'He told your father that the two of you were in love and wanted to be together, and that your father should give you both his blessing.' He leant backwards and started hooting with laughter. 'Isn't that the funniest thing you've ever heard?'

Charlotte stole another glance at her father, who met her eyes briefly, and she recoiled at the disappointment she saw there.

'So, is it true?' Floyd asked. He'd stopped laughing and stared at her.

She lifted her chin resolutely. 'It's true.'

Floyd's chest heaved in and out. 'You silly fool. What do you think you're playing at?'

'You're one to talk.' She shot him a withering look. 'Don't think I haven't spoken to Mrs Mayfair.'

Floyd's face turned pink.

She looked at her father. 'Please, isn't there another way we can salvage the business? I'll do anything. I'll sell everything I have. Just don't make me marry him.'

'The wedding is going ahead,' Floyd said.

'I wasn't talking to you.'

'Then talk to this.' He held up a hand, counting off the dilemmas with each finger. 'Huge debt. Unpaid workers. A breach of the bridge contract. Bankruptcy. You'll have more than a few hungry men coming after you soon.'

'Then I'll marry you and be unfaithful. I'll make a fool of you.' She sounded petulant but didn't care.

'There'll be no one to be unfaithful with,' Floyd said, smoothing back a strand of oily hair that had freed itself from the slick. 'I'm taking care of the engineer matter.'

Charlotte rounded on him. 'What does that mean?'

'It means I will do whatever is necessary to protect my investment.'

'What are you going to do?' She turned to her father, tears in her eyes.

Walter sighed heavily. 'Floyd, why don't you leave us for now? I want to talk to Charlotte alone.'

Floyd crossed his arms. 'I'm not going anywhere. I have a right to be part of this conversation.'

'Mr Clark,' Walter said firmly. 'I want to talk to my daughter alone. Please, will you leave us?'

Floyd met with Walter's determined gaze and snatched his hat and packet of cigarettes off the table. 'Fine. I'm a busy man anyway. Just get the situation under control.' He left in a huff.

At the sound of his Duesenberg gunning down Playfair Street, Walter leaned heavily against the fireplace. His brow glistened and he mopped it with his handkerchief.

'Papa.' Charlotte took a tentative step towards him.

'I'm disappointed in you, Charlotte,' he said, stuffing the handkerchief back into his pocket.

Charlotte hung her head. 'I'm sorry.'

'You went behind my back. You were with another man while engaged to Floyd. I'm appalled.'

'What will Floyd do to him?'

'I don't know and frankly, I don't care. It's none of our concern.'

Cold spread through her body. 'But it is my concern.'

'You are never to see Mr Young again, you hear?' he said adamantly.

'Please, would you just listen to me for a minute—'

'There's nothing more to say.'

'I won't stop seeing him.'

'Then I'll put a stop to it myself.' He shook his head. 'We've been over this before. What is it going to take for you to realise we need Floyd?'

'Floyd wants your business and once he has it, he'll cast us all out.'

'I won't let him do that,' he said firmly. 'We just need his money. He's planning to inject thousands into Greene Steel.'

'You think he's going to give you his money and not want something in return?' She almost scoffed. Her father's blind faith in Floyd was frustrating.

'I'll make him sign a contract. He won't act dishonourably.'

'He won't care for your contract,' she argued. 'He's too smart for you.'

'The man is about to become family.'

She stood her ground. 'I refuse to marry him.'

'That's too bad because you're going to! And you are to end it with that Young boy or so help me Charlotte, I'll end it for you.'

Walter stormed out of the parlour and Charlotte sank into the Chesterfield, not even bothering to wipe her tears.

***

Her father left the house soon after and Charlotte, desperate to get to

Alex, boarded a tram to Paddington in hopes of catching him before he left for work. But by the time she'd reached his house, he wasn't home and everything was locked.

She glanced at the time. It was eight am. She must have just missed him. She wondered if she should catch a ferry across to Milsons Point where he was stationed at the public works office, then decided against it. There were too many there who would question her presence, nor did she want to run into Floyd or her father on the off chance they were visiting the foundry. Instead, she slipped a note into Alex's mail slot, asking him to meet her that afternoon at six at Fort Street Public School, then she returned home.

While she'd been gone, the seamstress had returned the ivory dress, leaving it in its dress box by the front door. Charlotte's heart dropped at the sight of it, carrying it upstairs with her and hanging the gown from her wardrobe door, staring at it with what little fortitude she could conjure. Was there anything she could do to change what was to come? Alex's attempt had only fuelled the fire, and Floyd's words rushed over her in nauseating waves. *I'm taking care of the matter.* She didn't know what it meant, only that she had to find Alex and warn him. The time until six o'clock would be a long and agonising wait.

She filled the day with futile jobs, trying to pass the time, then at ten to six, she slipped on her hat and gloves and left the house. She hurried straight through Argyle Cut, cutting across to Upper Fort Street and in through the school gate. The grounds were quiet, a slight breeze whistling between the buildings. She sat on the hill, overlooking The Rocks and the bridge in the distance. Usually, it was quiet at that hour, the men long having returned to their homes for supper, but she could hear boats in the harbour, see beams of light sweeping the water as though they were searching for someone, their shouts echoing up the ridge. She watched for a while, unsure what the commotion was about, then her thoughts returned to Alex.

He usually finished work at four. She had given him more than enough time to get home to Five Ways, see her note on the floor of his hall and dash back out to catch the return tram to the city. But when six o'clock became six-thirty then seven o'clock, and the sun had slipped away, Charlotte resigned herself to the fact that he wasn't coming. She picked herself up off the hill and went home.

The next morning she woke early again, and this time caught the first tram at seven am to Paddington, disembarking at Five Ways and hurrying down Alex's street to his house. Once again, the house was locked. She pushed open the mail slot in his front door and peered through, noticing her letter still lying on the floor of his hall. She straightened, panic flooding her.

Her letter had been there an entire day, untouched, which meant Alex also hadn't been home for a day. Had he gone somewhere, to Canterbury perhaps to meet with his sister-in-law and nephew? Or, as her stomach flipped unpleasantly and she had to clutch the doorframe to stop herself weaving, had something befallen him? Something sinister?

It wasn't until she reached Playfair Street again that she realised she'd caught the tram home but hadn't remembered a second of it.

***

Later that afternoon, Charlotte walked back to Fort Street Public School to sit on the hill and wait for Alex. She hadn't dated her letter. In some weak endeavour of hope, she decided that if he arrived home to find it on the floor of his hall, there was still a chance he would meet her.

It was a feeble attempt to calm what was becoming a frightening thought. Where was he? Why hadn't he been home? What had Floyd done? She glanced out at the bridge, resolved to visit the public works office the next day, to check with Bradfield if he'd been to work.

She sat and waited until eight pm, her thoughts growing desperate in the dark, long after the streetlights had flickered on and terrace windows burned bright. She waited until it became obvious that he wasn't coming, then she picked herself up off the hill and walked home in a daze.

At the front of her house, Mrs Parsons and other neighbours were congregating in the street, huddled together in curlers and dressing robes.

'Did you hear?' she called out across the yard as Charlotte approached the front door.

'Hear what?' she called back.

'A young lad fell from the arch yesterday.'

Charlotte froze, her hand on the door handle. 'Fell from the arch?'

'One of the workers. A creeper crane struck him. They found his body in the water.'

Charlotte began to tremble, her hand lacking the strength suddenly to turn the handle.

'Are you all right, child?' Mrs Parsons asked, as all the neighbours turned to watch her.

Even in the dark, under the streetlights, Charlotte knew how pale she'd grown. She nodded, summoning the power to open the door and disappear into the house to escape their gawping.

It was quiet inside and she went straight to the kitchen, removed her hat and gloves and leant against the table. She clutched at her chest, her breath arriving in short, raspy bursts, a feeling of utter fear gripping her. *A young lad fell from the arch. They found his body in the water.* Her mouth grew dry, her throat ached.

'Charlotte?' Walter was beside her.

She lifted her head, hadn't heard him come down the hall.

'You're home,' he said.

'Help me!' she cried. 'I can't find Alex.'

Walter nodded gravely. 'We need to talk.'

Charlotte's stomach roiled. 'What is it?'

He swallowed, locked his large fingers together, then unlocked them. 'It's about Mr Young.'

She gripped the edge of the chair behind her, her whole body trembling.

'It all took place quickly,' her father said. 'You know Floyd, he had a score to settle.'

The room spun. Words blurred.

'He was trying to protect his investment. One thing led to another.'

Charlotte shook her head. 'What did he do?'

'I have a bag packed for you. I'll explain in the car.'

'Where are you taking me?'

'Somewhere I should have taken you months ago.' Walter leant forward, dropping his voice to a whisper. 'They're watching the house.'

The front door opened and shut and footsteps sounded down the hall. Floyd appeared in the kitchen, his eyes sweeping over them. 'What's going on in here?'

Charlotte, unable to contain herself, rushed forward and flung her fists at his chest. He held his hands up in defence, cowering, screaming at Walter to get her off him.

'Good grief, she's suffering female hysteria!' he cried once Walter had prised Charlotte off him, holding her while she sobbed. 'What in the devil's got into her?'

'It's the news of Mr Young,' Walter said.

'The engineer?' Floyd dusted off his lapel and straightened his suit. 'Hardly warrants that kind of reaction.'

'She needs rest. I'll take her up to her room.'

Charlotte clung to her father as he helped her up the stairs and into her bedroom. She sat on the edge of her bed, numb, her mind having departed someplace barren, where no thought existed. Floyd and her father were talking in front of her. She heard them mention Alex's name, the words seeping into her brain, but she was unable to put them into any logical sense.

'Try to get some sleep, love,' Walter said, kissing the top of her head and closing the door behind him.

Outside her room, Charlotte could hear them conversing again.

'Will she be all right by tomorrow? The wedding's at two.'

'She'll be fine,' Walter said. 'You can go home. I'll keep an eye on her.'

'I'm not going anywhere,' Floyd said defiantly. 'I don't trust her, or you. I'm staying right here in this house until we leave for Town Hall.'

'That won't be necessary.'

'Don't even try to talk me out of it, Greene.'

Walter sighed. 'I'll fix you a bed in the parlour.'

Their footsteps retreated downstairs. Charlotte glanced at the ivory satin dress hanging from her wardrobe, then down at her hands, then at the wall in front of her. She couldn't reconcile that Alex was gone. Only the day before last he'd kissed her, telling her he'd see her soon. That he was going to speak to her father and they would put things right. What had gone wrong? How could Alex no longer be? Surely her body would know if he ceased to exist. She would feel it, wouldn't she?

The light outside her window changed from dark to dawn, to a golden sunrise over a bridge she could never look at again. The colour of the walls changed, pale stretches of light drinking in the shadows. And not once did she move, perched on the edge of her bed the entire night, her heart in pieces.

***

'What do you mean she hasn't come out of her room yet? It's almost midday.'

Charlotte heard Floyd's anxious voice downstairs, turning her head towards it.

'I daresay she's almost catatonic,' replied Walter. 'She hasn't slept, hasn't moved from the one position all night.'

'Over this engineer business? Good lord.'

'I'm worried about her.'

'Do we need to call a doctor? Will she make it to Town Hall by two?'

'I'm not sure she's in a fit state to be married today. Can you imagine if the newspapers got wind of this?'

'What should we do then? We had a deal, Greene.'

There was no reply as the men moved into the front parlour and the door closed.

Charlotte, after fifteen hours sitting on the edge of her bed, finally laid down and rested her head against the pillow. It was an odd suspension of time she'd found herself in. The clock was still ticking, that she knew, but she seemed stuck somewhere, touching the edges of oblivion. She wanted to cry but was in shock. She wanted to scream but was disbelieving. She wanted to run to the tram stop, catch it to Five Ways and throw herself on Alex's doorstep, but she couldn't move a muscle.

She closed her eyes. Somehow, in some peculiar way, sleep prevailed, like a downy blanket, suffocating her thoughts. She allowed herself to fall into it, where there was no more pain.

CHAPTER
39

The insistent thrum of rain on the iron roof pulled Charlotte from somewhere deep, her eyes slowly opening. It was dark, the streetlights outside casting watery light across the walls. She let her vision adjust, saw her bedroom furniture gather shape and the silhouette of the ivory wedding gown still hanging from her wardrobe. It took a minute to register again what had happened, then it all came rushing back.

Alex. The bridge.

She rolled over and buried her face in her pillow and, unlike before, when she'd been too shocked to feel anything, great gulping sobs now wracked her slender frame as if reality had finally arrived to deal its swift and stunning blow.

Footsteps on the stairs, then in the hall, told her someone was approaching her room. The door opened and her father appeared, backlit by the hallway lamp. 'Charlotte, are you awake?'

She glanced up through puffy eyes and when she did, she noticed, in the spill of light, a leather suitcase by her door.

Her father stepped into the room. 'You've been asleep a long time.'

'I have?' Her voice emerged croaky in a dry throat. She closed her eyes, then opened them again. 'What day is it?'

'Wednesday.'

'But Floyd and Town Hall. Last weekend?'

'Don't worry yourself over it, love. Let's get you up.'

He went to her closet and opened the door, pulling a grey wool dress from a hanger. He laid it down on the end of her bed, sat a pair of gloves and a hat beside it and shoes to rest on the floor.

'Are we going somewhere?' she asked.

'Yes. Somewhere that will help you feel less sad.'

Less sad. Was there such a possibility?

'Alex?' she asked.

He shook his head sadly. 'He's gone, love. I'm sorry.'

'Are you sure? Maybe he's at home.'

'I'm sure.' His eyes darted towards the door. 'Floyd's downstairs.'

She closed her eyes, sorrow sweeping over her again.

'Come now. It's time to get up.' He reached down, gripped her gently around the arms and helped her to sit upright. She swung her feet to the side of the bed and lowered them to the floor. Her muscles were weak, her head lolling, limp curls falling over her face.

'I'll leave you to change.' He stepped back out into the hall and closed the door behind him.

She drew a shaky breath. She guessed her father had changed her out of last Friday's clothes for she was in a clean nightgown. She hadn't washed in days and saw that he'd set out a basin of fresh water on the dressing table. Her eyes strayed again to the suitcase by the door.

Charlotte stood, unpeeled her nightgown and dropped it to the floor, the room spinning as her stomach pined for food she couldn't tolerate but needed all the same. She sponged herself with the water in the basin and dressed in fresh undergarments and the clothes her father had laid out for her. Lastly, she pinned her hair, fixed her hat and gloves and slid on her shoes.

She wasn't sure where she was being taken or, by the looks of the suitcase, when she'd be back, and she thought longingly of the chest of letters beneath her bed. She wanted to take them with her but worried about their well-being. Her father didn't know they existed, and she wanted no harm to come to them. They were all she had left of Alex and decided the best place for them was where they were.

Instead, she took a pen and a slip of paper from her dressing table and wrote a few sentences down. She folded it, slipped it into her pocket and opened the bedroom door. The rain was coming down harder when she reached the downstairs hall and she saw her father on the telephone.

'We'll be there soon,' he said into the receiver. 'Uh-huh. Yes. I believe she'll go willingly.'

Charlotte squeezed past him and walked quickly to the kitchen. Her legs were unsteady from lack of use and she prayed they had enough strength to hold her up. She located the box under the sink that held loose coins for groceries and when her hand closed around the last shilling, she almost sank to the floor in relief.

Opening the back door, she let herself out into the yard. The iron awning only reached so far and there was no avoiding the deluge that quickly saturated her. She collected a handful of small stones from the garden, climbed up on the wooden fruit box stacked against the fence and tossed them one by one at Mrs Parsons' back door.

It took six stones for her to come out and investigate, and when she saw Charlotte waving her over to the fence, she hurried through the rain, wrapping her plaid robe tightly around herself.

'Are you crazy, child? It's pouring out here.'

'Can you please do something for me, Mrs Parsons?'

Mrs Parsons climbed up on her fruit box so they were face to face over the palings.

'I have a message I need to send my brother in England. Please, can you take it to the postmaster tomorrow?'

'You want me to send your brother a telegram?'

'Yes.'

'I can, but why can't you?'

'I have to go somewhere now.'

The rain was pelting down and they were both soaked through. Perhaps this was the only reason Mrs Parsons pursed her lips and didn't enquire further. 'All right then, hand it over.'

Charlotte reached into her pocket and pulled out the slip of paper, pressing it quickly into her neighbour's hand to keep it dry. 'Here is the message for James and details on where to send it. And a shilling for the fee.'

'It won't cost that much.'

'Please, take it.' Charlotte didn't wait for further protest but thanked her profusely and jumped down off the fruit box, scrambling back under the awning. When she looked back, Mrs Parsons had returned to her house, the note safely in the dry.

Back inside the kitchen, Walter was upon her. 'Where have you been? You're soaked through.'

'I thought I heard a noise outside,' Charlotte said.

Walter looked past her, then frowned. 'Come now, we mustn't keep Floyd waiting. He's out front and already in a mood. Are you hungry? I packed you something for the ride.'

'Where are we going?'

Walter put his hands around her arms. 'Do you trust me, love?'

She looked into her father's eyes and realised with great sadness that she didn't. That nothing he'd said or done in the past year had earned her confidence. Those delicate threads had long ago been severed.

It seemed he sensed this also, for he nodded sadly and shepherded her down the hall towards the front door, where her suitcase and coat waited. Outside, Walter extended an umbrella against the deluge and clutched Charlotte's arm, guiding her out to Floyd's Duesenberg. The back door opened and Walter helped her in.

'Why is she so wet?' Floyd barked. 'She's dripping water all over my seat.'

'I found her standing in the backyard,' Walter shouted over the rain.

Floyd shook his head. 'As mad as her mother.'

Walter closed the door and ran for her suitcase and coat. He locked the house door, tossed them and the sodden umbrella into the boot, and climbed into the passenger seat.

Floyd started the car and they moved down Playfair Street through the same sweeping torrent that swallowed up the house when Charlotte turned to look back at it. A small sob escaped her as she wondered if she would ever see her house again. A childhood memory came to mind, of the same suitcase waiting by the front door. Of her tearful mother being guided out by her father to his Studebaker and helped into the front seat, her eyes rimmed with grief as Charlotte watched from the front door. She remembered the song playing on their gramophone before they left—Victor Military Band's 'Poor Butterfly', an upbeat wartime melody that seemed far too cheerful for where her mother had been taken that night.

'This damn weather,' Floyd said, scowling at the sky.

Charlotte's attention returned to the car. They were somewhere south of the city, heading through Haymarket, towards Pyrmont, the curtain of rain not letting up, the wipers squeaking monotonously against the windscreen. Squally winds lashed the bays on either side of the road, the night turbulent, black and unforgiving.

'Did you hear?' Walter's voice came from the front seat. His head was turned towards Floyd's. 'The New York Stock Exchange.'

'It was on the wireless this afternoon.'

'It's not good news, Floyd.'

'We'll be fine.'

'I don't think any of us will be fine. They've called it Black Tuesday, the biggest stock crash in the history of the industrialised world. It's diabolical on Wall Street.'

'The Dow Jones will recover. It always does.'

'I don't think it will this time. It plummeted nearly ninety percent in one day. Billions of dollars have been lost. It's wiped out investors.'

'Our banks will hold up the economy.'

'The banks have been speculating on the stock market using deposited funds. They're set to lose money too. People will panic and take their funds out. Not to mention all the over-crediting.'

Floyd turned his head sharply. 'You've never complained about the bank's money before, Greene. All those loans I signed off on.'

'And I'm not complaining now,' Walter said quickly. 'I'm grateful, really. But I'm worried for my business. Maybe we should fold here in Australia and sell off the mill and foundry. I can pay my workers back.'

'We're not selling off anything. Don't get cold feet on me now.'

'Where will you get the money to prop things up if the bank can't come through? If it collapses? If a bank run occurs?'

'You're panicking.'

'We're thousands of pounds in debt. We can't operate like that.'

'I'm not an idiot!' But Floyd fell silent after that. He lit a cigarette, a quivering hand striking the match and touching it to the end, sizzling the tobacco. Rain lashed at the windows as they drove on. 'How long will she stay in this place?'

'Not long. The doctor will assess her and provide a course of treatment.'

'Your wife was in there for four years. And we all know how that turned out.'

Walter nodded solemnly. 'I do believe this is different.'

'Two weeks. I'll give you two weeks. Don't test me, Greene.'

'Of course, Floyd.'

They turned onto a long stretch of road slick with oily water and lined with trees buffeted by the wind. They crossed Gladesville Bridge over a choppy black bay and, after a further ten minutes, swung into a driveway, coming to rest at tall iron gates, a sign above a lichen-covered sandstone wall informing them to STOP. A larger sign affixed to a brown stone building announced Gladesville Mental Hospital and Charlotte's insides turned cold. She knew this place well, the monster of her young memories, the place that had taken her mother.

A guard in an oilskin approached the car. Floyd wound down the window, rain pouring in. He informed him of the psychiatrist's name and that they were expected.

The guard released the gates and let them through.

***

Little had changed inside the hospital waiting room. While Charlotte waited for her father to consult with the psychiatrist, she stared at the same grey walls and linoleum floors she had stared at as a child when they'd visited her mother on the weekends. The hardwood bench seat was still there, the one she and James used to kick the backs of their Mary Jane's against while waiting to be granted those rare and precious minutes with her. The austere woman with the severe bun was still behind the front desk, the one who used to dare them with her beady eyes to leave the bench and explore. She stared at Charlotte now, in the same way. Daring her to run.

Charlotte leant against the cold wall and sighed. Floyd was across the other side of the room, restlessly chain-smoking. Asylums, it would seem, were not for the likes of him.

A door in the waiting room opened and Walter and Dr Carmichael appeared. Charlotte remembered the psychiatrist well. He was older now, sandy coloured hair turned a shock of white, steel-rimmed spectacles over grey-blue eyes, but despite how he'd aged, she'd never forgotten the man who'd condemned her mother to that place.

'These things are often hereditary,' he explained to Walter. 'Her mother suffered it, so it's likely Charlotte has too.'

'I see,' Walter said.

'We'll give her the best medical treatment. Don't you worry about a thing.'

'Of course. I trust your advice explicitly.'

They walked towards her and Floyd crushed his cigarette in an ashtray and joined them.

'So this must be Charlotte.' The good doctor clapped his hands genially. 'Do you remember me? Why, you were just a little girl when I last saw you.'

Charlotte's teeth began to chatter, her clothes still soaked through from talking to Mrs Parsons over the fence.

'She got a bit wet in the backyard tonight,' Walter explained. 'I think she was standing in the rain.'

'Ah, yes,' Dr Carmichael said, as if this was to be completely expected of someone in her condition.

'This is her suitcase.' Walter handed him the bag.

The doctor took it. 'We'll keep it somewhere safe. She won't need anything from it.'

'How long is she going to be in this place?' Floyd asked impatiently.

Dr Carmichael shot him a firm look. 'As long as it takes.'

'Greene,' he growled.

'I'm sure Charlotte's recovery will be swift,' Walter said diplomatically. He turned to Charlotte and helped her to her feet. 'Now, love, you go with Dr Carmichael. He'll take good care of you.'

'When will you be back for me?' she asked. She was so tired, her thoughts were like fog, barely an ounce of energy to object. 'You will come back, won't you?'

'Of course, love. I promise.' He kissed the top of her head, and Dr Carmichael took her arm.

Together with her suitcase, he guided her to a large steel door that led to the wards beyond and, with a jangle of keys, a ward attendant appeared on the opposite side to slide it open.

Charlotte turned back once to see her father wave goodbye and found that same intriguing look in his eyes that once again said, *do you trust me?*

CHAPTER 40

PAIGE
Present Day

The sudden arrival of Delphine Beaumont at La Maison had taken Paige and Ryan by surprise. More so when she asked if there was somewhere quiet they could go to talk about the envelope. At the risk of this shy yet enigmatic woman leaving, they were quick to suggest a café close to the hotel, and they all left the lobby of La Maison, walking there.

A mild sun balanced in the sky, gently warming the cobblestones on the ground. It was not quite lunch when they arrived; the outside tables were full but inside was quiet. Perfect for listening to what Delphine had to say.

They sat in a booth at the back and ordered lattes and a plate of chouquettes that none of them would likely eat. They made small talk, Delphine slight and awkward in an oversized grey cardigan and ripped black jeans, her pale skin stark against the long dark plait that cascaded over one shoulder. They all seemed to breathe in relief when the coffee and puffs of pearl sugared pastry arrived.

'I'm sorry for the way I acted when you came to Ovillers,' Delphine said, her accent strong but English grammar perfect. 'I don't often get visitors and you surprised me. I used to live in Paris, you know. But my grandparents died a few years ago and I inherited the old place.'

'So they owned it?' Paige asked.

'Yes. And my great-grandparents before that, and so on. It's been in my family since it was built in the nineteenth century.'

'Your great-grandfather wasn't James Greene by any chance, was he?' Ryan asked.

Delphine shook her head. 'No, sorry. He was not called James.'

'Well, that rules him out as the sender,' Ryan said to Paige.

'What about your parents?' Paige asked.

'My mother was young when she met my father. Here in Paris, actually. After a brief affair, she returned home to Ovillers pregnant. After I was born, she left.' Delphine retreated into her cardigan a little. 'I don't blame her. She was young and not ready to be a mother. Eventually, she did marry and lives in Sweden now with her husband and children. We send each other cards sometimes.'

'And your father?'

'I've never met him.'

Paige smiled gently. 'I'm sorry to hear that.'

'Please don't be. I'm fine with it. My whole life to get used to it, in fact.'

'Well, your cottage is incredible,' Paige said, deftly changing the subject. 'It survived two world wars.'

'There were some near misses, especially during the Great War,' Delphine said. 'There is a huge crater behind the house. I can show you sometime if you find this sort of thing interesting. There are craters everywhere in Somme.' She wrapped her hands around her coffee and stared into it. 'You asked me when you came to Ovillers if I knew who sent that envelope.'

'Yes,' Ryan said, suddenly upright.

'I lied to you.' She glanced at them sheepishly. 'I do know.'

Paige gripped Ryan's hand underneath the table.

'It was a man called Alexander Young.'

Ryan almost knocked his coffee cup over. 'Alexander Young?'

'Yes. He was my great-grandfather.'

Paige gulped with astonishment. 'But how can that be?'

Delphine looked from Paige to Ryan with confusion. 'I'm sorry. I don't understand this question.'

'Well, it's just that we've done a lot of research on Alex Young,' Paige explained. 'We found a record that all but confirmed his death. He fell from the northern arch of the Sydney Harbour Bridge on October twenty-four, 1929, a few days before his lover was admitted to a mental hospital for grief. The timeline fits. How can he turn up in Paris in 1930 if he died in 1929?'

Delphine shrugged. 'I don't know about that record you found but I can assure you, Alexander Young was my great-grandfather. His daughter was my grandmother. And her daughter was my mother. Because of this line of females, I don't carry the Young name. I'm a Beaumont.'

'Incredible,' Ryan said, shaking his head. 'So Alex didn't die on the bridge that day. He came here to France.'

Paige was kicking herself for not verifying the fact properly. In her rush for the truth, she'd failed to follow up on the missing letters of the worker who had died the week before Charlotte was sent to Gladesville. Not Alex Young at all, but another man who'd fallen from the northern arch with the letters A, E and Y in his name.

'So tell me what you found out about Alex,' Delphine said.

'Well, he was an incredible asset to the design and construction of the Sydney Harbour Bridge,' Paige said. 'He also fell in love with a young woman there, only for a brief time, about six months. If what you're saying is right, then he must have left for France in October 1929. The young woman he was seeing died in a hospital a few months later in 1930. Her cause of death was suicide. We saw it on her medical report. She thought he was dead and she took her own life.'

'What made you start researching all this?' Delphine asked.

'My boss bought a house on Playfair Street in The Rocks in Sydney. Up in the attic, I discovered a chest containing old clues belonging to the young woman who lived there. The woman Alex loved, who also happened to be Ryan's great-aunt. I contacted Ryan in the UK to let him know what I'd found and it started from there. We've been researching it ever since.'

'This is fascinating,' Delphine said, her dark eyes lighting up.

'Even more so because my great-aunt was already engaged to another man,' Ryan explained. 'She and Alex were meeting in secret. They passed each other clues to arrange rendezvous points around the city. I imagine there would have been quite a thrill in it—solving the riddle and finding the person.'

'Like a game,' Delphine said, smiling.

'Exactly,' Paige said. 'And with those clues they also wrote small quotes from famous love letters to each other—Emily Dickinson, King Henry VIII, Oscar Wilde, Mary Wollstonecraft.'

'I know these people,' Delphine said. 'My great-grandfather recited letters from them. He was a bit of a hopeless romantic.'

Paige smiled. It warmed her to think that while Alex may have moved on with his life, he hadn't forgotten the game he'd played with Charlotte.

'And these letters and clues, the ones you found in the attic of the old house, were they in that wooden chest you brought to Ovillers?'

'Yes, they were,' Paige said.

'Do you still have them with you? I'd like to see what Alex wrote.'

'They're upstairs in my room,' Ryan said. 'I can go and get them.' He stood, declaring he'd be back in five minutes and dashed out of the café.

'So are you two married?' Delphine asked, sipping her coffee.

'Oh, no, we're just sort of dating.'

Delphine looked confused. 'Oh. He's British, right? And you're Australian. Which country do you live in together?'

'Well, we don't. I live in Australia and Ryan lives in the UK.'

'So you're together, but you're not?' She raised an eyebrow.

Paige grimaced at how accurately the girl had summed it up.

'My fiancé and I broke up last year,' Delphine said with surprising candour.

'You had a fiancé?'

'Yes, but after my grandparents died, I wanted to move to their house in Somme. He didn't like the idea of leaving Paris, so we ended it.'

'That's a shame.'

'My grandparents had thought I was too young anyway,' Delphine said. 'They were always telling me to travel and experience life. They were worried I'd arrive on their doorstep pregnant too.'

'I can understand their concern, given what happened.' Paige smiled softly. 'Your great-grandfather liked to travel. He travelled from England to Australia to France, in fact.'

'Yes, and yet, his French was terrible.' Delphine laughed. 'I even tried to teach him when I was a child, but he was hopeless. He was too English. What is this saying, you can't teach an old dog...'

'New tricks.' Paige laughed too. 'So you knew him well before he died?'

'*Oui*. As well as a child can. I was five when he passed away, but I remember him, of course. He fills my earliest memories.'

'When did he die?'

'In 2002. He was ninety-eight. He slipped away peacefully in his sleep one night.'

'And his wife?'

'She died the year before he did,' Delphine said sadly. 'She suffered a stroke and never recovered. To be honest, it's a miracle he lasted twelve months without her. They were inseparable.'

'I'm glad he found someone he could love that much,' Paige said. 'Do you live at the cottage on your own now?'

'Yes. Just me and the cow and the chickens.' She glanced down at her coffee, her expression sorrowful. 'There is no one left. My grandparents and great-grandparents are gone. I guess I have my mother and half-brothers and sisters in Sweden, but I never see them. And all my friends are still here in Paris.'

Paige thought of the immense sacrifice Delphine had undertaken to reside in her cottage of memories, the friends and fiancé she'd left behind. It seemed an unnecessarily lonely existence for a girl who should have been loving and laughing her way through her twenties in the heart of Paris, just as her grandparents had encouraged, but instead, she'd chosen to live on her own amongst the whispers of her departed. And whilst she seemed sad, there was also quiet resolve in her decisions, and Paige decided she must be one of the bravest young women she'd ever come across.

Ryan returned, holding the chest of letters in his hand. He set it down on the table and took his seat. 'Here it is, all the letters Charlotte and Alex wrote to each other, as well as the envelope that was sent from the Ovillers cottage to the Playfair Street house, attention to Charlotte.'

'Charlotte?' Delphine asked.

'Yes. That's the woman Alex fell in love with. The one he played the game with and who took her own life in the hospital,' Paige explained.

Delphine considered the envelope first, turning the plastic sleeve over in her hand. 'That's my address on the back. It definitely came from my cottage and yes, most likely from Alex. Dated February 1930.' Then she ran her palm over the Edwardian carvings of the chest and Charlotte's name engraved in the wood. 'May I?' she asked.

'Of course.' Ryan lifted the lid to the familiar sight of the letters tied in bundles with twine. He pulled the topmost one out and placed it in front of Delphine, wriggling the twine off gently so she could see the letters.

She took her time reading them, slight and nimble fingers touching the paper with the utmost care, as though she were handling delicate artefacts. And they were. A love between two people enshrined in a wooden chest, long after that love ceased to exist in the living.

Delphine's eyes misted over and she wiped a tear that spilled over her lashes and down her cheek. 'They are beautiful,' she said, wiping it away.

'Yes,' Paige said. 'They are. And we can't tell you what it means that you came to Paris to talk to us. Knowing that Alex sent this letter, that he didn't die on the bridge that day, was so worth the trip here.'

Delphine chewed her lip. 'There's something I need to show you.'

While Paige and Ryan exchanged a look she pulled from her bag a plain white envelope and extracted from it a piece of old tattered paper, yellowed with age. She slid it across the table and Ryan collected it gently and held it up to the light so they could make out the handwriting.

Paige was almost sure it was Alex's, and if Ryan's small gasp was anything to go by, he'd concluded the same.

> *Fifth February 1930*
> *To My Dearest Charlotte,*
> *Though still in bed, my thoughts go out to you, my Immortal Beloved. Be calm—love me—today—yesterday—what tearful longings for you—you—you—my life—my all— farewell. Oh continue to love me—never misjudge the most faithful heart of your beloved.*
> *Ever thine. Ever mine. Ever ours.*
> *Alex*

'Where did you get this from?' Paige asked, stunned.

'I found it in the house a couple of months ago,' Delphine said. 'I never knew what it meant until you arrived in Ovillers with your chest of Alex's letters and that envelope. I think this is the one that belongs to it.'

'*Ever thine, ever mine, ever ours,*' Paige said. 'It's Beethoven. And the date. February 1930. They're a match!'

'Read the clue,' Delphine urged.

> *I've spoken of it before, beneath the trees in Hyde Park.*
> *Do you remember?*
> *Oh, how I've missed you!*
> *Come find me. I'll be waiting...*

'Alex was asking her to join him in France,' Paige said. 'He must have told her about the cottage during one of their meetings. But by the time this letter arrived in Sydney, Charlotte had already died in hospital.'

'But hang on,' Ryan said, 'we found the envelope in Playfair Street. Delphine found the letter in the cottage. If Alex sent this letter to Charlotte in Sydney, how did it end up back here in France?'

'This is where I think you're missing some of the story,' Delphine said. She reached again for her bag and pulled from it a maroon hardcover book, its title in gold stamp. Paige caught a whiff of the ageing pages, stiff and gilt-edged, and the creak of its spine when Delphine opened it. 'I found the book first and the letter was inside.'

'*Love Through the Ages—A Collection of Timeless Love Letters*,' Paige read aloud.

'This was my great-grandmother's book,' Delphine said. 'She and Alex always read from it, until the day they died. It was her mother's, passed down to her, then to my grandmother and now me.'

Paige turned the pages gently, realisation dawning. They were all in there, the great love letters of old, the ones Charlotte and Alex used to write to each other—Emily Dickinson, King Henry VIII, Oscar Wilde, Mary Wollstonecraft and of course, Beethoven.

Paige looked up with emotion in her throat. 'She made it back to him, didn't she?'

Delphine smiled. 'Yes, she did.'

Ryan looked dumbfounded. 'Wait. Charlotte? Here? But how?'

Delphine leant forward in her oversized cardigan. 'Let me tell you what I know.'

CHAPTER 41

CHARLOTTE
Christmas Day 1929

Seven weeks had passed since Charlotte had been admitted to Gladesville Mental Hospital. Her treatment consisted of a weekly consultation with Dr Carmichael to discuss her condition, followed by a spell under the cold high-pressurised hose to restore her equilibrium, then a sedative that the nurses forced down her throat after dinner each evening, sending her into a boundless sleep that left her groggy the next morning. When she woke, she would eat a little breakfast with the other female patients and, if the weather was pleasant, take herself down as far as the grounds permitted, near Bedlam Point, to look out over the harbour and think of Alex.

She still pined for him, still cried when no one was around to see, for if having a mother in an asylum had taught Charlotte anything, it was to never let those around you know you were sad. Sadness was lunacy, the kind of female hysteria that landed you in a mental institution. But Charlotte didn't feel hysterical. She just missed Alex terribly. Sometimes her grief was so raw it scrubbed away all colour, other times the simple act of crying made her feel whole again.

Although their time together had been brief, it was a love that had changed her. As she stared out at the harbour, she would remember his whisper-like touch, his lips on her skin, the hours spent in his arms as if it were only yesterday. Sometimes, just to make sure it wasn't a dream, she would try to feel the moment his last breath left him, when he'd fallen from the bridge and left *her* and this earth, but she couldn't. It wouldn't come, almost as if it had never happened. She did know one thing for certain though, she would never know another man like Alexander Young.

Because Charlotte had been assigned to the female ward, she rarely interacted with the male patients except to pass them on the grounds. It was a curious thing to see their crazy out in the open. The females were not as spirited as the men, mostly having suffered a grieving condition like hers. Women who had lost babies through stillbirths or the sleeping death, who suffered anxiety or an unhealthy sexual appetite—or, inversely, a lack of sexual drive—and those who experienced insomnia or fluid retention. There were all sorts, but mostly the women were nice and they often shared snippets over the dinner table about the changing world outside, things they'd heard from visitors or the ward staff.

Black Thursday, followed by Black Tuesday, had come and gone. The stocks had crashed, banks failed everywhere, unemployment and breadlines had increased exponentially. But within the walls of the hospital, daily life remained a steady constant, a puzzling yet peaceful humdrum.

On Christmas Day, Walter arrived after lunch, bringing a small gift for her, a new wide-brimmed picture hat with a large blue ribbon.

'Thank you. It's lovely,' Charlotte said, putting it on. 'I'm sorry. I don't have anything for you. Well, other than this.' She handed him a photograph the matron had taken of her with Dr Carmichael, the night before on Christmas Eve. 'I thought you might like it. I did try to get one on my own but it wasn't to be.'

'Thank you, love.' He took the photograph and tucked it deep into his pocket, patting it fondly. 'I'll keep it someplace safe.'

They walked outside under a glaring December sun. Dark clouds hovered to the south, the threat of a summer storm to ring in Boxing Day.

'Sorry I haven't been back to visit since I brought you here,' her father said. 'You're looking well.'

'I feel well. Except when they give me medication at night. It's strong and knocks me out. I often wake dizzy from it.'

'I'll speak to Dr Carmichael about it.'

'Thank you.'

They reached the high iron fence near Bedlam Point and Charlotte wrapped her hands around the bars. The sun bounced off the surface of the water, turning it into a thousand tiny crystals, reminding her oddly of Estelle.

'Floyd lost his job at the bank,' her father said.

She wasn't ashamed to admit she was pleased. 'Good.'

'They're downsizing in light of the current economic times. And he's in a bit of strife for the number of loans he'd approved. Something in the vicinity of five million pounds throughout his career. All of it went to undesirables who couldn't hope to repay.'

'Like yourself?' she said, the hint of a smile.

He glanced at her sheepishly. 'Yes, I suppose like me.'

'I'm surprised he got away with it for so long.'

'He's a clever man. He would have continued to get away with it had the stock exchanges not crashed and the banks been scrutinised.'

Charlotte turned her gaze back to the water. 'What's going to happen to our mill and foundry?'

'Our contract with the bridge is all but torn up. I'm deciding whether to sell the mill and foundry. With the money we can pay back the bank at least, maybe some of our workers. Perhaps I'll let James decide.'

'What does Floyd think about that?'

'I'm not running things past Floyd anymore. He's still chasing me though, says I owe him. And of course, I do.' Walter sighed, looking exhausted.

'I won't marry him,' she said firmly. 'Not after what he did to Alex.'

Walter cleared his throat and looked down at his shoes. 'Love, there's something I need to tell you about Mr Young.'

The words sent a cold finger of ice down her spine. 'What is it?'

'Well.' He took off his homburg, scratched the top of his head and replaced it. 'I haven't been entirely honest with you.'

Charlotte's breakfast rose unpleasantly in her throat. She had only just managed to store Alex away in a safe place in her heart that felt less like sorrow and more like a beautiful memory. She wasn't sure she could handle any more painful news of him.

'You see, love, this is going to come as somewhat of a surprise to you.' He cleared his throat. 'Mr Young isn't dead.'

She blinked at him, taking a full minute to absorb what he'd just said.

'Come, sit over here.' He took her elbow and led her to a low wall by an enormous willow.

She sat beside her father, grateful not to be standing because her legs threatened to buckle. Her voice was a whisper. 'What do you mean he's not dead?'

'He didn't die that day on the bridge. He's very much alive.' He held up his hand when she attempted to interrupt. 'Just hear me out. That afternoon, when you came home, I was trying to tell you that Mr Young and I had come to an arrangement. But you were in such a state already and I had to get you out the door that there was no time to explain. Then Floyd arrived and our window of opportunity was lost. It all went downhill from there.'

Charlotte heard her sharp intake of breath, felt her pulse quicken in her wrists. *Alex was alive?*

'I know this is difficult to understand. You must be in shock,' Walter said.

'Shock?' she said, incredulously. 'Shock? I mourned him.'

'It was never my intention to mislead you. It just evolved that way. Then, ironically, it became our solution.'

Of all the rotten things her father had done, this had to be the worst. She felt a rage build inside her, and had she not been in the middle of the hospital grounds, where the threat of looking crazy was magnified, she might have flung herself at him and pummelled him senseless. 'So if he's not dead, where is he?'

'In France.'

'*France?*' She glared at him. 'And you didn't think to tell me this earlier? You had so many opportunities.'

'I didn't really. When we were at the house, Floyd wouldn't let us out of his sight. If I had told you, you would have become even more hysterical and given us away.'

'Hysterical?' Her voice rose with her anger. 'Hysterical!'

'Keep your voice down.'

Charlotte felt her world tilt as the revelation sunk in. 'But Floyd said he was going to take matters into his own hands to protect his investment. We both heard him say that.'

'Yes, that's right, and he did. He went to see Bradfield and demanded Alex be fired and sent back to England. When Bradfield tossed him out on his backside, Floyd had thugs follow Alex home.'

'What did they do to him?'

'A black eye and some broken ribs. The lad wasn't seriously hurt.'

'But Mrs Parsons told me a man fell from the northern arch. I saw the boats in the water looking for him.'

'A man did fall, but it wasn't Mr Young. Unrelated, a pure coincidence.'

Charlotte let out a trapped breath. Her head swam with the sweetest, most perfect kind of relief, but she was also confused. Why had no one told her this sooner? Why had she been left in this place to grieve?

'You see, Mr Young came to see me that night at a card game on Cleveland Street. He was a determined lad, tracking me down like that. He told me that you had feelings for each other and that he intended to marry you. He asked for my blessing.' He glanced at her with remorse. 'I had the poor boy thrown out. Not before he told me that he wanted to take you to France to get away from Floyd. You can imagine my reaction.'

He sighed deeply. 'Then I did something stupid. I took off home rotten drunk and called Floyd to tell him what happened. It was a mistake. I should have packed a bag for you then and there and sent you off with Mr Young.'

'Why didn't you?'

'Because I'm a pathetic old man who makes bad decisions. Always have been.' He hung his head, years of poor choices dragging at his shoulders. 'In any case, Mr Young had hit a nerve. What I was asking of you and the kind of life he was offering held no comparison. And when he told me he'd thought someone had followed you both home the previous evening from Fort Street Public School, my mind was made up.

'So I called Mr Young the next day and told him yes, that I'd pack a bag and bring you down to Finger Wharf that night where a passenger liner was leaving Sydney, bound for London. He'd already purchased your ticket and all we had to do was show up. As soon as I got home from work, I packed your suitcase and waited for you to come home.'

Charlotte had been at Fort Street Public School waiting for Alex to meet her. She'd had no idea he'd been waiting for her on the wharf. Their paths hadn't even come close to crossing.

'When you finally got home, there was no time to explain. It was late and I had to get you in the car and to the wharf. But then Floyd arrived and threw our plans into disarray. He couldn't understand why you were so hysterical over a bit of thuggery out the front of Mr Young's home. Of course, you thought something more sinister had happened, and I allowed the confusion, if only for the opportunity to get you up to your room so that Floyd would leave us and we could be on our way. But it didn't work out.'

Thunder rumbled in the distance and clouds began to charge towards the hospital. A brisk wind picked up, tossing the willow leaves around like untamed hair.

'Come, love. Let's head back so we don't get caught in the storm.'

They climbed to their feet and Walter guided her back towards the female ward.

'Floyd wouldn't leave the house that night,' he continued as they walked. 'Mr Young was waiting on the ship for you, but it was impossible to get you out. Even if I could, we were being watched. We wouldn't have made it two steps out the front door.'

'Why did Alex stay on the ship? Why didn't he get off and come back for me?' She was hurt that he could leave her behind.

'It was my fault, love.' He gave her another sheepish look. 'I told him that under no circumstances should he leave the boat. That I would make sure you boarded. I couldn't risk him getting off and you getting on, potentially missing each other. You would have been sent to the other side of the world on your own.'

'Oh God.' Charlotte dropped her head into her hands.

'He did as I said. He stayed on the ship.'

'You made him sail without me?' She lifted her head, boring her eyes into her father. Poor Alex! She could only imagine his panic as the ship set sail, realising too late that she hadn't made it aboard and that he was stuck on there, a six week journey to London, unable to get off and with no way of contacting her or knowing if she was safe. He would have been frantic.

'It wasn't my intention. Nothing went to plan.'

'Do you know if he got there okay? Have you heard from him?'

'There's been no word yet. I'm sure we'll hear soon.' He smiled reassuringly, but his eyes looked as uncertain as the storm clouds above.

The sliver of strength she'd built over the past month threatened to disintegrate. Alex was alive, news to warm her fragile heart, but they didn't know where he was or if he'd arrived safely. Charlotte couldn't even be sure he would want her anymore, that he hadn't got to France and realised too much time had passed and his feelings had changed. He might have met someone else.

'I'm sorry, love,' her father said, hanging his head ashamedly.

'What am I even doing here?' she asked through thinly veiled fury. 'You put me in this hospital for no good reason, then you left me here.'

'Not for no good reason,' he said. 'The state says you cannot marry someone under asylum care. You being in here meant your wedding to Floyd couldn't happen.'

Charlotte looked away. She supposed she should be grateful that he had thwarted Floyd. She wouldn't have to marry the man, although she was astonished at the lengths her father had gone to in order to gain the upper hand. She was in an asylum, Alex was on the other side of the world and the business was all but dissolved, leaving Floyd with nothing, not even his job.

'You know it wasn't just me Floyd's done this to,' her father said. 'He tried it on Augustus Baker as well, who wasn't so fortunate. Floyd's made a fortune exploiting the weaknesses of others, propping them up with loans they couldn't repay, taking over their businesses then selling them off for a tidy profit. He didn't get rich being a loans manager at the Bank of New South Wales, I can assure you.'

'I did try to tell you Floyd was bad news,' she said turning to face him again, 'but you were never any good at standing up to him.'

'I know.' He nodded glumly. 'I didn't want to admit I'd lost control.'

But he had and it had cost them dearly. His beloved company was in ruins, he was thousands of pounds in debt, and Floyd was no doubt vengeful having been cheated out of another takeover.

They were almost at the female ward again. Charlotte glanced at her father. 'Shall I run upstairs and get my things? I assume I'm coming home with you today.'

He sighed. 'No, love. Not today.'

She stopped walking. 'Why not?'

Her father stopped too and faced her. 'Because I have to go away for a while.'

'Where?'

'Out of town, until the dust settles.'

'What does that mean?'

He sighed wearily. 'It's not just Floyd I've upset, love. He's the least of my worries. There are a lot of bad men after me. I owe money, plenty of it.'

'Then take me out of here. I'll come with you,' she insisted.

'Believe me, you're safer in here, Charlotte.'

She frowned. 'How bad are these men?'

'Let's just say I didn't bring you here because of Floyd alone. It's bigger than that.'

His words left her cold inside. Just how many people had a score to settle with them?

'I've asked someone to watch over you. They'll be around to visit soon. In the meantime, keep to yourself. Don't tell anyone what we spoke of today.'

'And Alex. When can I see him?'

'Once we hear from him.'

They returned to the ward where the other visitors were congregating for their escort back to the main building. There he turned to her. 'A hundred apologies couldn't make up for what I've done,' he said, blinking back tears. 'Know only that I'm trying to right my wrongs.'

She blinked back tears too. She had no idea if Alex was safe or if her father would still be alive come nightfall or the next. Perhaps inside the hospital was the safest place for her, but it didn't stop her heart tripping on its beat from pure fear. 'How will I know when it's time to leave?'

'You'll know.'

'And where will I find you?'

'Don't worry, I'll find *you*.' He kissed her cheek and held her close. 'You have a merry Christmas, love.'

CHAPTER 42

CHARLOTTE
March 1930

It was three months later when Charlotte received her next bit of news from the outside world, in the form of a visitor. After breakfast, she was called to the lounge area where family members of female patients were being escorted in, and there, on a beaten old lounge, looking wildly out of place, was Estelle.

When she saw Charlotte she rose, smoothing down her mint green dress and arranging a string of pearls that looped several times around her throat before dropping to a knot at her navel. T-bar heels, silk stockings, white gloves and a white silk turban that she'd fashioned from a scarf made her look so extravagantly at odds with the hospital's muted tones that everyone in the room stopped to stare at her.

'Charlotte.' She moved to embrace her but halted.

Charlotte crossed her arms. 'What are you doing here, Estelle?'

She rolled her shoulders back with indignation. 'Your father sent me.'

So this was the person Walter had sent to 'watch over her'. This lying, no good schemer who played people to serve her interests. This woman whose name wasn't even Estelle Mayfair, rather Dorothea Baker. And yet, as Charlotte thought this, she also couldn't dismiss how alike they were. They'd both suffered the injustices of a loved one's gambling addiction, had both been pawns in Floyd's duplicitous games. Still,

Charlotte didn't trust her, and it would remain to be seen if Estelle was friend or foe.

The day outside was hot, with barely a breeze to break the heat. Charlotte suggested a walk to Bedlam Point but they stopped halfway when Estelle's heels kept sinking into the grass, and they sat instead beneath a willow tree. Estelle produced a fan to cool herself with, her expensive green dress a disparity against Charlotte's sombre hospital garb.

'You look well,' Estelle said. 'Better than I thought you would. I wasn't sure what to expect, to be honest.'

Charlotte remained silent, glaring at her, wondering what Estelle could possibly hope to gain from this visit. They weren't friends. There would be no heart-warming reunion.

'Your father sends his love.' She squirmed, working the fan harder against the stagnant heat.

'Is he safe?'

'Safe as can be for the mess he's found himself in.'

The nerve of the woman. 'No thanks to you and Floyd.'

'Come now.' Estelle gave her a syrupy smile. 'I can hardly be blamed for your father's gambling habit. He did that all on his own. You shouldn't think so poorly of me, Charlotte. You and I always had a common goal, despite what you think.'

'And that was?'

'To keep you and Floyd apart. I didn't want you marrying him any more than you did. So while you may find my actions abhorrent, remember that we shared the same objective.' She placed the fan down and dug around in her purse for her pack of Camels and a cigarette holder. She fitted the two together, struck a match to the end and puffed to ignite it. She blew a delicate smoke ring into the air, to be snatched quickly away.

'You know, you intrigued Floyd,' she said, pointing the cigarette at Charlotte. 'He didn't expect you to be so resistant. He found it charming, arousing even, until he became so desperately annoyed by it all.'

'Why did he want it so badly, the marriage? Surely there were other ways to acquire my father's company without going to such an extreme.'

Estelle inhaled contemplatively. 'I suppose there was. But when Augustus was alive, Floyd preyed upon his weaknesses, just as he preyed upon your father's. He'd almost secured our textile's business too. But what he didn't count on was Augustus taking his own life. The day that happened, the company folded. There was nothing left for Floyd to gain.

'He was furious. And he wasn't about to take that chance again. Marrying into the Greene family would have secured his position, allowing him to take the deeds right out from under you.'

'And you love this man?' Charlotte asked dumbfounded. 'After everything he did to you and Augustus? What he tried to do to us. What he will probably do to someone else.'

Estelle pressed her bright red lips together. 'It's not for us to judge what the heart wants, nor for us to understand why. Yes, Floyd destroyed my life, but I love him. I can't explain why. All I know is that you reap what you sow and for that, I will make sure Floyd is stuck with me and my children for the rest of his life.'

Brush away the gloss and glamour of Estelle and there was a woman who loved with one part of her soul and reprised with the other. Charlotte wasn't sure if she felt sorry for her or admired her resilience. Perhaps both. 'Do you know what's happened to our company?' she asked.

'Your contract with the bridge is over. Bradfield tore it up. He found another local supplier.'

Charlotte nodded, deducing as much. 'And our employees?'

'There wasn't enough money to pay them. They've moved on. What else is there to do in these times?' She exhaled before crushing the cigarette on the grass and flicking it away from the holder, looking absentmindedly across the hospital grounds. 'It's a changed world out there, Charlotte. Everybody's hungry. The breadlines are as awful as the food rations of The Great War. The world has gone to hell. You're lucky to be in here.'

Charlotte didn't feel all that lucky. 'Did my father send any information with you?' She wanted to ask about Alex, who had occupied her thoughts relentlessly since she'd discovered he was alive, but she was distrustful of Estelle, unsure of how much she knew.

'He did. That's why I'm here.' Estelle reached into her bag and pulled out an envelope. She handed it to her. 'Your father gave me a key to the Playfair house. I've been keeping an eye on things and tending to the mail. This arrived a few days ago, attention to you.'

Charlotte folded her fingers around it. 'Who's it from?'

'I think you know.'

She studied the envelope—the circle of water damage and the postmaster's stamp from almost six weeks earlier, the sender's address from France on the back. She tore it open, retrieving the letter from inside and unfolding it. One look at the handwriting sent her heart soaring.

Estelle watched with wide eyes. 'Looks like your beloved arrived safely.'

Charlotte smiled to herself. Yes, he had. And it seemed he hadn't forgotten her as she'd feared he would. She dropped her gaze to the letter and drank in the words. Alex had quoted Beethoven to his Immortal Beloved.

Fifth February 1930

To My Dearest Charlotte,

Though still in bed, my thoughts go out to you, my Immortal Beloved. Be calm—love me—today—yesterday—what tearful longings for you—you—you—my life—my all— farewell. Oh continue to love me—never misjudge the most faithful heart of your beloved.

Ever thine. Ever mine. Ever ours.

Alex

Followed by the clue:

I've spoken of it before, beneath the trees in Hyde Park.

Do you remember?

Oh, how I've missed you!

Come find me. I'll be waiting...

When she glanced up again, she felt tears collect on the brim of her lashes, spilling over onto her cheeks. She knew exactly where he was. He had told her of his family's country cottage in France during their walk around Hyde Park and she'd never forgotten. That's where he waited for her. That's where she would go.

Estelle lit another cigarette and watched with curiosity as Charlotte read and reread the letter. 'I loved someone like that once,' she said wistfully. 'My soldier.'

'When can I leave here?' Charlotte asked impatiently.

Estelle's expression became serious. 'Yes, we need to talk about that. Now pay attention. I will collect you from the western entrance of the hospital grounds at dawn in two days' time. I will drop you at the shipping port at Finger Wharf. There you will board your passage to London. But the ship doesn't leave until morning, so you will have to find somewhere safe to wait.'

It was a barrage of information yet all Charlotte could think to ask was, 'How will I get to the western entrance?'

'Dr Carmichael will come for you,' Estelle said. 'He will have your suitcase with him and show you safely through the gate.'

'And you'll be waiting for me? You'll drive me to Finger Wharf?'

'Yes. Your father will meet you just after sunrise on the wharf with your ticket. You can say goodbye to him then.'

Charlotte's heart thudded from all the instructions. This was really happening. 'Can I go back to my house first?'

'No,' Estelle said. 'To the wharf, wait somewhere safe for your father, then get on the ship.'

Charlotte's mind raced to catch up. 'There's a chest of letters under my bed. I need to take them with me.'

'You can't.'

'But I must. They're important.'

'Charlotte, let me be clear,' she said sternly, 'there are a lot of people who would like to get their hands on you and your father. Hundreds of thousands of pounds are owed. Do you understand what I'm saying?'

Charlotte swallowed. 'Yes.'

'No visits to the house. Stay near the wharf.'

'Fine. Can you collect the chest for me and put it somewhere safe? Hide it in the attic. Maybe one day it will find its way back to me.'

Estelle softened. 'I'll do it.'

Charlotte narrowed her eyes. That feeling of distrust had returned. 'Wait, why are you helping us? How do I know you won't hand me over to Floyd, or to someone my father owes money to?'

Estelle threw her head back and laughed. 'Goodness, Charlotte, I'm not a monster.' She stopped laughing when she saw Charlotte's dubious expression. 'Right, well I guess you're just going to have to trust me. Your father does.'

That was of little comfort. Walter had proven himself a lousy judge of character. Charlotte sighed, glancing out across the hospital grounds. She could take the risk and place her faith in Estelle, even though every fibre in her body screamed against it, or she could remain at the hospital and miss the ship that would take her to Alex. There was no doubt in her mind what she would do.

She returned the letter to the envelope and slipped it into her brassiere.

Estelle shot out a hand. 'I'll need to take that back. If you're caught here with it...'

'I won't be.'

'Your father was adamant I not leave it behind.'

Charlotte retrieved Alex's letter and tucked that into her brassiere instead, handing Estelle the empty envelope. 'I won't part with the letter. But you can have the envelope. Put it somewhere safe.'

Estelle hesitated, then took it and slid it into her handbag. 'Did you commit the Ovillers address to memory?'

'Every letter of it.'

The visitors were being rounded up by a ward attendant to be escorted back to the main building. They both stood and Estelle placed her arms around Charlotte in an unexpected embrace. 'I have to leave now. I will meet you by the western entrance in two days' time. Do not be late.' She let her go and walked towards the congregating group before looking back. 'You asked me last time if our friendship was real. Well, it was. Not at first, but you became the only true friend I've ever known.'

Something tugged inside Charlotte, an instinct to forgive and allow Estelle close again, but she pushed it down. 'It doesn't matter now.'

Estelle smiled regretfully. 'No, I suppose it doesn't.' She turned and climbed the hill back towards the ward, her patent leather heels sinking into the grass.

CHAPTER 43

WALTER
Two Days Later

A blazing orange ball burst onto the horizon as Walter drew his hat down low and stepped onto Finger Wharf. A telephone call from Mrs Mayfair had confirmed what he'd hoped for. That Charlotte had placed her blind faith in the woman and, with the help of Dr Carmichael, had met her at dawn at the western entrance of the hospital. If all went to plan, she'd be waiting somewhere there, on the wharf, with the suitcase he'd packed months ago for her and a pocketful of courage.

The SS Cathay, five-hundred and forty-six feet of mighty ocean liner, bound for London, was an impressive sight, hovering on the water like a gentle giant. It was only six-thirty in the morning but there were already passengers gathering on the wharf, and crew and deckhands were carting supplies up and down the gangway.

If Charlotte were indeed there, she would have arrived hours ago, during the first glimpses of dawn, and he hoped she'd found somewhere safe to take respite for the few hours in between. He silently thanked his good friend Dr Carmichael for forging Charlotte's death certificate, then cast his eyes upwards in gratitude to his late wife, Marianne. Once inspected, the Public Library of New South Wales had highly sought her impressive book collection and they'd been willing to pay handsomely for the rare first editions. It had secured the silence and willingness of

Carmichael as well as passage for Charlotte on the SS Cathay and beyond.

He had felt guilty about selling Marianne's books but reasoned that he had to travel light now and could not take them with him. They would have simply gathered dust back at the house, along with everything else he could not take, a meal for the rats and moths. And it wasn't the same as when he'd pawned her other treasures, the desperate, selfish, unthinking man he'd been. He felt certain that of this transaction, Marianne would wholeheartedly approve.

The sun rose higher, casting glaring rays across the city and the wharf was doused in burnt orange light. He put his hand up to shield his eyes, sweeping his gaze across the wharf. His heart beat a little harder in his chest, his ticker much too old for this cloak and dagger business. He should be enjoying retirement, his business thriving in the care of his son, the bridge proudly displaying his legacy like lights on Broadway. Instead, he had some of the meanest thugs in the city after him, the state's bank too, and he'd put his daughter in grave danger. He dropped his head and shook it. What a stupid old fool he'd been.

'Papa.'

Too busy wallowing in self-pity, he hadn't heard her approach, but now turned with relief at the sound of her voice. He broke into a smile, holding out a hand. 'Charlotte, love. You made it.'

She nodded but didn't embrace him, reluctance or perhaps distrust writ large across her face. She wore a pink dress and matching hat, clutching her suitcase she'd brought from the hospital in a single gloved hand. She seemed tired and bewildered, but otherwise fine. Carmichael and Mrs Mayfair had come through.

'Are you all right, love? Did you keep out of sight?'

She indicated westward. 'I waited in the botanic garden for daybreak. At Mrs Macquarie's Chair.'

'That's a fair walk from here.'

'Yes, but it had the loveliest sunrise. The sunsets are even better.'

He looked at her curiously, viewing her through different eyes. How changed his little girl was, no longer the meek, timid character of past years who'd refused to venture further than the grocery store, who'd been so thrown by the passing of her mother, then her childhood friend in the space of two weeks, that she'd melded into her own shadow.

Sighing, he reached into his jacket pocket and retrieved an envelope. 'This is your ticket for passage on the SS Cathay. It will get you to London with a stop in Mumbai.'

She placed the suitcase down and took the envelope. 'And from London?'

'You'll have to find your way. I've included extra pounds to see you through.'

She gasped. 'Find my own way? From London to Paris, then to Ovillers? But how will I do that?'

He smiled encouragingly. 'Someone told me that you are more than capable now.'

Her shoulders dropped from their momentary state of panic and she looked beyond him, towards the vessel. 'I wanted to go back to the house first.'

'You didn't, did you?' He had no doubt the house was being watched, that at some point, those he owed money to would help themselves to their belongings in an attempt to recover their losses. Estelle had been keeping an eye on things, collecting the mail and storing important items away in the attic, but he couldn't risk Charlotte going there.

She shook her head. 'Estelle said not to.'

'And she was right. It's best we stay away for now.'

Charlotte lifted her chin defiantly. 'Why is she helping us anyway? How do you know her and Floyd aren't scheming?'

'We can trust her. When it comes to Floyd, Mrs Mayfair has her own retribution to fulfil.'

Charlotte gave an infinitesimal shake of her head as though she was still unconvinced and reached into her coat pocket, retrieving her engagement ring. The sun glinted off the diamond. 'What should I do with this? I don't want it. I never did.'

Walter took the ring and stared at it. He knew Floyd sought its return for he'd mentioned it several times already to Mrs Mayfair, who'd told Walter. It was worth a fortune and as Floyd was jobless, he wanted to sell it and make his money back.

But now that its brilliance sat in Walter's hand, an old craving pulsed in his throat. He could sell it too, make the same money, try to double it on the hounds, a little something to set him up until he found work. But did he want to be in further debt to Floyd? Shouldn't he extend the olive branch and return it to him?

Resolved to decide later, he slipped it into his vest pocket and patted it.

Charlotte hadn't noticed his internal debate, her gaze fixed on the bridge instead. It stood resolute in its half-constructed form, sunlight shimmering off the steel. He knew she was thinking of Mr Young.

'He's going to miss the opening ceremony,' she said.

Walter nodded. 'Indeed. His passion was that bridge until he met you. I've never seen a lad quite so head over heels before. Reminds me of when I met your mother.' The emotion of the morning, of the past weeks, of the years he'd lived his life without Marianne, raising his children on his own and seeing her in their faces every day, weighed on his heart.

Charlotte's face softened. 'Won't you come with me? I'd feel better if you did.'

'I could only afford one ticket, love. Besides, I'd be no good at starting fresh someplace else. Too set in my ways.' Walter looked across to the SS Cathay as the wharf began to fill with passengers carrying suitcases and hatboxes, excited children racing along the planks. 'Looks like they're boarding. I guess it's time.'

Charlotte's bottom lip trembled. 'Where will you go?'

'Not sure. Maybe out west.'

'Will I ever see you again?'

He felt his heart crack in two. 'Probably not, love.'

Her eyes filled so abruptly with tears that she dabbed them quickly with the back of her gloved hand. She took a deep breath and picked up her suitcase. 'Well, goodbye then, Papa.'

'Goodbye.'

She gave him the saddest smile he'd ever seen before walking towards the passengers gathering around the gangway.

He watched her go, memories of her as a child, a teenager, a young woman, flooding his soul. He mourned her now as he had once mourned Marianne, the sudden gaping hole one leaves in your life when you know there will never be a tomorrow with them. He owed her a life free of his failings, of never having to worry about the demons he couldn't control. It would be his one precious final gift.

But then he remembered another gift he had for her as he turned to leave and the corner of its cover dug into his chest. He slipped his hand into his suit jacket and pulled from it the maroon book of love letters she'd always adored. He'd almost forgotten he'd had it. 'Love!' he called out to her, holding it up in the air.

Almost swallowed by the crowd waiting to embark, Charlotte turned and squinted into the sun. When her eyes fell on the book, he saw her visible intake of breath. Clutching her suitcase she ran back along the wharf like a gangly bird, holding onto her hat, her bag knocking against her knees and people exclaiming as she jostled past them.

She was out of breath when she reached him and he pressed the book into her hands. She looked so astounded that a full minute passed without words. 'But how?'

'I found the pawn dealer I'd sold it to. It just so happens that in this economy, no one has money for priceless books. I paid him a bit more than what I sold it for and he was happy for me to take it off his hands.' Another transaction Marianne would approve of.

Charlotte shook her head, so delighted that tears began to stream down her face. She didn't wipe them away, instead leaping forward to throw her arms around her father.

He held her close, tears springing to his own eyes. 'That book means a lot to you, doesn't it?'

'It's my past and my future,' she said, her voice muffled against his cheek.

After some time, he pulled away and took his handkerchief out of his pocket to mop up his face. 'Goodness, would you look at me?'

Charlotte laughed, dusting away her tears from the lapel of his tweed jacket.

The SS Cathay drowned out the wharf with a deep and resounding bellow of its horn.

'They're calling you,' Walter said, sniffing.

Charlotte held the book to her chest. It seemed she didn't want to leave, hesitating, wanting to extract the last of their minutes together.

'Go on,' he said bravely. 'Don't want them to leave without you.'

'I'll write,' she said through renewed tears.

'Sure, love.' He knew she didn't know where he was going.

'Can I contact James when I reach France?' she asked.

'Give it some time. Wait for the dust to settle.'

She nodded and hugged him again. She collected her suitcase and, with the book held close, she left him on the wharf, quickly enveloped again by the crowd.

He decided not to linger. He gave it ten minutes, enough time for the wharf to clear and for her to be safely on board, then he turned and left.

At the tram stop on Bourke Street, still quiet with barely a commuter, he was quickly circled by a group of men, a pair of hands bearing down on his collar and dragging him roughly into the Royal Botanic Garden.

'Steady on,' Walter said as they pushed him along the path, a gun pressed into his back. 'No need for that. I'm not resisting.'

Six brutes surrounded him, forming a tight circle as they walked, and he had no doubt what they'd come for. Retribution in that city was always swift and his day of reckoning had come. He eyed the circle, wondering briefly if his jolly old body could make a dash for it, but knew he'd only get a few feet before they caught him again.

The sun was higher now, cutting through the leaves of the trees, but it wasn't the heat that was causing beads of sweat to roll down his temples. It was the final rush of minutes. His end was near. Dead man walking.

The SS Cathay gave a final blare of her horn as she was tugged out into the harbour.

They walked faster, continuing along the path through the gardens until they reached Mrs Macquarie's Chair. There they sat him down, pulled rope from their pockets and bound his hands and feet tightly. He didn't struggle, didn't bother calling out. There was no one around to hear.

They tied a sack of rocks to his feet, the kind of weight to drag a body down. Walter could hear them clinking inside the hessian bag. He kept his emotions in check, even though his heart was beating like a rabid dog's. The SS Cathay was out in the middle of the harbour now, angling her sleek bow towards the Heads.

He kept his eyes fixed on it, as he was cupped under the armpits and hauled with strenuous grunts onto the harbour wall. The water below slapped against the sandstone, sunlight turning it blue, then green. He felt the diamond of the engagement ring dig into his ribs. Should he offer it to them in exchange for his life? Try to strike a deal? No, they'd take it and kill him anyway. The ring and its worth would go down with him, making him a richer man in death than he ever was in life.

'Any last words, Mr Greene?' the lout with the gun asked.

'Send my regards to Floyd,' he replied churlishly, from on top of the wall.

The lout looked confused. 'Who the hell is Floyd?'

They pushed him into the water.

He took one last gulp of air before the rocks dragged him under. He fought and kicked viciously, panic flooding him, muted pleas for help escaping his mouth in bubbles, but the rocks were too great a weight to struggle against, and they quickly sucked him down. As the surface pulled away and he exhaled the last of the air from his burning lungs, he caught a final watery glimpse of the SS Cathay, charging safely towards the Heads.

CHAPTER
44

PAIGE
Present Day

'Wait, that didn't happen. Did it?' Paige asked from the edge of her seat.

'It did. Charlotte said goodbye to her father on the wharf and left for France. She never saw him again.' Delphine brought a second cup of coffee to her lips and sipped. They'd ordered another round, too transfixed to leave after Delphine's explanation of the events that had led to Charlotte and Alex's break for freedom.

'That's one hell of a story,' Ryan said, shaking his head. 'Hard to believe it happened.'

'The Roaring Twenties were extraordinary times.'

'Do you know what happened to Walter after that?' Paige asked.

'No,' Delphine said sadly. 'Charlotte had always hoped that he'd made it out of the city like he'd planned to, waited years for a letter to arrive from him. But nothing ever came.'

Given the enormous debt he'd found himself in and the fact that the house had been ransacked when James arrived in Sydney, Paige felt certain Walter had met with a grisly end. Was it by Floyd's hand or someone else's? Who had settled their score with Walter Greene?

'Why didn't Charlotte send for James when she got here?' Ryan asked. 'Given he was in England and she was in France, she could have made contact.'

'What makes you think she didn't?' Delphine asked.

Ryan looked perplexed. 'Because it's always been said that he'd never heard from her.'

Delphine nodded with a thoughtful expression. 'I'm wondering if your family knew the whole story.' She gave an impish smile. 'From what I understand, Charlotte journeyed to Middlesbrough to find James shortly after she settled in France with Alex. Unfortunately, when she got there, James had already left for Sydney to search for her and Walter. They'd missed each other. Some years later, James visited her in Ovillers, when he was passing through northern France at the start of the Second World War.'

Realisation dawned on Ryan's face. 'But because he died early in the war, I'm guessing he never got the chance to tell his family he'd found her.'

'That must be what happened,' Delphine agreed.

'Tell us about Charlotte and Alex,' Paige said. 'What kind of life did they have?'

Delphine smiled. 'A beautiful one. They lived out their years at the house in Ovillers. They led a quiet life. Charlotte studied English Literature at a university in Paris for a year—quite an achievement for a woman back then. Paris always was a modern city, though. Then she returned to Ovillers to teach English and history at the local children's school.'

'And Alex?'

'He continued in construction, building infrastructure throughout northern France. Then he fought in World War II and helped the rebuild effort after that. And they continued to play the game. They left little clues around the farm for each other, playing it with their children too. I have a whole box of them at home if you'd like to see them.'

Paige and Ryan shared a smile. It was nice to know Charlotte and Alex had continued the game together, even in old age.

'How many children did they have?' Paige asked, deciding her appetite had returned and she should try one of the chouquettes that remained on the plate.

'They had three. Johnny was the eldest, Sophie the middle and Marianne, my grandmother, was the youngest.'

'You probably would have deduced by now that we're related,' Ryan said with a cautious smile.

Delphine dropped her gaze into her coffee and smiled too. '*Oui.*'

'I'm a Greene. Your great-grandmother, Charlotte, who was my great-aunt, was a Greene.'

'Yes.'

'What does that make us? Second cousins?'

'Third,' she said quickly, as if she'd already worked out the family tree back in Ovillers. 'We are third cousins.'

Ryan grinned broadly now. 'That's cool.'

Delphine was still staring shyly into her cup.

'Maybe you could come and meet my family in London,' he suggested. 'Or we could come to you if you'd prefer. No pressure.'

She looked up with a hopeful expression. 'I'd like that, yes.'

'Great.' Ryan sat back in his chair. He squeezed Paige's hand and his look of complete and utter elation, of not only having solved the mystery of Charlotte but of having gained family he never knew about, seemed to light the corner where they sat.

'I wish you could have known them,' Delphine said. 'Their love was so beautiful, the rarest kind that turned heads and made people want to share a piece of it. And it never waned. Not when the Depression hit, or they had three children, or when Alex went away to war. I've never known two people who were so meant for each other. And although I was young, I could tell what they had only happened once in a lifetime.'

Paige glanced at Ryan. He leant forward and kissed her cheek, and she knew what they had was their own kind of special. But Charlotte had crossed an ocean to find Alex, on her own, with no technology, no phones, no planes—just love and an address. Why was it so difficult, then, for Paige and Ryan to take that leap of faith? To trust in the same thing—love and an address.

Delphine smiled at them and it was in that moment that Paige saw her resemblance to Ryan, saw the way her dark plait over one shoulder was like that of Charlotte's in the photograph they'd found in the Playfair attic; the wistful eyes and almost playful smile that was like Alex's in the photograph in the bridge's southern pylon. After so many months, they'd come to the end. They'd found Charlotte and Alex and the delight of their descendant, Delphine, Ryan's third cousin, who seemed to brim with the prospect of acquiring a whole new chaotic but loving set of Greenes.

In many ways, Charlotte and Alex had brought them together.

Back on the street, Ryan and Paige walked Delphine to her car a block away.

'Are you sure you can't stay longer?' Ryan asked, shifting the chest of letters to his other arm. 'Maybe an early dinner?'

'I should get back. The chickens worry,' Delphine said.

Paige stifled a smile at her seriousness.

'But maybe before you leave France, you would like to come back to Ovillers?' she said, arriving at her small blue Volkswagen. 'I could show you where Charlotte and Alex are buried, show you some of their things at the house and take you to the crater out the back. It's quite something.'

'We'd love that,' Paige said, touched by Delphine's kindness.

'And I want you to have these.' Ryan held forth the chest of love letters.

Delphine's eyes widened and she shook her head. 'Oh, Ryan, I couldn't.'

'Please. I want you to. You're Charlotte and Alex's great-granddaughter. If anyone should have them, it's you.'

'But I couldn't possibly take them from you.'

'Charlotte would want you to have them,' Paige said. 'She'd want to know they made their way back to her.'

Delphine's eyes filled with tears as she took the chest of letters and held them close. '*Merci.*'

They said goodbye and Delphine climbed into her car. With a final wave, she turned on the ignition and drove down the cobbled lane, the exhaust spluttering.

Paige linked her arm with Ryan's, and they walked back to the hotel. 'Are you all right?' she asked.

He ran his free hand along his jaw. 'Yeah. Still a lot to absorb.'

'That was a nice thing you did for Delphine, giving her the letters. It meant a lot to her.'

'It's where they belong, with her in Ovillers.'

They rounded the corner onto the Rue Jean Goujon and into the lobby of La Maison.

'When we visited her house and you told her you were Ryan Greene, her relationship to you must have clicked straight away.'

'I'm just glad she drove down to meet us. Imagine if she'd kept the truth to herself. We'd be none the wiser.' Ryan grimaced at the thought.

'Will you really keep in contact with her?'

'I'd like to, if she'll have me and my crazy family.'

'I think she'd like nothing more.'

Ryan wore a sentimental look.

Paige reached for his hand. 'What is it?'

'I just can't believe we did it,' he said. 'Mystery solved.'

She nodded. 'Yes. I'm glad Charlotte and Alex found each other again. I can't say I feel positive about Walter's outcome, though. I think he may have ticked off one too many people in the end.'

'I also quite like that Floyd ended up in the dusty Outback with four children and a wife, a far cry from the lavish life he was used to,' Ryan said smugly.

'Indeed.' Then Paige grabbed Ryan's arm and stopped walking suddenly.

'What's wrong?'

Her mouth fell open. 'Floyd.'

'What about him?'

'The woman he married and moved to Alice Springs with. The one we saw in the obituary photo. Dorothea Baker.' She smacked her palm to her forehead. She couldn't believe it had taken her so long to put two and two together. 'I thought she looked familiar in that photograph, but I couldn't place why. Only that I knew her from somewhere. Ha!'

Ryan looked confused. 'I don't get it.'

'It was Estelle Mayfair. That's who Floyd married. That was the woman I saw in the obituary photo. She was much older then of course, and not quite so glamorous, but it was Estelle. The same woman who had the photo taken with Charlotte at Hubert Penny's.'

'Wait, Estelle is Dorothea?'

'Yes.'

'Are you sure?'

'I'll have to take another look at both photos when I get home, but yes, I believe so.'

Ryan's eyebrows went up. 'Well, it's the mystery that keeps on giving.'

They'd reached the lift and were stepping into it when Paige's phone rang. She dug into her back pocket and pulled it out, but the trip up in the lift extinguished the signal and the call went through to voicemail.

When they reached Ryan's room, signal restored and Paige rang through to her messages, surprised to hear the real estate agent's voice who had shown her the last rental property. She listened carefully, the chirpy woman explaining that the application form Paige had submitted had been accepted by the owner. She was the new tenant of a terrace not five minutes' walk from Playfair Street.

When Paige put the phone down, she sank onto Ryan's bed.

'What's wrong?' he asked.

'I have a place.' She glanced up at him. 'That was the real estate agent. I've been accepted for a rental property in The Rocks.'

'Oh.' Ryan looked crestfallen. 'That's great. Congratulations.'

'Thanks.'

The room fell silent, neither of them saying what was so clearly on their minds until Ryan spoke. 'Don't take it.'

'What?'

'You have a place with me in London.'

She smiled sadly. 'Ryan.'

He lowered himself down next to her on the edge of the bed.

She turned and grabbed his face in her hands, bringing his forehead to hers, her heart so full for him she thought it would burst. 'I love you.'

He smiled and kissed the tip of her nose. 'I love you too.'

'But I don't know how to do this.'

'It can be easy,' he said, leaning back to look at her. 'The question is, do you want to?'

She didn't even have to think about it. 'I do.'

'Then what's stopping you?'

'Lots of things. Like Xavier. I'd feel terrible for leaving him. And what about us? What if it doesn't work out or I don't make friends in London or I can't find a job? What if I have to go back to Sydney and start all over again?'

'That's a lot of what-ifs.'

Paige nudged him. 'I'm being serious.'

'I know you are,' he said. 'And I get that you're scared. I am too. What I'm asking of you is huge. But I think we're worth it.'

Paige tried to steady her breathing. Everything was rushing upon her at once, a decision that needed to be made. And it wasn't as though she'd never considered it before. She'd had months to think about it in the time Ryan had returned to London. But the moment was pivotal, now or never. She had a landlord waiting and a boss expecting her return, and Ryan watching her so expectantly it made the room spin.

'I just need a minute,' she said. 'Do you mind?'

Ryan smiled gently. 'Of course not.'

'I might go to my room.'

'Sure.'

She stood, then bent to kiss him and his hand found hers and squeezed it reassuringly.

'Dinner later?' he asked, dark eyes turned up to hers.

'I'd like that.'

She opened the adjoining door to her room and stepped inside, closing it behind her. Dropping down onto her bed, she exhaled everything in her lungs.

An incredible opportunity had been tabled before her, wide open and terrifying but ready to be embraced. Did she have the courage to wrap her arms around it? Was she brave enough to start fresh where there were no guarantees, no certainties, no rule books, just a step off a cliff into the unknown?

Was love enough to guide her? It had been for Charlotte and Alex. He'd made the agonising journey to France alone, sending for her when he got there. And Charlotte had responded, sailing across the world to find him.

Paige sighed and sat up, reaching for her phone in her back pocket. Whatever the case, she knew she couldn't think a second longer without first speaking to Xavier. She dialled his number, her heart thudding loudly in her chest.

The time was seven am in Sydney and he answered on the second ring. 'Hey you.'

'Good morning,' she said. 'Did I wake you?'

'Not a chance. Was up all night unpacking at the new place and back at Playfair Street this morning at six to work on the launch. I sent you some questions from the caterer. Have you seen them yet? Something about the gluten-free and vegetarian menus. Also, where's all that paperwork from the tax office? I thought it was filed under T, but couldn't find it.'

'It's filed under A for ATO. But Xavier...' She took a deep breath, her nerve threatening to break free and bolt. 'I need to talk to you about something.'

It sounded like he'd stopped what he was doing. 'Uh, oh. Okay.'

She swallowed and steeled herself. 'I've been invited to relocate to London. Permanently.'

Silence again, then, 'With Ryan?'

'Yes.' More silence, so deafening Paige's ears began to ring. 'Please say something.'

'You know I love you,' he said. She heard rustling and the familiar sound of his leather chair in the office squeaking. He'd sat down, elbows probably resting on the desk. Hopefully, his head hadn't dropped despairingly into his hands. 'I would never hold you back from anything you'd want to do. You know that, right?'

'I know.'

'And it *is* something you want to do?'

Paige nodded. 'Yes.'

'Then you don't have to be scared to tell me that. Of course you should explore what might be.'

'So what are you saying? I should go?'

'Yes, darling. You should absolutely go.'

Paige let out a breath she hadn't realised she'd been holding. 'But what about the business? The launch? Everything we've worked on?'

'Well, you still have to come home and collect all your things. If it's your resignation you're submitting to me now, then I accept. I'll give you the standard two weeks' notice period and, since the launch is next week, we still get to finish what we started.'

His generosity made her do something she almost never did, burst into tears. 'I feel awful.'

'Why?' he asked kindly. 'This business is mine, not yours. You are not tied to it out of obligation. You have already given me such an incredible gift. When I couldn't leave Albury, you came to Sydney and started it from the ground up, on your own. You have made this dream possible for me. What kind of a friend would I be to hold you back now?'

'Well, when you put it like that,' she joked through her tears. 'Thank you. For making me feel better.'

'There's no reason you should not feel excited about this.'

'I'm a bundle of mixed emotions right now, but excitement is one of them.'

'Good. So when are you coming back here?'

She sniffed and wiped her eyes. 'My flight home is the day after tomorrow. I'll stay for the launch, then I guess I'll leave for London.'

'And Charlotte and Alex?'

'All sorted, with some nice surprises. I'll fill you in when I get there.'

'Just be ready to work through your jet lag. We have a launch to throw next week.'

They spent the next few minutes reviewing work, then ended the call. Paige fell backwards onto her bed, turning the conversation over in her mind. She'd resigned. She'd actually resigned. Alarm shot through her, replaced by the slow and steady realisation of what she'd done, then waves of fizzy giddiness.

Before she could change her mind, she dialled the real estate agent's number but given the early hour, it went straight through to voicemail. She thanked her profusely for her help with the rental property, but politely declined the offer due to her changed circumstances.

Then she went next door to see Ryan, because dinner still felt like a long time away.

CHAPTER 45

CHARLOTTE
April 1930
Ovillers-la-Boiselle

On a lone war-torn road in the middle of Somme, the taxi wound its way through the French countryside. A decade on from Armistice, Charlotte could still see the battle scars of the war to end all wars. The landscape had never quite healed, with bowl-like craters and abandoned houses that had once been family homes, their walls crumbled and reclaimed by nature. And the deep pockmarks in the roads caused by tanks and heavy machinery that had never been filled.

She leant her head against the window and closed her eyes, her suitcase knocking against her leg every time they hit a pothole. Since they'd left Paris two hours ago, the driver had remained silent. He understood not a word of English and she spoke not a word of French. The quiet had been blessed.

She'd been a bundle of nerves when she'd left her father on the wharf in Sydney, the book of love letters and her ticket safely in her hands, weeks of uncertain travelling before her. She'd climbed the gangway, raced straight to the port side and waved as he'd watched from down below. Then when he'd turned to leave, her heart had squeezed so tightly in her chest, she'd had to force herself away from the edge to prevent herself from running back down to him. Her father had made some deplorable choices in the past year, wracked by weaknesses, but he was still her father and beneath it all, he had the most benevolent heart of anyone she knew.

As he'd left the wharf, heading towards the Bourke Street tram stop, she'd gone to find her room. She would hear from him soon enough, she was sure. He knew where to find her, then she would encourage him to make the journey to her where he would be safe. This thought alone filled her heart with hope.

The next six weeks on the SS Cathay had passed slowly. The passage by sea had at times been calm, other times so violently turbulent that Charlotte had been forced into her cabin with sickness, wondering if she'd made the right decision. At the port in London, with her feet at long last on dry land, she'd discovered a train was required to take her to Dover, then another boat was needed to sail her across the English Channel to Calais.

Having finally arrived in bustling Paris, she'd found a vendor who'd converted her pounds to francs, then a Parisian taxi driver parked on the side of the Avenue Montaigne to whom she'd given the Ovillers address, along with a handful of coins and a muted set of instructions. After some agonising minutes trying to communicate with him, he'd finally nodded his head, agreeing to take her.

Two hours later, as they bumped along the pockmarked road somewhere in northern France, with mist rising from the hills, she knew she was getting closer to Alex. He was out there somewhere, waiting for her. It had been six months since she'd last seen or spoken to him, but her every thought, waking and dreaming, had been of him, and she hoped he'd been the same. Hoped time hadn't dulled his feelings towards her or that he'd moved on.

She leant forward and tapped the driver on the shoulder before pointing to her watch.

'Cinq. Cinq,' he said, holding up five fingers.

She wasn't sure if he was saying five hours or five minutes. She hoped it was the latter for she had not nearly enough francs to travel any further. She leant back in the seat, exhausted yet trembling with anticipation.

Before too long, the taxi slowed and pulled over to the verge. The driver turned in his seat to look at her. He pointed across the road at a soggy track that led up through the fields by a copse of oaks.

Charlotte looked out the window. 'Is this it? Are we here?'

He pointed again.

She gripped an imaginary steering wheel in her hands, displaying the act of driving and pointed to the track, asking him to continue along it. He understood and turned the car through an open gate where unruly brambles ran unchecked along the fence line. The road led up through open fields, bordered by large stones. The way was as bumpy as the road they'd just left, Charlotte's body jostling from side to side in the back seat.

They drove for another two minutes when the track rose and fell over a hill and ended unexpectedly. Through an opening in a low wall, they rolled through to a two-storey house made of grey stone and white windowsills, with a steeply pitched, gabled roof. Chimney pots rose at either end and thin grey smoke swirled out of them, lasting a moment in the air before being stolen by the breeze.

Charlotte wasn't sure whether to get out of the car and allow the driver to leave or have him wait until she knew Alex was there. It occurred to her that the silent man in the front seat of the taxi may be the only person she knew this side of the world.

But then, the front door opened and there he stood. Alex, exactly as she remembered him, with a smile so wide she felt it open the car door for her. She burst out, rushed across the sodden ground to the front door and threw herself into his arms.

He caught her, his arms circling her tightly. She cried with relief, overcome by his familiarity and nearness, because all she'd had to exist on for so long was his memory.

'I wasn't sure I'd ever see you again.' She pulled away to take him in. His cheeks looked sharper and his frame leaner since the last time she saw him. Her face was just as gaunt, her waist thin, and she was embarrassed at the way her ribs poked through her back, for between seasickness and worry, she'd hardly eaten a thing in the last six weeks.

'I've been waiting by the window every day since I sent you the clue, hoping you'd come down that path.' He studied her closely, eyes drinking her in. 'Are you all right? Were you safe on the ship?'

'I'm fine,' she said. 'Just happy to have found you.'

He left her by the door to collect her suitcase from the taxi and reward the driver extra francs for her safe delivery. When he reached the front door again, they both watched him reverse and return the way he came.

'You must have a million questions,' Alex said, circling his arms around her again.

'My father explained it all.'

'I'm sorry I left you. He was supposed to bring you to the ship so we could sail together. He told me not to get off for any reason, that he'd get you on. I waited and waited. I thought maybe I'd missed you boarding, that you'd come on a different way. When the ship started to sail, I panicked, searching every inch of it, realising too late that you weren't there.' He was talking quickly, all the words he'd had bottled up for months pouring out.

'I'm so sorry,' she said, holding his face in her hands and bringing it to hers. She saw worry lines around his eyes, facial hair that he'd allowed to grow, exhaustion in his countenance. It spoke of the stress he'd endured, not knowing if she was safe, if something dire was unravelling on the other side of the world and he was powerless to do anything about it. She kissed his lips and cheeks, savouring the feel of him, bringing him close. 'You must have been frantic.'

She didn't tell him that she'd suffered too, believing he'd died, and mourning him in unfathomable ways, that she'd spent four months in an asylum and that she wasn't sure she would ever see her father again. Those were stories for another day.

She turned to look across Alex's backyard, acres of fields rolling towards a grey horizon. 'It's so peaceful out here, not at all like the bustle of Sydney.'

'And it's all ours, to live our best life, any way we choose.' He kept his eyes on her, as though not quite trusting that she wasn't a mirage. 'You have no idea how I've missed you.'

'I've missed you too.'

'You will marry me, won't you?' The words gushed out of him unexpectedly.

Her heart swelled. 'It depends. Is that a proposal?'

He laughed, rolling his eyes. 'Yes, but not a very good one. I'll make it better.'

She thought it was perfect, a world away from Floyd and his proposal in her parlour, fuelled by lies and greed and a business arrangement. There were no misgivings here. She loved Alex, the desire in his voice, his sweet, thoughtful words, the way he watched her now, pure and expectant, hoping she would say yes. And of course, she would.

Six torturous months. That's how long it had taken them to find each other again, bound by hope, a game and a prayer. Hilda would be proud, her mother too, but it was her father who would be most of all, from wherever he'd chosen to live out his days.

Alex kissed her and tucked her hand in his. Never would they be apart again. He pushed open the door and led her inside, to their home, and endless days that would belong to them.

Yes, Charlotte thought. *They are ours.*

THE END

Also by Michelle Montebello

The Quarantine Station

BLURB

The rules were crystal clear. She broke them all...

1918 ... When Londoner, Rose Porter, arrives on the shores of Sydney with little more than her suitcase, she is forced to take a job as a parlourmaid at the mysterious North Head Quarantine Station. It's a place of turmoil, segregated classes and strict rules concerning employee fraternisation.

But as Rose discovers, some rules were made to be broken.

2019 ... Over a century later, Emma Wilcott lives a secluded life in Sydney. Still reeling from a devastating loss, her one-hundred-year-old grandmother, Gwendoline, is all she has left. Suffering the early stages of dementia, Gwendoline's long-term memories take her wandering at night and Emma realises she is searching for something or someone from her past.

Emma's investigation leads her to the Quarantine Station where she meets Matt, the station carpenter, and together they begin to unravel a mystery so compelling it has the power to change lives, the power to change everything Emma ever knew about herself.

Set during the First World War and the height of the Spanish Influenza pandemic, The Quarantine Station is a captivating story of people who will love, no matter the cost.

Michelle Montebello

Beautiful, Fragile

BLURB

We'd hurt each other, my soulmate and me...

Faith James is found on a remote beach in the south of Spain with a head injury and no recollection of how she got there. Recovering in hospital, she is desperate to return to her twenty-five-year-old, single life in Sydney.

But Faith has lost ten years of memories and her world becomes unrecognisable.

Her husband, Will, arrives to collect her, and she is told she has three young children waiting at home in London.

So begins the emotional journey to reclaim the life she's forgotten, learn how to be a wife and mother, and mend a broken marriage. She wants to remember everything...

But are all memories worth fighting for, even the ones that hurt?

The Belle Series
Interwoven
A House of Lies
Beneath the Pepper Tree

AUTHOR'S NOTE

The idea of a lover's game played out across a city first came to me a few years ago but the storyline was very different. I'd planned to set it somewhere exotic like Cairo as a contemporary romance. Alas, it didn't take and so I parked it for another time.

Then the story of Charlotte and Alex began to emerge and I felt certain a lover's game of secret clues and renowned love letters belonged entirely to them. And what better setting to weave this magic than in the historical neighbourhood of The Rocks during the Roaring Twenties?

I consulted many sources to help develop this story. The complete list is too long to include here, so I've noted the primary ones. Thank you first and foremost to The Rocks Walking Tours at Clocktower Square for allowing me to spend a morning in your knowledgeable company. Although Sydney is my hometown and I've spent many a day in The Rocks, I was still shown pockets of wonder I'd never seen before, like the pre-plague fireplaces set in old foundations at Foundation Park and the crooked little alleyways that meander intricately between buildings. A huge thank you also to the volunteer in The Rocks (I'm sorry, I didn't catch your name) who passed me by and handed me a free map of the area. It served as my mouse pad and a quick and useful reference whenever I needed to get Charlotte to Alex!

Thank you to Sydney Living Museums for your wonderful tour of Susannah Place, and to the staff at Government House who imparted invaluable knowledge and who let me roam throughout the rooms and gardens. This was particularly helpful when building the scenes for the Governor's Ball Charlotte attended with Floyd. And my heartfelt thanks to Bianca Nash for her expertise in real estate contracts and rental applications, which helped the conversations between Paige and Jenny.

My go-to guide when detailing scenes about the Sydney Harbour Bridge was *The Sydney Harbour Bridge—A Life* by Peter Spearritt. This treasure-trove of a book describes every aspect of the bridge's build and was an essential reference point throughout the novel. I also paired this with a visit to the bridge's southern pylon, just like Paige and Ryan did, which had lots of informative displays. It is worth mentioning here that Dr JJC Bradfield was indeed the chief proponent of the Sydney Harbour Bridge, overseeing the design and construction, and Dorman Long and Co were the contractors who built it. All the other main characters are fictional.

There were a number of resources I consulted whilst writing this tale, *Old Sydney to Now* by Ian Collis, *The Roaring Twenties: A History from Beginning to End* by Hourly History, *The Great Crash 1929* by John Kenneth Galbraith, *The Great Depression* by Robert S McElvaine and *A History of Sydney Streets* by historians Dr Shirley Fitzgerald and Dr Lisa Murray, courtesy of the City of Sydney.

1920s Sydney contained a fantastically complex set of tram routes which extended to many suburbs well beyond the city proper. The tram lines are all gone now but it was a pleasure to transform Charlotte into a confident commuter of these routes. For a map of the tram lines, visit www.transitmap.net/1921-sydney-tramways.

Plotting the clues was undoubtedly the highlight of my first draft. It was fun to create playful riddles with accompanying love quotes for Charlotte and Alex to write to each other. To explore clue destinations, I consulted www.visitsydneyaustralia.com.au and for help with celebrated love letters, I visited www.theliteraryshed.co.uk, amongst other sites.

To research Sydney's history of lost cemeteries, the following site was invaluable, www.home.dictionaryofsydney.org. I also found a great article in *The Daily Telegraph* called Sydney's Shameful Asylums, which helped construct the scenes around Gladesville Mental Hospital. There were several sites too, that assisted me with the unfortunate diagnosis of female hysteria. Dousing a woman's genitalia with a cold high-pressurised hose to restore her equilibrium and 'make her feel better' was indeed a common treatment.

Lastly, it is worth noting the resources I used to assist with 1920's fashion. This part of my research was such a treat, especially when dressing Estelle, who was so glamorous. To help me construct the wardrobe, I consulted *1920s Jazz Age Fashion & Photographs* by Martin Pel and Terence Pepper, as well as www.glamourdaze.com/history-of-womens-fashion/1920-to-1929.

The Lost Letters of Playfair Street is an ode to a fascinating period in the twentieth century, between two wars, when the world lived fast and we forgot to be humble. It's also a love story and a nod to The Rocks, a place that is, as Paige aptly describes over lunch with Ryan, still trapped in time. It's worth a visit if you are ever in Sydney.

ACKNOWLEDGMENTS

None of my books would be possible without the support of my family. All my love and thanks to Brett, Eve and Connor for your boundless patience and the hours you afford me to write my stories.

To friend and editor extraordinaire, Lynne Stringer, thank you once again for lending me your wisdom and expertise.

Thanks always to my dearest cheer squad, Liz Butler, Natasha Booth, Jo Libreri and Bianca Nash, to whom this book is dedicated. To Erika Slaby, friend and research partner. Thank you for traipsing through The Rocks, for climbing two hundred steps to the top of the southern pylon and for getting lost near Fort Street Public School with me. It really was the best day.

To Eve Campbell, for touring Government House, Mrs Macquarie's Chair, the Royal Botanic Garden, NSW State Library, Susannah Place and the Sydney Harbour Bridge with your mother, thank you. I love you.

I have wonderful parents and in-laws who always indulge me when I want to talk about my books. To Carmen Montebello, Joe and Michelle Montebello, Rhonda Flynn, Roger Campbell and Paula Jeff, thank you for being as excited as I am about it all.

Writing the book is only part of the process. Many are involved in preparing it for the world. Thank you to my designer Kris Dallas, for creating another stunning cover and for discovering your inner cartographer, and to Kaylene and Kim Osborn at Swish Design & Editing for the flawless interiors. My immense gratitude also to my early reader,

Marcia Batton, for the feedback, wisdom and friendship.

There are a few individuals in the publishing world who are well worth a mention for their unwavering support, Helen Sibbritt, Phillipa Nefri Clark and Phil and Craig at HappyValley BooksRead. There are so many more in the Australian book community who I could easily fill a page by thanking. To all of you, you know who you are, and your encouragement means the world.

Lastly to my beautiful readers. Thank you for reading, reviewing and hopefully enjoying my latest story. You are some of the nicest people I know and I am eternally grateful for the kind messages and joy you share. Thanks for being with me on this journey.

CONNECT WITH ME ONLINE

Check these links for more books from Author
Michelle Montebello.

NEWSLETTER

Want to see what's next?
Sign up for my Newsletter.
https://michellemontebello.com.au/newsletter/

GOODREADS

Add my books to your TBR list
on my Goodreads profile.
http://www.goodreads.com/author/show/
17208833.Michelle_Montebello

AMAZON

Buy my books from my Amazon profile.
https://amzn.to/2LzG4Aj

WEBSITE

http://www.michellemontebello.com.au/

TWITTER
http://www.twitter.com/Michelle_Monteb

INSTAGRAM
http://www.instagram.com/
michellemontebelloauthor

EMAIL
michelle@michellemontebello.com.au

FACEBOOK
https://www.facebook.com/
michellemontebelloauthor

ABOUT
THE AUTHOR

Michelle Montebello is a writer from Sydney, Australia where she lives with her husband and two children. She is the internationally bestselling author of *The Quarantine Station*, *Beautiful, Fragile* and *The Lost Letters of Playfair Street*.

Her books have won numerous awards. Most recently *The Quarantine Station* and *Beautiful, Fragile* were shortlisted for the 2019 Australian Romance Readers Association Awards for Favourite Historical Fiction and Favourite Contemporary Romance. She was also shortlisted for Favourite Australian Author of the Year.

When Michelle is not writing, she has a keen passion for reading, tennis and travel.